TO VISIT EARTH

IAN HUGH MCALLISTER

ISBN - 978-0-9991690-2-5 (Paperback)
ISBN - 978-0-9991690-3-2 (Hardback)
ISBN - 978-0-9991690-4-9 (Ebook)
Library of Congress Control Number: 2018947706

Published by:
Cloaked Press, LLC
PO Box 341
Suring, WI 54174
Http://www.cloakedpress.com

Contact the author
http://www.facebook.com/scifimac
scifimac@gmail.com

This project would not have been possible without the support and dedication of a large group of friends and experts; too many to mention individually. If you don't appear in this list, you all know who you are. Thank you.

Every author has dozens of people to thank. In my cast that means Eric Johnson, Sheri Williams, Joanna 'Melfka' Maciejewska, Jennifer Worrell, Sandy Stuckless, Katharine Grubb, Jessica White, Brian Duxbury, Wendy Van Camp, Lydia MacKenzie, Lee Nelson, and Diane Dollin.

Thanks to my mother and editor, Sheila McAllister. You can take the English teacher out of the classroom, but...

Jonas Mayes-Steger, for the cosmic cover art.

Special mention to Drew Ferrell at Cloaked Press.

To Visit Earth is dedicated with love to my wife, soul-mate, and best friend, Simone McAllister. Without your support, none of this would have been possible.

TEXT NOTES

LATIN NAMES FOR LUNAR FEATURES ARE TRANSLATED ON FIRST USE ONLY.

LUNAR DAY = 29 DAYS, 12 ¾ HOURS, MEANING THAT FOR ANY FIXED POINT ON THE MOON, DAY AND NIGHT EACH LAST FOR JUST UNDER 15 EARTH DAYS.

TIME ZONES USED

LST = LUNAR STANDARD TIME
(LUNAR RESEARCH STATION / HOUSTON)

PST = PACIFIC STANDARD TIME
(LANCASTER - TWO HOURS BEHIND HOUSTON)

HST = HAWAIIAN STANDARD TIME
(MAUI – FOUR HOURS BEHIND HOUSTON)

Contents

PROLOGUE

The small piece of frozen detritus had orbited since the dawn of creation. After an unimaginable time some other unseen body started to influence its quiet, stable equilibrium. Imperceptibly, over many thousands of years, it slowed. The almost impossibly distant influence of the star, indistinguishable from the myriad other stars at this distance, called it home.

* * *

On the star's third planet, a long ice age retreated. Ape-like creatures spread across the warming land and started to group together. Slowly they learned to communicate and to influence their future.

* * *

A hundred thousand years passed before the object came close enough to its star to feel any real influence. Almost at the end of its long fall, the eternal darkness lessened. The Sun was a cold and faintly golden spark shining like a minute jewel; a tiny beacon to indicate the final destination.

* * *

On Earth, a great age of war and terrorism raged. At the end of the 21st Century, as counted in the Christian calendar, the First Age of civilisation ended abruptly and with devastating finality. Violence spiralled to a peak. Countless millions died in a desperate cycle of hatred and intolerance.

History failed to record the country or group responsible for the horrors of the end game. Without warning, the holiest shrines of every religion were destroyed. Each place was levelled by twin nuclear detonations. As a stunned world tried to come to terms with its losses, conventional weapon attacks razed the principal seats of government, most while in session. No counter attack systems functioned.

Shocked anarchy set in. Surviving religious leaders and governments were universally blamed and deposed and, in the final act of destruction, most local places of worship were destroyed, either by their own or rival congregations.

A brief but terrible epidemic raged through the world's major cities, spreading within weeks to every corner of the globe. Over half of mankind perished in three short months. It struck indiscriminately; every single person contracted it, half surviving and becoming immune. Four billion died. Over the next twenty years the population fell until it had been halved again.

There was an interregnum of around fifty years, as the human race stabilised and numbers increased once more. A sense of togetherness amongst the survivors saw new countries form out of the ruins. Organised religion was shunned, and people of faith congregated quietly, if at all. There were no bans and no interdicts; belief became a more private and dignified affair.

Mankind made a conscious decision to work with the resources of its beautiful planet, rather than exploiting them without a conscience. Although solar, wind, and water drove the Second Age, the damage was already done. Ice melted and sea levels rose inexorably, many low-lying places becoming inundated. The new young nations, some named after the originals, either worked to stem the tide or rise above it.

* * *

When the object was still many billions of kilometres from journey's end, the Sun began to make its presence felt, physically asserting its mastery as with all the other matter under its influence. Still a vast distance away, there was the gentlest brush against the object's surface. It began to feel the by-product of the continual titanic blast of nuclear fusion. It was now both pulled and pushed, as the mighty forces of gravity and the solar wind fought against each other to

2

destroy it. There would be no return to the edge of creation at the end of this journey. The object was so small, and it fell in such a way, that it would be sucked inexorably into the star. There, in the instant of an unseen flash, it would be silently absorbed.

* * *

War was a thing of the past. Stable nations flourished across the different continents. The Human Race looked at itself for the first time and saw a civilisation at peace. Like their recent ancestors at the end of the First Age, they started to explore the space around it.

* * *

For the first and only time since it was formed, the tiny object started to lose the cold of absolute zero. At first it seemed reluctant to surrender just a few atoms of its small mass to the hurricane force of electrons flowing outward from the beacon ahead. Almost imperceptibly, motes of gas started to surrender to the blast and were scraped away, forming a faint trail behind it and turning it into a visible object for the first time in creation.

* * *

On Earth, somebody looked straight at it.

1 - LUCY
7:25 AM (PST) 15th MAY

Fresh from her early morning run and shower, Lucy Grappelli savoured the warm air on her penthouse balcony at the Santa Ana Needle, California's tallest building. She had a stunning view across the ribbon city of Palmdale-Lancaster-Mojave, more commonly styled as PaLaMo. She watched idly as a SubOrbital ship lifted off almost directly towards her from Edwards International, a few kilometres away to the northeast. Even here, over 500 m above the desert floor, the day would soon be too hot for comfort, but for now she was able to enjoy the sights and sounds outside.

The last few days of her six-month rotation home on Earth were spent outside as much as possible. She loved to swim, or walk in the hills, but in two weeks Lucy was departing for her third tour of duty as senior field geologist at the Eugene Francis Kranz Research Station, usually known as "Gene's Place", near Crater Maskelyne on the Moon. At work she walked around the base with weights to keep fit, and the drug treatments stopped any loss of bone mass. It just wasn't the same. Although she lived for her job, she would miss desert breezes and swimming for the next six months.

The SubOrb turned eastwards. Already high enough to make a vapour trail in the cooler layers, the rumble of its departure finally reached her. Lucy visualised the wings pivoting to increase the already sharp sweep as it transitioned into rocket mode and streaked away towards to the fringes of space. The early morning clarity was already fading as the desert air soaked up the sun and started to rise and shimmer.

A tiny sensor in her right index finger buzzed, and she turned to point it at the nearest wall. SENTIENT (Secure Intelligent) recognised the gesture, and checked her fingerprint. If

4

she had been sleeping, it wouldn't wake her for calls except for those from certain numbers. The system knew she was awake, and the caller was on her approved list for video uplink. Any empty space on the apartment walls could provide a screen, and a camera nexus. The camera icon showed briefly on the wall next to the caller ID: "NASA / Leif Culver."

Lucy touched her second finger to her left thumb, unconsciously bringing two sensors together in acknowledgement, and the wall opened a screen. Culver smiled at her from the balcony wall. He looked pale and tired, and the usual easy smile crinkles were missing.

"Hey, Leif. Couldn't sleep?"

"Good morning Lucy, apologies for the early call. I know you have a few days of your leave left, so I shouldn't be asking for your time. Something important came up here overnight, and you definitely need to hear about it as soon as possible."

"What's the problem?"

"Not exactly a problem, but there's about to be a real sensation; to me it has 'Grappelli' written all over it. AusAstro at Woomera reported a new comet discovery by an Australian amateur two days ago. Some friend of Wilco's there called him for a confirmation sighting, which came late last night. According to his team it will make the closest Earth pass ever seen on Earth. Ed Seals has been up all night calculating trajectories, and his early math suggests an approach of between two and three million kilometres."

A shiver ran down her spine. "Oh wow. That'll be spectacular. Sensation may be an understatement."

Culver grinned at his geologist. He took in her long dark brown hair, curling slightly as it dried, and the strong cheekbones in her expressive face. Her brow tightened slightly, into what he thought of as work mode. She was handsome, rather than pretty.

5

"Indeed. The Astronomy team are all hopping with excitement. Wilco has asked the Australians to sit on it for another 48 hours while he and Ed try to run some more accurate numbers, but after that the news will get out very quickly. I'm trying to keep it in house until then. I want NASA and AusAstro to jointly break the news. I've just spoken to their management, and they are happy to work with us on that basis. Space Works India has had far too much publicity with that new space station of theirs, and a press coup like this would be good for us all."

The concept began to sink in properly. "Leif, two or three million klicks is way too close. How big is this thing? I know Ed's math is sharp, but could it hit us?"

"Well, as comets go it's apparently very small, and they are sure it has a high ice content but, in theory, yes, it could hit us. Ed says not, and that's not only down to the math. You already know how intuitive he is, and he's done the numbers and put his pencil down. I'd trust my life to his calculations. Everyone else is busy trying to check his analysis for official release. And if it does look like it's aiming right at us when all the numbers come in, we do have an option to move its orbit with the near-Earth object KICK protection system long before it gets here."

Lucy raised her voice. "Absolutely not, Leif! You know Comets aren't solid, and KICK would make it worse. I'd use it as an absolute last resort, and then only if the math comes up with a direct Earth hit. If so, then yes, I'd KICK it as soon as possible. Definitely not unless."

Culver nodded, and held up a calming hand. He looked twenty years younger when he smiled. "I'm right with you on that, and it's a first. I'll make a diary note; Culver and Grappelli agreed on something. Now, the specific reason I called you first is because of your post-grad paper on Cometary Geology. I know that was fifteen years ago, but it's been broken out again. Astronomy has already told Exploration of course. That office has gone into spasm trying to work out if they have time to design and build, or even maybe scavenge something from existing hardware to rendezvous with it. They will certainly want to talk to you as that effort progresses. Heck, we might be able to bring you a fresh comet rock."

Lucy moved to a sofa and sat down. The screen followed her, ducking to avoid a picture as it moved seamlessly across the wall, with the virtual camera keeping her in focus. "Stars! I don't know what to say. I'm shaking here. The only thing I've ever wanted was to study comet rocks that haven't been fried in the atmosphere or impacted on the Moon. I'd given up on the idea years ago. Right now I'd bet money that if we do retrieve anything, I'd have to rewrite the entire thesis. You're going to send a manned mission, right? My career priority just changed on that idea. I'll cast around for volunteers for my job, because someone else can pick up prospecting on the Moon. I have to go there, land on it, and choose my own pieces for sure!"

Culver gave a theatrical sigh. "Cancel the diary note, we're back to disagreeing as usual. You know that the risk to any manned vehicle approaching a comet this close to the sun is too high. Look, there's no use having a fight about it at this stage. I don't know exactly how we'll approach the problem because I only heard the news at midnight.

"My gut feeling is a remote exploration and retrieval probe to take samples. The pass is due around the fall equinox next year, so that only gives us sixteen months to get all our shit in one sock. It's a tall order even for an organisation as adaptable as we are."

Lucy pressed the point, shaking her head till damp hair flicked across her face. "No, Leif, no, unmanned isn't good enough, and anyway it's been done before. There has to be a safe way to get

7

a team there. I must have a piece of this; you know, literally, a proper piece!" She gave a wry laugh. "We can argue that one later. In the meantime what do you need? I've got thirteen days left before I lift back to Gene's, and I don't have any firm plans. You know me; I'm desperate to go back to work, and until then my time is yours."

"OK, argument parked and offer accepted. I just had an idea. Have you ever heard of Allen Percival?"

"Percival? I don't think so. Oh, maybe, wait a second. I might have met a Percival at one of those astronomy conventions Ed Seals took me to a couple of years ago when before we..." she paused. "Yes, at the observatory in Chile, I think it was. Why?"

"That's him. He's an Australian; owns the Wild Lives Theme Park and Zoo near Adelaide. I knew about the park but apparently it's the tip of an iceberg, the visible part of a global business empire. Percival is a wealthy and influential man. He's also a passionate amateur astronomer with a home observatory some countries couldn't afford. He discovered the comet."

"Now I remember him; nice guy, loud but charming. But what's he got to do with me?"

"Wilco called him last night to tell him the comet was being named after him. The guy was so excited he couldn't speak. He's flying in to join a staff meeting about it tomorrow evening. We're going to have a bit of fun with him. I don't believe he has any idea what we are predicting. He thinks it's just another comet, and only out of the ordinary because it's got his name on it.

"I'm going to spring our numbers on him at the meeting. I want to shock him and find out how he takes it. The guy may be rich, but he's not a publicity seeker. It's interesting that you'd met him and I'd heard his name mentioned in amateur astronomy circles, but neither of us really knew much about him. In two days he's going to be screen famous whether that suits him or not. I've been following up a vague idea and checking his credentials. He went to university in England and got himself a first in Volcanology. You and he might even be able to talk rocks. How would you feel about meeting him at Edwards tomorrow with Wilco? You could play host for me and bring him to the meeting."

"Sure, but, I'm walking over there this morning to offer my support to the exploration team. When I've seen them, I'm coming all the way up to Floor Fifty to talk to you about landing on Percival's pet comet."

"Why am I not surprised? Oh yes, I forgot to tell you. Percival recently booked a tourist visit to Gene's for next spring. Unlike most people who can afford the trip this guy wants to do some real work, and he's asked to be attached to the astronomy team there for the experience. I might have bigger plans for him."

2 – LANCASTER
11:55 AM (PST) 16th MAY

It was over a century since the old LAX airport slid into the Pacific along with parts of western Los Angeles, following a prolonged realignment of the local geological fault zones. East of the protective Coast Ranges, Edwards International rapidly became the long-haul hub serving the new world city of PaLaMo, plus much of the New American southwest. Now the second busiest SubOrbital departure terminal in the Americas, only OrbitOne at Dallas/Fort Worth launched more ballistic transports. To the northeast was AstroCal, the principal manned space launch facility for the New States of America.

Lucy watched as Allen Percival's private 'craft parked next to NASA 1, the organisation's own SubOrb. She stood airside outside their private terminal at Edwards, with NASA Astronomer the Honourable Arthur Stephen John La Grange Warrender, better known as Wilco. As the engines spooled down, Percival opened the drop-door, grinned at the pair, and bounded down the steps as they were still locking into place.

Wilco wasn't really stuffy, but he clung to an English liking of order and good manners. As soon as he laid eyes on their visitor, he half turned to Lucy. "Would you like to do the introductions?"

She stifled a smile as she noted Percival's look of recognition. "No, you're the senior here, Wilco. I'm just along to talk rocks with Mr. Percival. But thanks."

Wilco offered his hand, and greeted the visitor in his aristocratic English accent, "Ah, Allen Percival, I'm Arthur Warrender. Good to meet you at last."

"And you, Mr. Warrender. I'm still in shock."

Wilco managed a polite laugh. "We can dispense with the formality, Allen. I usually answer to 'Wilco' around here. They tell me it's the accent, but of course I don't even have one. It's all these New Americans. Allow me to introduce NASA's Senior Lunar Field Geologist, Lucy Grappelli."

Percival looked hard at the tall, attractive woman as he shook her hand, noting the firm, assertive grip. "Now I'm sure I know you from somewhere, Miss Grappelli."

"Please call me Lucy. As Wilco said, we're not too formal. We met in Chile a couple of years ago."

"Crikey, yes! I knew I'd seen you before. You're Ed Seals' girlfriend of course. I didn't even know you were a geologist."

"Ed and I split a while back, but it's OK. We're good friends."

A look of horror killed the grin, and he flushed. "Strewth! I've been here less than two minutes and already put me bloody foot in it. Might have to go home. Sorry."

Lucy felt contrite. "It's no problem. Really, it's not." She changed the subject. "Hey, Wilco here is astronomical aristocracy, practically Royalty. His father is the English Astronomer Royal. NASA had to bid high against Space Works India to get him. When I met you in Chile he was at the Lunar Observatory, otherwise he'd have been there too. He's also pretty hilarious."

"Oh, for pity's sake, you're an embarrassment, Lucy," complained Wilco, rolling his eyes as they walked indoors out of the searing heat. "Anyway Allen, are you looking forward to the meeting this evening? We have quite a high-powered crew working on your comet, and it seems like everybody at Lancaster wants to say hello." He turned to look at the Australian. "I do need to check something with you. I know you've just booked a trip to the Moon with us, but how flexible would you be, time-wise?"

"With a week's notice I can leave the company in safe hands any time. I spend half the year travelling on business anyway, and they don't miss me much. I took six weeks off once before and nobody even got killed." He still didn't know where the astronomer was heading with this. "What would change my plans?"

"Ah, now, we'll talk about that later on," was Wilco's cryptic reply.

* * *

Lucy and Percival entered the crowded and buzzing lecture theatre on the 10th floor of Space Tower One, NASA's high-rise headquarters building in Lancaster. About 200 people were crammed into the space. Moving the organisation from its traditional home in Houston to the New States was a direct result of Texas joining Spanish America, although NASA still had Mission Control and their University in that city.

NASA Director Leif Culver walked across to the lectern. He had real presence; exceptionally tall but well proportioned at over two metres. He held up one hand, and the audience fell silent.

"Good evening everybody and thanks for coming. We have a guest tonight; the Australian entrepreneur and amateur astronomer Allen Percival has kindly flown in to be with us. Allen, please step up here and join me on the stage."

Percival was surprised to find himself shaking hands with Culver to a polite round of applause. He was then seated at one side of the stage next to Seals. As Culver turned to the lectern, Seals said quietly, "It's good to see you again, Allen. Now, take a deep breath my friend, because your life is about to change."

Culver turned to the audience. "Allen has joined us to find out why we are all so excited about Comet Percival. These days, it's unusual to have an amateur discover one. Somehow everybody in the business missed it, but he has found us a rare treat. I have to say

12

that it's a long while since I've seen so much excitement here at HQ."

He handed Percival a microphone. "So, Allen, has anyone given our surprise away yet?"

Percival stood up. He sensed a real affinity with this forum. There was good humour here and they were obviously setting him up for something.

"Thanks for inviting me, Mr. Culver. I haven't got past being shocked out of me skin yet. To tell you the truth I've been mystified ever since Mr. Warrender called me yesterday. I decided to come straight here and see what all the bloody fuss was about."

There was a general laugh and the Director grinned back at him. "I'm sure Wilco told you we're not usually too formal here. Please call me Leif."

He turned to the forum. "OK, so let's introduce Allen to his comet. 3/A/72 Percival is a very small comet, and it's relatively close in already. We are projecting perihelion in the late fall of next year. Several observatories around the globe are watching it now, plus the Deep Space Telescope at Gene's Place on the Moon. The astronomy team are checking recent data to see if they can track it back any further.

"What's even more interesting about Percival is the lack of an orbit. There are two things that set it apart from the majority of comets we regularly monitor, or those we discover for the first time. Firstly, Ed's early calculations show it as a terminal run. He says that instead of passing perihelion and heading back out, it will fall directly into the Sun. And that's not even the most interesting part of it."

Astronomy and Exploration had been keeping the news quiet, and Culver was stopped short as a buzz of conversation started. He turned back to address Percival directly. "OK, folks, thanks. So, Allen, I am sure you will remember Comet Eckett, a few

13

years back. As with so many of its predecessors, it was billed as 'The Comet of The Century'. It turned out to be barely visible at best. Percival is small, but already showing a tail. We believe it contains more ice than most. The downside of all these suppositions is that, if they're correct, it may still lose most of that gas before it gets close enough to become a naked-eye object.

"On the other hand, we already know this one will be visible. If Ed's numbers are right, Comet Percival is going to pass less than three million kilometres away from the Earth. We are in for a genuine visual treat, and you, sir, have assured yourself of a place in astronomical history."

Percival sat stunned as the room erupted into applause. *Astronomical history? Crikey, rock star treatment from some of the planet's cleverest people.*

Even for Director Culver, it took a while to bring the room back to peace. "Thanks, team, that'll do. All right, now." He waited for quiet. "Allen, Wilco does a regular June to December tour at Gene's, so he will be at the Lunar Observatory during the pass next year. He's already refusing offers to swap, because there are people here, and at Houston SpaceTech, who would sell their kids for the chance to go. We've talked it over, and I am offering you the opportunity to reschedule your lunar visit to coincide with the pass, because Wilco says you ought to be there to see it. I see it as a fantastic publicity exercise; I can already picture him interviewing you out on the surface with your comet in the background. He tells me you have some flexibility into your busy life."

Percival was left in shock. "Uh? Well, yeah. I could go whenever Wilco says. Look, Leif, I'll need some time to take all this in. I blame jetlag, but me head is spinning here. I'm stunned."

Culver put a hand on his shoulder and turned to the forum. "OK, I think we surprised him, folks. I have one more unusual duty to perform this evening before we can accept you into the organisation. Many people around here have a unique nickname, or call sign. Mine is Stretch, on account of the height d'you see? It doesn't get used much now as I'm usually on Earth. Most of the paying tourists who visit the Moon proudly arrive back with one as a rare and priceless souvenir.

"I received an unusual suggestion today that we tag you before you go. One of my scientists, Kent Warwick, and his wife spent their honeymoon in Australia last year and visited your park. He's told us that apart from the night sky, your other passion is Australian bird life. Where are you, Kent?"

A young man with heavily spiked bright red hair stood up and waved. He was wearing such a badly fitting vintage tweed jacket that it looked like it might have been designed for an alien species.

"Allen, the strange creature waving down there is Kent. He's easy to spot and you can blame him for this at your leisure. He pointed out how tricky it would be if we have to call both you and your comet Percival. He suggested that we identify you as 'Pelican', like your park mascot."

Percival roared laughing, and the room joined him. His fate was sealed. "OK, Kent, what's yours?" he called when he got his breath back.

"They've tried several," was the reply from the floor, "but nothing has stuck yet. I'm too unique!"

"OK, I can't argue on that score. Did you know I got called Pelican in school? I had a pet one when I was a kid and my feet stuck out like his."

"No, I didn't. But I'd still say it," admitted Kent.

"Pelican it is, then, but take note that I reserve the right to get you back."

15

Kent made an exaggerated shrug and sat down, still laughing.

Culver spread his arms. "OK, team, that's the main business over for now. It seems to me that a celebration is in order, so let's reconvene on the 36th in fifteen minutes." He turned to their guest once more. "Pelican, that's the bar. Would you like have a drink with us?"

Pelican waved the new ID pass that doubled as a charge card while on NASA property. "Drinks? Bloody right, fellas, drinks are on the Pelican."

3 – RECRUIT
7:22 AM (PST) 17th MAY

Lucy woke with the desert sun on her face. SENTIENT was buzzing a call but it soon stopped. It would wait. She didn't foresee the best of mornings. Shuffling to one side of the big bed to get out of the sun, she kicked off the remaining shoe, and lay for a while with shut eyes, wondering if her head would stop spinning. What an evening. Pelican had insisted on putting his card behind the bar and then declared it well and truly open. Beyond that her memory of the affair was pretty fuzzy. There might have been a taxi. Finally she opened her eyes and found herself in her own bedroom at the Needle.

On her way to the bathroom, she switched on the coffee maker. After half a litre of water, a long shower, and a couple of cups of coffee she decided she might live. She finally picked up the message from Leif Culver, reminding her to collect Pelican for a meeting at 9:00 AM on Floor Fifty, across at Space Tower One. The clock said 8:25 AM; just enough time to get over there. The walk through Seventy Palms Park might do her some good.

In the Point NASA hotel area of Space Tower One she rapped hard on the door of suite 2024. "Come on, Pelican! It's Lucy Grappelli. You up yet?"

The door opened.

"Hey there Lucy! What a cracking evening. Did you stay here at the hotel?"

The guy had no right to look 100% fit and healthy. The deep tan probably helped, but it still wasn't fair. She'd begun to recall some of the evening's hilarity and was sure he'd had a skinful too. "No, I got a taxi home, and I'm delicate this morning. You look OK."

17

"It's a front, I'm good at hiding it but I feel like death." They both laughed a little.

She called the elevator. "You took it all in good humour last night. I'm sure Leif was testing your reactions because you're a bit of an unknown quantity. If it was a test you obviously cheated, buying the bar like that. You'd have aced it anyway. Even before that you'd made a lot of friends at the staff meeting."

"I've never been so bloody excited. Look, I'm 48 years old and I've been successful enough to be bored half to death. Now I'm going to have to keep notes and write a book. You know, the park and the import business just pay for stuff, but the stars are where me passion lives. I booked this trip to the Moon as a once in a lifetime treat, because even for a fella like me it's expensive. Now I've been pitched right into the middle of this comet event."

"Is there a Mrs. Percival?" Lucy asked, "What does she think of you going off planet?"

He darkened a little. "She and I don't see much of each other these days. We signed a twenty-year contract just before Kyle was born, but we let it lapse. She still lives at the park but we have separate lives. We're friends, but not close."

"Oh, I'm sorry. Guess that pays me back for embarrassing you over Ed yesterday. Call it evens?"

He laughed, "You'd keep score? OK, evens it is then. You're a hard case, Grappelli."

They arrived on Floor Fifty to be greeted by an elegantly dressed woman of about sixty.

"Hi Lucy, and a very good morning to you Mr. Percival, I'm so glad you could join us. I'm Penny Tipton, Leif Culver's Assistant. Now, might anybody need medication? I hear there was some sort of party last night. The description 'world class' was offered a few

18

minutes ago. Anyway, the Director would like you to join him in the office. There's a small breakfast gathering and a buffet."

Lucy gratefully accepted some pills and then ushered Pelican into a spectacular and huge office space. It featured double aspect full length windows, plus a large glass balcony. About twenty people were present, standing around or sitting with cups of coffee. Pelican spotted Wilco and Seals among them. Culver approached them.

"Good morning Lucy. Ah, there you are, Pelican," said the Director warmly. "Well then, you two don't look so badly off. I was hoping the whole inner circle would be up here but apparently we took some casualties. Kent called in from his bathroom floor a few minutes ago to excuse himself. Lightweight!"

Pelican laughed with him. "Thanks, Leif. I do have a bit of a head going here, but I'll live. I think I was delivered to me room by a person, or persons unknown. I must owe somebody thanks or an apology, or both, but I don't know who or which."

Culver waved that away as he led them to a well-stocked buffet, "Hey, they had to deliver Kent too. At least you didn't have to be put in a shower. That young man is a complete liability at a party. Maybe we should include the ability to hold a drink as a prerequisite for joining the business. Anyway, I'm getting ahead of myself. Come and have some breakfast."

Lucy started to feel better as the pills kicked in and she picked at something to eat. "Bacon cures everything," she declared, indicating a steel-haired man with a heavily lined but young-looking face. "Here, this is my boss. Pelican, meet Gene's Base Commander Andrew 'Ajax' Thibodeaux. We missed you at the party last night, Ajax."

"Great to meet you, Pelican," said Ajax, meeting his eye with a direct look. "I hear you are visiting us next year."

19

"That's what we need to discuss this morning," interjected Wilco, joining them. "You look OK, Pelican, but I'm going to have to go and lie down again, I'm afraid." His face was almost as grey as his hair. After exchanging a few more words, he excused himself and left in a hurry.

The breakfast meeting broke up around 10:30 AM. After the others went off to ride desks, Lucy, Culver and Pelican were left in the office with Seals and Thibodeaux. They sat casually on a three quarter square of sofas just inside from the balcony. The glass wall was open, admitting a warm breeze.

Culver put his coffee cup down. "So, Pelican, we have a proposition to make to you and it's great that we are all here to discuss it. We rarely manage to get together in one place, although Ed is sitting in for Wilco, well you saw what he looked like. Usually at least one of us is either on the Moon or dealing with some sort of business elsewhere.

"There's no doubt that your comet is going to be a major sensation. We have a news conference tomorrow. NASA would like to use you to enhance our own publicity and I've got a proposal to make. I know you have a four-week stay at Gene's Place booked for next spring, more like six weeks off Earth when travel is taken into consideration. As I said last night, if your schedule allows and you would be keen, we would like you to be there at Gene's during Comet Percival's closest approach."

"That's what I thought you said," Pelican replied, "but this morning me head was so confused I wondered if I'd been dreaming." They all laughed.

"No, I said it alright," Culver told him. "So, we seem to be looking at the fall equinox for a core date of September 20th, give or take. We already have a planned tourist flight departing in the middle of August, but we want you to consider something radically

20

different, depending on your availability." He turned to the astronomer. "Over to you, Ed."

Seals was on the edge of his seat, desperate to get in on the conversation. "As Leif says, we've only had a couple of days to come up with a plan. Unfortunately you managed to break Wilco last night, as well as Kent. I was hoping he would be here to ask you this himself. He's on duty at Gene's from the end of June through December next year. I'd chew off my own leg to be there, but the rosters were set ages ago and I will be based here at Lancaster. He usually ropes in anyone he can for assistance, as the based astronomy department there is normally a one-man show.

"This was Leif's idea, but in his very English way Wilco declared it 'absolutely wizard'. He noted that you had asked for observatory experience during your visit. He wants to take you on as his official astronomy assistant for the whole six-month rotation. Now we have no real idea about your situation with regard—"

Pelican was already out of his seat, waving his arms. "For crying out loud, yes mate! Absolutely yes! I've been trying to find an excuse to let me boy Kyle take over and run the business at home. I'll bloody well do it!"

Culver looked delighted. "That's great news. Now, we need to work around some red tape. To make any stay on the Moon beyond the usual tourist visit legitimate, we need to take you on as a NASA employee. Prior to us ratifying a work permit you will need a two-day visit to the Flight Surgeon here at Lancaster to assess your fitness. Before you can go into space there will be some intense training too, a good deal more than those doing the four-week tourist trips receive, but we can get most of that done in about six weeks. We already have NASA University training courses scheduled in Houston for September/October and February/March. I can place you on either of those to suit you and your business, but again, we can discuss all that later. In principle, are you are willing to commit nine months of your life to training, shuttling to the Moon and back, and working with Wilco?"

"Again, absolutely yes!" Like Lucy, Pelican had woken with a hangover just a few hours ago wondering how bad his day would be. *Not bad, but definitely weird.*

Culver had one more comment to make on the subject. "Of course, if we put you on the payroll, it will be on a Space Tech 2B grade level; that's the lowest that will get you a work permit for the Moon. The money isn't that much, but the juniors take it because it all counts to seniority and better bids for trips. The thing is, to make the visit legal we have to be paying you, and we won't be able to take your money for the tourist trip."

"Oh, come on, Leif. I can afford it."

Thibodeaux spoke for the first time. "This isn't about money, Pelican. It's to do with the Red Book; Space rules and regs. If we took you as a tourist and kept you there longer than a month, we break about 28 of Deputy Director Will Redwood's precious rules. Space knows, he's difficult enough half the time even when we follow them!"

The NASA team laughed among themselves. Lucy added: "Yeah, Leif, where is my least favourite manager this morning anyway?"

"Oh, my!" said Culver theatrically. "He must have slipped my mind. I unexpectedly dispatched him to Boston yesterday afternoon to report in person to the President and break the news about Comet Percival. He's due back later, which is why we had to get this meeting in so early after what was always going to be a hard night. Anyway, we're all settled on how we'll handle this, and my Precious Deputy will receive precisely worded paperwork to that effect through the correct channels as soon as we are finished here.

"If the truth be told, it's been the easiest job interview I've ever conducted. This candidate fills all the requirements for an off planet assignment with NASA. In fact, as the discoverer of a major new comet, I recommend to the interview board present that we offer him the position of Astronomy Lab. Assistant, grade 2B, with immediate effect. All those in favour?" Lucy, Thibodeaux and Seals immediately raised their hands to join his.

Culver called Penny, who appeared with a ready-prepared sheaf of paperwork for Percival to sign. The Director stood and offered his hand to the Australian.

"Space Tech Grade 2B, A/72-00453 Allen Randall Percival, welcome to NASA. I hope you enjoy the Experience."

A neatly suited man wearing expensive shoes joined them, bustling in from the outer office wielding a large briefcase and complaining loudly. "Director, I wasn't made aware that we had a breakfast meeting scheduled here this morning. Oh." He stopped as the Director stood up.

Culver had his back to the door, and clearly rolled his eyes at them all before turning to greet the new arrival. "Allen Percival, meet NASA Deputy Director Will Redwood."

There was a cursory handshake, and Redwood managed a brief nod to Percival, wearing a sour expression that looked like a poor attempt at a forced smile. He carried straight on complaining to Culver. "I caught an earlier flight, and I read your message on the way. I do work when I'm travelling, it isn't all for fun you know. Look, Leif, it's just a comet. There's no need to be changing the tourist rules and sending an observer to the Lunar Observatory to get underfoot. We're not running a science exchange here, for star's sake."

"Oh, calm down Will. Pelican's a highly respected international amateur astronomer, you know. He's just discovered the comet of the millennium and I think having him there during the pass will give us some great publicity. Actually, Wilco wants him to do the whole six-month tour and we've just interviewed him for the job of astronomy lab assistant. He passed with flying colours."

"You've done what? Oh for the sake of the Galaxy, Leif, he's a fucking tourist. You can't just go around—"

"That's enough," interrupted the Director sharply. "Actually I can, with a properly accredited recruitment team such as Grappelli, Thibodeaux, and Seals. I was about to say that *we*, and in this instance that specifically means *not you*, have offered him a Tech Grade 2B position at Gene's for a six month trial, starting in June next year."

"You're recruiting amateurs now?" Redwood demanded. "We have standards. It's not as if—"

"Quiet!" Culver shouted over him. "The decision is made. Mr. Percival has a more than acceptable science degree; for your precious records he actually holds a First in Volcanology from Oxford, England. He is also a highly respected and published astronomer. You will therefore be satisfied that I have carefully complied with every single one of your precious recruitment and employment clauses. Show him your new ID, Pelican."

"Pelican?" Redwood's face screwed up even further and he looked like he'd bitten an onion.

"Ho yes, matey! It's me new handle," said Pelican jovially, slapping Redwood on the back. He knew the man wouldn't like it. "Kent Warwick's bright idea, apparently. When they told me I laughed like a bloody nutter. Have you got one?"

"One what?"

"Nickname? Handle?"

"Of course not, childish nonsense."

24

"Oh, yes he has," put in Lucy. But we never tell on you, do we Will?"

"Tell you what, sunshine," Pelican said amiably to Redwood, "I'm an employee here now, just like you. If you swore at your colleagues in my office like you just did here, I'd fire you on the spot."

"Oh you would, would you? So why don't you fuck right off back to your office in Australia and do exactly that then." Even as Culver demanded he apologise, Redwood turned on his heel and stalked out, still muttering loudly.

Culver sat down with a weary sigh. "Allen, I apologise on his behalf. I should just fire him, but I badly need some of his skills. He'd snap up my job and destroy the ethos we have in ten minutes if I gave him the chance. I'm working on it, but right now I can't replace him and it irritates me."

"It's fine, Leif." He's a run-of-the-mill asshole. I employ a few, and for the same reasons, but I keep 'em at arm's length. I don't really fire people for language excess though. Attitude, yes."

He grinned at Culver. "I was just giving his strings a tweak to gauge him, a bit like you did with me last night. Looks like one of the bugger's strings broke."

Culver laughed back, "It certainly does."

"Vom," said Thibodeaux suddenly, causing them all to giggle like teenagers.

"I missed that one, fellas," admitted Percival.

"Vom Redwood, but of course we don't ever tell on him," chimed in Lucy. "His nickname is Vom because he only ever got off planet twice. He's a hotshot desk pilot and a software and system genius, but zero-G never suited poor Will."

Lucy's pre-launch cocktail party was one of the highlights of her year. It gave the core team she worked with an opportunity for a get-together a couple of days before they left for their six-month rotation off planet. She went to the door herself, rather than touching finger sensor three with her thumb and letting SENTIENT do it. She was nearly bowled over by a skinny red-headed kid of thirteen.

"Lucy! Wow, the building is so high. My Dad said your Dad built it, it's amazing!"

"Hey there, Andrew McEwan. You're getting so darn tall, young man." She exchanged hugs with the kid's parents. "I bet you're heading straight outside, Drew McQ. The best view is from my bedroom balcony, and the door is open. Go that way and left. We'll be out in a few minutes." The three of them watched as the boy disappeared. For Sara's benefit Lucy added, "It's perfectly safe. At this kind of elevation there has to be a high screen to keep the breeze out. Come on in."

She sought out Pelican. "I've been waiting for ages to introduce you to my best friends. This is Evan McEwan and his wife Sara from Toronto. Evan is my deputy field geologist at NASA, and my right hand man on the Moon. We travel thousands of kilometres each season on survey work and Leif will tell you we're far and away the best geology team they've ever had. Their thirteen year-old next generation astronaut Andrew is here too, but he headed straight for the balcony to take in the view."

Lucy caught sight of Sara's face and saw "help" written all over it. She turned quickly to Evan.

"You fellas get acquainted. I can't believe it's a whole year since Pelican joined NASA, and you haven't had a chance to meet him yet. He's got a degree in volcanology and a strong personal dislike of Vom Redwood, so he's definitely on our team."

The men both laughed, as she caught Sara's arm. "Come on, let's leave these boys to talk."

She steered her friend into an impressive bathroom. "Are you OK?"

Sara looked at her for a second and swallowed hard. "No I'm not. You know how I hate flying. I wanted to take the train, but Evan booked us on the SubOrb as a surprise for Andrew. StratoCanada did upgrade us into first when they spotted him checking in though. To tell you the truth, I'm queasy today. I'll be good in a few minutes. I can't..." She flushed and started to cry as Lucy put an arm round her.

It took a minute or two for Sara to recover enough to speak. "I'm lying to you, Lucy; I feel like death. I haven't told him yet, so you're the first to hear because I only found out this week. Andrew is getting a surprise brother or sister."

Lucy felt her own tears starting as they hugged. "That's great news, Sara. Oh, magic! I thought Evan said it could never happen."

"Not after Andrew. Well at least the doctor said so anyway. Look, I'm not going to tell him until you two are safely on the Moon. He'll be upset to miss the birth but if I tell him now I know he won't go, and that would be all wrong. Anyway, he was a nightmare when I was so ill carrying Andrew and I know he'd be far worse this time as soon as he heard. I'll be better off away from his fussing. Honestly, it's easier for me without that extra stress. Do you think you could manage not to say anything yet? I'll find out by accident, maybe next week sometime, OK?

"He'll be so mad."

"Only if he finds out I knew before he went, but more so if he knew I'd told you. I do feel better for telling you though."

"That's not a problem. I may be loud, but I'm good at controlling what I say." She chuckled. "Well, unless I'm dealing with management, of course. Reason does let me down there sometimes."

Sara managed a weak smile. "You know me, Lucy. I'm frightened of everything. I hate the risk every day Evan is out there but I would never stop him going; not even now when I'm expecting his miracle child. I'm scared of my emotions; I don't even know if feeling like this makes me weak and foolish, or brave and stupid."

"Strong, Sara. You're putting him first by letting him go, but if what you need most is not having him fussing around you, then it's the right thing for you too. He might have a flash of panic, but nobody would ever know. He'll get over it in ten minutes because that's how he is; the supreme pragmatist."

Sara snapped at her. "And I wish everyone would stop telling me Andrew is the next generation of NASA. I don't want him out there like Evan. I wish you'd all stop with this Drew McQ business. It makes me feel like he has no choice, you know, tag him and he's yours, er, theirs. Oh, blast it, now I've gone and yelled at my best friend. I'm sorry Lucy, I don't know what's the matter with..." She started to cry again.

"Come on, It should be me apologising. The nickname was my idea, and it sort of caught on. I can hold my hand up for that; my fault."

Sara's tears turned to laughter. "What am I doing? Look at the state of me. I never get angry. I think the hormones are fighting. Watch out, pregnant lady with attitude. With Andrew I did nothing but throw up and cry for seven months and here I am picking fights."

28

"It's OK. Maybe letting it all out is good, and you know I'm not easily upset. I bet feeling different means the pregnancy will be easier than before. I bet you it's a girl." She held her friend's shoulders and looked into her eyes. "Look, I promise I'll try and get them to call him Andrew. Now you've tested out every emotion in the book on me, do you still want me to take Evan for six months? Zeph Waggoner is mission prepped and he'd go at a moment's notice."

Sara nodded firmly. "Yes I do. He must go with you, but next year I may want him to stay home."

"That's how we'll do it then. Look, I need to host, so let's get presentable and go back in, shall we?"

"I get strength from you I think. Love you, Lucy. Not a word to anyone, though. Promise me?"

As they came back into the living room Lucy caught Culver saying in a stage whisper, "Quiet now or she'll hear me. Oh, rats." There was a laugh as they joined the group.

Culver pretended to double-take the pair and it was obvious he'd had a couple of cocktails. "What a spectacular place, Lucy. I was just telling this lot how my astronauts shouldn't be allowed to live in a penthouse over twice as high as my famous Floor Fifty office, even if their dad did build it. And there you are, Sara, I'm so pleased to see you." He took the Canadian woman's hand. "You look great. I saw Evan was here, but I thought you weren't coming across this time. Where is the next generation astronaut? How's the best boy?"

Usually, Sara would freeze, mumble something, and make a rapid exit. She didn't like parties, and loathed being the centre of attention, but Culver always brought out the best in her.

"Andrew is on the balcony. Evan wanted to bring him. You know I hate the fuss and I'd rather be home, but Evan did promise

29

that he could come and see his dad off on a Corona launch. He's been nagging about visiting Lucy in the Needle ever since he heard she was moving in. He's having a major rush about buildings. Right now the Needle is a thirteen year-old would-be architect's dream. He headed straight out for the view she promised him on the screen last night, but I'll check on him in a minute."

"He won't be back any time soon," Culver assured her. "Chermak and Fancy are out there and I'd be willing to bet they're sounding off at him about rocketry. Those two are taking most of this gang to work on Tuesday aboard the St. Louis. Anyway, Lucy always has the SubOrb schedule on a screen out there. There are several due off in the next half hour or so. He'll see those OK, but Corona launches at AstroCal, way out east of here. You two will have to ride out there with me to watch it go on Tuesday."

Sara was impressed, although she loathed watching any launch carrying her husband. "Are thirteen year olds allowed over there, Leif?"

"Not normally, but god-children of lunar base commanders most certainly are, especially as guests of the NASA Director. My precious Deputy will have far too much on his hands to do any complaining. It's still not 'what you know', as they say." He waved his glass around, indicating that it was empty.

Lucy laughed with the others, but she knew Sara would struggle keeping up a conversation for long.

"Sara and I are just heading outside to see if Andrew is OK. I'll be back soon."

Outside, Andrew had indeed made a beeline for the astronauts, and was still busy pounding them with questions. Both men looked like they were enjoying themselves. Sara moved to retrieve him, but Lucy laid a hand on her arm and shook her head.

30

"Mom! MAGENTA stands for MAGnetic ENergy TAkeoff. It launches straight up the peak at Mount Rainier. Mr Fancy says it's like a cross between the Hoover Dam and a huge concrete gutter full of magnets. At the top it fires its rockets, but it's already supersonic and halfway out of the atmosphere!

He turned back to the astronauts. "Can visitors come and watch? Have you been on a MAGENTA launch, Mr. Fancy?"

"Yes, son, I have," the astronaut admitted. "It's brutal. Evan at the lowest 6G acceleration I nearly swallowed my wisdom teeth. I'm a Spacewing driver these days, that's the big shuttlecraft we launch on top of a Corona rocket just over there at AstroCal." He pointed northeast. "Much more civilised."

"What about the TUGs, where do they go?"

Sara looked at Lucy again, but the geologist shook her head and whispered, "Leave him, Sara. Let him soak it all in. Dean volunteers at the visitor centre whenever he's home. He loves it."

Dean Fancy turned to wink at the two women as he continued. "TUG is a brilliant tool. There are still three of the small Low Earth Orbit vehicles. They haul everything into place once we deliver it to orbit. When the lunar base was built, the TUGs were upgraded to make them capable of reaching the Moon from LEO space, that's what we call Low Earth Orbit, hauling a cargo POD."

"Haven't you had enough yet, Dean?" asked Lucy, knowing he hadn't. "I need to borrow Andrew and show him and his mom around a bit. I keep hearing he's the next top architect, and I promised him a trip up two more levels to the Sky Deck."

Lucy knew Sara would hear about nothing else for weeks. The kid was just like his Dad, with a head for numbers and statistics. After half an hour with Fancy, she knew there would be no more excitement about big buildings. In spite of his mother's misgivings,

Drew would eventually want to be a lot further off planet than the Santa Ana Needle Sky Deck.

5 – LAUNCH
10:45 AM (PST) 3ʳᵈ JUNE

"Ready, Pelican?"

"Sure am, Lucy. I'm so bloody excited here I can hardly breathe."

"There's not much to see I'm afraid. You'll get a spectacular view when we reach LEO-NINE though."

They were strapped in the passenger lounge aboard the Spacewing shuttle St. Louis, with Wilco, Evan, and a Communications Specialist called Paula Everett, who Pelican had been introduced to briefly as they boarded.

Chermak and Fancy were in final preparation to launch the stack known as COR466/SSL122/DS331. That stood for the 466th Corona launch, the 122nd mission by the St. Louis and the 331st in the current series of PODs transporting supplies to the Gene's Place at Maskelyne.

The PODs were spartan, with six seats separated from the cargo by a simple restraining net. The lunar astronauts wouldn't have to use it until the final hours of the trip. They would leave LEO-NINE aboard one of the TUG vehicles for the lunar transit, only entering the POD for the remotely controlled descent and landing at Gene's Place.

Various other commercial outfits on Earth also operated as far as LEO space, but NASA, or New American Space Affairs, always lifted its people by either Corona or the much more punishing, high acceleration MAGENTA.

Corona was a hybrid based on two of the early launch systems; the first genuine heavy lifter Apollo, and the later Space Shuttle. It was a direct descendent of both; an advanced lightweight shuttle sitting on top of a conventional rocket.

The beauty of the system was in its adaptability. While the Spacewing landed back at AstroCal in the Mojave Desert, the Corona rockets were also 95% recyclable. Various complete Corona cylinders and half-pipes formed the major components of most orbital hardware, together with the lunar base. All the complex valves and technical components from the engine systems were modular; easily retrieved from the rockets for return to Earth aboard the Spacewings for re-use.

Fancy checked on the crew for the last time and the countdown was un-held at minus two minutes. Pelican's heart started to race. This was a lifetime's ambition, plus the means to pay for it, elevated to the status of a free ride and an invitation to work at the lunar observatory as a lab assistant for six months.

At the viewing facility, Sara McEwan couldn't even watch the launch. Her breakfast was fighting back and she had retreated to the restroom, leaving Andrew to enjoy the show as he stood on the Mission Control balcony with Uncle Leif. He knew several people on the rocket apart from his dad and Lucy. He liked Wilco a lot, and the Englishman was always fascinating about stars and planets and stuff. At Lucy's party, Pelican had said he owned a theme park, and then invited him and his parents on a VIP visit to Wild Lives Australia when his dad got back from the Moon.

Aboard the St. Louis, Lucy followed the centuries-old litany. "Ten, nine, eight, ignition sequence start, five, engines running, two, one, zero." There was a distant rumble outside and the machine started to vibrate; it felt as if every component had been disturbed from a pleasant sleep and woken grouchy.

"Lift-off was timed at 12:33 PM, Houston time. Corona is clear of the tower."

Pelican glanced outside, looking across the comms specialist who had the window seat but was still dozing. He couldn't believe that here was an astronaut so laid back she'd actually needed prodding before replying to the roster call with a brief "Uh-huh," before slipping back into her nap. Outside, all he could see was sky. The pressure increased, pushing him down into the couch.

On the viewing deck, Drew was still yelling in sheer excitement, waving to his dad and Lucy as the huge rocket spread its impossible thunder across the searing desert. The sound hollowed as it receded, more rapidly than any of the SubOrbs he had watched from Lucy's balcony.

"Throttles up, please."

Pelican felt the discordant vibration fade into a more coherent dull buzz, but all the noise seemed to be receding into the distance. The early rockets had been much less refined, slamming and jerking as they accelerated. Dean Fancy had told him that Corona was the smoothest ride to orbit ever taken.

"Stage 1 DISCON stand by."

This would be the first real jolt although, where they were sitting aboard the St. Louis, they were a long way from the action.

"In five... four... three... two... one."

He was ejected off the couch a couple of centimetres, and then jerked to a sudden halt by the wide straps. A moment later there was a huge gong sound as the used stage disconnected, and then absolute silence for a second or two.

"Uh?" Everett opened an eye. "Nuke was that? Oh, staging." She shut the eye, relaxing back into apparent slumber.

There was another sudden jolt, back into the couch but with less pressure than before. This time there was very little shake and almost no sound. It was dark outside.

"How are you doing, Pelican?" asked Lucy.

"I'm dying of excitement here."

"No conversation from Paula. Is she sleeping?"

He chuckled, "So you know her pretty well then?"

"Yes, I've known her for years. She's sharp as a blade, so don't let the dumb act fool you. She'll act sullen, but somehow has the gift to put three words together and express a whole concept. She's a great friend to have if you're in a real jam though."

"Enough!" Paula's exclamation made Pelican jump.

Lucy laughed. "Not so fast asleep then, Paula?"

"Awake now. Yada yada yada. No peace."

The other geologist chimed in cheerfully, the friendly Canadian guy with the red hair, Evan McEwan. "Yeah, chatty this morning ain't she?"

Percival looked anxiously at Paula only to find a huge grin inside the big dome helmet.

"Yo, Pelican," said the grin, "we there yet?"

"Don't ask me," he said. "I'm the tourist around here. I'm enjoying you guys bantering."

Lucy laughed again from behind them. "Come on, Paula. Talk to the visitor, make him feel welcome."

"In edgeways, Grappelli," Paula said pointedly.

"Sorry, Pelican," said Lucy. "She wakes grouchy."

"Ain't grouchy. Ain't asleep is what." He realised these two were joshing each other, probably for his benefit.

"Were you actually asleep when we launched?" Pelican asked, fascinated by the strange woman.

"Ain't dumb," Paula said, looking at him intensely. "Ain't no tourist neither. You that Pelican found the comet!"

"Well, you're correct on that one. Strictly I'm not a tourist, I guess. I'm officially a Space Tech 2B on me first assignment to Gene's Place as Wilco's able lab assistant. That makes me a company man."

Paula laughed. She had a rich, from-your-boots deep laugh and a South Carolina accent. "Oh yeah! Our puppy now is what. Hey, new boy, y'all."

Wilco chimed in. "Paula, it's a jolly good thing NASA doesn't hold initiations or anything like that. You'd make people do horrible forfeits, or worse."

"Yeah, frat stuff. I say, wizard wheeze old boy." Her Wilco impression made them all laugh, "But hey, he done survival already."

He had indeed done survival; four days of team building in Marble Canyon, on a trail hike with his training course. Seven girls and five guys trying to live off the land and get from a drop point to a pick-up in time to catch a ride. He'd found it hard work but fun, especially as the others were all half his age or less. Papa Pelican, they'd immediately called him.

He'd had the last laugh though; they were all either waiting for assignments, starting at NASA U in Houston, or apprenticed to tech specialists. Papa Pelican was going straight to the Moon.

By the time the conversation subsided they had slipped easily into weightlessness, and he spent the next hour or so gambolling about the passenger cabin with the others as they taught him some zero-G tricks and played games.

Corona 466 caught up with LEO-NINE after four orbits, six hours after launch. The crew transferred from the St. Louis to the station via a flexible airlock. Lucy took Pelican to watch as their POD was removed from the St. Louis' cargo bay and vac-parked on a short tether next to the station. TUG 4 was due in to pick them up in a few hours.

Unlike the other two current NASA space stations which used their reference numbers, LEO-NINE was always spelled out in full. The mission badge for a tour or transit there showed a regal looking lion, and the station was rightly proud of its name. It was made up from dozens of Corona shells, fitted together in a cross, and converging on a central docking hub capable of handling four SPACEWING category ships or similar. The spokes supported two rings of the shells, forming a double-rimmed wheel with some light centrifugal gravity. To Pelican it represented hundreds of years of science fiction brought to life.

The sleeping area was situated in the outer rim of the wheel and consisted of small individual cubicles with plenty of tie-down space for luggage. There was a sleeping bag with lots of Velcro patches on the outside and the walls also had the stuff in larger panels. Pelican fell asleep stuck to the outer wall in microgravity and feeling very comfortable, but what followed was a bit of a shocker. He woke in a blind panic after a dreadful falling dream. It took a few minutes to get calm, but once he got used to the idea of low- or zero-G it was mind over matter.

TUG 4 was docked by the time he woke up, so he was able to watch from a large floor to ceiling Perspex window in a nearby unit as it connected to their POD and prepared to haul it and them off to the Moon. The TUGs were not designed for in-atmosphere work, so there were no streamlining or aerodynamic qualities about them. In fact it could best be described as looking like a gigantic tractor section from an eighteen-wheel semi, with the wheels replaced by various grappling hooks, arms and antennae. The POD attached to an open framework behind the piece that looked like a cab, and connected to an airlock there. It was a basic vehicle, but there were small sleeping spaces. They would spend most of the journey sitting around in the control cabin.

The voyage from LEO-NINE to the Moon was uneventful. He spent as much time as possible watching as the Earth receded and the Moon got closer. The TUG crew turned the vehicle so that Earth and Moon could both be visible from the side windows. Paula lightened up a bit between sleeps, and the crew quickly assimilated Pelican into their team. He became proficient in zero-G, but still had trouble with his head free falling when he tried to sleep. He was fortunate to avoid getting space-sick, the one embarrassment he had worried about.

A burn on the pair of large rockets established TUG4 in lunar orbit, where it would stay until the DS331 POD had been dropped off, and the returning DS329 launched and captured. The five astronauts going to Gene's were strapped into the remotely piloted POD, and disconnected for the final leg of the journey. It was an uninteresting hour, stuck in a seat with no window. Pelican did a "Paula", falling asleep and only waking up as the collection of small rockets underneath brought DS331 to a gentle stop on the surface.

"DS331 system shutdown at 10:52 AM. Welcome to the Moon, Pelican," announced Commander Thibodeaux.

Paula got in first, "Heck, Ajax, now you done woke the guy."

"Bloody rich coming from you!" Pelican retorted, laughing with her. "At least I don't wake grouchy. Thanks a lot, Ajax."

They sent him through the airlock first and he enjoyed a practice bounce-around on the surface while the old hands were catching him up. They were driven the five kilometres to the base aboard two vehicles that looked like a pair of ancient electric golf carts. Pelican and Wilco were taken through the airlock by the base Recycling Specialist, a First Nation American by the name of Lincoln Todd Eagle Jeffs. Ajax was there to meet him for a brief guided tour of the facilities. The place was huge, much larger than he had visualised it, and there were a lot of people about.

After unpacking in his allocated room N4/5, Pelican arrived in the lounge. There was nobody there he recognised, so he drifted around checking the notice boards and screens. One was looping a short bio on himself, with an introduction from Leif Culver. "Make Pelican welcome, folks. We are treating him as a regular NASA employee on a trial deployment. He will be Wilco's lab tech at the observatory for the next six months."

He followed a delicious baking aroma and was welcomed into the galley by a blond Canadian guy of around forty. "Hey, I know you; Pelican Percival the comet guy. Welcome aboard, dude. I'm head cook Bryan Downey, but they call me Bird." He laughed. "Pelican and Bird, eh, makes me feel like I'm your cousin, or something."

"Thanks Bird, I reckon it does. It smells great in here."

"Oh, it's English afternoon tea today, to celebrate Wilco getting back. I made scones and there's double cream and strawberry preserve. We don't do too badly. I'm serving it up outside in about fifteen so you can help yourself then. Anything else you need?"

"Information, actually. Ajax said you were the top local historian, and the go-to guy for the full tour."

"Wanna do the tour? Most of the tourists miss it out and start complaining there ain't enough picture windows after about two days. If you're here to work and learn, you'll make friends. I get off around 7:30 PM and I'd be delighted to walk ya through."

* * *

After dinner Pelican waited in the dining area for Bird. The cook launched straight into his routine.

"See the shapes of these six units set in the wall? They look like Quonset huts, but they're Corona rocket half-pipes bonded to the floor. They form the main rigid base, six each side of the central area. The ends have these airtight doors. Two of the units located at opposite sides of the square each contain an external airlock, suit storage and changing areas.

"Those kinda 'Y' shaped mouldings between 'em complete the inner walls and corners of the main square. To roof the central area of the base, a sealed carbon fibre roll was stretched and bonded to the top of the walls.

"There are four poles holding the roof taut above the space, anchored deep into the lunar regolith. At the top of each you'll see the ring holding a Perspex half globe, lifted from Earth by moulding it to fit over the dome end of a Corona fuel tank. Pre-cut holes in the roof roll fitted over the domes exactly before they were glued into place."

Pelican was amazed. "Wow, Bird, it's like a toy rocket kit all glued together properly. I could never finish 'em."

They both laughed. Bird was enjoying this as much as his guest. "Sure is, I guess. So, the boxes and sails fixed below each dome are diffusers and filters, which soften, break up, and scatter the sunlight through the living areas during the lunar day. We catch sunlight from the domes and reflect it into the corridors through each of the huts.

"The east wing contains the main laboratories and work rooms plus an airlock, North and South are living quarters, bathrooms and store rooms." He pointed along the row of doors. "In the west wing we have the kitchen, stores, medical centre, comms, the project offices and an airlock. The central square has this dining area, a general living zone round there to the right, then a comfortable lounge and finally a gym, bringing you back here. A

41

walk round the marked perimeter is 170 m, so six circuits for a kilometre. There's our cartographer, Ace Horowitz, walking round in one of the lead-weighted suits and counting. He usually does thirty circuits for a five klick walk. All the gym equipment is muscle-powered; we scavenge electricity from the treadmills etc. back into the system.

"Both airlocks open into the covered garages, built from six more Corona half-shells. Two pairs face away from the lengthways, with the others across the end of the opening leaving room for a roller door to open to the surface. Each garage has strengthening arches, lifting the roof to allow the exploration vehicles access. This gives the structures a Conestoga appearance from outside. Although pressure capable, to save air the garages are usually kept in vacuum. The outer doors can be rolled down and secured when we need them pressurised. In an emergency they double as temporary shelters if the base suffers a vacuum breach.

"Follow me through here, Pelican. This corridor runs for 42 m past all these workshops and stores, to the outer end of the structure. We are walking along the two shells that make up one side of the west garage, to reach this full size window, the one the tourists like so much.

"Outside here, you can see another set of six building units. Those are an alternative variation of the spacecraft parts, featuring filtered Perspex top halves which allow sufficient sunlight in to grow hydroponic plants. We call it the greenhouse, and it's my favourite part of the whole base. Intensive farming and water-looping over there has proved to be a massive success in supplying fresh food to the galley. On the downside, during the lunar night, the need for daylight provision draws deeply on the power reserves piped in from the remote solar stations. When the Far Side Array is built we'll have power all the time."

42

"Crikey, I can't believe paying guests don't like the tour," Pelican said in amazement. "You could make money selling tickets for this. You know, Bird, selling tickets is how I make a living, I run a zoo and theme park."

"I know about that," Bird replied. "There's a piece about you playing on the lounge info screen. Leif wanted us to be prepared to receive a proper observer rather than a tourist. You come highly recommended. Did you meet Kent Warwick?"

Pelican laughed, "Oh, yes, I met Kent. He's an original."

"Too true. I was at his wedding last year. He and Helen had their honeymoon at your place. She's into the rides and he's a wildlife geek. Well, to be fair that guy's a geek about everything he touches. I've heard all about you scoring points off of Vom Redwood too. The Director doesn't usually do gossip, eh, but he couldn't wait to share that with us up here. Following that success you're already in the core team, as far as we're concerned."

Back in Bird's office behind the kitchen, they sat with a late cup of coffee. "I'll tell you my dream, Pelican. I'd like to open a museum and a proper hotel up here. Maybe I should ask you in on that deal."

"That's a cracking vision, you know. I'd be happy to take on a consultancy for that. I'll give it some thought. No charge for ideas. Between you and me I'm considering getting out of the park altogether and finding something new to amuse me."

"Wow! Thanks, it's a cool dream but realistically my long-term place here is in the kitchen. Anyway, I've saved my favourite useless fact about building the base.

"The entire structure, apart from the ends of the two garages and the four light domes, was covered with sifted regolith, or moon dust. It fills in all the space between the huts and covers the roof to a minimum depth of 30 cm. One of the exercise bikes from the new gym was placed outside and hooked up to a lightweight conveyor belt, lifting dirt and tipping it over the roof. Naturally that prompted an immediate competition to see who on the crew could lift the most dirt in an hour. It's typical of the attitude the place seems to bring out in people. Makes you wonder how Vom would react if he ever stopped upchucking long enough to get here, eh?

7 – NEIL
11:15 AM (LST) 9th JUNE

After prepping one of the Lunar Exploration Vehicles for the first of their planned survey tours of the season, Lucy and Evan invited Pelican on the required short refresher and test-drive with the Indian LXV Engineer, Kyran Mukherjee. They were departing in the afternoon for a two week trip breaking new trails and surveying up north.

"This is like being at home," Lucy told him, as they sat round the table in back while Evan drove and Kyran checked him. "We spend far more time aboard NEIL or BUZZ than we do at the base. Last season we did nine two-week trips in our six months."

"I love it. Such a cool piece of machinery," said Pelican. "I've seen so much great stuff in the past two days I can't get over it all. Is it old?"

"Not really, LXV-252 NEIL was the first to arrive, twenty years ago. LXV-253 BUZZ is a year younger. Those equipment numbers lie in a sequence that Bird has been compiling, right back to the Apollo 15 Lunar Rover, LRV-1. The letters vary to reflect the changing mission, but the numbers are still sequential. These were named for the first two people to walk on the moon. Properly they are NEIL IV and BUZZ IV, as the fourth pair of vehicles to be named so, but we never usually bother with the numbers.

"These two measure 10x4 m, the largest vehicles ever used here. They have a single stiffened carbon-fibre structure, covered in a sandwich layer of protective foil. Bird tells me the chrome finish gives them a resemblance to old Airstream trailers, but when he goes all historical on me I have no idea what he is talking about.

"Each of the eight wheels is a metre high and the solid tyres protrude out beyond the main body for stability. The centre pairs of drive wheels are independently powered. The end pairs steer in opposition. They came up from Earth in pieces for assembly in the base garages.

"During testing, they developed an uncomfortable bounce at certain speeds in the lunar gravity. For some unknown reason BUZZ resonated at a slightly lower speed than NEIL, eventually reinforcing that observation by flipping over on one side while being driven at 35 km/h. BUZZ lay on the landing field for a day or two before they hoisted it upright.

"There was no real damage; in fact it demonstrated the durability of the design. They added extra suspension dampers, and with new centre axles to push the four non-steering drive wheels another half metre outboard. That's why they look so odd, with the snaggle-tooth wheels. That work delayed their service entry for a year.

"I heard a great story. Some wit at Lancaster reckoned they were named the wrong way round. Apparently, Neil Armstrong had a famously slow heart rate and, according to legend, always resonated a bit more slowly than Buzz Aldrin."

Kyran spent a minute or two signing Evan off as competent. He turned to speak to the others, flashing a huge grin filled with ultra-white teeth.

"That is the both of you done. Now do you think Mr. Pelican here should be allowed a small try at driving NEIL, isn't it? Most certainly I shall not be making a fuss about it with Ajax. As Mr. Pelican is a team member who is not so very keen on Vom, I am minded to be suggesting we should probably ignore every one of his rules in this case."

8 - KICK
5:35 PM (PST) 11th AUGUST

Culver and Seals sat in the executive office on Floor Fifty of Space Tower One. Most of Culver's business was done in the restaurant, or in the various coffee shops and lounges up and down the building. He only used the Floor Fifty office for high level meetings or anything involving his Deputy Will Redwood, who wouldn't be seen dead in a coffee shop. Since the comet discovery, the Director and his best friend had enjoyed the occasional quiet meeting out of the spotlight as they kept up to date.

Culver spread his arms and shrugged. "Is it, or is it not, going to hit the Earth? Do we need to KICK it? If so, when? Come on Edwin, Percival is due to shoot through here at the end of next month. We only have about a week to decide if we need to use KICK, and four more till we find out if that was a good decision. If we do need to fire the KICK system I need to make that decision now. Vom smarmed right in here yesterday and told me to KICK it or resign. I'm actively looking for a way to get rid of him. If I manage it, what about you taking the Deputy role?"

"To be honest I don't think it's really me, but if you redeploy him I might feel obliged to give it a shot. I'd certainly stand in for a while if the board wanted it."

"We'll see, but I digress. Talk to me about KICK."

KICK, the Kinetic Intervention Collision Killer, was a set of rockets with partially directional nuclear explosive devices. The system had waited outside Earth orbit, for over half a century. In theory, one of the rockets would intercept and literally kick a target into a less threatening trajectory if necessary.

The original joke acronym had stuck. KICK had been intended for dealing with near-Earth asteroids, but deploying it against a comet had never been considered. Until now it had never been used.

Seals was philosophical. "Look at it this way. Vom's opinion is irrelevant. He's got no real ideas beyond simple confrontation. We know for sure there isn't much hard stuff in the nucleus. It's all snow and ice. If we used KICK it might smash whatever is in there to pieces and spread a meteor shower across Earth's path. Most of that might miss us this time around but it would be there waiting, every September. To my mind, with the data we have available, we are better off leaving it intact and watching it slide by while we enjoy the show. That way we can watch it drag most of its ass straight into the Sun. I know it's close to call, but my math still says exactly what it did three months ago.

"The numbers have drifted a bit, at the moment they are decidedly closer, so we're probably looking at around half a million kilometres. I know that's a lot less comfortable than we originally projected and yes, astronomically it's scary close. I'm still staking my reputation on a miss."

"I believe you. Your reputation is sound, but if Earth takes a direct hit I'll be the one that gets nailed to the wall. So are we recommending, 'No KICK,' to the board tomorrow?"

Seals gave a wry laugh. "Yes, we are.

"There's something else I wanted to talk to you about. The probe will rendezvous with Percival on September 20th. I've offered Lucy a ground posting here next year to analyse the data and samples. After all, she's the cometary geology expert. She was still griping about me refusing her a manned mission organised before she left here in June, you know. She's so intense. I've got her marked as a possible future Deputy, or even Director, and she certainly carries enough weight with the folks, but I need her to focus a little differently."

48

"She'd make a great Deputy," Seals assured him, "but I agree she needs to learn better control. Tell you what; when she gets back I'd better ask her out again and try to get her to think management. I've regretted the split, but it was me that called it. I can't say I'm sure why it happened, and I wish it hadn't."

"My, we are philosophical this afternoon. Maybe we should get out of here and go for a beer."

Seals took a deep breath, and Culver wondered what was coming next. "Leif, I'm officially on leave, but I want to go to Gene's and photograph the event. This is a first in history. I've never asked you for any favours, but I am ready to get on my knees and beg you to send me."

Culver was impressed. The astronomer wasn't usually that passionate. "We need to be seen to be doing the right things here. Sending you might make everybody think we are casual enough to be planning a photo-shoot. On the other hand, it might look like we are splitting our resources in case the Earth gets wasted. You'll have to let me sleep on that idea. I suppose you've already checked for uplift."

"Come on, what do you think? You know there's a MAGENTA due out on the 19th. At the moment it's an unmanned direct supply run planned for a 16G push off so you would need to authorise a seat and re-arrange the departure to be human capable. I spoke to Tavis and he said if I was going they could do it easily."

"Galaxy, Ed! You're streets ahead of the possibilities here. All right, I'll think it over. If I thought it would do any good I'd tell you to switch your head off and get some rest. Do you know what? I'm tired, and I'm also tired of talking sense. Let's get out of here and catch that beer. Maybe I'll calm down enough that I might know what to do next."

49

The phone rang, and he rolled his eyes at the younger man. "Yes Penny? No, we were just leaving. What, right now? OK, put him through."

He looked at Seals and mouthed, "White House."

Seals mouthed back, "Wow." He came closer to the phone, but Culver waved him off and switched on the speaker.

"Good evening, Mr. President."

"Ah, good evening to you Leif. I do hope I haven't caught you in a meeting," the Southern Caribbean accent rolled gently.

"No sir, we were packing up for the day."

"I want to be sure that your mathematician has been checked and double-checked on the approach distance for this blasted comet. My military people are all shouting 'KICK', although I do know that all they want is the chance to set off a proper firework."

"We are confident, sir. My technical math specialist Ed Seals is here in the office with me. He confirms a near miss. At this point I don't believe we need to KICK it."

"Good. I just wanted to be certain that inaction is the right course of action, if you catch my meaning. I understand we are in for a celestial show this fall."

"Yes sir, we believe so. Spectacular is the word Seals used. Earth may be grazed by the comet's tail, and that would trigger vast displays of shooting stars caused by miniscule ice particles hitting the atmosphere."

"I'm pleased to be appraised of Mr. Seals' confidence," said the President.

"He is absolutely certain. Edwin Seals is one of the best orbital mathematicians on the planet. He's also a well known space photographer, and he has just told me he wants to go to the Moon himself to take some grandstand photos of the event."

50

"Is he, now? Hmm, I think my office here in Boston could use a properly commissioned photograph or two. You said he was there, can I speak to him please?"

"I've switched the speakers on, sir. Go ahead."

"Good evening Edwin. I hear you want to go to the Moon and take some shots of the comet."

"Good evening Mr. President. I had mentioned it to Mr. Culver. Space photography is my passion."

"What do you think, Leif?" asked the President.

"I know Wilco Warrender has more than enough to do at the observatory. If we send Ed, quite apart from photography it would be an extra pair of hands."

Braithwaite considered that for a second. "In that case young man, you are officially deputised to go and do that. Leif, would you make arrangements?"

"I certainly will, sir." said Culver.

"Very well, I shall bid you gentlemen good night."

"And a good night to you too, Mr President." Culver exhaled deeply and turned to Seals. "That, I never expected."

"Orders from the White House! By the Stars, I'm in shock," said Seals, shaking his head. "Spencer Braithwaite II wants a photograph for the New Oval Office and I just got deputised. I don't believe it."

The NASA Director looked at his friend. "If you were kidding Ed, it backfired on you. On the other hand, if you were wrong with those numbers, don't come back! Now, about that beer..."

9 – SPLIT
8:25 AM (PST) 12th SEPTEMBER

Culver dumped his briefcase on the desk and walked across to admire the view from his glass balcony on Floor Fifty. It faced east across Edwards, the very place where man had first broken the sound barrier. Along the road at Mojave there had been a small airfield where some of the first air-dropped spacecraft had been tested. It was an area rich in flying and space travel history.

He had dropped his daughter at the PaLaMo AmTransCon station to catch her train to NASA U. The MAGLEV trains travelled at up to 95% of the speed of sound, connecting most major cities across the New States and Spanish America. His Houston staff often caught the train to Lancaster for meetings, returning home the same day.

It was a fabulous clear morning with the hot sun already riding high. Tiny patches of desert cirrus hung stationary in the blue like so many strands of spun sugar. A high altitude contrail streaked westbound overhead. It felt good to stand and observe for a minute. *An old Sonic Clipper maybe? No, smaller than a Clipper. More likely a later model Savannah SratoBiz IV by the shape of that contrail vortex. East coast to Hawaii. After all these years I'm still a transport nerd.*

He used to sit out on the old sea wall at San Mateo with his dad and watch the transcontinental Sonics taking off from San Francisco International. That set him to thinking about when he was six. Dad managed to book places on the Golden Gate Bridge, so they could watch the new CalPac Sea Wall and shipping locks being dedicated below.

San Francisco still had its airport in the bay, but nearly sixty years had passed since then. These days fresh water surrounded the runways, two metres below sea level.

He was tired. Not the superficial lack of sleep kind of tired but the deep down, long term, bone-weary fatigue from carrying it all on his shoulders. At 64 he was feeling the strain. The trail disappeared out of sight above his window. *Hawaii... Maybe when this comet panic is over we should go to Hawaii and have a real break.*

The phone had been ringing for some time; he turned to the desk. He never shut the office door and as he spun round he caught Penny coming in to see why he wasn't answering. He waved her off with a grin. The phone stopped.

"Sorry, Penny, you caught me deep in thought."

"You need a break."

"I know. That was part of it. When this all dies down I'm going to take some time off." Even as he said it, the plan changed. "I think I'm considering retirement."

Penny closed the door. She had been his right hand for fifteen years and he knew what was coming. "I didn't hear that. You're under too much pressure over this." She switched to the firm tone he thought of as Telling Leif Off. "Does the President actually think the comet was your fault? That you are responsible for it? Because he damn well better hadn't, and he shouldn't keep on hounding you for information you don't have."

She gestured towards the closed door, losing the tone a bit and taking a deep breath "Leif, you look exhausted. The people out there in the office are worried. Why not take Sunny away and have a real vacation? Retirement is a much bigger step, so take the time to think it through. Anyway, when was the last time you were off duty for more than three days? I'm going to call her right now and tell her you are under orders from me. You're impossible, you know." She was right on all counts.

"Thanks, Penny." He gestured at the door. "You know I couldn't do any of this without you or them. I always know where I stand with you guys and I appreciate it. I promise we will plan a proper break; I'd like to take at least three weeks. Ed can get back from his Moon jaunt and help Redwood to run this for a while. Maybe we could contrive to assign Redwood somewhere else and let Ed run it. When I think about it, things might be a lot easier that way. I guess I'll feel better for a break. Now, would you happen to know who that was calling?"

"No," she laughed," but I hope it was The White House. Make him wait. I'll rustle up some coffee."

He sat down at the desk as the phone rang again. Not normally intuitive, he sensed bad news. He switched on audio. "Culver." He knew from the time lag exactly who it would be.

"Leif, it's Ed. The comet split up."

Culver shot out of the chair. "WHAT?" He stopped for a reply but Seals remained silent. After a second or two, denial set in. "Oh Galaxy, no! Come on Ed; tell me you're kidding."

"No." Seals said flatly. "For once I wish I was."

Culver's skin crawled with horror and his heart skipped a beat, leaving a vacant feeling behind in his chest. "Oh Edwin, I'm sorry, If there's a God, please save us all. We made the big mistake, and I called it wrong. We should have used KICK when we could and now it's too late. Stand by, I need a minute here."

He put his hands to his face and sighed. Penny had left the door open and he looked up to see anxious faces gathering in the doorway. Well, there was no point having to tell it all again; everybody on Floor Fifty knew the score. He waved them in and switched on the conference speakers and the 3D. Seals' hologram appeared life size in front of the whole wall screen opposite the door. He was in the base commander's office accompanied by Ajax and Wilco. He waved briefly at the team filling the office as he could now see them all.

Culver was grateful for the distraction. It allowed him to get a firmer grip on the growing sense of horror and guilt. He addressed the expectant crowd.

"Come on in, gang. Blake, would you fetch the rest of them in here, please. As you can see, Ed is calling from Gene's Place. The comet split up."

There was an immediate gasp and a buzz started, but he waved them sharply back into silence. "OK, you can see we have most of the team here Ed. If I know you the numbers are in your hand, so hit me. What does it mean?"

Seals sounded calm, and he certainly looked calmer than Culver felt. "There was a major outgassing event and then it split, well I guess the word should be cracked. It came apart in two pieces. To be honest it's both better and worse. The more I think about it, the more it looks like good news.

"The larger piece will still go right by, 200,000 km out. The other piece, and thank goodness it's the smaller one, was ejected off one side and now looks like it will be seriously close to earth. A quick stab at the math suggests maybe as near as 5,000 km. As I said it's much smaller than the nucleus, but I don't have any firm numbers as yet. I reckon we are talking about house size rather than a whole mountain. With some calculation error it could even be an atmosphere grazer, which would be an amazing visual treat.

He looked straight at his boss. "Leif, don't panic. We still have time to calculate the orbits for manned junk and evacuate anything if necessary. However close it looks now, I honestly still don't think we are looking at an impact scenario. You have to believe that and try to relax a bit. The President can't crucify you for this; after all it's not even your comet."

Culver rubbed his face. "OK, Ed. You sound like you've been talking to Penny."

That provoked a nervous laugh or two in the office. It was obvious that even if Seals hadn't, some of the team had. One look brought quiet. "I have two immediate questions; One: Is it stable now? Two: how long till you can get more accurate numbers on the Earth pass? I'll need to talk to the White House and that is all they will want to know."

"It's still twelve days out Leif, but that's very close now. We will do the math again in six and twelve hours. That should give me better accuracy. I'll call you back at 9:30 PM. We have a great set of tools here and the next series of measurements is due in another hour. I'll call Hawaii and get some parallax readings."

"Thanks. I'd better warn the White House." He turned to the crowd. "All right then, questions, people?" For the first time ever there were none. "Wow, Ed, did you see that? You seem to have stunned this lot into silence, and that's a certifiable first. I've never once managed it."

Seals laughed, "Guys, it was a major event visually. Get it on the screen. Everyone on the planet looking at it will have seen something so it's no big secret. It happened, er, 38 minutes ago now. I'd call the White House immediately, Leif, but I'm not in your seat. Also, we still have tourists in situ here, and I don't think comms security is as tight as it might be."

He turned to Thibodeaux. "Sorry Ajax, but..."

"No, you could be right," was the commander's reply. "Leif, we will get straight back to work here."

"Thanks. It sounds like you're lucky to have him and Wilco there together, Ajax. At least that was a lucky call. I'll speak to the White House in the next ten minutes." He suddenly became aware that several phones were ringing in the outer office. He knew he wasn't going to need to make that call. Penny had gone to take charge.

56

"OK, Leif," added Seals. He desperately wanted to lessen the tension around Culver, so he let them in on a snippet he hadn't been planning to share. "Incidentally, I'm not coming up here again. I need a ground job. It was awful. It's never happened in ten round trips, but for some reason this time I puked all the way from LEO." That did the trick; there was a universal howl of derision.

The Eugene Francis Kranz Lunar Research Station was located north-west of Crater Maskelyne in the Southern part of the Mare Tranquillitatis (Sea of Tranquility), 200 km from the site of Man's first landing on the Moon. A few years previously, Evan McEwan had been lucky enough to take part in a ceremony at the site to mark the anniversary of that event.

The Earth-facing side of the Moon had over 8,000 km of marked trails. The main east-west route, stretched all the way from Crater Kastner in the east to Crater Hermann in the west. It was known as the East- or West Way depending on which side of Gene's you travelled.

The other main route was an extended exploration trail stretching through the vast network of ancient lava fields known as the Lunar Seas. From the south-western corner of the Mare Tranquillitatis it ran north and west through the Mare Serenitatis (Sea of Serenity) before turning west to wind through a fractured and folded area between the great craters Archimedes and Aristillus. Finally it looped around the northerly Mare Imbrium (Sea of Rains). These areas had been explored during the previous century by various teams using all sorts of vehicles.

Since Gene's had been established as the permanent base fifty years previously, the emphasis had been on connecting east and west, with the idea of harvesting solar power during the entire lunar cycle. Supplies had been dropped at strategic locations, with teams of astronauts whose job it was to unload and stockpile rolls of cable and solar panels, together with their associated equipment.

Once all the required hardware was in place, ground missions started to work their way westwards from the south-western corner of Tranquillitatis. Even with low-orbit high-resolution mapping and computerised photographs it took over ten years to connect the system all the way west. Eventually the decision was taken to include another solar facility known as the Central Array, almost exactly in the centre of the Moon as seen from Earth, in the Sinus Medeii (Central Bay).

Once the Central Array had come on line, adding to the East Array at Crater Kastner, plus its own local setup, Gene's had solar power for 23 out of 29 days each lunar cycle. When the West Array was finally completed, the base was down to a three day break in power generation every 29 days. There was enough battery storage available to make ends meet. The current power project would extend the East Way and include a new Far Side Array. This would finally ensure a constant power supply.

After the junction with the Seas Road, as it was known, the West Way ran for 500 km along the northern edge of the long sinuous canyon Rima Hyginus, to where it joined the Mare Vaporum (Sea of Mists). Here, about 900 km down-trail from Gene's, it turned sharp left to head almost due south on the other side of the Hyginus, gradually turning west again into the Sinus Medeii.

Passing the Central Solar Array, the West Way entered an area of extensive cratering and folding that had held up progress for several years. Eventually a route was pushed through, exiting into a long bay extending from the Southern edge of the Sinus Aestuum (Bay of Tides). At this point there was another junction, where the Copernicus Road headed off northwest to that mighty crater. The West Way then turned south again for several hundred kilometres before once again curving west to pass south of Crater Guericke and across the Southern edge of the Mare Cognitum (Sea of Knowledge). The last 1,500 km of the trail followed various interlocking lowlands and lava-inundated craters to reach the site of the West Array at Crater Hermann.

NEIL rolled along, following the brightly coloured plastic traffic cones to the left every 100 m. There was a simple system; if you had cones on the left of any marked trail you were heading away from the base, if they were on the right you were homebound. Junctions were marked by a line of five cones opposite the turn and at each side of the joining trail. They would never blow away or get stolen here.

Lucy Grappelli was arguing with her best friend and fellow geologist Evan McEwan as she drove NEIL through a wide space between two crater walls. Here, 1,400 km from the base, the pair had turned off the Seas Road. Approaching the end of a two week tour, they were once again heading off road to visit an unexplored area south-west of Crater Aristillus.

She looked across at the red-headed Canadian. He'd pulled that damned unsettling trick of his again, the one where he stopped arguing with her and waited while she ranted on into thin air. Every time he did it he scored a point as the argument blew itself out and died. She knew he would be wearing the wide grin, and looking across she was right. Evan could be irritating, but she would never have missed the chance to have him on her team.

"Guess you're tired, Lucy-Lu. So let's quit driving for today. How about stopping for a meal and a full break, eh? I could do with some proper sleep.

"OK, you win," she replied, the tension gone. "We'll have to rest up sooner or later. If we start fresh we could put in a long day tomorrow. We've only got two days left before we need to start back. We could still stay up here four more days though."

Evan sighed heavily. "Lucy, leave it for a bit, will ya? We're starting back on schedule. You may be senior here but I'm your conscience. So don't let's have another fight with the commander when we check in. Please?"

"But it's so unnecessary, Evan. We've got days of spare supplies and air. It seems so wasteful when it takes so damn long to even get this far from the base. I know it's a safety margin but even if we worked here for the four days we would still arrive back with days to spare." She pulled to a stop.

"Ah, here we go again," he complained, "Will you *please* stop venting for a bit. 'S like sitting next to Old Faithful; every thirty minutes you blow steam. Give me a break here and stop wasting the air."

"Hey, I'm sorry, Evan. I'll fix food, that way I'll get my mind off it."

The two old hands were over halfway through their third six-month survey tour on the Moon. They had cemented their reputation as a solid team and enjoyed the work. If only Lucy would calm down and relax a bit more Evan's life would be perfect.

He delegated himself to call the base with the details of their rest stop. That would usually keep Lucy from picking another real fight, but not this time. Ajax asked to speak to his senior geologist.

"Hi, Ajax."

"Hey, Lucy. I can't believe you two manage to drive so far on these trips. My geology team never ceases to amaze me. I need to preempt the usual fight by reminding you that we need the expedition to start back to base in exactly 58 hours. How you use that time is not up to us, but please break camp and start rolling back here by then."

"Roger. As usual I'm frustrated about it. Instead of arguing can we plan a meeting to work on closing the gap between the procedure and the practical implications of the over-generous safety margin?"

"That's fair, Lucy, and scores points with me because it's a much better opening than you made last time. We'll all work together on the procedure. As for now, you've already bought yourselves two extra days on this tour by travelling hard and resting in rotation. You do far more work than the other team because they sleep at the same time and therefore don't travel so efficiently.

"Look, personally I wouldn't have a problem changing to a 24 hour buffer but, as you know, I don't make the decisions. We'll talk to the systems department at Lancaster and Houston when you get back here. Best I can do."

"Thanks boss. So we're going to take a proper break and sleep before we do the last ten kilometres and get working."

11 – BREAKUP
8:30 AM (PST) 19th SEPTEMBER

Culver accepted the regular morning call from the Moon and made their standard joke. "Hey, guys, how's the weather today?"

For once, Seals let it pass. "For the first time I don't know if I want to be here. I wish I was going to be on Earth to see it."

"Oh, for pity's sake, Ed, you got the grandstand seat and you're there by Presidential Decree. You paid your money and took your choice." He studied Seals and Wilco, sitting in Thibodeaux' office. They didn't laugh with him.

Ed shook his head. "Choice didn't come into it, and you said it right there. Whatever happens please keep that thought in mind; that I was sent here by the President and not by you."

Culver began to wonder where this was going. "I know. Right now I wish this thing would get by here and piss right off into the sun forever. I'm exhausted and stressed, and I need a vacation. If your numbers are right and it loses a bit more momentum, you might even be the ones to get the better show. It's not going to be that far from you on the run-in."

The two scientists exchanged a quick glance as Seals carried on. "You do look tired Leif, but I promise that you guys will get your vacations. Wilco and I have spent the last 48 hours busting our collective brain cells on some fresh math. We've done a new set of observations and attacked the numbers from the top every three hours, day and night. As of now, we are still confirming an Earth miss, and we're staking our reputations on that."

"That's fantastic news, Ed. I'm–oh, sorry."

He caught himself as he saw his friend stop. They hadn't done it much over the years, but Seals was still talking and they had crossed in the time lag.

Seals' face fell as he held up a hand to ward off Culver's speech. His voice started to crack. "Sorry Leif. You have to listen to me for one more minute, because I've got notes, and a prepared statement to make. Apologies in advance, but we need to deliver one more piece of bad news."

Culver thought all that was behind him. He felt a hollow tug inside his chest. For a second he thought he might stop breathing and die. Ed looked emotional. Wilco swallowed hard and he could have sworn that the chatty Englishman was keeping a proverbial stiff upper lip, explaining why he hadn't joined in the exchange so far.

"Galaxy, Ed! For pity's sake what's happening? Are you guys OK?"

Seals pulled himself together, sat up straight, and look straight at his boss. "We're OK for now, Leif. This will be straight from the top, and I'm not taking any questions after the conference, as they say.

"It's you guys Earthside that will have the grandstand seats, not us. The smaller piece, officially Percival B, but we're calling it the Shard, is definitely going to provide the show of the millennium on Earth as it grazes the high atmosphere. There's not enough ice left in it to boil off and alter its course now. The numbers on that are as firm as the rock itself, and we're no longer worried about it. After that it's thanks for the show and bon voyage, straight into the Sun.

"We are watching the nucleus, now termed Percival A. Our math indicates that after drifting towards a closer Earth approach for some weeks, the recent splitting event pushed it a little further out. On the face of it that should be good news. However, after the new burst of outgassing two days ago we suggested a ballpark 200,000 km Earth miss figure.

64

"That's changed. Wilco wasn't sure what we were seeing at first so we've been sitting on it since the event so we could give you the hardest data we can. There was something in the math we hadn't allowed for. Aside from the trajectory change when it split, Percival A kicked itself in the head and slowed down some. That places the pass in a different part of the day, and therefore local orbital positions vary."

He paused long enough for Culver to speak again. "Am I missing something significant here?"

"We missed it too, until a few minutes ago, but here is the precise figure, Percival A will never get that close to you. It's going to miss the Earth by 375,500 km. That's the good news, and that exact distance will be familiar. In fact that number is also the bad news. Leif, in five days time, exactly three hours and seven minutes before the Shard gives you the big firework show, what's left of that comet is going to smack the Moon."

Culver looked at his friend and knew that the usually unflappable Seals had already recovered from coming close to losing his cool a few moments before. The two men in the office at Gene's waited respectfully as the NASA Director held up a hand to them, shut his eyes, and gave himself ten seconds of thinking time. He finally looked up at them and spoke. "Ed, Wilco. Thanks for the report. Give me two hours and I will figure a way to get you all off safely. That is, if you don't have a plan ready. I just need time to make some calls and talk to the brains."

Wilco surprised him by replying. "Leif, we've been working on that here, too. As usual there are two of the DS PODs outside here on the surface. If we strip everything out, and I mean everything, they would lift more people than usual into orbit to await a rendezvous. The underlying difficulty in this instance is that none of the three TUG vehicles can get here. One left two days ago, but

65

it only took the four tourists we decided to send home early. Nobody else was due a shift change. To act as lifeboats the PODs would need to lift extra oxygen and so forth, depending on how long we would need to wait for a TUG or MAGENTA. Even stripped, that would reduce the payload, but I don't have the numbers. Added to that, if we chose to use them there would be a severe risk from orbital debris after the comet impact. I, for one, am staying right here."

Seals took up the dialogue. "There's a top brainstorming team here too, and believe me we are working on the impact. Our best guess places the impact about 90 degrees west of Gene's, here at Maskelyne, and a little further north. My gut feeling suggests a new crater somewhere in the Oceanus Procellarum. It seems fitting that it should hit The Ocean of Storms, because it will the biggest event here for thousands of years.

"We have to allow for some calculating error so that may narrow down some. Ajax is confident that, barring a direct local impact, we will be able to survive in the shelter below the base. He and his team are already moving equipment and supplies down there, and placing as much outside gear as possible under cover.

"As usual, you asked us about the weather." He gave a wry laugh. "Well, OK. For the first time ever, we have a lunar weather forecast for you. There will be a possibility of it raining rocks, pebbles and gravel, together with cooling lava, for several days. We anticipate severe dust contamination across half the surface, quantities uncertain. With no atmosphere things will cool down quickly, but the 1/6G means we have a working prediction that during the impact some debris may even go orbital, and we have no idea how long to expect incoming from that.

"The fact is that what we have here is a certified geologists dream. Lucy and Evan are doing two things. The first is jumping for joy at the prospect. The second is protesting about the fact that Ajax has ordered them back from their deployment up north. He wants them here in the shelter, and Lucy wants to stay outside and watch the show."

Culver found his breath coming more easily. He felt dog-tired and his chest was doing that dull ache thing again, the one that he had been waking with for the last few weeks. Seals was back in scientist mode and the lunar team was working on every aspect of the problem. "OK Ed. I'll reinforce Ajax' instructions to the field team to get back to the shelter. Aside from all that I still think we need to consider a complete evacuation. Observation and science equipment can be left to watch the show there and gather data, but I want you guys as far away as possible. That is how I want to go, and if we have the means those will be my orders."

The reply was formal. "Roger, Director Culver. But we've looked at the data. I'm not being in any way insubordinate if I tell you it simply can't be done."

"I know you well enough to say I believe you, but I am compelled to refuse to accept your decision until I have had that verified here. Is that fair? As I said, give me two hours."

"Agreed. Do you know what? The hardest part of this was telling you, but we are hopping with ideas and plans too. Speak to you later."

"Gene's calling NEIL, anybody awake?"

"Hey there, Ajax, it's Evan, go ahead."

"Is Lucy sleeping?"

"Sure is, man. We worked fourteen straight and she crashed right after we ate. I'm going soon, too."

"OK, that's good. Now listen up because we have a new situation breaking here and you have to get moving. Never mind the comet splitting in two, Wilco and Ed say that event changed its trajectory and the nucleus is going to hit the Moon. We don't know exactly where yet, but we are 'Amber/Standby Red' here at the base. I'm preparing the shelter for sealed occupation. I want you to start back here right now, and I mean immediately. Get on it. Is there any equipment outside?"

"Hit the ol' Moon? Are they for real?"

"Absolutely, yes. Time is tight and I need you to drive hard in shifts. So how long will it take you to get rolling, and are you fit to drive after a long day? I'm 100% serious here, Evan."

Evan finally got the message, and started initiating the drive motors. "Nothing outside is vital or expensive, and none of it plugged in externally. I guess we could leave it all here for later."

"That's good, so move, right now! That's an executive order. I don't care what's outside, drive. I expect Lucy will scream but do what you can with her. I'll stay here in comms until the dust settles on that. If you slam-drive like you did on the way out I figure you can be here at impact minus six hours. Evan, I can't emphasise how concerned I am about this, so please keep the pressure on for me. There will be a high level meeting at Lancaster shortly and I want a firm ETA from you by then.

"OK, copied. NEIL is already rolling. I am inbound to the base and showing 1422 km to run. I can update you better when we hit the Seas Road and then we'll see if we can't shave any time off our old record, eh?"

Thibodeaux sighed with relief. "Good man. I appreciate your level head. That's one item off my immediate worry list."

The Canadian laughed a little. "Tick off another one, Ajax. Don't fret about Lucy, I can handle her, so you don't need to sit there and watch us. Anyway, she won't wake up for hours, and you've got demands on your time."

"Damn right I have, but if you have any problems call me immediately. Break that speed record for me, dude, but do it safely.

* * *

"What's up? We're rolling? Evan! What's going on?"

"Hush, will ya? It's an emergency change of plan. Ajax ordered us back to Gene's and we have to break the ol' Lunar speed record."

"How so?"

He laughed at her. "You sound like Paula. It's legit though, Wilco says the comet is actually gonna impact right here on the ol' Moon. We have to be in the shelter. We have time to spare if we push hard like usual, but Ajax told us to kick ass. I'm not surprised you stayed asleep; resting on the roll feels natural to us hardened trailheads. I've been in the saddle four hours already and I'll need a bathroom break soon. We're under orders not to stop for anything, so will you take a rolling handover when you've eaten?"

"Oh for the Galaxy! There goes another two week's work. Did you stow the survey gear?"

"No, they're pretty worked up at Lancaster and my orders were to drive immediately. I scored us a few slick points by getting the wheels turning while Ajax was telling me. Anyhow, the gear can

69

stay there; ain't like it's gonna get stolen by the moon cheese guys. We'll be back up there by the end of next week. It'll be fine."

"Why couldn't we stay and watch it from there?"

"Because, dummy, it might land on us." He rolled his eyes.

Lucy could do indignation like nobody else. "Oh come on, who's the dummy in this outfit? It might land on Gene's."

"OK, granted, but you've got to admit the shelter there has to be the safest spot on the map.

She stared hard at him across the space between the seats. "Do you know what, Evan? This is galaxy-spanning cosmic bullshit. We have to be out on the surface with Ed filming the comet, not in the freaking shelter. I don't see how we could be safer there than anywhere else. Let's face the physics; if that comet hits the Moon everything within, I don't know, say fifty kilometres, will be vapourised. The President sent Ed here to get that picture."

"Twist it round any way you want Lucy-Lu, but Ajax has ordered us back and that's how it's gonna be. Change of plan already, I need the bathroom now, and then I'll fix food and coffee. Get over here and keep driving max up as you can, eh? We got power to waste as we're going straight back. Hey, they'll be taking bets on when we'll roll in, y'know."

He half turned and looked right at her. "Lucy, do not stop or, so help me, I will airlock you!" He gave a grim laugh at their private joke, and she joined in as he shut the bathroom door.

* * *

"Gene's, NEIL. Can I speak to the commander please?"

"Hey, baby," Paula looked tired. "He said you'd be stabbin' his ear. Stand by." She usually chatted to Lucy in her shorthand style, but for once she sat with her eyes closed as she waited. Thibodeaux appeared in a few seconds and pulled up a chair.

"Thanks Paula. You OK?"

70

"Tired. Hard day."

"OK, get a break and eat. I need to chat to Lucy for a while so I'll stay."

"Thanks boss." She left.

"Hi Lucy, Tracking says you're twenty minutes behind on our projected arrival. I've got the horrors here. Evan resting?"

"Yes he is. Look, boss, I've been thinking all this through since he hit the bunk. He and I should plan on staying outside in NEIL with Ed, to get those photos the President wanted. I'm talking right by the base so we could pull a rapid resupply and head out to wherever the comet hits as soon as possible after the impact. I wanted to visit the thing but Lancaster didn't have the balls for that. Now it's inbound to visit me. I can't wait. A cooling impact crater, that's certifiable warm geology, man!"

He was already shaking his head. "OK, Grappelli. I've been expecting that speech, almost verbatim, and you will note that I let you deliver the whole show. It's an absolute negative on that request. It wasn't my order, that came direct from Leif Culver. When the comet hits, everybody in my command will be in the shelter, so keep driving and make up time."

"But Ajax, we need to—"

"No, you don't. You don't *need* to..." He stopped, rolled his eyes, then closed them and took a couple of deep breaths. "Look, what you *need* to do is follow my specific orders, as reinforced by The Director. I have too much to do here to waste time on another sparring session right now; this is actual life or death, nothing more, nothing less. Get it, and get here. Am I clear?"

"Yes, Commander."

"That's better. For once in your life will you please shut up and drive, Grappelli? Just drive."

13 – BRAINS
10:00 AM (PST) 19th SEPTEMBER

Sixty Space Tower specialists assembled in the lecture theatre with less than an hour's notice. More of the science team were on their way in, but Culver needed this forum up and running immediately. The MAGENTA management at Mt. Rainier were waiting on the main screen, and the Houston SpaceTech specialists were present in holo at stage left.

He wondered how he would get through this; his heart ached, both emotionally and with a dull throbbing that promised more bad news sooner or later. That Hawaiian vacation was out of the picture already; when the comet crisis was over he was heading for a hospital. *I was so flippant with Ed and Wilco about my own problems and the need for a vacation. How crass and selfish am I? Those guys could get killed up there.*

A respectful silence fell, and everybody looked at him. His chest stabbed as he drew a ragged breath.

"Good morning everybody, and thanks for assembling at such short notice. I've asked for closed doors, so nobody leaves here until we are ready with a statement. We paged people so there are others inbound to join us, but we have to get working.

"This morning we are facing a new and ultimately more dangerous problem. For the third time we seem to have had our eye off the ball. The outgassing events have slowed the comet significantly. In August it looked like a near miss. The predictions suggested a ballpark figure of 200,000 km, but Wilco and Ed called from the Moon an hour ago with an update to those numbers.

"On their fresh math it will never get that close, because three hours and seven minutes before the Shard's firework display happens here, the nucleus is going to collide with the Moon."

There was a roar of disbelief. It took several minutes to calm the room down. He gave them time, but finally had to call for order. Something stabbed him in the chest again, and he had to catch his breath before calling for calm. For the first time ever he had to shout them down. "OK, people, please! Can I get some quiet? QUIET! Ssshhh! We are not done here yet. Thanks.

"I can hear expressions from the floor about perturbation, orbit, destabilisation, and all manner of other technical stuff. People, park that science right now."

He waited a couple of seconds, and then spread his arms. "I said No! Please, please pay attention for a minute, team, because we need to work together. Nobody is calculating anything, and I do mean anything, until we deal with the next problem. We need to work on my agenda first, OK?" He waved his notes. A ragged silence descended, and around him heads nodded as several team members shushed their colleagues.

"Thanks, people. Now, we have 35 people on the Moon. They are all desperate to stay and observe the impact, but I have made an executive decision to order their evacuation. As soon AS POSSIBLE." He raised his voice over the renewed din, and waited for quiet.

"I spoke to the President 45 minutes ago. He said, and I quote: 'I don't give a shit what this costs in money or equipment. This office will cover the cost, but we must have those people extracted safely.'

He stood still, trying to get deep breaths to stem the dizzy feeling. Something was going wrong in his chest; it felt hollow, and each breath hurt. He realised he was sweating heavily. "So there's today's challenge for you. If we can do it, I want them off, even just clear of the surface into space if necessary until we can retrieve them. Whether it's on the Moon, here on Earth, or in orbit, you can wreck and cannibalise anything you need. Everything else here, everything, goes on hold until we get a working plan together for that, and I need you to fire your imaginations. Wilco says it can't be done, and I have to say that from where I'm standing I don't see any real options. I absolutely refuse... Sshh! I refuse to believe that it's not possible until every single one of you here in Lancaster, at Rainer and at Houston says so.

"If we can't pull our team out, we switch to preservation in situ, using the hurricane shelter at Gene's. Ajax is preparing for that as we speak. Now, don't shout, think. Does anybody have any instant thoughts?"

There was a sudden deep hush, startling him after the recent noise level. Scientists of every persuasion stopped discussing their specialities and sat stunned. Culver saw a single hand raised.

"Talk to me, Kent."

Kent Warwick stood up. "Leif, I'm sorry to hit you with negativity straight off, but the TUG Team can't do it and there is no maybe about that I'm afraid. I started making notes the moment you said it would hit the Moon. TUG 4 is inbound LEO 7 from the Moon. It can't stop and turn back; minimum time to LEO and return to the Moon is five days. TUG 1 is halfway to the Elevator Station with supplies. It will have to return to LEO space for fuel. Minimum time to the Moon is, uh?" he closed his eyes for a moment, "twelve days. TUG 3 is still in refit at LEO-NINE; planned unavailability is currently 31 days. We can expedite that, maybe by ten days, but there is no way to have it ready in time and that's a bottom line. All sorts of stuff for the refit is still scattered about here on Earth. I said at the time we should have replaced TUG 2 after the accident, but there it is."

"OK, thanks for the report, Kent. If anyone can find a solution out of the box it's the TUG Team." He looked at Kent's compass-point haircut. "You might be out on paper, but you keep those red spikes whirling, Sunshine. Crash my office door immediately they spark an idea, eh?"

There was a ripple of amusement.

"OK, so get out there and break things. The President wants the rules abused, so abuse them. Steal government equipment if you have to and, if you do, make sure we get to keep it." Another laugh.

"Steal ideas, but above all work together. If your department can't help, then make your grey matter available and give the other departments anything they need.

"Actually I'm already thinking on my feet here and I've got a better plan. I'm back to you already, Kent. I want you to take control of this effort for me please. People, run any ideas you have past the TUG office and see if he can pick something out of it all."

There was already some furious note-taking, and he noted a general murmer around the room in approval of his decision. Kent waved up at him and gave a firm nod.

Culver turned to the big screen, saying. "Let's talk to Mt. Rainier."

MAGENTA manager Tavis Sarkasian looked like a true zombie, as if he had never managed to sleep in his whole life. Two metres in height and with dead-looking pale skin, his eyes always looked like they had lost a fist-fight. On a visual scan, you might consider it wise never to let him near tools in case he turned violent. On the other hand, he could do accurate orbital and launch mathematics in his head.

"Hey, Tavis! Can you launch any bright ideas at me from MAGENTA?" The audience groaned.

Sarkasian spoke in a slow, bass Texas drawl. "Leif, we have a regular MAGENTA DS delivery shot due out next week. If I ditch everything else and then load, stack and push it, we are looking at minus," his dead eyes rolled up while he mouthed numbers, "sixteen hours plus thirty two. If I cattle-prod some people around here it might even get off faster, depending if you need to adjust the load. All other PODS are in rotation off planet. Even at max drive the one I have still can't get there in time for a retrieve. I can overload the POD that's ready and recalculate the shot. Hell, they are only ever sent filled at half bulk. But sorry, no. I have no new ideas for recovery beyond that."

Culver refused to give up. "OK, here's the deal. We have 35 people at Gene's. They have the usual two regular orbital PODs available that could meet MAGENTA. You say overloading PODs will work. Can we get them to orbit in those?"

Sarkasian rolled his eyes again and Culver watched the lips working in silence. The shaved head tilted forwards for a few seconds, showing a series of ancient witchcraft tattoos on his bald pate. He came back to life. "That's assuming loads of eighteen and seventeen in each of two six-man PODs. That's a negative. They won't lift that sort of mass off the Moon; six is about maximum stretch. If they strip out seats and fittings to leave straps on a bare floor, we could still only get 9 off in each POD, so no, we can't lift them all out.

"Anyhow, It would be mighty uncomfortable, especially if they have to sit in orbit and wait a few days. You mentioned possible orbital comet debris there too, so I wouldn't say a parking orbit was advisable either. And it would take longer to fit the MAGENTA we have ready to retrieve two PODS. I'd say the risks are significantly lower using the hurricane shelter."

"Thanks, Tavis. Work on minus sixteen hours something and max fill the supply POD for me, would you? If they are going to have to hold out underground, start thinking about sending a second POD as soon as possible. Work up a checklist of supplies

76

and survival gear for that mission. Ditch all other launches for now and stand by for a 'Go' order on the first shot. We will call you back."

"Sure Lancaster. Call you back with an earliest ready time. Can I get guys in?"

"Definitely, overtime anybody you need. What's your stack and launch record?"

"Sixteen plus thirty-two, man, I already said so."

"OK, sir. It felt like I was issuing a challenge to MAGENTA there."

Tavis grinned like a movie star doing the deranged murderer scene, making himself look even more dangerous and wild. He gave a deep, villainous chuckle. "It sure did, and my guys'll love that idea. MAGENTA is on the case."

Culver felt a bit better for it. He knew that Tavis would get supplies out as soon as he could, which would also place an extra lifeboat at Gene's. Getting a second run planned with an option to tailor the manifest and launch after the impact was sound backup. It was small comfort, because nothing had improved the immediate rescue or recovery possibilities. He turned to the holos of the Houston team. "'Morning, Anton."

"Hey, Leif." It was always reassuring to see Senior Mission Director Anton Levine. Another of NASA's bright minds, Anton looked far more like a regular human than either Kent or Tavis. "We don't have anything as yet, but there's a lot of muttering and pencil work going on here. I will call Gene's after this and speak to my guys there."

"Thanks, Anton. Call back if you get anything."

He addressed the room again "There's a press conference at 1:00 PM back here, so it would be good to have a plan ready. All right people, that's it for now. Thanks for your time. Let's go to work."

Penny and Chief Flight Surgeon Eric Tunstall both came up to the lectern immediately he had finished speaking. Tunstall caught his arm in a firm grip and led him off the side of the stage, talking as if he was discussing some aspect of the meeting.

"Good Morning, Leif. Walk over this way for me, would you?" He indicated an office chair. "Sit there. Now. You look dreadful and Penny says you have chest pains. Roll up your sleeve."

He produced an infuser and it hissed as he pressed it to Culver's inner wrist.

"Oh, for crying out loud, Eric—"

"Hush, and listen to me." Tunstall looked over a pair of old-fashioned glasses. Culver knew that like everybody else his eyes had been fixed, but that he wore them to look more professional. "You have two hours until the press turn up. You are coming up to Medical with me and Penny for a once-over, or so help me you will not be hosting a press conference. That's Doctor's Orders and you have no say in the matter. Redwood can manage it if necessary, and we will keep you 'on other projects.' Nobody will know. In spite of appearances and his attitude, he isn't so stupid. Now, how do you feel?"

Culver managed a deeper breath. He realised he had been panting to keep his chest as still as possible. "The pain went away while you were reading me my rights." He hadn't realised how bad it had been.

"That's a good sign. I mean it, Leif, I suspect you might be having an angina attack, but I need to check you over and be certain. If it is, I will dose you, and then let you run the press conference under my watchful eye. Otherwise it's hospital for you, because a heart attack won't wait until after lunch. You must understand that and let me be the judge. Now, let them finish getting out of the way and we take a slow walk to the elevator."

"OK, I give in. I've had a nagging chest pain on and off for over a week. I need to get through this and make sure the guys at Gene's are going to be safe. After that I was coming to you, honest."

Tunstall grinned at him. "Too late, buster. I have come to you, and where your health is concerned I outrank you, so do as you are told. You have good people around you. Don't carry it all on your own. Penny called me yesterday and told me you were close to collapse. She says you're exhausted. I came up to Floor Fifty to collect you this morning but I was too late. You can't avoid us two, you know."

Culver looked at his secretary. "Thanks, Penny," he said with a wry grin. "Look, Eric, can't I just come and lie down for half an hour, then do the press conference?"

"I have already said so, provided I check you over first. It depends if we can get you fit enough to stand on the stage. Come on then, let's go.

"Ed!" Wilco shot out of the Astronomy office yelling. "Seals! Where are you?" He bounce-ran the fifteen metres to the main doorway, opened it into the square and shouted again "Ed!"

"What's up?" Seals appeared from the lounge.

"It's happened again. This time it looks like the nucleus broke up. I'm already willing it to be good news for a change."

Bird appeared from the kitchen. "Ajax is in the science lab, d'you need him?"

"Please, Bird, and warn everybody. Any idea who's outside?" Seals looked frantic.

"Levon and Eagle are on recovery and tidy detail out there. I'll check and assemble the troops. Hey, that inbound supply pod we swapped for the tourists brought me some more chocolate, and I've been making brownies all morning. Must've known, eh?"

"Did you say there was chocolate? We love you, Bird," Wilco informed him earnestly. "I'll clear it with Ajax, but call for a meeting in the lounge, say, 45 minutes from now?"

"You got it!" The amiable cook grinned at him, and bounced off.

It took an hour to get the surface party inside. They were still busy stacking the last of the outside junk in the east garage. Thibodeaux had decided that until the last six hours prior to impact, every single piece of recoverable material would be brought in and stored. The whole team had bent to that task, pairs working round the clock in four hour shifts. His deputy, the African New American astronaut Levon Haines DuPage had been leading that effort while Ajax and Life Science Specialist Tobin Pengelly supervised the preparations in the shelter

Following a debate on splitting resources, in case fallout damaged the base, a disused open-fronted garage outside the perimeter now housed a lot of recovered equipment. One of the two Lunar Exploration Vehicles, LXV 253 BUZZ, was driven there, freeing a lot more room at the base garages to stow local items. As an added contingency, a supply of oxygen and emergency gear was packed inside BUZZ in case there was any damage at Gene's. The other vehicle, LXV 252 NEIL, was inbound carrying Lucy and Evan, still complaining about having their precious survey mission cut short.

Bird was amazed to see the sheer amount of debris scattered around by previous visitors, most of it within a rough circle five kilometres across. With two days left till the impact, all sorts of stuff was already stored in both locations; experiments long forgotten, skeletal remains of stripped and abandoned historic landing and surface vehicles, the list went on.

He had started a catalogue, concentrating at first on the items with interesting histories. He planned on editing a full report for Lancaster, before writing a book about it all. He recognised several of the recovered items from his knowledge of former versions of the base, and photographed many others. At least two pieces were tagged "historic/museum", keeping them out of the general heap.

The team drifted in from one direction or the other, helping themselves to brownies and drinks. The entire central square of Gene's Place smelled of warm chocolate, guaranteed to lift the mood a bit. Although apprehensive, nobody seemed depressed. The evacuation scenario had been a double-edged sword. Head for Earth and miss the show, or risk their lives to stay put, ready to do some real science. Staying was the pragmatic thing to do; on occasion scientists prepare to risk their lives. There was a collective sense of

81

impending heroism. No scientists in living memory had been in such a situation, and the collective world press loved it.

As a group of science geeks, most were delighted that Culver's Last Stand, as it had already become known, had failed. As predicted when Seals and Wilco had broken news of the impending impact, an evacuation attempt had not been a possible option.

There was also major concern for their much-admired Director. The NASA boss was recovering after having a stent fitted in one of the veins around his heart to combat severe angina, but might be on his feet in time to see the show. He was hospitalised for the procedure after the meetings following the breakup of the comet. Flight Surgeon Eric Tunstall had issued a statement to the effect that, as soon as the comet crisis was over, he would receive an artificial heart.

Ajax insisted on a one-to-one meeting with every member of his staff, to check whether they wanted recovery to orbit in one of the PODs. Up to eighteen people could volunteer for the uncomfortable wait, but the outbound MAGENTA DS wasn't due into orbit with emergency equipment and supplies until two days after the comet impact.

Sarkasian had done good work, and the mission had been ready to launch barely fourteen hours after Culver's challenge. In the event Houston took the decision to hold it for another 24 hours. The later departure from Earth was calculated to allow time for high altitude impact debris to fall back to the surface before the rocket arrived in lunar orbit. Using the PODs would mean leaving the Moon with no chance of return except via LEO, or even all the way to Earth. Not one single person had asked to go.

Acting NASA Director Will Redwood had also asked each of them to consider the options for leaving the surface, but the team was working tight and refused to split up. Nobody at Gene's was much of a Redwood supporter, so their assigned meetings with him had varied from short and terse at best, to Paula who cancelled hers at the last minute and refused to speak to him.

He stopped short of issuing direct orders for any sort of forced evacuation, for once realising that he might do better to back down a bit than to force the open mutiny he was sure would result. In the end, he gave up on trying to persuade anybody to leave, and stopped talking to the base completely.

* * *

Thibodeaux called the meeting to order. "So, once again our fate changes, it would seem. Wilco was watching as the comet nucleus, Percival A, broke up an hour ago. They are still busy doing math and observations, so it falls to me to deliver the news, and this time it looks better. According to Ed, this comet is more than 95% ice, hence the huge amount of melting and disintegration we have seen. The tail and corona have got larger every time this happens. In fact, today's event was so violent that a quick calculation from Ed suggests that most of it will actually miss the Moon and fly right by. A small piece of the nucleus, I suppose the name Percival A is still valid, seems to be heading for an impact in the same general area, but has lost a vast amount of mass. We can expect a random scatter of smaller impacts over a wide area.

"The Shard is still on course for a spectacular atmosphere graze across the Earth three hours after what's left of the comet itself arrives here. We will have to watch that event on screen, because we will need to be in the shelter due to the fallout risk. Ed is as horrified as Lucy and Evan, because the President sent him here to record the event and he will be stuck inside with us."

He looked them over. Nobody seemed too tense or nervous about the impact. He wondered what was going through their thoughts. "I'm not afraid, people. The expected impact will be 90

83

degrees west of here, so we will get through it fine. Does anybody have any issues at all?" The reply came as a general shaking of heads.

"That's good. Oh, here's one more piece of disappointing news. Houston called with a message for the geology team aboard NEIL, but I don't think we'll share it with them until after they get back here. The final split of the comet destroyed the landing probe before touchdown, so there will be no undisturbed samples for Lucy."

15 – IMPACT
2:21 AM (LST) 25th SEPTEMBER

"Ten minutes to go, Ajax." Wilco sounded as calm as if he'd said "More tea?"

"Roger, Wilco. Oh,, see now, I did it again!" The Englishman laughed with him.

They were sitting in the sarcastically named hurricane shelter below the lunar surface under Gene's Place. Although pretty crowded, the three storey 7x21m cylinder would be comfortable enough for the planned 48 hour stay. Everybody had a space in one of the shared twin cabins located on the narrower bottom floor, together with the bathrooms. On the top floor, there was storage for consumables, water and safety gear, along with the multi-purpose offices. One of these would receive camera and seismic data from every instrument left outside. The other doubled as a comms and medical room.

The main floor had a galley and open lounge with chairs, a comms access desk and screens. The entrance end had two independent airlocks, located at the sides and which were usually left unused in favour of two pairs of normal air-tight entrance doors located each end of an entrance hallway in between the airlocks. Today they were sealed and the airlocks activated, in case the base above lost pressure.

Above ground, every airlock and interior door was locked. Most of the base was left empty, operating on very low air pressure, with the air recovered and stored. If the base suffered an impact, the decompression would be less violent and damaging than a full pressure escape. Everything necessary, plus most other loose items, had been repositioned underground into any available space in the shelter.

With a day to spare, most of the base furnishings were stacked between the entrance stairway and the shelter airlocks. For those not directly involved in the observation and measuring of comet data it had been easier to have something to do than sit and wait. Most people had removed their personal goods into the tiny sleep spaces below.

Bird and his assistant had spent the last three days working round the clock, preparing as much food as possible to keep 35 mouths fed. The shelter had a basic galley, but there was plenty of cool storage. He felt an unexpected excitement, rather than apprehension. Whatever happened he planned to make proper observations as a historian.

Thibodeaux thought back over his day so far. He had issued an absolute deadline for the cessation of all outside activity. Everybody was to be in through the two base airlocks at impact minus four hours. With about two hours to go to that deadline he had initiated a roll call. As expected, every single one of the 35 base staff was on the surface. It took about two minutes to cycle the airlocks, each located inside the garages. They held two people in the suits, three at a pinch. He would call time thirty minutes before his deadline.

They were waiting to see the NEIL roll in carrying the geology exploration team. True to form, Lucy and Evan had made remarkable time and were ninety minutes ahead of the original estimate. Finally, somebody reported seeing the dust thrown up by the LXV. A few minutes later NEIL turned into the open east garage.

Seals had a tripod camera set up. Pelican had already posed with his comet in the background, for the picture predicted by Culver the previous year. Everybody was waiting to converge for a group photo against the same backdrop. Thibodeaux liked the idea of a bit of fun, and the photo opportunity would create a few laughs; a valuable release of tension before the waiting game started. He was fatalistic enough not to worry about survival. If they took a hit and he had injuries in the crew, well that would be altogether different.

As a young spaceman, Thibodeaux had survived a near disaster on his second mission. A fuel cell exploded during MAGENTA test flight DM 5, as it left LEO for a practice lunar supply drop. The crew of six survived the fire, but two were severely injured by a loose panel which detached during an EVA to assess the damage. The only way to recover was via a lunar slingshot, the exact manoeuvre that brought the historic Apollo 13 mission home after a similar scenario, right at the dawn of space travel.

It was a desperate five days. The medikit was woefully inadequate for such a disaster, with only enough painkillers for a two day headache. A crushed and splintered leg was way beyond their ability to treat. The mission commander had died in extreme agony from his injuries, a scant twelve hours before they reached Earth orbit for a rendezvous with a TUG and recovery to LEO 6.

Thibodeaux spent months in psyche recuperation at NASA before the horrors of his commander's fading screams stopped stalking him. Even so, many years later he would still wake on occasion to a thin grey ghost of that pain echoing from deep in the night. It took him a long time to persuade the Flight Surgeons to allow him into orbit again.

He shivered. As a quiet, non-church aligned New Faith Christian he wasn't given to praying much, but there was a time for everything. Standing outside for a while, away from the people milling around the base he offered up a silent prayer. *Please God, no injuries.*

A crowd gathered in the general area of the camera tripod. He checked the head up display. Less than seventy minutes to his deadline. Time to get this photo in the can.

"Gene's Team surface picnic, this is Ajax. Are you guys all ready to do this picture and then scoot on down to the playhouse? Anybody still not near the photo spot please report in."

"Ajax, Doc. Half a klick inbound."

Several of them had bounced out to the nominal 2,000 m footfall perimeter and back, just for the joy of movement. The next few days were likely to be pretty confined.

"Ajax, it's Ace, I'll be there in five."

"Ajax, this is Tobin with Bird, north perimeter and hopping in now."

Those two explorers! "Any more? OK then, who's handing out those name cards? That you Lucy? Welcome back." There was a wave. "Good. Roll up, gang. Find your card and stand by for the big picture." In typical local style the usual mix of real names, nicknames, and callsigns adorned the cards.

Once the four stragglers had arrived and taken their positions, Seals readied himself by the camera. The usual nonsense broke out as they tried to get into rows. It was almost like a school photo, with the tallest at the back, the shorter ones in front and a row of ten kneeling at front with Mario Silva, the dwarf Communications Specialist, standing at centre. Mario was a favourite among the regular crew at Gene's, one of the many dwarf astronauts that worked off planet.

Seals had placed the camera the day before so little adjustment was necessary. He pleaded with everybody to keep still and bounded off to his place in the back row.

"Thanks. I'm doing this on remote, crew, so I'll take a few. In fact I am already recording video. Don't leap about until I say so,

88

eh? Ready, One shot. Everybody, the Sun is off your faces, so dark visors up for a few moments and I can get a mug-shot. Oh yeah, that's real nasty. Say, 'Moon cheese'. That's two shots. Visors down again, three shots. Point at the comet, good, that's four. OK then, do something for this last one. When I say go, throw those cards as high straight up as you can. Ready, steady, Go! That's brilliant, folks. Thanks a lot, people."

Thibodeaux had decided the time was right to round 'em up. "Picnic Team, Ajax. Someone grab those cards for me. Levon and I are going to head for the airlocks now, so for those staying out here you have ten more minutes for your own photos and a quick walk if you want. Please report to myself or Levon at your designated airlocks no more than twenty minutes from my mark, that is a stop watch order. Three... two... one... Mark! That is all."

His channel had chimed, the head-up display said LEVO. "Go, Levon."

"Well handled, Ajax. I'd wondered if we were out here too late."

"No, we're fine, I needed to start the process for my own sake. After NEIL rolled in I got jumpy. We do have some time to spare so we needn't bust asses if they drift in a few minutes behind."

"Roger. See you inside."

After a meal, at impact minus three hours, there was an orderly withdrawal to the shelter. He reflected as he sealed the airlock. Overall, it had been a good day, relaxed and cheerful. He didn't believe any single one of them was suffering much real anxiety.

* * *

"Five minutes, Ajax."

"Thanks, Wilco. See how I managed to avoid it that time?"

"Want to have another go at three?"

"OK, then, try me..."

"Three minutes."

"Roger."

"One Minute, now."

"Roger." Ajax turned to the company. "This is it. Let's wish ourselves good luck."

"Ajax, the clock says zero."

"Thanks, Wilco."

For the first time since they had sealed the shelter there was complete silence. Everyone held their breath, as if they might hear the impact. The screen showed the view towards the projected impact site from the Space Telescope at LEO 6, Earth's scientific research space station. The telescope would collect eight minutes of film before the station slipped behind the Earth.

The last surviving piece of ice-covered rock from Percival A appeared to crawl across the surface of the Moon. At this range, the corona was too nebulous to see, or perhaps there was a little fuzziness to the entire picture. It stopped moving. There was an almighty flash of light that overloaded and blacked out the camera shot. It faded over perhaps three seconds, replaced by a slowly widening black circle on the face of the sunlit Moon.

"That's impact at 2:33 AM Houston time, Ajax," called Team Leader Anton Levine from the control room there. "Are you guys getting pictures?"

"Yes thanks," said Thibodeaux. "Spectacular! No other indications here as yet."

Across the globe most of the population either waited outside, or watched on screens. In three more hours the worst of the danger would pass, as the Percival B Shard scorched through the high atmosphere and departed towards the Sun.

"Seismographs are waking up," said Tobin, sitting with Evan at the science console alongside Thibodeaux. "I'm seeing big quakes at some of the outstations."

Billions of people glued to screens across the Earth watched the telescope shot, as a massive cloud of steam, dust, and lava expanded across the impact zone. With negligible rotation and no atmosphere, the fallout resulting from the huge impact fell in an almost perfect circle. The vast majority of the debris fell back to the surface over the following hour, dust and ice crystals settling at the same rate as the larger pieces of rock and cooling lava.

At Gene's, the team waited, and wondered if being more than six metres below the surface would be enough to protect them from any serious damage. Houston confirmed the distance to the impact as 1,382 km, far enough away to be safe from most of the larger debris. An alarm rang. Immediately everybody at a console bent over their keyboards.

"Ajax, there's a pressure loss in module N6/10, a minor impact so somebody may get a souvenir," Tobin called across the lounge. "Everywhere else is still tight. Who lives in N6/10?"

Kyran called back, "Room 10 in N6? Hey, that is mine. Do I get a rock? Most fortunately my stuff is all down here so I'm OK for damage, isn't it."

Thibodeaux laughed with everybody else. "First rock to Kyran. Ace, did you have odds?"

Cartographer Asa "Ace" Horowitz laughed with everybody else. His bookmaking was legendary. "Kyran wins the $500 prize."

The base got lucky. Kyran's rock, a tiny fragment later confirmed as a bit of Moon rather than comet, was the only damage the actual station received. There was a distinct thump somewhere nearby, as a larger piece hit the surface and set off the local seismograph, but no damage showed up on the system. A few minutes later Wilco, Seals, and Pelican all howled in protest as the observatory feed shut down. That suggested either damage to the facility itself or severed cables somewhere outside.

A pale-looking Culver put in a surprise call from Maui. Houston reported that there were a few fragments in orbit around the Moon but a lot less than first predicted. Also, one of the three lunar orbit comms satellites, TEL 2, was no longer responding to commands, presumably either damaged or destroyed by debris.

Thibodeaux, Culver in Hawaii, and Anton in Houston held a conference. They decided the team at Gene's would stay underground for at least 24 hours after the impact, while the risk of a debris strike receded. There would still be a diminishing risk over time as lunar gravity sucked in the comet tail.

The science team were all itching to get out on the surface and make observations, but Thibodeaux asserted his authority, supported by Culver. Until at least 2:33 AM Houston time on September 25th, the team would stay downstairs.

Lucy and Evan seethed in a corner of the lounge. They were desperate to visit the impact site, where they were expecting to find a new crater and the first ever molten lava recorded on the Moon. They had prospected a lot of craters and impact sites, with some major success in charting rare metal finds for a planned mining operation. Every one of those sites was millions of years old. The chance to be the first geologists to visit a brand new one was a career topper. Lucy in particular was furious that Thibodeaux was keeping them underground. She was desperate to get back on the trail in one of the LXVs. The pair argued in a quiet whisper.

"Lucy, it's not safe outside yet. It's not just Ajax, y'know. Lancaster and Houston have a say in it too, eh. It's only for a day, although I guess it might end up being two."

"Two? Oh, Stars! It's our one chance to ever do this. We are the people on the ground. Fresh geology, man! Science needs us to get there. I was desperate to go to the comet but nobody had the balls to plan a mission. Now it's followed me here and I can't even go and visit the hole. It's not fair."

He sighed. They had been round this twice already. "You'd have had the balls, yes, but you'd be dead. Come on now, please don't pick a fight with the commander today. He is a fair guy, but he's prepared to step on you if you cross him again. You, we, need to be a bit careful here. If we work on him *quietly*, together, he will let us go as soon as it's safe. I know Ajax as well as I know anybody. Did you know Sara and I named Andrew for him? He's the future astronaut Drew McQ's godfather. He's also the best balanced man I have ever met."

"So, he's a good guy and he's your friend. I get that Evan, but he's still dead wrong about this. We need to be outside because we have important work to do, and he needs to understand that."

"He will, but will you *please* let me speak to him first before you do, eh? I promise you he will listen to me. Not immediately, but in the morning I will catch him and ask if we can get going soon. Most of the science team will be busy here and we are the only ones who need to request transport."

"All right then, but if he says no he will have me to deal with. And I'm in no mood for a long fight over it. We must get there before it's as dead as every other site we visit. I'd take an LXV whatever he said."

Evan rolled his eyes. "Look, that kind of talk will get you fired for sure. You're the geology boss and the comet guru, but I can't operate the survey solo. I need you here working, so don't get yourself suspended from duty. Please, Lucy-Lu, eh?"

"We'll see. Just try and work on him."

16 – OBSERVATORY
10:20 PM (HST) 24th SEPTEMBER

Leif Culver stood with his wife Sunny, on the visitors terrace outside the Haleakala Observatory on Maui. It was late evening on September 24th, three days before the full moon and a date to mark in history. Like countless millions of people in places with a view of the moon, they were waiting to see the end of the show.

The visible part of Comet Percival's tail hung across the evening sky like a wedding veil. Over the past few days it had begun to twist and fold around as it came under the influence of both Earth and lunar gravity, as if the veil had caught a light breeze. To the naked eye the tiny bright spot that was the last piece of Percival A was already invisible, outshone by the background illumination as it started to cross in front of the Moon's sunlit surface.

Hawaii was one of the places where the comet impact on the moon, and the subsequent transit of the ejected Shard through Earth's upper atmosphere would be best viewed. The party had arrived from Edwards the previous day aboard NASA 1, the organisation's own SubOrb craft.

Twenty of the NASA management team, plus a few partners, joined several hundred invited guests at the observatory. In the morning they would head back to Lancaster for a huge round of meetings and press conferences.

The predicted meteor shower, spawned by solar wind attrition and the subsequent breakup of Comet Percival, had started bombarding the Earth two days before. The spectacular free display was still causing great delight all around the planet.

As the party stood watching the Moon and the great comet tail, a constant stream of shooting stars sparkled and coruscated in the upper atmosphere. Every flash heralded the destruction of tiny particles of dust and ice crystals torn from the comet.

There were an increasing number of ground impacts around the planet. Most were small enough to cause minor damage and sensation, but earlier in the day one had sparked a near disaster. A direct hit on one of the Panama Canal locks caused major damage. The upper section of the canal was still draining, with several other locks out of action and a lot of ships aground. Incredibly, there had only been a handful of casualties. There were also reports of a large meteor filmed crossing South America, towards an impact deep in the Amazon basin.

The Percival A impact wasn't expected to be as dramatic as the atmosphere-grazing light show of the Percival B Shard just over three hours later. When the last piece of the diminished nucleus hit the Moon, there was a sudden, almost blinding flash from a point close to the centre of the disc. Within a few seconds it started to fade into to a small dark stain, and that was it; to the naked eye the show was over. The name Percival had been transferred from the comet to a brand new lunar crater formed in that instant.

At this altitude, the clear air 3,000 m above the Pacific Ocean felt sharp and cold after the parching heat of the Mojave Desert. Before returning outside to watch Percival B, the group moved into the Visitor Center for an informal meal. Chief Astronomer Ringtone Buchanan approached Culver.

"I still can't believe it, Leif. 'Phut!' and there it was gone, just like that. It feels like we got away with it."

"I wish it were so but we can't say that yet. I don't think we can claim we got away with it until the folks at Gene's are out of danger and the meteor shower finishes here. Even if they don't sustain any gross damage at the base, we have no real idea what the comet tail might do. There's still a huge amount of stuff moving about at enormous velocities up there, never mind here."

Culver felt no enthusiasm for the show; he just wanted it to be over. He was jet-lagged and tired. In spite of having the stent fitted, plus all the drugs he was absorbing, his chest still ached. Even after a week of resting, persuading Doc Tunstall to allow him to fly out for the show had been tricky. He tried to put on a brave face, but knew he needed more treatment.

Redwood pushed past some other guests to join them, and Culver's failing heart sank even further. He had left his deputy behind at Lancaster, so he must have made his own way to Maui. He sensed Redwood's antagonistic mood.

"They've taken major damage on the Panama Canal this afternoon, Director. People are getting killed. I was right. I told you, and you should have used KICK when you had the chance. You need to resign."

"No, Will," Culver said as calmly as he could manage. "You were dead wrong then and you're still dead wrong now. We've been through this already. We did exactly the right thing with regard to KICK. Ed's math was right all along. Overall the comet was 98% ice and snow, with almost no rock inside. If we'd actually done it back then, the whole thing might have split up and shot a much larger collection of smoking holes in both the Earth and the Moon. As it is, the vast majority of the material boiled off to give us a harmless light show, without intervention. So far we've only had one significant hit here, and it missed Gene's. As far as I'm concerned, as long as the people on the Moon stay safe and we don't get any major hits on Earth, Ringtone will be right. With those qualifications we will have got away with it."

Redwood staggered a little. He wasn't satisfied and it was obvious that he had been drinking. He started jabbing a finger at his boss's face and raised his voice. "That was more by luck than judgement on your part. That's gross incompetence. You gambled with the safety of the entire planet and so far you got lucky is all."

"What's with making this personal, Will?" asked Culver, sounding calmer than he felt. The hollow ache in his chest was back, and it produced a brief warning stab of real pain. "Not using KICK was a decision made in conference and you were there. We all accepted responsibility for that course of action. You're being antagonistic and you've had too much to drink." He spoke with great care into the stunned silence that had fallen around them. "I'm not prepared to fight you here in public while we are guests of the observatory. If you still feel the need to discuss it *when you get sober*, I'll see you in the office back at Lancaster tomorrow."

TUG System manager Kent Warwick heard the exchange, and arrived on the scene with a couple of the other young guns in tow. For everything that was eccentric about him, he had a strong sense of fairness, respected Culver, and was obviously furious. He caught Redwood by the shoulder.

"Will, why can't you leave him alone? You're acting like a complete dick."

Redwood spun around to face him. "You keep out of this, you fucking weirdo."

"That's enough!" Culver came close to losing his famous cool. "Will, you're creating a ridiculous scene here and you need to leave right now, or I'll ask these guys to see you off the premises. I mean it, get out!"

"You can't—" began Redwood, as he swung back unsteadily to face Culver, but Kent and his buddies weren't prepared to wait for the order. By mutual consent they placed themselves in front of the Director. Kent turned and pushed Redwood hard in the chest, making him stagger back into Ringtone. Kent pulled back his arm in a clear threat. "Out of his face, right now. Back off, Redwood."

Culver was delighted that they had intervened, because he had come as close to actual violence as Kent. The pain subsided a little as his heart pounded with adrenaline. He could hear the rush of blood in his ears. The dizziness started to pass as he gripped a chair back to steady himself. As he looked on, Ringtone joined the youngsters and took hold of Redwood's arm. He stopped shouting and submitted, caught in a steely grip on both sides.

Forcing himself to stay calm, Culver apologised to the onlookers and took a few deep breaths as he tried to recover his composure. He went inside to the museum lobby, where a satcom kit and a screen had been set up. Calling Gene's, he found the crew hanging out in the shelter as planned. Anton Levine joined the call from Mission Control at Houston.

Culver had to reach deep inside himself to muster up a jovial greeting. "Ajax, man, there you are! Well, from our point of view the Percival A show is all over. Ringtone described it as a 'Phut!' We're high up here on Maui and it's cold outside, so we've all retreated inside until the Shard show. How are you doing?"

Thibodeaux gestured to his crew, scattered about the Hurricane Shelter living area. "We're good, Leif.

Locally we had some mild seismic reaction, and one room upstairs suffered a minor decompression. There was one big rattle nearby a few minutes ago which made us all jump, but no damage showed up on the system. We've lost visual links from the external setup and the observatory feed is down so it could be that it suffered a hit. We have no way to see if there's any other damage."

Culver could feel his heart starting to slow a little. The dull throbbing returned, but in spite of it his confidence rose. "That's great so far. The best field estimate we have for potential damage suggests that the risk will lessen by half with every passing hour. I'm taking, 'an hour after impact and we're relaxed and happy', as good news. Please keep us informed if anything changes, would you? Yes, Anton?"

At Houston, Levine was holding some sheets he had received from the shop floor a few moments before. "Guys, we have some scattered rocks in orbit, and there's been a whole band of impacts across the lunar surface, but all the big stuff looks like it came straight down. There's a lot less orbital matter than we estimated. I'd still recommend the full 24 hour wait before leaving the shelter. After that it's on a calculated risk basis. Their luck has been amazing so far with the one minor pressure loss."

"Good call, Anton, I'm comfortable with that," said Culver. "Ajax?"

"Absolutely," agreed the commander. "I'll have to give the scientists a talking to; those guys are already nipping at my ankles. I reckon you're right Anton, 24 hours matches my gut feeling here."

Half the Hawaiian press were in the lobby trying to grab interviews. Kent was always a good man to offer up but as yet he hadn't reappeared, so Culver set a couple of the other department heads onto them. He usually helped the media as much as possible, and had a reputation for going out of his way to do it, but for once he didn't feel like it.

Making an attempt to shrug off the chest pains he found Sunny, and they wandered outside with a glass of red wine. It was a good job they were wrapped up against the cool night because this high up the day's warmth evaporated quickly after sunset. She snuggled against him to wait for the final act of the show.

"How are you doing, big guy?"

Culver sighed. "I'm tired, love. It's been hard these last few weeks. I'm grateful everybody has carried some of the load for me. Eric says I shouldn't be here and I still don't feel well, but I'm seeing this show before we leave if it's the last thing I do. I promise I'm going to do two things. He said the stent would keep me going for a while, but it feels weird and I know I need the replacement heart immediately. I'll give myself up to him tomorrow and get it seen to. That might take a while, but afterwards you and I will have a proper vacation."

She squeezed him a bit harder. "Oh, Leif, I've been so hoping you would say that sooner or later. Eve Meredith from NASA U said she wants us to use her house here on Maui for as long as you need to recover. She's been plotting with Penny. Your training manager and P.A. are both adamant that you should get some proper rest. And yes, of course your people will lift the load for a while."

"That's fine as far as it goes. It would be much easier if I didn't have Redwood hanging about trying to grab the reins so he can whip the folks. He's the only reason I didn't stay in the hospital and get this old heart properly fixed yet. I wish I could find something for him to do, but nobody wants him." He sighed. "I wish I hadn't got stuck with him as deputy, but there was no choice at the time. After we lost Eb Stanford to ill health I had no better options available at short notice. If I'd had a few months to firm up a plan I could have avoided having him."

"Who would you want running it?" she asked.

"They could all do it," he mused. "Ringtone is sound, or Ed, although he's younger. I know he can deal with Redwood. Ajax has the tools, but he's going to need rest after what they've been through on the Moon. Actually, if we need someone to control Redwood, Eve Meredith would make a great caretaker, although she's even older than me. She takes no nonsense, that's for sure. Everybody would back her up and be respectful, and she has no enemies. I think that might be what I'd want."

"You should get them all together and talk about it," his wife commented. "I don't understand about how it works with Will, would he take over as of right? Is that the problem?"

"The way the rules stand, yes. He'd be sure to sue and create mayhem otherwise. That's why he keeps trying to force me into retiring or resigning. I'm sure he knows I'll replace him, after some of the trouble he's caused. I came close to breaking some knuckles on him about an hour ago, before Kent and Ringtone threw him out of here drunk. You missed the best of that show. He has all the right credentials, but he can't manage people. I've said it before; management skills can be learned, sadly people skills can't. It's a bit of a mantra where he's concerned. That's the bottom line; I keel over and he walks right in."

She hugged him again. "Hey hey, now, don't keel over just yet, big guy!"

Flight Surgeon Eric Tunstall joined them. "Leif, Kent tells me he had to get between you and your drunken deputy before. I missed it, but it's only a few days since you had that stent fitted. I only allowed you to come along provided you didn't get stressed. I don't suppose there's any use asking if you are feeling OK?"

"No, I'm calm Eric, but I amazed myself by coming close to actually smacking him one. Kent was right; he and Ringtone hauled him away before I could get my jacket off."

Eric laughed at that. "The Culver cool was nearly shattered? Now I'm impressed. It was a good deal letting those guys eject him. I've been outside attending to a graze on his head. He did some ejecting himself; lived up to that notorious nickname of his and threw up all over Kent's favourite red shoes. Following that drama he passed out in some style as I understand it, hence the head injury. You'd think a man of 52 would know better."

"Eric, it may have done some good in the long run because I've made my mind up. Tomorrow morning we'll hold a meeting at Lancaster and I'll nominate a team to try and hold it together under him while I get the surgery. After lunch you and I are catching the train to visit your friend the heart surgeon in New York, OK?"

The terrace was filling for the final act of the show. It was already past 1:00 AM and if predictions were correct the Shard was due to do its skipping-stone act off the atmosphere to the south at 1:42 AM. It was time to check the accuracy of Ed Seals' math. The news of Culver's altercation with Redwood was hot gossip, and he found himself accepting unexpected handshakes and hugs from some of his closest friends and colleagues. There was a shared sense of destiny as the group waited on the top layer of the terrace along with the observatory staff. He noticed with interest that people were standing a little closer together than they usually might, surrounding their boss in a show of solidarity.

They wouldn't need a physical countdown; the comet fragment would show itself in good time. As the minutes passed, conversation died away to the occasional whispered words. Just before show time Sunny caught his hand, unexpectedly followed by Penny standing on the other side. All around them, people were holding hands or resting arms around each other's shoulders waiting for the moment of shared destiny.

There was a flash of light and the final act of the Greatest Ever Show on Earth commenced. A vast fireball swept from left to right before them, blazing a path of ionisation through the Southern sky. It increased in intensity almost immediately; from orange, to fierce yellow, to a blinding, eye-watering white hot. As it seared through, showers of multicoloured sparks exploded and danced away from it in every direction, as tons of ice and dust ripped away in the slipstream. In a matter of seconds it was halfway across the sky.

In the utter silence Culver gasped, along with many others, as the precious Earth came so close to an epochal disaster of unimaginable proportions. For less than half a minute the Shard grazed the tenuous upper atmosphere, blazing a neon-bright path that would take over fifteen more minutes to fade away into the cool darkness.

Then it was gone, away into the night. The fireworks shimmered out to the odd spark, leaving the watching crowd stunned into silence as they watched the trail of near destruction begin to cool and fade.

Somebody in the crowd on the lower terrace started to clap, and in a few moments the quiet evening was a mass of applause. As it died away, the show came to an astounding finale, an ear-splitting crescendo to the loudest sound anybody present had ever heard. The hammer of Thor himself couldn't have struck a more terrifying or discordant blow, as something akin to a volley of simultaneous thunder claps and multiple supersonic booms crashed across the islands like a physical punch-line. It literally shook the ground and struck a cold, primeval fear into the hearts of even the most hardened scientists present.

It was the final straw. Culver felt as if the Shard had ejected something diamond-sharp and intensely cold as it passed. It plunged deep into his chest like some cruel dagger; the venom of interstellar ice at absolute zero. It was like pure hatred, drilled into his very being from the heavens with the force of an ancient and angry god.

He couldn't speak. His heart gave one massive beat, then another. The next one was slower coming and then there was an ominous pause. He willed it to beat again as his head started to lighten towards faintness. There! It gave one final ragged shudder, a physical jolt that made his vision blur and dim. In that single instant he knew that his heart had stopped.

"Leif!" Sunny screamed as his hand slipped from hers, and her husband slowly folded to a kneeling position on the cold tiles. She and Penny both scrambled to try and break his forward topple.

The doctor skidded to his knees as he pulled out a small emergency kit he had brought for just such an event. Sunny was in tears as they turned Culver onto his back. He felt for a pulse, shook his head, and yanked the shirt open, buttons scattering as he did so. He pumped two diffusers directly into Culver's chest.

Sunny shrieked at him. "Eric, don't let him die. Oh, Leif!"

Tunstall started CPR, and turned to the stunned group looking on in disbelief. He raised his voice, pumping the chest in threes and calling out a word with each press. "One, two, three - Call, ambulance, now." He took a breath. "Get, van, head -

104

Down,to, meet." He gasped. "Come, on, people - Some, body, move." Another breath. "Don't, die, here - On, me, Leif."

Several people departed at a flat run. After a few more seconds he checked the man's pulse again and turned to the two women, speaking in gasps as he got his breath back.

"Sunny, I've stabilised him. He has a weak pulse. Phew! Not as young as I was either. Altitude doesn't help, him or me. His heart is beating. Uhh! I know where the trouble is, so we can have him, under treatment as soon as we get him to a hospital. I asked him not to come, and we're bloody miles from help. I'm hoping we can transport him part way down the mountain, to meet an ambulance and save time. I'm making no promises here."

"Thanks, Eric." She nodded and clung to Penny.

Houston liaison manager Blake Shermann arrived back on the terrace. He was panting hard too.

"Doc, one of the observatory guys has a surfing van. He's got help dumping out his gear in the parking lot and it'll be out front in one minute. They're getting a mattress from the bunk-house and an ambulance will meet us half-way down to Kula hospital. What can we do, Eric? Can we lift him in a sun lounger?"

"OK, that'll have to do," said Tunstall. "Come on folks, lend a hand here."

18 – GEOLOGISTS
11:00 AM (LST) 26th SEPTEMBER

"Nobody goes out? Another twelve hours? What in the Galaxy are you talking about? Evan and I have to get over there!" Lucy was more furious than she could ever remember. She refused the seat Thibodeaux was indicating, and stood in the lounge waving her arms and shouting at her boss, surrounded by shocked friends and colleagues.

"Commander, in case you weren't aware of it we are geologists. In the last hundred years all the resident geology teams have managed to do here on the Moon is pick up billion year old rocks and the occasional billion year old meteorite. The comet missed us, and most of the pieces have stopped flying around. We are about as likely to get hit sitting here as anywhere else. Everybody volunteered to stay because we are all scientists. For pity's sake, we observe and record and explore and examine and take samples and document and photograph. That's what we do! Nobody has ever had a real live dead comet to examine and sample. How much longer do you think you can you go on making us sit here with *nothing to do?*"

The final question had come out at a full shriek.

He pointed. "Sit." She sat. Thibodeaux could be assertive when he chose to, which wasn't often. He was on his feet facing the growing crowd, as people drifted in from other parts of the communal area to see what the fuss was about. They had started to bring their belongings and supplies up from the shelter. Bird was due to serve a meal shortly, and most people were stretching out in the lounge after 36 hours in the cramped emergency space.

"I will not, repeat not, be yelled at," he insisted, trying to catch a couple of eyes around the room. There were others around who agreed with her, and it was important to stay professional. "Senior management has deemed it unsafe to be outside, and we are all grounded until the new deadline. It's twelve extra hours, that's all. We will continue this discussion in my office after lunch. Not here, and not now. Do I make myself crystal clear?"

"What's with all this racket? Say, what's going on in here?" Bird broke the tension, putting his head round the corner from the dining area. "Do you folks wanna eat or not? Brunch coming up next door in two, people."

Thibodeaux was grateful for his friend's ability to defuse a row. It was a skill that occasionally came in handy. Grappelli would calm down soon enough.

* * *

Lucy put her head round the office door. "Commander Thibodeaux, I owe you an apology."

"Get in here and grab a seat, you. Apology accepted, all right? Look, I can take the occasional hit but it wasn't the best choice of venue. You could have yelled at me in here all you liked and we wouldn't have had such a scene."

She sat down and sighed. "I know. I just blew. I even surprised myself and now I'm embarrassed to the soles of my feet. But from where we are sitting it's so frustrating."

"Do you think I'm happy stuck inside? We're all stir crazy, but with the camera lines cut we are blind. We have to accept guidance from Earth on what's happening overhead. Nobody is more frustrated than Wilco, but have you seen him yelling at people in public? The moment we get the all clear, you can follow me outside for a look."

She nodded. "OK, but the minute we can go outside Evan and I need to commandeer an LXV and get as close to the impact site as we can. There is so much out there we need to do."

107

"Look, I get it. And I will cut you a deal. As my senior field geologist, it is always going to be your team that has first call on the LXVs. I have no problem with that. As soon as possible you and Evan can get there and report. For the meantime, like me, like the rest of us, you will have to be patient."

"Thanks, Commander."

"All right. Now get back out there to the lounge and relax for a while. Go and tell them I kicked you from one end of this office to the other and then let you off with a warning." He actually winked. "By the way Lucy, I'm sure I overheard some talk out there before; the usual old nonsense about a well hidden bootleg stash being discovered in the shelter, and some sort of party later. The time-honoured moonshine rumour, I suspect. Nobody claimed ownership, and I wouldn't know a thing about it of course."

She turned to ask what on the Moon he was talking about. He was holding out a bottle of Scotch whisky.

He was laughing. "Go and join the survival party. There'll be some other stuff appearing in the lounge shortly too. By the way, that was all a line about the moonshine. Lancaster gave me the combination to a well hidden lock-box behind some hardware downstairs. Inside was a stash marked 'Strictly for Emergencies.' Seems they do think of everything."

* * *

Against advice from the management team, Acting NASA Director Will Redwood extended the lockdown at Gene's to 36 hours. He enjoyed twelve self-satisfied hours, having asserted his new authority. When he attempted to stretch it to 48 hours, his new regime ran into trouble.

Evan arrived in Thibodeaux' office with a sudden outburst that was right out of character.

"Enough, Ajax! Everybody knows the risks. Why another twelve hours? At least let the science teams get out long enough to check over their kit. I've never seen Wilco in despair before. Poor guy would be in tears if his English emotions were ever allowed out into the open."

Ajax snapped back. "Give over telling me what to do here. Of all the people, Evan, why do you become the spokesman? I expect it from Grappelli because she's fiery, but not you. You're making it even harder for me because you're my friend."

Evan was furious. "That's crap and you know it. I'm the voice of reason for the entire crew here, eh? 36 hours is way more than enough time shut inside. No significant impacts in the last twelve hours and now you say twelve more. Round it up, make it a bloody week, why don't you?"

He was raising his voice. "Even I'm backing Lucy's effort to stock up and head back out with NEIL. We'd be off the blocks faster if we took BUZZ though. The LXV guys got it mission-ready before they stowed it up north at the shed. They used their heads, and now it's time for you to use yours!"

Thibodeaux stood up and faced the Canadian. "The decision was not made here. Orders came from Lancaster. Against my better judgement the Acting Director asserted his authority, and it's going to be the full 48 hours before we open the door. Don't lay it all on me. For your information, a significant chunk of the comet shot a new hole in the surface about ten klicks from where you were sat when I ordered you back. That means you two have dodged it once already. I don't want you out there hoping to dodge it again, and I am not allowed to send anybody out until it is as safe as possible. That's how it's going to be."

"OK, so 'as safe as possible' you say? Still not totally safe though, eh? I know how Lucy feels sometimes, man. You're like a brick wall. Listen to reason here, because your team is coming apart and going stir-crazy. You need to give all these intelligent people the numbers and let them make their own choices."

"That's enough. You're goading me into a fight, and you won't get one. I think you've said plenty on the subject, OK?"

"Nah, I won't fight you, but Ill tell you this, Andrew Thibodeaux. Lucy and I *will* be starting our external departure prep for a mission to the comet crater at precisely 2:33 AM. That's your oh-so-precious 48 hours after the impact. If you try and stretch that deadline one more time, we will both cancel our tasks for the rest of this tour and invoke the team breakdown safety clause as per our contracts.

"This is your one and only warning, because we're not the only ones by a long way. I checked and, since NASA became a commercial outfit, no single person has ever invoked that clause. If you decide to play hardball with us you'll be the first commander ever to lose his team. Bottom line? If we're not outside by 2:35 AM Lucy, me, Wilco, and at least six others, will immediately quit and request transport home at the earliest convenience. Want to make a prediction for your management career based on that?"

Thibodeaux sat down, open-mouthed and completely side-swiped by his usually jovial friend. "Come on, Evan. We—"

Evan was fuming. "No! I'm not done. Now we both know what this is called, of course; mutiny, out-and-out blackmail. I'm done pissing around waiting for over-cautious managers, both here and downstairs, to make a credible decision. Incidentally, I'll deny ever talking to you so don't try and bring it back to me. I wasn't even in here. I'm the rock steady Canadian joker who never said a bad word to anyone.

"Oh yeah, and something tripped in comms so your office area voice recorder ain't running." Evan flashed his sunniest smile, then stalked out and slammed the office door, leaving Thibodeaux shaking.

After a long talk with Anton Levine at Houston and Ringtone at Lancaster, Thibodeaux called a staff meeting at 10:00 PM to announce that the lockdown would cease with effect from 10:33, exactly 44 hours after the impact. Within thirty minutes he had a call from a furious Redwood.

"Thibodeaux, We agreed to keep you inside for 48 hours."

"We didn't, Vom. Against the advice of the department heads you did, but the orbital debris has lessened significantly today and the teams here have a lot of work to do. Wilco needs to survey the observatory for damage and my field team must start out to the impact crater."

"You have not been officially authorised to change that timing. You are all grounded inside the base until 2:33 AM. A possible extension to that deadline will also be subject to a full meeting of the management heads of department for approval before I sign off on it. That is final."

"So come up here and say that. Oh, I forgot. You can't, can you, Vom? And while we're on the subject of your nickname, did you pay for Kent's shoes?" Thibodeaux gave a loud puke impression, and cut the connection. If they could avoid it, nobody in the company was speaking to Redwood after the news of his row with Culver leaked out. Many believed it had led directly to the Director's heart attack.

Redwood had spent most of his first day in charge wondering why the Floor Fifty office smelled so bad. He finally discovered Kent's red shoes in the top drawer of the desk. Some wit had brought them back from Maui for him, still covered in vomit and stuffed with most of the tissues they had used to clean him up afterwards.

19 – BUZZ
11:20 PM (LST) 26th SEPTEMBER

Although it was approaching the normal sleep period as they followed Houston time, most of the scientists headed out to check over their equipment as soon as they could. Unlike the morning of the impact when they had all been out for the group photo, the base was manned. With a constant dialogue between Gene's and Houston, Paula Everett and Mario Silva stayed in the comms office. Since Culver's hospital admission in Maui everybody was trying to avoid talking to Lancaster, where they would have to deal with Redwood.

The main focus was still orbiting debris. The orbital team at Houston were already planning how to attach hardware to larger individual pieces and move them, either away into space or more likely to planned lunar impacts. The vast majority of debris had cooled and fallen back to the surface as a mixture of rocks and dust, plus fine strands of cooled lava and glass. There was also a significant amount of ice and snow in places, the first ever water detected on the lunar surface.

As soon as the surface teams went outside Houston received some good news. The external dome containing the astronomical observatory was completely undamaged. A small piece of falling debris had cut the heavy feed line from there into the base. The installation had its own set of solar panels and had kept on watching and recording, even as poor Wilco sat underground for two days fretting about it.

Wilco and Seals were already busy over there retrieving data, aided by the ever-willing Pelican. The damaged cable was a standard stock item and there were spares, making for a straightforward fix.

Thibodeaux was also outside checking on his teams. He took a call from base Recycling Specialist Eagle.

"Ajax, it's not good news at the old hangar. BUZZ has been trashed and the rest of the stuff out here is knee deep in gravel and shit. There's a hole in the shed roof and an even bigger one in the back wall. Whatever made it went straight through the rear end of BUZZ too. It looks like most of the emergency stores over here are intact, but we'll have a major clearing up operation before we can retrieve anything."

"Roger, Eagle. Can you do me a rapid survey and a damage estimate we can put in the plan?"

"OK, no problem."

So in spite of the amazing escape, they did have a casualty after all. Losing BUZZ, now that was a real blow. Another chime sounded in his ear. The icon in the headup said GRAP.

"Ajax. Go ahead."

"Commander, I just asked Eagle about BUZZ. Does having one LXV out of action mean Evan and I are grounded here at the base?"

He tried to keep the usual calm and cheerful tone, but he felt himself breaking into a sweat about his exchange with Evan. Somehow he managed a slight chuckle as he replied. "Why am I not surprised? I knew I'd find you stabbing my ear again sooner or later. Don't panic, Grappelli. I've only just heard about BUZZ too, and if the damage is severe then that's a real nuisance. It's lucky for you that the geology department at Houston is almost as desperate as you are to start getting data in from the impact site, so that's the one operation I can't restrict.

With no injuries and only minor damage here we need to start getting the science in. I'm going to let you take NEIL out and start your survey."

113

"Thanks, Ajax, that's great news. I'll alert the LXV team and get prepped immediately. Can we take Kyran Mukherjee? He's great for morale, always cheerful, and even helps us with the science. He's a much better trail buddy than Ellis, who just sits and stares at nothing if he's not driving. That dude's really creepy. We'll be out of here in a couple of hours."

"Not so fast." Thibodeaux rolled his eyes. "First, it'll take some proper planning. It's going to be a long trip, so I'm minded to despatch you and Evan as a pair again to conserve supplies and stretch your trail time. I know Kyran likes to go along, but I'm going to need both him and Ellis here to work on BUZZ. Second, before we can despatch you I will need to deal with Redwood, but he's my problem."

"OK, boss, Evan and I are cool with that too; probably better on mission duration grounds."

"So go and get your equipment list organised and prep NEIL. Then get some rest. I want you and Evan to meet me in the office with the LXV team at 9:00 AM for a comprehensive planning meeting. I'm guessing that will mean a late morning departure at best. I am not prepared to rush round cutting corners; not for you, not for Houston, and not for anybody else. But Lucy, you need to acknowledge the risks. Without BUZZ available, there can be no backup at that kind of range if you encounter any problems."

"OK, I understand all that, NEIL will look after us, and I promise we will take good care of NEIL too. I'll get on it, and thanks boss. Lucy out."

He called his deputy, who was surveying the north shed with Eagle. "Levon, what does it look like with BUZZ?"

"Well, BUZZ might not be a complete write-off but it's a major job. We haven't found whatever hit the garage yet, but it went right on through the back wall and made a crater about three metres across. BUZZ has an entry hole in the rear part of the roof, the whole of the sleeping space is trashed, and there is a half-metre wide exit hole on the starboard rear corner. I think we'll be looking at a new body shell and that's a spare part we don't have. The good news is that the chassis, drive motors, and steering all look fine, but two tyres are shot. Nothing switches on so we can't even move it until we get some system work done. We called the LXV guys and they both rushed over here. Kyran is already hopping about with a checklist pulling fuses and circuits, but Ellis is just sitting in the cabin and muttering to himself. He looks devastated."

"OK, It's not difficult to understand how he feels. Those guys are in love with their machinery. He's an ace for procedures so he can organise the repair operation. In the meantime I will need both him and Kyran in the office for a 9:00 AM meeting. Would you pass on to them that Lucy and Evan are prepping NEIL and stocking up for a departure later towards Crater Pelican. I'll have to keep the LXV Engineering team here working on BUZZ. Also if I send the Geology team as a pair they can have more time down-trail."

Levon wasn't sure. "Is that wise? They're having a bad day already, and you're going to ground them from the expedition?"

"I know. It makes me wish I'd sent Kyran with them on the last one. Come to think of it, if I had the trip would have been shorter and we wouldn't have had to drag them back in like we did. I'll make it right with those guys face to face later. I think that working on BUZZ will have the greater draw, at least that's my hope. Ellis will be fine with that but Kyran is a bit of a would-be pioneer. He'll be disappointed but you know him, ever the optimist. He'll say something almost comprehensible, blind us all with the teeth in that grin, and go back to work."

115

"OK, sounds like good logic. So, was Lucy yelling about it?" Levon was well aware how much the fiery geologist had upset his commander.

"No. She was all up for a hasty kick-off but I slapped that down and made it crystal clear that the correct procedures and checklists will be followed. Now I sound like Redwood, and for that I apologise. I may have to go and kick myself in the butt!"

Evan eased NEIL out of the garage and turned to head for the base perimeter. Lucy sat in the passenger seat, ecstatic at the prospect of doing some cutting-edge geology. He had waited with as much excitement as his colleague, but was usually more laid-back. They glanced at each other, took a deep breath and sighed at the same time.

"Say, Lucy-Lu, aren't you so glad to be out of there? All that excitement and fuss, and then the embarrassment of watching you pick a fight with Ajax. I'm relieved we've left all that behind for a couple of weeks, eh. Don't you think it feels like the holidays at last?"

She grinned back at him across the cabin. As they crossed the 2,000 m perimeter markers they both "went on vacation", taking off their regulation space helmets and attaching them to clips low down on each side of the control panel. More basic decompression hoods were stowed at the necks of their suits. They were there for emergency use only, but the pair popped them out to hang down, folded behind the suits in case of any incident. They could be pulled over and sealed in five seconds if required. It was a compromise that was officially frowned upon, but acknowledged as standard operating procedure if travelling any distance.

"I'll tell you what," she said. "We're going to end up well known after this. We'll be on every talk show on the planet."

"Now come on, you know the publicity circus isn't my scene. I'll watch you soak it all up though."

"No way. I'll need you along as my straight man."

Evan grimaced, and then laughed unexpectedly. "Hey now, I forgot about this. I've got some special home news to tell you. I'd been waiting for a chance to share it since before we hit the shelter, eh. I had a call from Sara the day before we went to lockdown, and I've been saving it for when we finally escaped out of there. Guess what? Drew McQ is going to have a new baby sister."

She reached over and rubbed his arm. "Oh, Evan, that's such great news. I'm so glad for you." She didn't dare let on that she had known for months.

"She's already 26 weeks. Says she knew before we even left AstroCal back in June, but she didn't tell me then in case I wanted to stay home. Then she worried for weeks and thought she'd miscarry. Then she didn't want me to worry, then she wasn't well, then the comet, and... Well, it's only now the doctor thinks she'll be OK. We never thought she could get pregnant again after Andrew, you know."

"That makes it even more exciting for you both. I can't tell you how delighted I am. I wish we had some champagne."

"Thanks, Lucy. I'm over the... Well, the ol' Moon, I guess. I did say we could call her Sue McQ, but Sara's sense of humour was never too good when she was carrying Andrew and, well it didn't go down so good, eh." They shared the laugh.

Following the West Way for 2,000 km, they planned to turn off 310 km southwest of the Copernicus Road junction. Leaving the road, the plan took them almost due west across the floor of the wide Fra Mauro Crater, breaking a new trail to locate the comet impact. Evan reckoned on three days out and two days back to the Central Solar Array where there was a charging station. They had thirteen days to reach the impact site and beat the sunset back as far as the Array. That would allow eight days to break trail to the impact site and work on the science. Apart from the last 200 km or so of off road travel it looked like an easy trip. After charging NEIL they would travel slowly back to Gene's through the dark of the lunar night, although Earthlight always helped.

At Gene's, Thibodeaux knew they would travel hard to give themselves extra time on-site. His instructions, made crystal clear to Evan, were to leave the site not less than 72 hours before sundown was due at the Central Array. Evan would stick to that deadline. The man was careful, and blessed with enough common sense to keep the much more volatile Lucy out of trouble.

Evan had been pretty fired up over the lockdown. Thibodeaux had let the subject rest for now but, close friend or not, there would be a difficult management conversation about it after the mission.

Four hours out from the base, Evan was ready for a shift change. "So, it's no use both of us sitting up here if we are going to drive solid all the way. Want to drive or sleep, eh?"

Lucy had been dozing in the big seat for two hours. "Sorry, Evan. Stars! I must have dropped off. What's the time?"

"We're already plus 4:15 outbound from Genes, so that's 5:45 PM Houston."

"OK, let me take a leak and then I can drive. Want me to take an eight and change at 2:00 AM?"

"Sure. I'll sleep till then."

A few minutes later Evan settled into one of the two small bunks stacked at the right rear corner of the vehicle. Evan had the top space, and everything he brought on the trip fitted into the 3x1x1 metre cubicle. He pulled the light plastic slats across to seal it off. It was comfortable, and he found it easy to settle and rest. The LXV suspension and low gravity made for a smooth ride.

Lucy was finally on her own up front. She and Evan were great friends and worked well together, but she relished this solo time driving across the face of the Moon.

119

Sharp as knives, the shadows seemed to menace the view. Unlike at home on Earth, objects were either in or out of the shadow; there was no lighter shade anywhere. The shadow would slice clean through a rock, one half visible, one half hiding, There was no dust, no haze, no air. The obvious lack of atmosphere would kill you in an instant. Discounting that, without a spacesuit the sheer cold behind a boulder would freeze you to death in minutes. In front of it you would fry in the solar radiation. She both loved the landscape and was terrified of it.

The Apollo astronauts had struggled to describe the colours all those years ago. Now she was finally out on the surface again her eyes caught the many different shades in an ever-changing palette of soft hues. Here, the landscape was washed in shades of beige and grey. Ten kilometres closer to the base it was more brown and ochre. The rocks were generally smaller this far out too; there was a lot more gravel these last ten minutes. Even so she was kept busy steering NEIL to avoid larger the pieces of ejecta, which had created their own small indentations when the surface was young, who knew how long ago?

Two weeks off the base prospecting with her best friend. Two weeks without fighting management for the right to do their job, setting their own timescales and travelling as they preferred. She was excited to spend some quality time documenting a unique event in Mankind's history. She could write another paper, perhaps even take the time to write a book about it. Lucy started to hum a few of her favourite songs as NEIL rolled on past the traffic cones. In some areas they looked a bit more grey and dusty than they had a few days previously, as she and Evan rolled in from the curtailed field trip. What would she find out here this time?

"Hey Lucy-Lu, stop a minute, would ya?"

"Stand by." They were travelling at over 30 km/h and it took a few seconds to stop. She turned around and retraced their tracks until Evan called out again. Once again she turned, and brought NEIL to a standstill to see what he had spotted.

"Look back over there, maybe fifty metres. See a dark patch? I bet that's another fragment for the comet collection."

In places where the lunar dust had been thrown up so recently there was a definite colour change, so the impact sites were easy to spot. Looking to the left Lucy noted that NEIL stood 200 m from the edge of a crater with a shallow lip, possibly three kilometres across. They were between that and the high outer rim wall of a much larger crater to the right. A lot of shattered scree was piled against it, stretching down almost to the trail. They had made good time in a day and a half, and with 1,400 km of trail behind them they were just under 1,000 km due West of Gene's.

"We've got five already and they're scattered all over the place. The outside storage will be full soon. Where we are going there will be millions. Do we need to pick up another one?"

"You're right; we probably need to keep on moving. Tell you what though, let me go fetch that one and then we'll have three each?"

"Oh get out of here, you hero." Lucy laughed at him and waved towards the airlock "Let's make it a proper rest stop. I'll nuke some of Bird's dinners."

As usual they had taken it in turns to drive and rest, only stopping to take samples. It would be good to have a meal together and get some proper sleep. She reported in as she ate.

"Gene's, Lucy."

"Hey, Lucy, it's Mario."

"Hey, Mario, according to NAV we are 1,412 km down range. Evan is presently on assignment outside gathering another comet rock. We'll take a six hour food and rest stop here and call in again not later than 4:00 AM.

"Good, Lucy. Say, would you have time to bring me a small comet rock? A couple of the guys found them here and everybody has been out looking for one. I didn't get lucky."

Everybody wanted one, and on the way back she meant to check how many the team had collected near Gene's so she could pick up enough to give out. "Sure, Mario. I will keep looking. Good night."

She liked the hard-working young dwarf who always had a smile and a pleasant word for everybody. He was fun to be around and played a mean poker game. She had met him once before on LEO-NINE, but they had only become friends since she arrived at Gene's.

It was time to check on Evan. "I couldn't wait so I've been eating while I gave Mario a position report. Want me to heat something up for you?"

"Yeah, if you would. I'm walking in now. I had to dig around some, but it was worth it. There were three fragments. I'm walking in... Whoa-hah!"

Inside NEIL there was a definite movement as if a sharp breeze had caught the vehicle. There were no breezes on the Moon.

"Shit, wow, I saw it, Lucy. I spotted that one inbound. A big rock hit the top lip of that crater wall right above here. The ground shook and I'm on my knees."

She made for the driving seat. "Get inside. MOVE!"

"Shit, landslide. It's coming off the ridge on your right, a big one. Brace and hold on, I'm running."

No time to reply. She hurled herself into the left seat, got one arm into a shoulder strap and fumbled for the webs. She glanced out to the right, and then abandoned the effort to strap in properly as she worked to get the electric motors live and move NEIL. The entire crater rim above had given way and there was a huge wall of rocks bearing down on her. Lucy knew that there was no chance of escape.

"You have about ten seconds. Hang on to something. I might outrun it if... Oh, shit, sorry, Lucy. I fell. Uhhh..."

There was a sharp jolt, then another. NEIL lifted, moved to the left and rolled sharply. She still wasn't webbed in and screamed as she reached round the seat to find something to hold on to. She flailed, half in and half out of the seat. Then her head whipped back around and collided with something hard. Lucy tumbled into blackness.

* * *

Black... Turning... Grey... Spinning... Dimness... Pain...

Vision returned. Two pictures overlapping, but she had to keep her eyes shut against the insistent whirling in her head. She hadn't felt so ill since a bout of food poisoning when she was a teenager. She was hanging in the straps at an awkward angle, unable to feel anything from her left arm. Everything else hurt; bruised, stiff, sprained. She faded away, back to the greyness, suffering a misery of discomfort.

* * *

Trapped... Arm trapped... Lucy trapped...

Conscious. Trapped in the LXV which was on its side. She'd hit her head hard. Her brain whirled and even through closed eyes she sickened with the rotation as nausea gripped her. Trying to look

123

around, her eyes went spinning off one way and her mind the other. Faster and faster her head turned until she knew her stomach was about to reject her dinner. She was almost upside-down and now she was going to puke.

There was nowhere she could aim for to prevent making a mess, and even thinking about it made her briefly check the up-rush. She vomited through both her mouth and nose. She couldn't turn her poor head the right way up. As she heaved and tried not to choke there was a dreadful, deathly stabbing pain in her side. After several more rounds of retching and torture, each worse than the last, she was once again ready to welcome the blackness closing in around the edges of her spinning vision. The rotation slowed until she lapsed back into merciful oblivion.

22 – CRISIS
3:01 AM (LST) 29th SEPTEMBER

Thibodeaux woke to the emergency message siren in his room. The red priority light was flashing. In all these years he'd never seen it before. He pressed the accept button. "Thibodeaux, go ahead."

"Boss, it's Mario in comms. NEIL was caught in a landslide. Lucy is badly hurt and Evan is missing outside. I need help here. They need help."

"There in one minute."

"Roger."

He snapped on the light. 3:01 AM. He flung on a T shirt and ran to the comms office barefoot.

"What happened?"

"Boss, Lucy said NEIL is lying on its side with the airlock underneath. She reckons there is still some rock movement outside and that the fall is unstable. NEIL might flip upright, or upside down. Either might free the airlock, depending on the nature of the debris. On the other hand, she's worried that it will all move again and NEIL will roll down into a nearby crater."

Thibodeaux decided he was still half asleep. "OK, what about Evan? Can we locate him?"

"Telemetry is patchy, TEL 3 picked up some signals a few minutes ago but I guess NEIL's antennae are either under the rocks or damaged. Lucy was talking and I didn't get a chance to check the recovered data. Evan was outside taking rock samples when the fall hit, and he is not responding. He told her he was running, and then she was knocked out for hours. Even if he is alive and has oxygen, he can't get back inside unless they can right NEIL. It's not good."

Thibodeaux could see tears forming in Mario's eyes. He and Evan were good buddies and he was facing up to losing a close

125

friend. "Take a minute, Mario, deep breaths. We need the tech boys up and some coffee in here. Then I need you to stay sharp."

The comms specialist nodded and swallowed hard. "I'll be OK, boss."

Thibodeaux was already calling for help. "Bird, sorry to wake you, we have a developing external situation. I need coffee available immediately, plus a full breakfast meeting ASAP. Yes, dude, it's a 3:00 AM crash call, so wake up and help me here, would you? I'm going to ring the base alarm. As people arrive in the central area, make them aware it's not a fire drill, would you?"

He listened for a moment. "Good idea. I'll cancel the alarm in one minute and you make a general P.A. announcement from the kitchen. I'll be out there real soon. No, details later. You're deputised, so tell them there's a full system emergency aboard NEIL. Can you get the coffee on, stat, and we'll get a full team canteen meeting in twenty minutes if we can manage it. Get cracking. Thanks." He pressed the base fire alarm button and heard the sirens start outside.

"I'm good, thanks. I'll be OK." Mario rubbed his eyes.

"All right, I need you to stay strong. Whatever happens here everybody is going to feel shaken. Now, you said Lucy is injured. What about that?"

"She was trying to report but had to stop because she was puking. She said she's broken a rib, banged her head real bad, and her left arm is trapped in the seat. That was fifteen minutes ago when I woke you."

"Let's get a report." He picked up the mike and took a deep breath "Lucy, Ajax, over..."

"Lucy, this is Ajax, over..."

"Lucy, Ajax, over..."

The speaker clicked twice.

"Lucy, it's Ajax, was that you?"

Two more clicks.

"Lucy, using the oldest code, click once for yes, twice for no. Are you OK?"

One click. Mario exhaled.

The speaker clicked on. "Ajax, Lucy, concussed. Uh, I keep being sick. NEIL is slowly rolling over, call you... back. Uh... ugkh! ickk..."

Mario went pale. "She sounds awful. Ugh! I don't do sick."

Thibodeaux stopped at his room to put on a one-piece. When he arrived, the canteen was full of staff; almost everyone was present, with a few stragglers arriving and taking seats. Bird was a bloody magician, he and his assistant had warm pastries and hot coffee all set up ready. He knew he'd called the right man first.

There was silence as they waited for the report. "OK, people, apologies for the early call, but we have a crisis with the field trip. NEIL was caught in a landslide and rolled over. Lucy is trapped and hurt some. She is conscious, but very nauseous. We don't have an exact time-frame because we only heard from her a few minutes ago as she was knocked out. NEIL is holding pressure, which is a miracle."

LXV Engineer Ellis Ransome stood up and tried to make a comment. "Boss—"

"Not yet, Ellis, please let me finish this report and I'll get to what we need soon, OK? Look, I am so sorry it has to come to you like this, and there's never an easy way to deliver bad news, so I'm going to give it to you straight. Evan was outside at the time of the landslide and we can't confirm his current situation."

There was a collective gasp, and an, "Oh, no!"

Thibodeaux felt no emotion. That would kick in later. The room fell quiet again, several of his people with hands clasped over mouths in horror.

"I'm sorry, team. Lucy reported that he saw the trouble coming and ran, but he's not answering calls. TEL 1 and TEL 3 are only receiving patchy computer telemetry, so we think at least one of NEIL's antennas is damaged. Luckily the direct radio link is OK, at least for now."

Hands were raised, and several people had stood up, but he shook his head at them.

"Please let me get you all up to date. At the moment, Mario is listening out for Lucy. So far she's not been able to talk much. Five minutes ago she reported that NEIL was rolling again, so with regard to damage it might not be over yet. That's all the information we have for now. Bird is in the kitchen working on breakfast, so get something to eat first and then we will work on a rescue plan. Think solo and collective specialities. Think out of the box."

Ellis couldn't contain his horror any longer. "Ajax, I can't drive a rescue mission because BUZZ is inop. Shit, what've we done?"

"I know. That's where you come in, Ell. Now we're up to what we need. Can you guys engineer us out of this? Can we rig something to get us out there? Is BUZZ useable in any way? Can we patch the holes and get it airtight? That is what we need. Drop all other work. Pressurise the garage immediately and recover BUZZ back here any way you can, so you can get on the case. If you can fix it, I need a timescale, preferably in single figures of hours. Ace, I know you're good with the tech team when you're not mapping. Hit the garage and see what you can do to help. Eagle, as chief scavenger I need you on component planning with that crew. Make and mend, we don't need pretty, we just need to drive it, and soon. You people

128

have first call on anybody, and cannibalise anything you need." Ellis nodded in approval.

"Kyran, I want you to leave Ellis and Ace to work on BUZZ. From now you have responsibility for NEIL and checking the systems if we can get data. Tobin, work with Kyran on NEIL. I need timings from you on supplies and oxygen aboard. All of you, I want to know what works, what doesn't, and if there is any chance we might be able to get NEIL upright.

"Levon, manage both those efforts for me. I'll be based in comms. Wilco, do we have anything scheduled in from Earth or in orbit either here, or even at LEO, that we can use? Paula, for pity's sake, why are you on a fire drill callout in a T shirt and shorts? Get dressed and then please relieve Mario for me and send him out here. I will spell you in comms, but he's shaken up and I need him to take a break. Doc, with me to comms, I want you to coax a full medical report out of Lucy.

"Any questions? Is everybody OK? Lives depend on us here today, team, so let's eat and get thinking."

* * *

"Anything?" Thibodeaux handed the dwarf a cup of coffee as he and Doc Fisher took seats. Doctor Donald Eaves Fisher was well known in the organisation for not suffering fools, or being kept waiting. He was also respected for his total honesty. The fact was that he still took rotations out here on the Moon after a fifty year career. Somehow he brought an air of calm optimism into the office.

Mario accepted the coffee. "There's good news Ajax; she's not trapped. Actually NEIL is almost upside down now, and she says she kind of worked her arm free as it happened. I think she is hurting more but feeling better if you know what I mean. She said she was going for some water, and to take a leak." He consulted a notepad.

129

"That was at 3:45 AM, and she promised to call again in, er, eight more minutes, at 4:10."

"Good idea to keep a log, well done." He looked at the pale face. It was obvious that his comms operator was in shock. "Mario, will you take a break please? At least freshen up and eat; the canteen is open. Paula will be here in a minute."

Mario picked up the coffee and spun the chair round to face his commander. "Andrew, we will rescue her." He had never once called Thibodeaux by his first name and, unlike when Evan had used in anger, he was touched by the unexpected familiarity.

"You bet we will."

"Please can I wait here till she reports again? I won't be able to think unless I know."

"Sure you can. Then go eat."

Paula ran in and stood behind them. "Sorry, boss. I was sleepy."

"It's OK, Paula. To be honest, when Mario called I arrived here in my shorts. I'd only just got changed when I got to the meeting and I was being grouchy. Forget it." In typical style she gave a curt nod.

The speaker clicked a couple of times. "Gene's, this is Lucy."

"Lucy, it's Ajax. How are you?"

"I'm feeling better than I was. A bathroom break helped. Well, not the bathroom, we're upside-down. I had to make do. I had some water and painkillers."

"Lucy, Doc Fisher is here. Can you give him a medical report? We can all step outside if you need."

"I'm good to report now and you can all stay. Doc, I'm glad you're there. I'm better than I was. I probably took a slight concussion. I have a huge egg above my left temple from head-butting something when NEIL rolled over. I wasn't properly strapped in and I must've whipped around some. I'm still a bit nauseous, but I'm lying down on what was the roof and I feel a lot better than I did stuck upside down. My arm still has serious pins and needles and my left shoulder is wrenched. The arm will be OK in a bit and I can try and strap the shoulder. I think I might have cracked a rib, maybe even two, and throwing up was painful. I will need to get a blanket and sleep for a while soon as I'm still dizzy."

Doc nodded at Ajax. "That's good, Lucy. Sounds like a concise self-diagnosis. Is there any chance you could make it as far as a mirror and see if your pupils are dilating evenly. If they are, your concussion is very light at worst. Having you conscious and able to think straight is also a good sign."

There was a pause. "I'll take a look now, but it might take me a couple of minutes."

She was back in three minutes. "I'll be OK. Not so dizzy now, and my eyes look even. We're airtight and I can brace if we move again. There are oxygen alarms flashing on the panel. Tanks three and five are empty, two is down some and dropping, but the others are tight. I'm using tank two while I can. There must be damage underneath somewhere. Well, meaning on top now. I wish I knew about Evan..." The transmission ended in a cut-off sob.

"OK," said Doc. "I know it's hard, but you're doing really well so far. Try to drink plenty, and I don't recommend any more pain killers on an empty stomach. Eat something when you can manage it."

Ajax gestured at Doc for the mike. "Lucy, we're all awake here and working on a recovery plan. Until then we can do nothing about Evan. Believe me, we will be out there as soon as possible. When you are able, can you have a look around outside and try to give us a report on your position and the state of the rock fall. Any information will help us to help you."

131

Mario poked his arm and indicated Doc, who was making obvious "stop" gestures at him. "Stand by a minute, Lucy." He turned. "Sorry Doc."

"Don't overload her. She is obviously in shock. Sleep will help her more than any tasks. Can we give her some time to rest?"

"Yes, OK. It's 4:30 AM, what do you suggest?"

"I'd say you should give her at least four hours. There's nothing she can do at the moment unless NEIL starts moving again."

"Agreed, you or me?"

"It should come from you, but via me. That way it's a direct command reinforced by a medical recommendation."

Ajax handed over the mike. "Lucy, it's Doc again. Belay that last request. We don't need anything else from you for the next four hours at least. See if you can sleep. After that, try and eat something if you can, and drink plenty of water. If you do eat and you need it, take another pain killer. I bet you will feel less knocked about by then. If we don't hear from you by 9:00 AM I shall get Bird to rattle pans in here."

"Thanks, Doc. I'm still dizzy and I may puke again. There is such a mess in here. I'll rest if I can, but call me back immediately if you hear from Evan."

Lucy woke and sat straight up, felt her head start to spin again, and laid it back down. *Dizzy, only dizzy.* It took a couple of minutes to stop, and when she dared open her eyes again there was no sign of the earlier nausea. She was relieved to feel hungry. Sitting up with more care, she took stock for a few moments, rotating the shoulder and finding it stiff and sore. Pain stabbed her left side and she was held together by bruises. It helped when she discovered the pins and needles in her left arm had gone. No lasting damage, so it must have only been stuck behind the seat and not crushed.

The cabin was a complete bomb-site. There was equipment all around her on what had been the ceiling, and the smell was dreadful. She was going to have to do some housekeeping. Being an assistant medic made her immune to most things, but cleaning her own half-dried vomit off the business end of the cabin was going to be quite a chore. She would report in first.

"Gene's, Lucy's awake."

"Lucy, Bird here."

"Hey Bird, they got you on the comms rota now?"

"I volunteered. Mario has been looking over BUZZ with the tech boys, and Paula was here until just now. There was some patchy telemetry from NEIL but it faded out. Anyhow, Doc said to let you sleep. You had five hours, and it's 9:54 AM."

"Bird, did telemetry pick up anything from Evan?"

"I'm so sorry, Lucy. We know for sure that Evan's implant stopped transmitting and sent a shutdown message at 11:07 PM."

"11:07 PM would be almost exactly the time of the landslide, so that's that then. I've been facing up to it as inevitable, but it's..." She took her finger off the button.

"Lucy, I'm..." He did too.

There was a long pause. She pulled herself together because she had to survive first and do her crying later.

"Bird, thanks buddy. I'll be OK. I need to put off thinking about that for now and concentrate here. I'm bruised to death but better than I was. The nausea seems to have settled down a lot. Do you have the video downlink there from Neil?"

"Stand by. No, the screen is blank and I think the link is off. The camera is either damaged or disconnected. It says NEIL CAM 1 UNLINK on the main fault panel screen."

"That's OK. Do you know the panels?"

"No, sorry. I only do pans."

She shut her eyes and tried to visualise the comms room as well as she could remember. It wasn't a place she would know blindfold like she did NEIL.

"Would you find the LXV SYSCON panel over on your left for me? Is there a NEIL CAM 1 rocker switch showing green or red?"

"Got it, and that's in the on position and showing green, but on the screen it still says UNLINK. What does that mean?"

"It means the camera is working but the data is not reaching you. In case it resets itself in the next few minutes, can you select the NEIL CAM 1 rocker switch to OFF for me please? It should turn red. I'll try and fix the link here and then we'll recycle it, but before we do I'm going to strip down, wash, change, and eat. I will report in again at 10:45 AM."

"Copy. Gene's out."

She needed to visit the bathroom by this time but the prospects in the tiny, multi-purpose upside-down cubicle didn't look too promising. The chemical toilet had a magnetic lid, but it was leaking and there didn't seem to be an obvious way to stop it. Lucy reckoned that opening the lid would make it ten times worse, so she shut the door on the whole sorry business and decided she would have to improvise, and soon.

At least she could strip and have a full clean-up with some antiseptic body wipes. She had a couple of spare one-piece suits in her locker. It wasn't ideal, but there was an empty ten litre water container with a wide screw top in the trash locker which had already seen service as a makeshift toilet.

After a cereal bar and a chocolate bar, plus a litre of water, she began to feel less feeble. The residual dizziness she put down to shock and low blood sugar. A wash and some clean clothes helped too.

Nobody out on a field trip expected to spring-clean NEIL inside, so she sacrificed the medical antiseptic spray to help wash the place down a bit. She piled everything non-tech and loose into Evan's bunk for the meantime. Most of the tech stuff had stayed clipped or Velcroed in place.

By 10:35 AM, Neil's interior looked a lot better. What had been the bathroom ceiling, now the floor, was a mess of paper towels, plus the two driving seat covers which she had unbuttoned and used as rags. Before calling base again, she had a proper look outside.

"Gene's, it's Lucy reporting."

"Good Morning Lucy, it's Ajax. I've got Paula, Doc, and Bird here in the comms room."

"Good Morning Ajax. I have three reports for you; medical, situation interior, and situation exterior."

"We are taking notes. Go ahead and report."

"Roger. Situation, medical: I'm bruised and sore. My left shoulder is stiff and strained but my arm is fine this morning. This headache is probably due to mild dehydration and shock, but I have

135

been eating and drinking. I checked my eyes again and pupil dilation is even both sides. I'm nausea-free which is good. I had a full wash down and inspected for other injuries but I feel OK. I've put a T shirt on under a clean one-piece and tied some bandage around my ribs as tight as I could comfortably pull it.

"Situation, interior: Neil must have moved again because we are flat upside down now. When you told me to sleep last night there was about a ten degree list. I just about passed out right after that. I've cleaned up some and piled a lot of non-essentials in Evan's bunk. It was a mess in here, mostly mine I'm afraid. When we've finished here I will see if I can fix the video feed. Oxygen tank two is lower, but if that's a leak, it's a slow one. I'm using it now to recover what I can, and as per the emergency checklist I haven't opened any cross-feeds. I also used it to recharge my surface suit and top off the spares.

"Situation, exterior: Upslope, i.e. north towards the high crater wall where the landslide started, the windows are completely covered. I think Neil is stuck on a big rock downslope. There are rocks and boulders of all sizes in that direction, probably as far as and into a nearby crater with almost no rim. I can't quite believe NEIL is still intact and airtight. The stuff is still moving past in fits and starts, and it's got to be about half way up the airlock which is now on the down side. Neil must have been spun right round as well as rolled. The left front centre wheel, axle two wheel three, is hanging down against window L2. Boss, I can't see any sign of Evan. That's all."

"Thanks Lucy," said Thibodeaux, impressed at the concise report. "We are all thinking about Evan, but it's twelve hours now and we have to be realistic. Priority one is to get out there and extract you. We have several avenues open, but any attempt to reach you will take more time and careful planning.

136

"Even with two tanks gone and one leaking, solo you have plenty of on-board oxygen plus that in the suits, and general supplies are not a problem. All I can say is hang in there for now. Please would you helmet up and try to keep a workable escape plan in your head just in case. You know the drills, but as a reminder; if you do need to evacuate through a window there will be no way to repressurise NEIL."

Lucy had already put some thought to that. "I will get organised and report again. I'm going to try and fix the video feed. Please would you reset NEIL CAM 1 back to ON?"

She dismantled the panel and accessed the small camera fitting to check for wiring damage. It looked OK. At least it was easy enough to reach as it had been above the forward windows and was therefore on what was now the floor. If Neil was the right way up she would have had trouble getting to it on the ceiling. Putting it all back together was a lot trickier than it looked. She stopped for a cup of coffee and sat on her mattress. Then the tears came. Evan's last three messages ran round her head, over and over. She wished he would leave her alone.

"Shit. Wow! I saw it, Lucy! I spotted that one inbound. A big rock hit the top lip of that crater wall right above here. The ground shook and I'm on my knees." Then: "Shit! Landslide. It's coming off the ridge on your right, a big one. Brace and hold on, I'm running!" Finally, the awful: "You have about ten seconds. Hang on to something. I might outrun it if... Oh, shit! Sorry, Lucy. I fell. Uhhh..." After that, nothing. No telemetry pick-up, no radio static, nothing. The implanted medical data chip in his finger had reported shutting down within a minute.

She had worried that he might have felt pain, or worse, been stuck outside the rock fall with a broken aerial. Now she was almost certain that he had been killed instantly and the thought did help a bit. There, she had accepted the word. Killed. It knifed her to the core, leaving her feeling cold and alone.

"OK, he's dead, now pull yourself together." She tried to make it official, vocalising the sad finality with surprising force. Did it help? Somehow she thought it might.

"Lucy, it's Paula. You OK, baby?"

Paula had been calling for several minutes, but her head had been too busy trying to rationalise her loss. She hadn't heard.

"Hey, I'm so sorry. I was thinking about Evan. There's no chance now, he's dead. I've accepted it."

"Oh, baby, we know. Can't deny it."

"I think I'm beginning to deal with it now, Paula. I need to put it away somewhere for a while so we can work on the situation here. Can you help me out?"

"Yup. Video feed on? Blank here."

Lucy reached up to the panel, "No. On now."

"Well, you done good. We got video, but it's upside... oh, duh! I can fix that."

Lucy laughed with her. Somehow it eased the anguish the same way as crying. Wasn't there an expression about laughing and crying being the same release? She thought it might have been an old song lyric because it made her hum a tune. She'd work on that and see if she could remember it.

Her screen came to life. "Oh, Paula, there you are. You're upside down too."

Then she started screaming.

"EVAN!"

"Lucy, what the . . ? WHAT?"

"Wait."

"Lucy, what's going on?"

"Ssh, Paula. He's knocking outside."

Lucy leapt across to the windows; there was nothing to see but rocks. She knew she couldn't open the airlock from inside; he would have to move all the rocks from outside. She had kept his frequency on the other channel, and she had been calling him every half hour she was awake. But there it was, a definite scraping sound. She tapped back and selected his channel on the local radio kit.

"Evan? Evan, bang on something if you can hear me. Evan? Oh I can't do this."

She could hear Paula calling on the other box, but couldn't reply through the tears.

"Lucy? Gene's calling NEIL."

"Oh Paula," she sobbed, "I thought I heard knocking. The rocks must still be moving. How could he be here in the middle of the rock field? I'm beginning to hallucinate."

"Face up, girl. Can't be him, you said so. Air gone hours ago."

"I'm feeling dizzy again. I think my head is still injured, that's part of it I guess. I'm going to lie on my mattress and watch the rocks for a while. Maybe I'll sleep, or maybe I'll think of an escape plan."

"I'll be here. Ain't goin' nowhere soon."

"Thanks. Don't tell the others I'm stupid, please?"

"Baby, stupid you ain't."

Thibodeaux had been on a constant round of conference calls between Gene's, Lancaster and Houston since Lucy reported the accident at 3:00 AM. There were now separate staff meetings at both the concentrations of NASA brain-power, plus Mt. Rainier where the MAGENTA team had taken on the challenge. It was after midday by the time the base commander found a few minutes to visit the canteen again and eat something.

He reached the big space and found a full-scale meeting. Several tables had been pulled together and large-scale system prints of BUZZ taped across them. There was a spirited debate ongoing between LXV engineer Kyran Mukherjee and various other members of the engineering and technical staff.

After avoiding an attempt to draw him into the conversation, Thibodeaux managed to tear himself free with a tray of supplies, and retired to his office for half an hour of peace. It was going to be at least a 24 hour day, and he sat outside the mainstream for a few minutes to try and mull over all the different strands of thoughts and ideas before he could make any further decisions.

The news of NEIL's accident had reached the press with surprising speed. Lancaster had a press office, so at least he could refer any calls that arrived at Gene's. That was one relief. He ate while working through the list of both sensible and hare-brained recovery schemes that he had heard during the past six hours.

The door opened and the base cook leaped through it. "Boss, what about Bouncer?"

Thibodeaux was starting a headache. "Bird, what are you yelling at me for? What on Earth, OK, on the Moon, is Bouncer?"

"It's a jump rig they were experimenting with years ago, here on the base. I read about it in 'Based on The Moon', you know, Robin Van Kampen's autobiography." He was hopping about like a kid at a birthday party.

Thibodeaux shook his tired head. Bird wasn't usually as daft as he made out and it was always worth paying attention when he got excited. "Van Kampen was the first base commander here. For goodness sake, Sunshine, that was a hundred years ago. Will you *please* stop leaping about and sit down. I was already starting a headache before you bounded in here. For pity's sake man, sit!"

"I know all that." Bird settled on the edge of a chair. "Van Kampen arrived 84 years ago. The base was right here; well about three kilometres further north than where we are today, to be exact, over by that big hangar where the rock trashed BUZZ. They also had an underground storage area, and they played about testing a revolutionary jump platform, LJP-44, which they called Bouncer. It was a gyro-stabilised four-seat open vehicle driven by air bottles pressurised with waste CO_2 from the base. Clever, eh? It must still be here somewhere. So are there any plans from the old base? Can we find the underground garage? Bouncer was never lifted out of here, I do know that."

"Give me a break here and slow down for a moment." He held up his hands for a pause, and mulled it over for a few seconds.

"OK, now let me think out loud, because I've heard some even wilder stuff already today. So, if this old rig is still garaged or hidden here somewhere, what kind of state would it be in? How would we use it? Is there a manual? What did the gyros run on? Who could fly it? Would it be safe? All that was off the top of my head, and that's providing the thing is still here. Over to you, my archaeologist extraordinaire."

For the first time since his precipitous arrival Bird sat still and looked his base commander straight in the eyes. They had known and liked each other for twenty years and he held Thibodeaux in high regard. He did know that the man would listen to him if he spoke with all the gravity he could muster.

"Look, Andrew, if I can locate it somewhere, all it would be is dusty. Wouldn't finding it be better than sitting around in the canteen worrying about repairing one obviously smashed vehicle to retrieve another obviously smashed vehicle? As the commander here, do you want the opinion of a simple cook?"

"Of course I do, Bird. I take everybody's feelings and opinions into account. You know that."

Bird nodded. "Sure do. I'm no tech, but they already know cobbling BUZZ together isn't going to work in a month of blue moons. All I can do is keep you fed. What I do know about is the history of this place. As for flying it, heck, I would fly the damn thing if I had to, eh. I'd rather kill myself doing that than leave her out there. So, do we have access to local historical data or not?"

Thibodeaux broke into a grin. "OK, you. That's the second time I've been called Andrew today. What is it with all this familiarity? If that data is here it would be on my link. We have nothing to lose by looking. Do you want to view it here?"

"Can you let me use it in the galley office? I'm making a lot of chocolate cake. They all need it. Wish there was some way I could get a slice to Lucy."

"OK, I'll add you as authorised staff on the management links. It'll take me a few minutes to set codes and stuff. Use your staff number and we'll make the password 'chocolate'. It's not strictly allowed, but the rule book is somewhere in this office and I can't find it. Leif would be fine, but I won't even consult Vom. Just stick to looking up historic stuff, would you?"

142

They stood, and he rested a hand on the younger man's shoulder. "And Bryan, we will fetch her back here. We will do whatever we have to. There are serious amounts of brain-power working on this one."

The reply was even quieter. "You know me better than anybody here. I need to tell you something. I've just realised that I would actually walk all the way there, you know, to where she is, and carry that cake too, eh. We need her back. I need her back."

"We'll get her back. Everyone is feeling the same, you know."

Bird shook his head slowly. "Nobody knows how I feel today. I'm only the coffee boy. In fact I didn't even know how I felt about her till after it happened. And it's not another crush; I can't describe it to you. The Galaxy knows there have been a few, but I need Lucy back here safely. She and I have been making friends instead of... Well, you know, we've actually been making friends. There's nothing in it yet, but when you woke me this morning and told me what had happened I knew, Ajax. I think she's the one."

He had turned away until he was facing the corridor. He slipped from under the resting hand and made his escape.

Thibodeaux watched his cook leave, and saw the hand covering his eyes. He had long thought of himself and Bird as cousins. It had started years ago because of his own nickname, Ajax.

It was a contraction of his first two names, "Andrew Jackson Thibodeaux", but it made him sound like one of the heroes of mythology. He and Bird had played a lot of chess over the years, rather than the mythological pair of Ajax and Achilles, whom legend said had played dice. The Canadian actually made a good Achilles to his Ajax. The man had a weak spot, but this Achilles' heel was his heart. Bird had a fearsome reputation as a womaniser. His nickname came from two separate sources, the obvious initials (Bryan Richard

Downey) and the fact that he had a well-documented tendency to swoop and snatch a prize from the available females.

It gave Ajax one more problem to keep an eye on. For the first time he could pinpoint, Bird had trouble with his emotions in regard to a woman. After some weeks he hadn't actually made a move, but had been busy making friends. Maybe it was the unusual situation at the base, but to Ajax' knowledge it had never held him up before. This time it looked serious.

25 – DELUSION
10:00 PM (LST) 29ᵗʰ SEPTEMBER

"Hey, Gene's, it's Lucy. Who's on?"

"Hi, Lucy, it's Mario. Are you all right? What are you whispering for?"

"Ssh! Quiet. I'm lying on my mattress on the ceiling looking out across the rock field. Something is moving out there and I'm really scared..."

"Don't cry. You'll be fine in a day or two. You hit your head."

"I know but it's not my head, that's good now. Mario, something out there is coming for me. I've been staying still and watching. It started right by the edge of the crater and now it's come about fifty metres closer. At first I thought it was just another rock, but they are all brownish red here. I'm good at colours and shapes, you know. There is definitely a round greyish something creeping over the rocks out there."

"Lucy, can you get it on camera?" Mario had already called Ajax and Doc to comms.

"I'm too scared to even move."

"OK, your call. I don't know how to advise you."

Ajax ran in with Doc hard on his heels. "What is it, Mario?"

"Lucy says something is moving outside NEIL. She sounds terrified. She says it's round, greyish and creeping towards her over the rocks from the crater. She thinks it's coming to get her."

Doc gestured, and Mario vacated the seat.

"Lucy, this is Doc."

"Doc, before you start I absolutely am not hallucinating. The thing has stopped moving and it's out of sight now behind a big rock. I'm watching to see if it moves again. I'm scared and I need the bathroom, but I don't want to move."

"That's OK Lucy. How fast would you say this thing was moving?"

"It's come more than fifty metres in the last half hour. Now it's hiding."

"Get up and go to the bathroom. Those are Doctor's Orders. Drink some water and then have another look. Come on, it's not going to move far in the next five minutes, is it?"

"I need to keep watching."

"Lucy, you need to pee."

"Yes I do. Will you keep listening while I move around? I'm switching to area pickup. I wish the external camera was working."

"Keep a commentary up, Lucy. We'll be here."

"OK, I'll move if it's still out of sight in two more minutes, OK?"

"Good plan. Tell me before you do."

"Roger."

Doc turned to them and whispered, "She's wound tight. I think she's seeing shadows."

Mario agreed. "She sounded so scared when she first called in. She was crying and whispering so I could hardly hear. Could she have been dozing and had a daydream?"

Thibodeaux' worries about his geologist were increasing with every passing hour. There was no possible way to reach her with the resources and equipment they had. Even the combined brain-power available on the Moon and across Earth nobody had devised a working plan. He didn't know whether to break the news to her or sit on it. He was wound pretty tight himself. Now she was beginning to hallucinate, at best. It could be the suspected concussion, or the fear of being there alone, far from any

146

possible help. Like everyone at Gene's she was devastated about Evan, but what private hell she must be going through he couldn't even begin to guess. For the first time in his entire NASA career, he didn't want his job.

"Ajax." Doc had been speaking to deaf ears.

"Sorry, I was miles away."

"Look, you're the one who has to keep up the appearance of control. The base, everybody here, needs that now. I've sent Mario for supplies because the three of us are going to sit through the night with her. You know we can't get there. We know we can't get there. Lucy's not stupid; she knows we can't get there. Lancaster and Houston know they can't get here in time to get there."

"Doc, I'm moving now."

"Go, Lucy, and switch the internal camera on."

"After I pee, OK? You know I can't go in the bathroom. Galaxy, you boys!"

"Of course. Sorry, I wasn't thinking. Yes, after you pee would be fine."

Doc turned to Thibodeaux and broached the subject they were all dreading. "We need a reality check here. I want you to speak to her in a minute. Be honest, and give it to her in straightforward language. We need everybody to be on the same page right now, otherwise we create false hope and even that spread far too thin. There are people who will need to speak to her, say goodbyes, as much for themselves as for her. Although they already know the score on an intellectual level, some of them don't know that they will want to do that yet. We all have an emotional minefield to cross here.

Thibodeaux shuddered, and covered his face.

"Oh, come here Andrew." Doc put an arm round the commander and took him to a seat.

147

"Doc, Bird says he'll bring... Oh shit! What happened?"

"It's OK Mario. Thanks." Doc waved the dwarf to a seat too. "We were discussing reality."

"Reality? Like, we can't help her?" asked Mario. "There's no way, I know that."

"Mario, it's my job to tell Lucy but I can't bring myself to do it," said Thibodeaux.

"I will if you need me to, Ajax, I can tell her. I think she knows already. Is that why she is so scared of the shadows, Doc?"

"I think it is. You're her friend and it's hard on you too. You don't have to do it."

Thibodeaux looked even worse. "Mario, I want to bring her back, but I can't help her. I shouldn't have let them go in the first place. With BUZZ totalled we simply don't have the resources here. I am so sorry."

"Ajax, don't apologise to me or her. How can this be your fault?"

"What commander in his right mind would approve an external mission with no back-up available? Ultimately I'm responsible for safety, and when this is over I'll resign and return to Earth. Nobody needs a commander who sends scientists out into the field to die."

"No Ajax, you're wrong," the dwarf asserted. "I'll tell you something, because it doesn't matter now. You could never have stopped them going, even if you'd tried. After the row you two had she was fixing to take NEIL anyway. And I'd have bet Ace Horowitz that Evan would have gone with her too."

Doc stifled a laugh. "No! Seriously? Well, in that case I'll hand it to her for having some real balls, that's for sure."

Thibodeaux couldn't bring himself to laugh, but he was somehow glad. "D'you know what? You don't

148

surprise me, Mario. I knew about Evan because he actually came into my office and tore strips off me. But she's a tough one. Let's hope she has the balls to face the next few days."

"Gene's, Lucy. I'm done, and switching the camera back on now."

Mario clicked the link on. "There you are Lucy. You look good."

Thibodeaux intervened. "Lucy?"

"Yes, Commander?"

"I need to make you aware of an ongoing problem we are having here at Gene's."

"If you want to tell me that with BUZZ fritzed I am stuck here unless I can get myself back, save yourself the trouble. I can't do that because nobody has ever walked 1,400 km on the Moon. Physically I could do it, but I couldn't carry the air I'd need. I already worked it out."

"But— "

"I realised when I woke up this morning. You have nothing in stores, in the old junk, or inbound that could help me turn NEIL over. To the core of my soul I am both frightened and exhilarated at the same time. I'm already so far gone from reality that I'm beginning to see movement in the shadows and rocks outside. I had a nightmare is all. I need to rest my sore head, but somehow I can't settle. I am utterly, dead tired. It's seeing the Earth that's so hard. I could almost touch it from here. Feels like my home is here on the Moon, but I just want to visit Earth one more time."

She straightened up and spoke with more conviction. "Commander Thibodeaux, I am planning to break out of NEIL when the time comes to use the oxygen in the last suit. I'll try to locate Evan's body and say a few words for him. I know roughly where he was, and which way he would have run. Then I'm going

149

to work my way up that slope to the top of the big crater and say goodbye to the Earth. I'll take the helmet off at a time of my own choosing. I refuse to sit and gasp as the air supply runs out and leaves me begging for another breath with some oxygen in the CO_2. More than anything else, that death terrifies me. Right now I need rest, and I am no longer afraid. Good night." Without warning she cut both the audio and video uplinks.

Thibodeaux leapt out of the chair. "No, Lucy, no. Mario, get her back."

The short man also stood up and stretched to his full height. He had to look a lot further up to the base commander. "No, Commander Thibodeaux, I will not 'get her back'. The fact is we can't get her back. Now we all know that she knows. Let her sleep. Go; you look awful too, and you need to rest. I'll stay right here and monitor till she wakes."

Doc nodded to the stunned Thibodeaux and gestured for him to leave. In the corridor outside they passed Bird carrying supplies and blankets. Doc waved him in.

Mario looked up from the panel. "Hey, Bird. Thanks, man. Say, are you busy? Would you sit with me for a while? We've had a weird half hour here. I need to tell you what just happened with Lucy."

Doc Fisher walked Thibodeaux to the central area. "Mario is right. You heard, she was going on that mission whether you liked it or not. Now I don't know if you're feeling like handing out discipline tonight, but I have a confession to make. There's a suspicious looking bottle in my office emergency supplies marked 'Medicinal', one that didn't make it to the moonshine party the other day. We need to check it out and decide if it's contraband. If so, I guess we'll have to destroy the evidence. Let's stop by the kitchen and fetch a couple of glasses for that purpose. More than anyone else I have treated here, you need a drink, my friend."

A couple of drinks with Doc helped him calm down. He was still smarting from the feeling of helplessness, plus a dose of what seemed like calculated insolence from his stranded geologist. The likelihood was that there would be no rescue, but he had not expected the extreme reaction. Everybody in the organisation, both here on the Moon and all over Earth, was working on the problem. Something would come up. At least he had to believe that, because the alternatives were too dire to consider.

He wondered if Lucy had any idea that he would trade places with her if he could. He couldn't sleep, because he knew all too well the screaming horrors of a slow and painful death that waited for him if he dared to go there.

He studied his drinking buddy. Like himself, Doc Fisher wasn't enough of a liar to rise into senior management. A fit and healthy 72, he both looked and acted like a much younger man. They had been friends for almost all of Thibodeaux' own long career. Doc was sitting back and looked relaxed, waiting patiently for him to speak.

"What's the likelihood of her walking away to sit on the crater rim and give up?" he asked. "I don't think I could cope, and the idea makes me feel sick."

"Pure filibuster is how I see it. I don't think she has it in her. She's a pretty strong kid though. You might think I'm out of line because she ruffles your feathers, but I'm telling you I admire her for having the guts to think that far ahead. She's worked her way under your skin, that's for sure."

Thibodeaux mulled that one over for a few seconds. "I'll tell you exactly why that is, too. I run a fair system here. After her outburst in the lounge the day after the comet I shouldn't have let her go out. Now I'm hearing that she might have actually taken an LXV if I'd denied her and Evan my permission to go prospecting. From my position she looks more like the proverbial loose cannon every time she opens her mouth. And the way Evan yelled at me after that, I'd been planning to keel-haul him across my desk when they got back. Now..." he swallowed hard.

He started waving his arms and his voice rose. "It isn't even her. It's the knowledge that somehow I allowed her to bully me into making a series of poor decisions. Now one of my crew is dead and another is injured, stranded beyond our ability to help her. How do you think I should feel?" He put his face in his hands. "I can't even think straight. I'm finished."

Sitting in the medical room drinking brandy was a therapy as old as medicine itself. Doc knew Thibodeaux well enough to realise that it was worse than he had hoped. Either the base commander was about to give up and collapse into hopeless depression or, maybe with his help, find the grit to pull himself together and take control. How he steered the conversation in the next few minutes was crucial. He studied the vintage bottle standing on the desk for a few seconds.

152

"Look, young man. I think I need to prescribe another drink." He poured them both a small one. "We also need clear heads in the morning, so after this one it's closing time at this bar. Anyway, this bottle has to go back where it came from for real emergencies. I need to sleep, and you have to get some rest too. If you want my opinion, I'm betting on the brains at Lancaster coming up with a plan. The spiky-haired guy, what's his name? Oh yes, Kent. Wacky in the extreme, but he'll solve it for us. So, what are you going to do in the morning?"

Thibodeaux accepted the proffered glass and looked into it, then opened up and started to confide properly.

"I'm frightened to sleep. I've been having the daylight horrors about Vic French and the MAGENTA DM 5 ever since Lucy had her accident. It wasn't losing Evan that started it, because we knew almost immediately that he was killed outright. There's a line drawn there and we can come to terms with it. My horror stems from the prospect of what will happen to Lucy. I'm scared to death that she will die slowly in pieces, beyond help, like Vic."

The Doctor remembered that incident all too well. He shook his head. "I wish you'd told me that before, Andrew. I would have prescribed something other than the brandy, but after what you've had I can't do that now. Tomorrow evening I will give you something if you need it. Hell, you can sleep here in Medical tonight and I'll sit with you if you want. We veterans have little use for sleep."

"I appreciate that. I'll get past it, but I may take you up on the medication if it happens again though.

We'll have a full staff meeting at 10:00 AM. If Lucy decides to grow up and call us in the meantime I suppose I will have to take a firm line with her. Even in her situation I can't afford to have her running the whole show and dictating terms."

The Doctor was nodding. "I do agree on reining her in some. I'd recommend that you wait until she's back here before you give her a proper kicking. She's far more scared and emotional than you or I, and she's also hurt. I suspect shock and pain helped to fuel this evening's outburst. Make no mistake about this, Lucy is the last person who would ever blame you for her situation, so you can strike that idea. Give yourself a break and stop fretting over it because it's fogging you up. That's why you can't think straight. Come on now, finish that drink and try to catch some rest."

"OK, well, cheers then." They both knocked them back and Thibodeaux stood up to leave. "Thanks, Doc. I guess things will look better in the morning. That's good brandy, and you say it's actually medicinal too. I'm amazed."

"Oh, it's medicinal all right, and I'll tell you when it was last used. Ed Seals arrived here after suffering zero-G vertigo all the way from LEO. He got a dose and he's been fine since. In fact he says he ain't ever going back in case he has a relapse. His head spun and he was nauseous for 43 straight hours, and he's been a spacer for fifteen years. Odd how it happens sometimes, but I suspect he may have had a slight ear infection. I've given people some of this to help them cope on the return leg before, too. Not this bottle usually. I have a more suitable and far less expensive version under lock and key."

"Another one?" Thibodeaux feigned horror. "For crying out loud, Doc, this whole station is like a Speakeasy. Next thing it'll be 20th century jazz music!"

"Oh, don't even go there," said Doc. "Your Life Scientist Tobin Pengelly is a old-time jazz player. I hear he has a saxophone under his bunk."

Doc wore a poker face, and Thibodeaux couldn't tell if he was being joshed. "I can't cope with that. I'm off. Thanks again."

154

Doc laughed. "Go on, rest if you can. If not, buzz me and we can talk till late. As I said, we oldsters don't use much sleep."

Thibodeaux still wasn't ready to settle, so he fished in the kitchen for supplies and wandered back to the comms office. The screen links from NEIL were still off and Paula was watching a movie.

He put down the cake and drinks. "Hey, Paula, need a break?"

"Uh, yeah. Dude never sleep?"

"I've been visiting with Doc and I'm not ready to rest yet," he answered. "Anything new?"

"Lucy ain't called. Sleepin' I guess."

"I presume you know already, but I don't think we can pull off a recovery."

"We all know, man. Tech guys hangin' on fixin' BUZZ, they know. Workin' so they don't think about her. Rest of us can't do much." She rested a hand on his arm. "Ain't easy, but we'll be OK. Get through together. They worryin' about you, some of 'em. How you doin'?" It was the longest piece he'd ever heard her speak.

"Well, to be honest with you I feel like a loser right now. Because of poor decision making on my part I've already lost a team member. Rumour has it that after chewing me out in public Lucy was fixing to take NEIL whether I approved or not. I'd like to know if Evan had a part in that, but I suspect he didn't and I'm happy to park that idea. Now it's beginning to look like I'm going to lose her too."

Paula helped herself to a piece of Bird's cake. "You're a good boss. Was accident is all. Tell you what. Bird goin' insane with worry. He ain't slept since. He's cookin' heaps o' treats. Does great cake. Gonna need a new jumpsuit if this goes on. As for coffee, theory states usage directly proportional to crisis. Ajax, will you hang five while I go? All this talk o' coffee..."

They both laughed. "Go, I'll wait." That's twice, he thought. Twice she'd made a real speech. Was she trying to jolly him along, or covering up the fact that she was dying a little inside like everybody else?

"Say, we ain't gonna run outta coffee?" she asked as she came back in.

"If that was the most important thing to worry about, we'd be laughing, wouldn't we? No, we have that supply run inbound. There's another problem. You and Mario work well together. Is he coping?"

"Worked together years. Good friends. Quieter than normal. Others too."

"Paula, I wouldn't usually tell anyone the gossip, but I can see problems ahead and I need your help. This will need careful handling. Bird and Lucy have become good friends since she arrived. There's nothing serious yet, and I'm dead certain she knows about his reputation. Galaxy, every female arriving here gets briefed on that. I don't know, maybe it's an old flame at Lancaster, or Rainier, or Houston, or in LEO space for all I know!" They laughed. She rarely used that rich, deep, infectious laugh.

"Ain't me," she chuckled, turning to him. "I'm the one he never hit on."

Thibodeaux didn't know how to deal with that. Paula was passable, if a little boyish. Like Lucy with her long dark hair, she stood out from the crew-cut regulars by having a short bob. Granted, she did put a lot of people off with the chopped speech and sharp wit, but she burned brightly for her real friends. Personally he thought she was sometimes a bit scary. Bird usually liked them a bit less forthright, but even that didn't exactly fit with what he knew about the cook's feelings for Lucy. Maybe that was why Bird was so surprised at his attraction to her; Lucy wasn't at all what Thibodeaux looked at and thought "Here we go again, Bird food."

"Well," he began, "Bird comes to see me with his idea about an old float rig he wants look for outside, 'Bouncer'. Then he starts telling me that 'she is the one', and he's pretty frantic. The man is so tight he could snap. We need to let him cook because he has to keep busy like the engineers and techs, but I will have to keep an eye on him. Now, I've known him well for twenty years or more and I can deal with him OK. He will get over this."

She put down her coffee. "With you so far. Open secret, how he feels. People know."

"The point is this; Mario is in pieces, which is why I called you to take over from him at 10:00 PM. He and I have had a talk and I stood him down until 8:00 AM. He will take the day shift. He is realistic about the chances of rescuing Lucy, but we need to keep an eye on him too because I think his emotions are less robust than Bird's, well, than Bird's under normal circumstances. Can you help me?"

"Sure. Oh, it's why the cake, I'm here till 8:00 AM." She was laughing at him now.

"No, I'm grateful you stood an extra watch this evening. Thanks for doing that, Paula. Pelican is desperate to help and keeps telling me he feels useless, so I asked him to relieve you at 3:00 AM. It's only a listening watch, but he's a qualified pilot and has a comms ticket, so he can handle it. I'll stay here now till he pitches up. When I crossed the lounge, Mario was sitting there on his own, staring into space. Would you see if he is still there and talk to him please?"

"Sure. Find him now."

Mario wasn't in the lounge. Paula couldn't find him anywhere. Her search ended outside his door, two rooms along

157

from her own in N2. The "Do Not Disturb" light was on. It was 2:53 AM but she buzzed anyway. Usually he would open the door to any call, but tonight the tiny speaker clicked on.

"Who's there?"

"Paula. I come in?"

The door slid aside. He was sitting on the bunk wearing just his shorts, and he looked awful. She sat down next to him and put her arm around his shoulders. He gave in easily and cried for a while before making an effort to pull himself together.

"Man, I feel better. Thanks Paula."

"Who else ya got?"

She had told Thibodeaux that they worked well together, but it was much more than that. The pair went back to day one at NASA U in Houston. They had worked in four different locations as a team over the years, selecting posts at the same station.

"Tell."

He was hesitant. "She's not coming back, Paula." He sighed and put both hands over his face. "She's so much braver than we all are. Ajax is in shock too, and we need him to be strong for us all. Evan was my friend for eight..." He couldn't go on.

"Oh, little bro," was all she could manage.

"Paula I need to sleep. I'm due back in comms at 8:00 AM. Stay?"

She had known he would ask. They'd never been lovers, or even dated, but sleeping in the same bed was an old comfort they had shared sometimes over the years. He climbed into the bunk, and she took off her coverall, dimmed the light and slipped in behind him. She put an arm round the small body.

"Mario, Bird worryin' about her too. He wanted to ask her out."

"I know. We had a talk about that, Bird and me. She's not coming back Paula, and that means it doesn't matter."

"It does. They'll do it OK."

"I can't deal with all this. Please let's just sleep."

Pelican arrived in comms to find Thibodeaux waiting.

"Oh, I was expecting to find Paula in here. Is everything OK?"

"I guess so. I sent her to check on Mario. He's in a mess. I've been mulling it all over and I can't see any way to reach Lucy. Have you just got up?"

"No, I've been with Engineering in the garage all night. They're all at it. Ellis and Ace are there with Eagle and Levon. Kyran is crashed out on that old sofa of theirs. They've been working on BUZZ for eighteen straight hours. They're convinced they'll come up with something, and they're running on adrenaline and coffee. I'm not much use in the practical sense so I've been running supplies and trying to keep a conversation going."

Thibodeaux was impressed. "Everybody here will need to sleep for a week when we crack this. Look, I've been thinking hard today. I'm struggling under the pressure. I can't sleep because I'm getting the horrors about where we are heading with the situation out there.

"Look, would you help me lift some of the management load? I know you're here as a paid observer, but I'm hearing universal appreciation for how you've helped and looked after people. I think it's because you're not 'the management' as such, but you do have a certain authority about you. A quiet word from you throws a lot of weight. This team would accept some more official direction from you for a while if necessary. I'm surrounded by specialists, and Levon didn't even want to be my deputy in the first place. He's been staying out of sight, and so hands-on in the garage I haven't seen him inside the base in two days."

It was the first time Thibodeaux had seen Pelican actually consider a reply. The guy had a fast head and was always ready to go before anyone finished speaking, sometimes even cutting over the end of a sentence.

"Ajax, I'm touched by the sentiment. Sure, I've got management skills, but I don't belong here. I'd do it for you, for the base, for Lucy. I'd do it because I believe Leif might ask me to if he wasn't grounded. I can't help you though, because Vom Redwood would actually come up here with a bazooka and start shooting people. In case you weren't aware, that shithead doesn't like me."

Thibodeaux shook his head. "This isn't about Lancaster. This is about keeping us all together up here where the work is getting done. The core management team on Earth are keeping him off our backs as much as possible. He's as out of date as the dinosaurs. Earth dispensed with power hungry government and greed management after the Fall. We're so far on from that culture, who could ever predict a throwback like him?"

Pelican shrugged. "Then I'm jammed here, because you said I'm pretty much doing it already, kind of comes naturally. OK, I'll go for this on two conditions. One: If you ask the team at the next meeting and they want me to, I'll pitch in and help you as I can. Two: It has to stay off the comms between here and Lancaster."

Thibodeaux looked him in the eye. "You should know that there was a discussion about the idea in the lounge earlier. Paula said, and I quote: 'Pelican 'stead a Vom? Yeah!' Look, did you say you came straight from the garage? Do you need a break?"

"I could use some food. Do you want anything?"

"No, but thanks for asking. Go and take a proper meal break and I'll sit here. Don't rush though."

He wanted to check on Houston before he finally tried to catch a couple of hours sleep. It was 3:45 AM in Texas. It cheered

161

him to find Eve Meredith in the hot seat. It was his night for looking up old friends.

Like Doc Fisher, Eve was another veteran with a fifty year NASA badge. She was a tiny, energetic blonde woman of 74, but looking about 45. He loved the fact that she still kicked around at SpaceTech after a career that had started as a TUG Assistant hauling pieces of the lunar base. Eve reckoned she was the missing link between the crews and the dwarves that were so numerous on the staff in space. A diminutive 1.51 m, she commanded huge respect from her team, looking up and fixing them with a pair of huge blue-grey eyes that had seen through many a soul. She grinned and waved at the screen.

"Ajax! Hey there, it's good to see you, fella. I've promised my team a week at my place in Maui if we come up with a rescue plan. Ain't seen so many manuals and engineerin' books on the desks here in years." She nodded towards the rows of consoles and the bowed heads manning them. "Listen to that... it's the sound of brain cells keepin' warm. Anyhow, y'all holdin' together up there?"

"Hey, Eve. So, they've got you on nights. I thought you were done with all that."

"Oh, you wouldn't believe what's goin' on down here. These guys are workin' harder than they ever have. Most of the night crew roster took the train out to Lancaster for a tech conference, and I'm so bored in trainin' I said I'd chuck in some late time this week to help out. I think I'm gonna stay with this team for a while."

He loved her energy, which she somehow managed to share with others. Anywhere Eve Meredith was working the team around her fizzed with enthusiasm.

"I wish you were here, Eve. The team are all right so far, but I'm struggling. I've been getting a Doc Fisher pep talk. I'm so far gone he prescribed some medicinal brandy. I wanted to check with you and see if those brain cells were giving anything off yet."

"Not yet, but we will. I promise you that. And 'Yo!' for the Fisher brandy treatment, I had it once. Now where that's concerned, it's important to make a distinction between his medical supply and the special bottle. How is Lucy doing?"

He laughed with her. "As an old friend he told me I have enough privilege points to rate drinking the good stuff. As for Lucy, she's pretty knocked about but nothing needing hospital treatment. It's fortunate, because we could never get her to one."

He passed a hand across his eyes, which were prickling towards more tears. "She also had a bit of a tantrum with us tonight and has now switched off the feed completely. I have to say that hurt me deeply. It shouldn't have, but I feel a lot of responsibility over what happened. Put in the simplest terms, with BUZZ out of service I should never have let them go. As for losing Evan, I don't think any of us can begin to deal with that until we sort out the situation with Lucy. I need to call Sara McEwan, but I can't face that yet."

"Oh, Ajax, that's so hard. Would you like me to call Sara in the morning and let her know you are thinking about her. The folks from Lancaster are takin' care of her, but I know her well enough to call. She and the boy are in Ontario with Evan's Mom."

"I'd appreciate that." He had to wipe his eyes again. "Did you know that young Andrew McEwan is my Godson? And I've gone and lost his Dad. I'm so devastated I can't begin to describe how I feel. I have to hold it together for my team, and somehow keep them going. For the first time ever I don't want my job. I want to crawl away and come home.

"Did Donald Fisher tell you things would look better in the morning?"

163

"Of course he did. Tell you what though, even if we don't come up with a plan today I've got enthusiasm coming from every direction. My cook, Bird, wants to find a discarded jump rig from years back. He reckons it's stashed somewhere here. It's a cobbled-up thing that's supposed to have run on waste CO_2. He's busy making us fat on comfort food and searching the records for a hidden garage."

"Heck, yeah! I remember that; Bouncer, it was called. Wasn't that long ago. Oh wait, I was haulin' PODs and that would have been, oh, 35 years back, maybe more." She laughed. "OK, forty years ago then, but I don't feel that old. I might have some data that'd help him, send me his link would ya?"

"You don't look it either, Eve. Age is a state of mind, you know. Bird would appreciate any help," he laughed. "Actually he's desperate because I think he has plans for my geologist. He says he'd walk to where she is carrying chocolate cake."

"Oh, that Bird. I know him; he was at LEO 6 when my team worked there a while back. He had plans for one of my engineers too. Does she know his rep?"

"Oh, yes," he replied. "She's too smart for him, I reckon." *What's the matter with me tonight? I'm not one for gossip and rumour, and I'm unpicking love lives in front of Eve. Ah, the brandy. Get a grip, Ajax.* "Anyway, good to chat to you Eve. I'm so stretched for man hours I've accepted an offer from Pelican Percival to work the graveyard shift in comms after a meal break. He flies and he's comms rated for that. OK with you? As soon as he gets back in here I'm off to get a few hours, so can I take a regular report while I'm here?"

"Sure thing; a comms Pelican won't cause any panic here. The only hardware you have inbound is the MAGENTA 471/DS335 supply run. That's due to drop as per the flight plan tomorrow evening, and extra coffee is on the 'Mission Critical'

164

delivery list. Sarkasian says he included some spares that were lying around on site, whatever that means. He's so weird, but under the tattoos he's another of those odd guys we seem to attract who all do great work."

"Thanks, Eve. It's great going out for beer with Sarkasian. Nobody ever gives us any bother."

"Hey, before you go, they're workin' up a mission to send you a support team and change over some staff. With my seniority I still have good biddin' rights, *even* for my extreme age and *even* from my big important desk in the trainin' office. Why do you think I'm doin' some real work for a change? How 'bout I come up and put in a support tour with ya for a month or two when this blows over? I miss the place and you ain't serious about rotatin' back early, are ya?"

His spirits lifted at the thought. "Now that's an absolute yes! Please do that if they will let you. It would give us all a boost, whether we pull this off or not. Actually if we fail your presence would be even more vital, but in this organisation that scenario, as you well know, is not an option. Did you know that not one of them has asked to go home? And I couldn't do it even if I thought it was what I wanted. I think it's the brandy making me feel maudlin."

"All right, we'll put some thought into that, Ajax. Listen buddy, I know you're carryin' a heavy load. Doc can help, and it sounds like he's the guy to lean

on, OK? But if you need to talk at all just call me, or get someone here to patch you to my home. I'm always there for ya, 24/7."

"I appreciate that, Eve. Good night then."

Pelican had come back in during the exchange. "Lovely lady, Eve Meredith, I met her during training at Houston. She's a genuine original, and she's dead right. It's hard on you, but I can't see any

165

way it could have been your fault. Do you want to go and rest, or tell me how you want me to get involved?”

“Thanks a lot. Eve and I go way back and she can pull a team along like nobody else. According to her report, Mt. Rainier has sent us treats aboard our inbound supply drop. I wish we could have Lucy back here to share them. Yes, I might go and lie down for a while if you can cope here.”

For the second time in less than an hour, the reply didn’t come immediately. He looked round to see why just as Pelican spoke.

“Ajax, tell me if I’m being stupid here. Didn’t Bird take me downstairs and show me about four months of supplies stacked up? Do we really need any of that inbound stuff? I’m just a sky watcher and I don’t understand orbital math and stuff, but is there any reason why Houston couldn’t drop the whole thing over by NEIL?”

Thibodeaux whirled round out of the chair, open mouthed. Then he leapt up and clapped the other man on the back. “Shit! Yes, Pelican. Galaxy, it’s us regulars who are stupid, man. Who’s paying attention and putting two and two together? Vom Redwood’s ‘fucking tourist’. Ha! You just saved her life. Go on record right now and call Eve back yourself to suggest it.”

“Oh, it was bound to come up sooner or later,” Pelican said. “I’m the lowly lab assistant here.”

“How many more times? Come on! we’ve never met anyone like you. You’re as team as the rest of us. Now call Houston.”

Pelican shrugged and pressed the button.

“Houston, it’s Gene’s again.”

“Oh, hi there, young Pelican. He said they got you doin’ nights now too.”

"Eve, hi. Look, I just asked Ajax if there was a good reason why you couldn't drop that inbound POD near NEIL instead of here."

Eve echoed Thibodeaux' reaction, and was already out of her chair yelling; all around the control room specialist's heads popped up above their consoles like so many meerkats.

"OH WOW YES! Why haven't we...? Too many brains and no lateral thinkin'. Oh, Pelican you're a superstar! We can do that. Give me about twenty minutes and I will call back with a decision and some timings. That's the best news I've heard in years. I'm gone."

The screen went blank. Thibodeaux stood grinning at the lab assistant.

"I'm going to make sure you get the proper recognition for that idea. Imagine if someone had thought of it *after* the POD dropped here."

"Come on, dude, I don't need recognition, I want to see this team back in one piece. You look dead tired. I can take the call back from Houston. Now we have progress, will you please go and rest for a while? You need to be fit to function in the morning."

"OK, OK, I'm going. I'm out on my feet here. Now I wish even more that she'd stayed in touch and not been so childish. If she does climb down and decide to call us, tell her all about it, would you?"

28 – MESSAGE
7:44 AM (LST) 30ᵗʰ SEPTEMBER

Lucy woke up slowly and yawned, feeling rested for the first time since the crash. The view from her mattress on the ceiling was quite strange to wake up to. Until the last two days stuck here she had always slept well on the Moon. The low gravity meant she was never uncomfortable in bed.

She reflected on the wisdom of hanging up on Ajax, Doc, and Mario. She had meant to stay off line for an hour or so, but she must have been asleep for ages. She checked the clock: 7:44 AM. *Oh no, oh shit! Nine hours.* Now Ajax would burn her for sure. Still, the way her future looked it was unlikely that she would ever have to stand and face his anger.

The toilet had stopped dripping from around its lid. She had kept the mess under control using most of Evan's clothes, plus the removable seat covers. She did a final clean-up with the diminishing antiseptic spray and paper towels, double-sealing it all in bags with the dirty stuff stored in Evan's bunk.

NEIL had turned out to be tough and durable way beyond any design parameters because, apart from the oxygen tank damage, everything still seemed to be working. She was still using tank 2, which was a lot lower than she'd hoped. That would be gone in a couple of hours. Given time, the air purifier should take care of the smell.

There was no need for her to make the stale air problem any worse, so she stripped and had a wet-wipe bath. There was a single clean one-piece left, but she wanted to save that to wear in the surface suit for her final walk if it came to that. To hell with the rules, it didn't matter if she was ready for a decompression any more either. She got comfortable in some shorts and a T shirt.

There were plenty of supplies left; food and drink were not going to be a problem. Breakfast was two cereal bars and coffee as usual. She decided the creeping horrors in the rocks outside had all been in her head. On balance Doc was right; a combination of a slight concussion, shock, stress, and fatigue. Who knew what you might think you saw? She lay back on the mattress to work up the courage to call Gene's and face the music. She glanced outside.

There was a message.

She froze with immediate, skin-crawling fright. Horror movie terrors rippled along her spine, and gooseflesh crept across her body like a million spiders. She couldn't catch a breath. Her heart pounded and she was overcome with a deep, writhing nausea. The cereal bars threatened to make another appearance. *Think, Lucy, think.*

She couldn't rationalise. Everything started to recede into a fuzzy tunnel and her stomach lurched. She was going to faint, and then she was definitely going to throw up.

* * *

She came to, crouched one corner of the tiny bathroom with her hands clasped round her drawn-up knees. There was cereal bar and coffee squish everywhere. It wasn't fair because she had only just finished cleaning in here, and now she had messed it up again. Was it the concussion, or were there words written outside NEIL? Was the morning real, or had she slept and had nightmares?

Lucy crept out of the bathroom and had a glass of water. She decided to get herself organised and as calm as possible before looking outside again. There was enough spray and kitchen paper left to clean up in the bathroom one more time, but this throwing up would have to stop soon or the supplies would run out.

She didn't fancy eating anything. The clock said 9:12 AM. She stood by the mattress, knowing that when she sat down there

169

would only be a load of old rocks outside. *Get brave, stupid girl, it was only a dream.*

The message was still there, scratched roughly on a big rock that she knew hadn't been right outside the window the night before:

HAVE AIR WE
NO SHIP DIE WE
IN SHIP HELP WE

Beside the message there was an alien creature. It looked something like a cross between an old motorcycle helmet and a large horseshoe crab with too many claws.

There was a brief return of the gut-wrenching fear, but even as the creature terrified her, the scene was fascinating. The horrors began to fade away. In a few seconds, intellect started to win the struggle against instinct and she was no longer as frightened.

If this thing was trying to communicate, it hadn't been sneaking up thinking about how best to eat her. The fact that it appeared to be asking for her help was a fascinating conundrum. Surely it must live here on the lunar surface.

The scientist in her started to beg for more information, and she scrambled to find some paper and marker pens so she could write her own message back.

DO YOU LIVE HERE

She left out the question mark for simplicity. It disappeared out of sight for a moment, before coming back into view and scratching underneath the first message. The reply surprised and intrigued her even more:

LIVE AWAY AWAY FAR FAR WE
ROCK FALL ON SHIP WE
MANY DIE WE
NEED HELP IIII WE

Lucy wrote:

HOW DO YOU KNOW WORDS

Again it ran off; this time it returned with three others, one of which was rolling a new rock into view. The creature scratched a new message:

NO WORD USE WE
MOVE CONTACT WE
STUDY FROM SOON AGO HERE WE
OTHER MOON MANY WE
HERE IIII NO SHIP WE
NO SHIP DIE WE

She needed time to work it through. It needed interpretation, and there were several ways it could make at least some sense. They could presumably see her working and waited without any discernible movement. "WE" seemed to end a phrase. By using a written version and playing with variations of the message as phrases she had a possible meaning, which she copied onto paper. Above it she wrote their original message and crossed through their words, hoping to indicate the translation. It now said:

WE USE NO WORDS

WE TALK USING MOVEMENT
WE ARE HERE TO STUDY
WE HERE FROM SOON AGO
MANY MORE LIKE WE ON ANOTHER MOON
WE IIII NEED HELP
WE HAVE NO SHIP
WITH NO SHIP WE WILL DIE

She held up the paper. All four of them stood still for a few seconds, tapping with lightning speed on the corner of each other's shells using claws on one of their two pairs of arms on each side. They moved to stand in a line abreast with their shells touching, facing the window. Together they stretched up about twenty centimetres taller on a lot of small legs, presumably standing at their full height. Each raised the four multi-jointed claw-like appendages, which she was already thinking of as arms. Together they stretched out the arms towards her. Each arm ended in two pairs of the claws, small and large, which they held pointing upwards. Four arms; eight sets of claws.

Lucy couldn't stretch up to her own full height and still see them, because the window was too shallow. She stood up for a few seconds, allowing them to see her legs and feet. Then she knelt down facing the window and held her arms out, palms down, towards them. Reflecting their gesture, she tilted her hands upwards to show the palms, and spread her fingers in two pairs.

There was an instant reaction. Three of the crab-like aliens sat down again, tucking their larger rear arms and claws under their carapaces. Their forward arms rested on the surface. The other one scratched at the back of the rock. After a few minutes it rolled the rock around to show the new message:

NO WORDS USE WE
CONTACT MOVEMENT WE
STUDY HERE TO PLANET FROM SOON AGO WE
THANK HELP WORDS WE

Lucy drew a picture of herself as a stick figure cartoon, with the four crab-like aliens next to her as half circles with lots of small legs and four arms each. Below she wrote:

SAME AIR

Again the reply amazed her. It was the same drawing on a new rock, but it showed Lucy and all four of them inside a shape that had to represent the upside-down NEIL. The message underneath said:

SAME AIR
HAVE AIR WE
AIR IN SHIP HELP WE
ROCK FALL ON SHIP WE
IN SHIP HELP WE
NO SHIP DIE WE

The message was crystal clear. Lucy made an executive decision in less than three seconds. She drew a series of cartoons:

1. The aliens rolling rocks away from the door.

2. One alien entering the airlock.

3. Lucy opening the inside door.

4. Lucy and one alien inside.

5. Lucy and four aliens inside.

6. NEIL the right way up with the wheels on the ground, Lucy in the front seat driving all four aliens.

7. NEIL with Lucy and her passengers inside next to another stick figure human. This one was lying under some rocks.

The scribe scratched one more message, while the other three immediately set to and started to move rocks:

IIIIIIII IIIIIIII
IIIIIIII IIIIIIII
IIIIIIII IIIIIIII
IIIIIIII IIIIIIII
IIIIIIII
DIE IN SHIP WE
I IN SHIP SEE WE
I IN SHIP DIE SEE WE
I IN SHIP DIE IN SHIP HELP WE

Numbering in groups of eight: four arms, eight claws, fair enough. She took this to mean that 9 x 8 of them were dead, leaving four left from the entire crew. If she took the meaning, they also knew where Evan's body was, and it looked like they were offering to help recover him aboard NEIL.

She drew one more picture. It repeated the lines of marks representing the lost alien crew, together with the stick-figure Evan. They were all shown below the surface of a line, with rocks piled above. NEIL and the five living beings were driving away.

The single watching alien once again saluted her with the claws-up gesture. She replied with her own outstretched hands, and then waved. It waved back with one arm and two claws, then moved away to help the others roll rocks away from the door.

"Gene's, it's Lucy."

"Oh, thank the Stars." Paula was speaking; she and Mario were both at the desk. "Why no calls?"

"I slept for ten hours straight, Paula. I have some important news to report and I need Commander Thibodeaux and Doc to be there when I do. Would you call them please?"

"Lucy, he so mad. Ain't kiddin'. Report to us?"

"Paula, I am in control of my destiny here and it just changed. Something important has happened and I need to tell him urgently. Please will you just fetch them in for me."

"We got news for ya..."

"Please, not until Ajax gets there, OK?"

"OK. Warned you. He got stuff to tell, but he'll burn ya good. Take time to get him, outside with Bird. Suit up, no? A few rules, Lucy."

"Roger." Paula had given her an idea.

She was watching as Thibodeaux arrived in the office, actually 'crashed into' might have been more appropriate. He didn't even acknowledge his comms crew before he started shouting.

"So there you are, Grappelli. Alive, although we hadn't bothered to worry about that of course. I don't think anybody here has slept since your childish stunt last night. And then, after more than thirteen hours of radio silence, I find myself ordered to attend you while you report. Do you have any idea how worried we are? Don't answer that, because it's clear that you don't."

"Commander—

"No, Grappelli. Keep quiet and listen to me."

"Yes, sir."

"First off, you will not break communications with this station again under any circumstances. If you sleep, we will watch. If you need to pee, we will look the other way. But the camera stays on and you will not cut the links again. Is that crystal clear?"

"Yes."

"It's 'Yes, Commander Thibodeaux.' I'm through playing games with you, Grappelli. I *will* have order here, and I *will* be shown due respect."

"Yes, Commander Thibodeaux."

"Better." He sat down and looked at Paula and Mario, who were both staring. Paula's mouth was open, but Mario had clenched fists. Thibodeaux took a few deep breaths and apologised to them for his entrance before looking back at Lucy.

"You will give me an ulcer," he started, calmer after the rant. "We actually have good news for you. In fact you would have had it about six hours ago if you'd bothered to keep in contact with us. We have an outline rescue plan complete with options."

"Commander— "

"No, Grappelli!" The anger was still there, so she shut up. "I haven't finished with you yet. I was talking and you were listening. Carry on listening in silence until I have finished, or so help me..." He stood up with balled fists.

Mario stood next to him and put a small hand on his commander's arm. "Come on, Ajax. She's OK now. Sit down with us, please?"

"Mario, I..." Thibodeaux seemed to relax and sank back into the seat, hands over his face. Paula looked at Lucy and shrugged.

He tried again. "Look, I have been so worried because..." he wiped his eyes again. "I lost a crew member once before. When you get back here I will tell you that story. In the meantime we have a plan. I'm sorry to say it doesn't involve retrieving you back here to

Gene's so I can kick you round my office like I should have done last time. You will of course remember how, on that particular occasion I felt disposed to give you the benefit of the doubt. You, young lady, are going straight home to Earth, and I don't feel any guilt about it being Redwood who gets to deal with you first hand at Lancaster. After the way you have treated this team and your friends, you deserve him."

"But I can't go home now Comman. . . "

"WHAT?" He started to shout again. "What are you...? Grappelli, you are going to be so fired from this organisation that I'm actually amazed they're bothering with the expenditure to get you back. And now you 'can't go home'. It's in my service record that I don't have a temper, lady, but right now I am about to find one and then lose it for the first time ever. You have one minute to explain yourself."

"Please, Commander Thibodeaux, please, I only need thirty seconds of that minute. The external camera on NEIL is smashed, but the surface suits have them."

Thibodeaux noticed that she was suited up.

"I just need to kneel down on my ceiling mattress and show you the view outside. Don't talk; look."

She switched the uplink to SUIT 1 EXT CAM and pointed the camera through the window so they could see the message. Each side of the scratched rock outside the window stood an alien. She panned to the left, to show the other two.

Thibodeaux sat down hard in the nearest chair, and the mood in the comms office changed completely. There was a long pause while the watchers took in the scene outside the upturned LXV.

He looked at her out of the screen for a few seconds, open mouthed. "I'm at a loss here, I don't know what to say." Then the

177

penny dropped and he broke into a huge grin. "Lucy, is that what was coming to get you yesterday?"

"Yes, sir." She said quietly. "These guys are friendly, have air supplies, and are in a far worse mess than I am. They say they are not Moon people, but visitors from afar. Debris fell on their ship and the remains are somewhere nearby. They need my help. Can I make some suggestions?"

"How can you be sure they are friendly?"

"We've been busy this morning, communicating via written messages. And what choice would I have had if they weren't? If hunger or violence was their motive those claws would have been through NEIL's shell in no time. It's clear to me that they are intelligent, in trouble, and pleading for my help. I don't think they have any idea what a jam I'm in."

"Lucy, how in the name of the Galaxy did you manage to find aliens and make friends with them?" Thibodeaux looked bemused.

"I'm happy to report that I wasn't hallucinating when I saw one of them out there in the boulder field. After talking to you and Doc I did wonder if I was losing it." She wanted to make it right with him if she could.

"OK, Lucy, I'm sideswiped by all this." He looked across to Paula and Mario. "You're on the ground there and I have no experience to call on; I mean, nobody does. So what are we, you, going to do? This changes everything. Galaxy, girl, this even changes history."

She thought about it for a few seconds. "Can we sit on it until I find out as much as I can about them? In a few hours we've made strides in communication and started to think together about our situation. I'd like to be able to introduce them as a known

178

quantity. I haven't a clue about the right thing to do here. Yes, I'm on the ground, but you are still the boss."

"I don't believe that we can, or even should, keep the lid on this," he said. "It's a unique event and will affect Earth as a whole. Lucy, we are not alone, and of all people, you are the Human Race's First Contact. Your life changes forever from here on. I, we, NASA, the Government, the Reunited Nations, everybody, will be supporting you, but that all comes later. For now it's my belief that we need to get as much external help as we can muster. Anyway we'd never keep it quiet, even if we tried."

"OK, so do we have a meeting with Lancaster today?" she asked.

"Yes, it's 11:50 AM now and that's scheduled for 1:00 PM. Tell you what we'll do here, you maverick. I'll buy you some more time to find out what you can about them before we convene. I'll get you two hours, that's your time limit. I'll let you know how I get on with that. You know how Vom likes organisation; there's bound to be some fantastic reason why he won't approve a delay."

"You still look as if you're in shock," she said, smiling. "It's not taken long, but I'm already getting used to the idea. These guys are intelligent, resourceful, and pretty cool. When you think about it, they came across all these rocks to ask me for help. Their only other option was death. It must have been equally scary for them. Finding out that the only possible source of help is already in dire straits will be a major disappointment for them. We have shared issues. They have lost their ship and most of their crew, I'm trapped in NEIL and I've lost Evan. I think we are already beginning to feel like a team."

* * *

Thibodeaux wasn't about to talk to Redwood if he could help it. After some consideration he called the Houston control room and

179

asked if Lancaster would mind him delaying the joint conference for another two hours until 3:00 PM. He didn't tell them about the new development, because even after all the anguish and distress she had caused her colleagues, he thought that piece of news should be for Lucy herself to deliver. It was her show out there, and denying her the moment would be mean.

He was taking five quiet minutes in the office with a cup of coffee when comms buzzed him.

"Ajax, go."

"Paula. Vom on screen. Yellin'. I'm fired for not seein' him 'bout evac."

"Fired? That's not happening. Put him on and I'll tell him to eat shit and die."

"Too late!"

He laughed. "OK, make him wait. Put the call here on my screen in two minutes."

"Oh *yeah*!"

The screen chimed and Redwood appeared. He was sitting at Culver's desk, which in itself offended Thibodeaux. He wasn't feeling conversational.

"Why is that woman so rude? She's fired, so suspend her. She's on the first trip back."

Thibodeaux favoured him with a sweet smile. "She's not getting fired. I won't do it, and I dare you to try. You were rude first and it's on the tape. Everyone here is working double shifts and I can't afford any suspensions. Our situation here is too tense to have you messing with my team. Anyway, did you follow your own rules on contract termination?"

"I won't have her talking to me like she does."

"Let's take that as a no then, Vom. I'll tell Paula you were kidding."

"I don't kid, and you can stick to 'Mr. Redwood' when you address me, Thibodeaux."

"You're being a complete dick, *Vom*. We're not ready for a meeting yet and we have some developments to report regarding the situation aboard NEIL. You can reschedule it for 3:00 PM."

"This particular meeting is time-critical. We'll take what you have, on schedule, at 1:00 PM. That's in 45 minutes. You don't need to fancy it up, just report."

"I'm not ready, and I'm not interested. You'll get your report at 3:00 PM or we'll take a rain check and keep working till tomorrow. You can shit all you like, but don't do it on Leif's chair. If you call at 1:00 PM and we don't respond you're solid jammed. So what's it to be?"

"Look, Ajax, we've got high level visitors this afternoon." He looked around, as if checking for spies, before speaking through his teeth. "Our biggest account holder is sending the head man; the one whose office isn't quite circular. He's coming across here in a big blue SubOrb and he will be in the lecture theatre at 1:00 PM.

"You can stick to 'Commander Thibodeaux' when you address me, Vom. I don't care who's coming, that's *your* problem. You will receive a special report direct from Lucy Grappelli, supported by us here, at 3:00 PM. I am willing to stick my neck out here and promise you a world class show-stopper. That's how it is. Now get off my ass and let me work here, or I'll delay it till 4:00 PM.

The screen went blank. Ajax allowed himself a brief smile, before starting on a few extra arrangements. Whatever happened, he was going to have the last laugh, because his stranded geologist was about to turn trumps on anything the officious Redwood could cook up.

He also found time to put in a call to the Department for Alien Affairs in Lancaster. It had become a sort of joke title for an

181

office that had developed in the hopeful and excited days of the early 21st Century. Back then the combined might of the world's space agencies supported SETI (Search for Extra-Terrestrial Intelligence). Put as kindly as possible, it had never found anything.

These days there was just NASA left holding the task open, and the DAA spent most of its time trawling fruitless archive data from observations outside the Solar System. Their practical work relied on standard and pretty cursory computer-driven searches gathered by several space agencies. Thibodeaux never understood how they still received funding. The DAA office was one of those seconded to study Comet Percival photographs and data, as the ground-based organisation worked to better understand the events of the past few weeks.

Thibodeaux spoke to his old NASA U classmate Sol Duke, who had previously worked on the LXV design team as a pressurisation specialist. Apart from some aerial issues, NEIL appeared to be functioning upside-down just as if it was upright. So far the on-board systems didn't require any external technical help.

"Alien Affairs?"

"Hey, Sol, it's Ajax."

"Ajax, oh yeah. Good to hear from you, pal. How's Grappelli doing? That old LXV's looking like a real winner, hey?"

"Look, Sol, we're stumped here and I'm getting desperate. There's stuff going on with NEIL we don't understand now. I'm searching for any field expertise I can drag in. I know you were close to the LXV program and I'm clutching at straws where I can. There's a full meeting at 3:00 PM. Would you and the team do me a favour and drop in?"

"We could manage that. OK, we'll be there. Man, I was so sorry to hear about Evan. Great guy."

"Thanks, Sol. So far we've kept that parked until we find time to deal with it. I'm planning to say a few words for him later, too."

"Sure. Stay strong, Ajax."

There was one call left to make, but he was dreading another shouting match. After putting it off once and wondering about asking Paula to cover it, he managed to pull himself together. He picked up his coffee, but it wouldn't help.

"Lucy, Ajax."

"Go ahead, Commander."

Good, she was still feeling chastised enough to be respectful. "I've pushed the time back to 3:00 PM. Vom was being difficult so I had to threaten him. He tried to fire Paula. Now, today's staff meeting is going out live to a wide audience. I want you to report in person from NEIL. You will turn out for it in full standard dress, meaning surface suit and boots with emergency hood deployed as per procedure. That is not a casual suggestion, Grappelli. That is an order."

"Yes, Commander Thibodeaux."

Lucy faced the camera in the upturned LXV. The cabin was tidy and she wore regulation kit. She checked her notes again. The idea of springing her news on the lecture theatre at NASA in Lancaster had her panting with excitement. As the last minute ticked by, she concentrated on deep breaths and tried to stop grinning.

Paula switched on her feed and immediately laughed. "Yeah? Oh no! Shaved head? What the...? We ain't the military!" For her it was a long speech.

Lucy laughed with her friend. "Simple hygiene. I'm running out of ways to keep clean in here and I can't afford the time or water to look after long hair. It's my new hero survivor look."

"Space pirate movie thug. Ajax'll laugh or shit!"

"Warn him if you want, Paula. Actually it might be best if you did, I guess."

"Yeah."

Paula had reorganised the comms links so that whichever forum Lucy was talking to would show on NEIL's big screen, with the other link shunted to NEIL's main navigation screen on the forward control console. The LXV team were still working round the clock trying to get data from NEIL. Comms could still access the screens, but the NAV link was still off.

Having sound and vision was a massive plus. Lucy watched the Gene's crew waiting for the meeting. Paula would switch on the screen there when Thibodeaux stood up, so as yet nobody had seen her. They also wore regulation gear. *He must be pissed at them too if he's making that happen.*

At 3:00 PM Thibodeaux stood up to face his team, and the general hum of conversation subsided. "Thank you. Good afternoon everybody. For those of you joining us from Lancaster today, this is coming to you from the lounge at The Eugene Francis Kranz Lunar Research Station. Welcome one and all to Gene's Place."

Thibodeaux was acting out of character with all that formality. Maybe he was also expecting to find himself lynched and thrown to the dogs with her, if and when they all got home.

"I want to sober the mood a little before we deal with today's reports, and then we'll spring a surprise or two. What we have not had time for so far is to reflect on the loss of Evan McEwan. Evan was our fun Canadian, and Lucy's support geologist. He was also a personal friend of mine and I had worked with him for many years. We were shocked at the sudden loss of a team member when we had all managed to escape the comet impact unscathed.

"When we realised the comet would hit the Moon, nobody requested a recovery to Earth, even with the higher risk in staying here. There is a sad irony in having the courage to stand your ground and face the unknown, only to be killed doing what you know and love. We will each take time to come to terms with our loss after this crisis, but from everybody here and at Lancaster, I would like to put it on the record that our thoughts are with Evan's family in Ontario this afternoon. I would also like to formally mark his passing. Please would you all be upstanding and join me in observing a quiet minute while we remember him. Evan John McEwan."

On board NEIL, Lucy died a little as each of the sixty long seconds passed. She expected tears, but none came. At the end of the minute, "Oh Canada" rang out at Lancaster. Then Thibodeaux on the Moon, and Redwood on Earth, led another minute of applause before gesturing for silence. Lucy was glad there was no video feed from on board NEIL just at that moment, because finally the tears came. She dried her eyes, noticing from the screens that she wasn't the only one by a long way.

After a pause to wipe a hand across his own eyes, Thibodeaux carried on. "Thank you. Now, we have another ceremony to carry out; a much more informal one, I hasten to add. I was reminded yesterday that the LXVs, 252 NEIL and 253 BUZZ, bear unofficial spray tags. Both vehicles display Gene Kranz' famous quote from the Apollo 13 recovery episode, way back at the dawn of space travel in 1972. Nobody seems to know when they acquired them; neither has anybody ever claimed ownership."

He held up a book. "I am holding a special item today, as a talisman for that saying. This is a very rare, genuine, and I am assured priceless, hand-signed antique hardback copy of Gene Kranz' autobiography. It belongs to our cook, expert space exploration memorabilia collector, and now base historian, Bryan 'Bird' Downey.

"It is fair to say that many people here already know what I am talking about. It is a line that is occasionally quoted here at NASA in times of crisis over the years, and is also the title of this historic book. I would like us all to stand together and retrieve it from across the centuries as a joint statement of our intent today." They stood as one. "The line, anybody?"

There was an almost reverent chant of Gene Kranz' short, but unique legacy to space-faring mankind in the lounge on the Moon: "Failure Is Not An Option." A time-lagged echo from Earth followed it. Lucy joined in, choked at the sentiment. They were pledging to save her life. She didn't feel all that worthy.

"Well done, and from my heart a sincere thank you," said Thibodeaux to the now hushed audience. "We have never been, and we are still not, prepared to give up on Lucy Grappelli." There was another round of applause.

186

Lucy couldn't believe what she was witnessing. *The man is on fire, this is the speech of a lifetime.*

Thibodeaux waited for quiet. "Now, on to current affairs. Yesterday, we were still considering all the options regarding a possible rescue and/or recovery of crashed Lunar Exploration Vehicle LXV-252 'NEIL', together with its surviving occupant, Senior Field Geologist Lucy Grappelli. At the close of yesterday's long round of meetings we were still without a viable plan.

"Overnight, it became apparent that the MAGENTA supply rocket from Earth was in a position where it could be re-tasked to drop the attached DS335 resupply POD as close to NEIL as possible, instead of over here at Gene's, 1,000 km further east. Credit for that idea must go to Allen 'Pelican' Percival who, as an observer standing outside the team, was able to employ the lateral thinking that none of us tech-heads saw. That afforded us the chance to work on several options to help Lucy's situation.

"We came up with two basic plans, but either would require Lucy to break out of NEIL through a window, because she couldn't open the airlock on the LXV as it is covered with rocks. This would leave her with no backup if she couldn't access the POD, and are both therefore considered as last chance options.

"The initial idea was to use the POD as a place to hang out until we could get help to the area. This would only be a viable option if the POD could land close enough to the LXV to establish a cross-feed line for NEIL's air supply, because that is the one resupply item this POD wasn't scheduled to carry.

"Within a couple of hours of those suggestions, another alternative emerged. Lucy could empty the POD and return to the MAGENTA rocket parked in orbit, thereby achieving a recovery to Earth. She couldn't use it to return to us here at Gene's because the PODs have a single down-and-up capability from lunar orbit to the

187

surface. There is also the possibility of colliding with orbital debris from the comet, and even bringing an unmanned MAGENTA here attracts a real risk of losing the rocket. We've already lost the TEL 2 comms satellite in this manner.

"One other item of note. Apart from all the regular stores, POD DS335 was carrying a vital delivery item for us to be able to guarantee the continued safe operation here at the Research Station. The fact is that the stress levels here at Gene's have been so severe during the last few days that we are fast running out of coffee." There followed the predictable outbreak of mirth at Gene's, Lancaster, and inside NEIL. Lucy felt some of her tension release as she found herself enjoying a good laugh with everybody.

"Yes, OK, thanks people." He waited for quiet. "And in fact that's not all. Since well before the comet impact, Bird Downey has been so busy making us comfort food that we're going to need a re-order of larger jumpsuits."

That did it. This time there was a complete collapse. She watched as her team launched several empty styro coffee cups at the commander, and by the sound of it he was receiving a huge round of applause from Lancaster.

"All right, thanks again people. I can see a few smiles, and I think we needed that tension release. So, settle down for a minute and we'll move on to this afternoon's business. That is the background so far. In 24 hours we have moved on from a hopeless situation. Now we are weighing up the risks for at least two different recovery scenarios, and cracking jokes. On both counts that's real progress.

"Before we move on to today's agenda, which is a report from Lucy, I need to hand you over to Will Redwood at Lancaster for a few minutes. Uncle Willard says he has a surprise." There was a gentle, possibly sarcastic, "Oohh!" from the audience. "OK, Go ahead, Will."

Lucy's screen switched to the lecture theatre in Lancaster. Redwood took to the stage as applause rang out for Thibodeaux. He stood firm, wearing his most miserable expression, and tried to stare them down, but if he wanted calm to return it wasn't the correct approach. Lucy winced as soon as he spoke.

"Quiet, now. Enough of this frivolity, for Galaxy's sake. This is a planning meeting, not the old friends' society." There was a quiet but definite hiss. "I said, that will do!"

He was forced to raise his voice over the persistent undercurrent of dissent. "I have a piece of information to add, and which you might want to hear, and then we will get on with business. I was able to speak to Leif this morning. He is watching this, but he will be out of action for a while yet."

A defiant round of applause started to gather pace again, but he was ready for it. "Quiet down! I'm not hosting a stage show." He had to raise his voice once more. "Do you want to meet our visitors?" The noise gradually died away. "That's better. Show some proper respect for a change, as you welcome the President of the New American States and The First Lady."

In both meeting rooms everybody leaped to their feet in total surprise, and as "Hail to The Chief" rang out there was a rapturous welcome from both Earth and Moon. Spencer Braithwaite II walked to the lectern and waved to them. He beamed down amiably and raised a hand for silence.

"Good afternoon, NASA. Thank you so much, Willard. Now I am not going to take up more than a few minutes of your valuable time. I am well aware that we are part, but not all, of the way to rescuing Miss Grappelli from her predicament. We wanted to drop by and tell you all as personally as we could what a fantastic

189

effort you are pulling off here. I wish I could also stop in at Gene's Place, but I don't think Air Force One could make that trip, and anyway I'm not sure the First Lady would ever allow me that far out of her sight."

There was a smattering of polite applause. "Evelyn and I would like to add our condolences on the death of Evan McEwan. We know that Evan died following his scientific passion. We also know that to you all, NASA is more than just a job; it is a family. We are sorry for your loss." There was another polite, but less restrained, round of applause.

"The concept of putting together a rescue package such as this seems to bring out the very best in all of us New Americans. Over the last few weeks we have seen so many crises, and potential crises, that we have become used to looking to you folks at Lancaster, together with Houston, Mount Rainier, and at Gene's Place, for what always seems to us laymen like an easy answer. Yet I found myself drawn here today to see if I could personally witness the process of developing a solution to every problem. What do I find? A team of vast intelligence spread across Earth, Moon, and space, working together with great humour and dedication. I am extremely proud of you all.

"I wish I had been at Gene's Place a few minutes ago. I would love to have been able to throw a coffee cup at you, Andrew. I will arrange for you to receive extra coffee supplies, and maybe a treat or two as soon as possible." There was applause from the Moon. "Now, is Bryan Downey there?"

Bird stood up, nervous and uncertain. Thibodeaux enjoyed seeing his super-confident cook unsettled. It was a rare treat.

"Ah, Bryan. Have they appointed you to this historian position yet?"

"Er, no, sir. I think Commander Thibodeaux was making a joke, sorta."

"As I thought. Andrew, the new office of lunar historian is no longer a joke. It rates a Deputy Head of Department ticket. I want Bryan appointed immediately. Please attach him to your Science department and I will see to it that Willard, here, makes that official. After what I have heard of his work it is apparent that we need to document the history of the place. You can work on whether his catering duties need reassigning or modifying later. Oh, thank you Bryan." He waved Bird back into his seat. Bird mumbled something and sat down.

"Now, Evelyn and I dropped in to see Leif Culver earlier. I am hoping your Director will be back on his feet in time to attend a proper celebration, which you will all be invited to attend in Boston when we can arrange it." This time, the main applause was from the much larger live audience in Lancaster.

"Please believe me when I say that I honestly wanted to keep this as low-key as possible, so to that end there was no press fanfare, and there will be no TV coverage. It's not even in my diary, and Air Force One is on a planned crew training mission out to Edwards today. This is a genuine pop-up, from the heart visit to thank you all for the work you are doing.

"Now, folks, we really do have to leave soon, but first I would like to hear that report from Miss Grappelli. And I had expected today's treat would actually be me. Just for once I shall be content to find myself upstaged."

He leaned in towards the microphone. "You know, when you are the President, everything is usually planned so far in advance that there are few real surprises left to enjoy." He actually winked at them.

191

31 – REPORT
3:00 PM (LST) 30th SEPTEMBER

"Now, where is she? Ah, there you are, Lucy." The President paused for a second "Oh!"

Paula switched screens and cameras at the right second. Lucy heard the collective gasp from Gene's when they saw her shaved head, followed by a louder one from Lancaster. A close-up of the President filled her screen.

He recovered quickly. "Er, good afternoon. I hear that you are a remarkable and resourceful young lady. You must be as proud as I am of your extended team, both there on the Moon and here on Earth. I'm so glad they have a plan to help you. Now, I've been promised an interesting report today."

"Good afternoon, Mr President. Yes, I am privileged to have the team behind me. I knew they would come up with a rescue plan sooner or later." She paused. "I'd like to settle one item before we go any further. After yours, and Commander Thibodeaux' speeches, I want to beg a favour. I would like this place to officially become 'The Evan John McEwan Station', and call it 'Evan's Place'." That provoked ahuge round of applause.

"Oh, certainly. That's a fine idea, Lucy," the President was beaming. "Do we have any objections?" Apart from Redwood's famous pained grimace there were none. "In that case, Miss Grappelli, would you like to go right ahead and deliver your first report from Evan's Place?"

"Thank you all so much. Yes, sir, I do have a guaranteed show stopper for everybody. I have a lot of notes prepared, so please bear with me as I read through, after which we can cover each point separately..." She caught sight of Thibodeaux on the small screen. He was gesturing at her to stop talking.

"Why of course, Lucy," said the President. "If it is as exciting as it all sounds, we will most certainly stay and hear the complete report. Once you and the team start work on it, I imagine it would be best if Evelyn and I slip away quietly and let you folks with the brains get to work without any distraction. Would that seem like a sensible course of action to you?"

"Certainly, Mr. President. That sounds like a good working plan."

"Thank you Lucy. In that case, please go ahead."

Under the circumstances, and considering what she was about to say, Lucy thought she had better formalise the introduction. She had the idea it might be on screens everywhere within a few hours. She was glad Thibodeaux had ordered her into regulation gear. It dawned on her that he knew what was about to happen.

"Mr. President, Director Culver, Deputy Director Redwood, Commander Thibodeaux, Ladies and Gentlemen, I understand that a MAGENTA DS mission is due to deliver a resupply POD close to my position shortly. I cannot fully express my gratitude for all the effort and lost sleep that has gone into making that possible. The situation regarding the chances of my rescue had been somewhat tense, and it was a massive relief this morning when I heard the news that help is on the way. For a while I didn't think I would be going anywhere. What's more, if the POD lands within walking distance, I will be able to reach it, while retaining NEIL as a backup. This is because the airlock door will soon be free." The audiences in both locations started to buzz. She glanced at Thibodeaux, who nodded her to go on.

"Before I clarify that statement, I must post a brief medical report for Dr. Fisher, because if I don't speak to him soon, he will probably die from suspense." It was the President's turn to chuckle.

193

Most others didn't, especially the ones who knew what Fisher was like if kept waiting.

"Doc, I had a much better night and managed to get some proper rest for the first time since the accident. This morning my head felt much better and there has been no return of the nausea I had been suffering. Apart from that, I think the worst of the damage is bruising. By the way, I heard a sharp intake of breath there when you first saw me. No, I haven't had a psychotic episode. The prospect of living rather than dying has made me take stock of my situation much more pragmatically than yesterday. I shaved my hair off because I don't have the time and resources available to look after it.

"As Commander Thibodeaux suggested, I do have an important scientific discovery to present to you, Mr. President. It needs a brief clarifying introduction. I had the horrors last night and imagined I was seeing things; for a while I convinced myself that there were moving shadows in the rubble field. After consulting Dr. Fisher we decided it was either an optical illusion, or the effects of shock and a mild concussion." *There, Ajax will be happier that I'm not being controversial. Time to start the fun.*

"Early this morning I had another real scare when I looked outside NEIL and found a message scratched onto a rock. There are aliens here. Of that there can be no doubt."

There was total uproar. She waited while Thibodeaux and Redwood both tried to call their respective meetings to order. In the end it took several minutes. Thibodeaux tried to calm them. "OK, people. No, we're not taking any questions yet. Later. Quiet please! Thanks folks. Yes, we have a completely unprecedented situation here, but we need to proceed as planned and hear Lucy's report in full. I just need to add a few words from Gene's before you all start yelling again. No. I WILL HAVE QUIET!"

He waited while Redwood sourly reinforced the order at Lancaster. Finally there was a tense silence, allowing him to finish. "Thank you. I promise you that we will address every single question, and yes it will be a long meeting. From here on we go 'closed doors', and that means nobody in or out.

"I want to make it clear that Lucy is not hallucinating. There are definitely aliens outside NEIL, so listen to what she has to say about them before we start any further discussion. There are several witnesses here and we have film and photographs to show. Quiet! You are not getting anything else until you have all listened to Lucy's full report. . . in silence, OK?"

He scanned the audience. "Is Sol Duke there?"

There was a shout, and Duke was on his feet. "For Galaxy's sake will you be quiet for me, guys? I'm re-evaluating data and history here. WILL YOU ALL just let her speak? Go, Ajax!"

"I did tell you to be here, Sol. That was the best I could do." He turned to the President. "Do you need to leave, Mr. President? The closed-doors order doesn't apply to you of course."

"I'm not going anywhere, any time soon, Andrew. You have my full and undivided attention." Under the usual deep tan, Spencer Braithwaite II had gone pale. "I need to know if she is safe? Are we all safe?"

"Yes, Mr. President, we believe so and you will hear why soon. In fact the aliens are communicating with Lucy, and we understand their predicament is far more serious than hers. Even I haven't heard the full report yet. Shall we ask her to continue?"

"Please, yes." The President nodded, and then shook his head and sat down, fidgeting with his folder and paperwork.

"OK, Lucy," said Thibodeaux. "As the President said, you now have our full and undivided attention. Please go ahead and deliver your report."

"Thank you, Commander." She carried on, in the desperate hope that she was following the correct protocol. "Mr. President, for sake of argument I have christened them 'The Rock People' for now, and according to what I can glean from their messages it seems they are stranded here like me. Their spaceship was somewhere close by this position, and was destroyed either during or shortly after the comet impact. They say they lost over seventy of their crew, and the four of them outside NEIL are the only survivors.

"They use the same air as us and have good supplies of it. They have offered to share it with me in return for entry into NEIL, because otherwise they will soon die outside on the surface. I have air supplies left at the moment, but I took their offer at face value, as a genuine gesture of friendship and understanding. Right or wrong, I have accepted that as fair and invited them in."

Once again Redwood and Thibodeaux shouted for quiet. Both rooms subsided into hushed whispers.

"Now, if I understand correctly, they were part of an exploration team on the Moon. There are others of their race elsewhere. They used the expression, 'other moon'. I'm not sure whether they are actually talking about a moon or a planet, or even whether it is here in the Solar System or further away. It's on my list of items to clarify with them."

The President raised a hand, and Lucy stopped. "Yes, sir?"

"Andrew says you are safe. I am still frightened for you, Lucy. Could you defend yourself against these... creatures?"

"I will be quite honest with you and say no, sir. However, all the signs so far have been positive, and in my position I have little choice but to accept what they say at face value. At the moment they are moving the last of the rocks from outside the airlock, and then they will come inside. When that happens, I guess we shall see." For

196

the first time since she had started on the report, both rooms fell silent.

"That's for later, and I'm trying not to give it too much thought. I'm not afraid now." She took one deep breath. "Where was I? Oh, yes, rocks. The four creatures rolled some rocks of certain shapes away to one side, I imagine for use later. They lifted the rest of the rubble and threw it all some distance across the larger rock field. Some pieces sailed clear out into the crater. They have also cleared a large space to the side of NEIL, where they are working.

"These are small, powerful guys with eight multi-use, dexterous claws. You will see, but the best description I can offer is that they look like very large, more rounded, horseshoe crabs.

"So far it has been a slow and laborious conversation because it takes them some time to scratch their messages on a rock. They have a working vocabulary in English capitals, but their message construction is strange. I think the language they are trying to use has been part of their Earth studies as a research team. I have to think carefully about it and then send back interpretations until we agree on a meaning. I'm using a notebook and marker pen, holding my responses up to the window. The good news is that we've made remarkable progress since this morning.

The first task once they are inside NEIL is to try and find a more efficient way to communicate. I see no reason why they shouldn't be able to use a pen and paper, but they don't communicate using words as such. I have noticed that they tap on each other's shells with lightning speed when they are discussing something. They also know the exact location of Evan's body, which they have already offered to help me recover. That concludes my report for now. Are there any questions?"

Redwood managed to indicate that the President wanted to say something before he had to leave. It was yet another case of waiting for quiet before the highly charged proceedings could continue. At Gene's there was somewhat less of a panic. Lucy's news had been seeping out all morning, so the surprise development had not exploded with the nuclear force that it had in Lancaster. Most of the team at Gene's were busy slapping Bird on the back and insisting that he make them more cake.

At long last the President was able to address the electric atmosphere at Lancaster.

"Well, as punchlines go that was the biggie, young lady. Aliens on our Moon. I am almost at a loss to know what to say. Do I understand that they don't belong there, that they are not Moon men? And have you asked them what they want?"

"Yes I have, Mr. President. If my interpretation is correct, they were part of a visiting research and exploration team from somewhere far outside our solar system. They say that they are here because they want to visit Earth."

I said it to Ajax last night. All I wanted when I was certain I would die here was to visit Earth one last time.

"What is your official title, Lucy?"

"Senior Field Geologist, Eugene Francis Kranz Lunar Research Station, Mr. President."

"Thank you Lucy. I must leave for Boston in a minute, but I want to make you an offer before I go. Would you do me a singular honour, and accept the role of base commander at the newly established Evan John McEwan Research Station? I suspect we should add Exo-Sociological Scientist to your c.v."

Lucy lost the confident and cool demeanour she had kept up, more or less, for the previous two hours. Caught in the emotional maelstrom of losing, and then honouring, one old friend,

198

helping her four new-found friends, and then accepting a personal honour from her President, her emotions finally won. She nodded at the screen, shrugged one final smile, and buried her face in her hands.

32 – HANDSHAKE
6:00 PM (LST) 30th SEPTEMBER

Lucy wasn't sure if the Rock People would manage the airlock controls. The chamber wasn't designed for over-sized horseshoe crabs and, even with NEIL upside-down, she reckoned the panel would be out of their reach. It would be a lot easier if she showed them how it worked. She decided to meet them outside; at least it would save time. She waited by the window until they had finished rock-rolling. One of them brought the final rock to the window. It said:

READY WE

A few days ago Lucy had left Gene's to chase her dream; fresh comet debris for study. Now she was the first human to meet a real life alien. Looking outside, she had a déjà vu moment, more like a distant echo from one of the many science fiction books and movies she had devoured as a teenager. She felt like she was starring in a sci-fi movie. It felt strange to be Lucy Grappelli, First Contact. She doubted that she would ever have been selected for the job, partly as she was a geologist, but mainly after falling out with Commander Thibodeaux. *Too hot-headed to be an ambassador.* She allowed herself a wry grin.

There was a brief moment of doubt as she entered the airlock, sealed the inner door, and recovered the air. As a scientist and a pragmatist what else was she going to do? The worry passed as the pressure dropped away.

She was surprised at her lack of real nerves. Once she had decided that the creatures were stranded and in danger, there was no choice other than to help them.

She opened the external door and stood in the doorway with her arms held out, making the salute that she had learned from them. The four creatures were waiting, and saluted back. Three of them were sitting in line abreast about 20 m away from the door; the other waited in front of them.

NEIL had a fixed external ladder, but this now stretched upwards above the door. It was also fortunate that the door was side-hinged. If it had been a fold-down design it would have been tricky to open it upwards. The pop-out ramp was also useless. She had watched the creatures survey each rock as they removed it, leaving selected examples to one side before discarding the rest.

Using the saved examples, they had fashioned a rough ramp down the metre drop from the door to the surface. Lucy hadn't even considered that problem, but here it was already solved. She stepped out onto the packed pebbles and gravel, and walked down to meet them.

The nearest creature moved to the bottom of the ramp to greet her. It stood up to its full height and half raised one arm towards her with both the claws closed and held together. She faced it and held out her gloved hand, fingers closed, placing it against the claws. It didn't feel like a true handshake, but the gesture was made. The two species met, and studied each other for a moment.

Lucy turned and walked back up into the airlock, standing in the far corner and facing out. The creature followed, reaching the door just behind her. By catching the side of the opening with a small claw and lifting itself at an angle, it was able to fit its shell through. Lucy stepped around it to pull the external door shut. Once that was done she pressed the cycle button and monitored the system board as pressure returned. The inner door swung open and she hopped down to a storage box she had used as a step. She realised that she hadn't thought to organise a proper ramp on the inside. *Points to them.*

She turned back to see the creature do exactly the same as her and hop, landing on its many legs. It turned and walked to sit in front of her. Lucy took off her mittens, before standing and repeating the hand out gesture with her fingers together. The creature stood and touched its claws to her hand. They were freezing cold.

Lucy had put careful thought into what she would need to do next. She hadn't organised a ramp, but she was ready with two writing pads and a couple of marker pens. She knelt where she knew the creature would see her and wrote in two lines:

SHARE THIS SHIP AIR
LUCY

Next to her name she added her stick figure drawing. She passed the pen and pad across, and was immediately rewarded with a new message:

LUCY

It pointed its closed claws at her. It wrote with remarkable speed:

W-W-IIII-IIII-II-II-I

Then it drew the little monogram she had invented for the creatures. It pointed to itself:

SHARE AIR LUCY
W-W-IIII-IIII-II-II-I THANK

Next it did something different. It pointed to its name, bringing a rear claw from the tucked position behind its shell and tapping a sharp rhythm on the top. It was fast and loud.

Lucy picked up the pen and tapped sharply on the ceiling beneath her, copying the pattern:

4,4,2,2,1.

The other rear claw appeared, and it tapped both sets twice on its shell. Then it pointed at her again and wrote:

LUCY

She tapped on her head twice with both index fingers, hoping that meant either "yes", or "Me."

It pointed outside and tapped again:

5,4,3,4,2
5,4,3,1,5
5,4,2,5,1

Then it wrote on the paper:

W-W-IIIII-IIII-III-IIII-II W-W-IIIII-IIII-III-I-IIIII
SHIP WE AIR LUCY AIR WE
W-W-IIIII-IIII-II-IIIII-I SHIP LUCY

She had to look for a moment or two before catching the message. If she was right, two of them had gone for air, the other was ready to come in. Lucy went back to the airlock.

33 – BOUNCER
8:00 PM (LST) 30th SEPTEMBER

Bird was determined to make something of the President's offer. Promoted beyond any expected career aspiration he was walking on air; well here on the Moon he was actually walking on a vacuum, even more impressive.

Extensive research through the history files had furnished him with a good idea of the former base dimensions. He pinned a big printed wall map in the dining area and superimposed outlines of both the present and original facilities on it. Several members of the team offered suggestions and it immediately became one of those leisure time tasks that take on a life of their own. It also doubled as a way to take people's minds off the developing emergency for a few minutes.

"Yo, Bird."

"Hey," he replied as he turned. "Gracious, way to go, Everett. So you shaved your head too, eh? She'll get that. Anyway you look way cooler. On you it's actually very attractive."

She pointed a finger. "Uh-uh. Don't you be gettin' ideas, Downey. Solidarity is all. New map?"

"Yeah. I'm charting the history of the base to see if I can find an old jump rig that used to be here. I was hoping people may add stuff. Everybody knows something, but I've never captured it all."

"Bouncer? Ajax said."

"Yeah. That's one target, but you heard the President. He made it an official historian job. I need to start collecting stories and hearsay about what happened here."

"My dad worked here at Gene's. Met mom here."

"Wow, was he in comms?"

"Nope. Tenniel Zander, base commander."

Bird gasped. "Galaxy, Paula. TeeZee was your dad? He's a bloody legend. You're space royalty. Was your Mom an Everett, then?"

"Royalty, huh? Nah, simple comms chick. Mom was Melly Everett, medic. They never contracted."

"Are they still around? Can I talk to them about the base? Data from that era would be gold dust."

"Mom died years back. He in SpanAm, place called Belize on the Carib. 93 now, but he'd tell ya."

Paula was typical of those who had connections to former NASA people, actually knew something, or had been told something about the base and its history. He was surprised that a lot of tales that sounded apocryphal led to firm data if carefully researched. There were plenty of coloured pencils available. He soon moved up to a much larger version of the map, adding everything he knew for sure in marker pen.

He also found time to get outside and confirm things for himself. He had always loved being on the surface prospecting for bits of history. Ajax had asked at the morning meeting if anybody outside with nothing better to do would mind picking up any external scrap still remaining, log its location, and bring it in for Bird to catalogue and examine. Even before the official backing, there was a growing pile of treasure trove in the east garage. Some of it was readily identifiable; much more seemed to be broken and discarded bits of equipment which would require further investigation.

On Earth, several other people were keen to make a contribution. Bird arrived in from his first surface trawl as base historian to find a message. Astronaut training manager Eve Meredith had some information for him about Bouncer. He'd never considered it, but there were NASA staff still working who had started their careers setting up the present base some fifty years before. Eve was one such veteran. He called her back.

"Hi there Bird Downey, Historian guy. I guessed you'd burn my ears real soon."

"Eve, hi. Thanks for getting in touch. I'm getting a great response here. Everyone is taking time off from the Lucy problem for a few minutes at mealtimes. I've got wall charts up and they're covered in notes already."

"You're keen enough. It'll do 'em good to think about somethin' else for a bit. Be interestin' to see a proper history written too. I'll ask around here, there are a few of us vets left who saw it all. Heck, I hauled shells up there myself with the TUGs early on."

She was laughing. Bird remembered an awkward exchange with her early in his career, when she called him out for distracting one of her staff to the detriment of her duties. Maybe she had forgotten that incident; at least she had the grace not to mention it.

"That's great, Eve. I'm in awe of all you people doing that early stuff. Talking to you has given me a great idea. I'm going to dedicate the book to the teams who built the place."

"Still a smooth talker after all this time, Downey. So, Ajax told me why you want to find this rig."

Damn, she remembered. "I've grown up a bit in the last fifteen years."

"Yeah? I heard tell you'd walk to where NEIL is, an' carryin' cake, too. You ain't grown up, kid."

"OK, you've got me. Did Ajax tell you I think she's the one? Don't laugh; we've been making friends the last couple of months,

206

but friends is all. When I spoke to Ajax I'd just realised I needed her back."

"All right, I accept that, subject to confirmation at a later date. Hey now, I called to tell you I know where Bouncer is stored. There's a 30 m wide crater close outside the official boundary, beyond that open garage where BUZZ was hit. I believe it's in a zone marked as 'unsafe' on the current map. Before my time it was partially excavated at one side to make a ramp down to the floor, and then roofed in by stretchin' and peggin' heavy canvas sail. There was another large piece of canvas that rolled out from the roof, coverin' the ramp and makin' the crater almost invisible when closed. The sail started out green, but faded to grey within a year or two. Somehow the Moon seems to suck the colour out of things.

"The crater is so well hidden because it's where they tested the equipment that spray-covered your roof with the dust there at Gene's. It camouflaged the whole area. It'd be hard to spot if you didn't have a clue. The 'unsafe' tag on the map refers to the hidden crater hazard. I believe Bouncer was stored there, but Stars only know what else you may find."

Bird's heart was racing as he made notes. "That I will find, Eve. I'm indebted to you."

"I'm delighted to help, son. I'm copyin' a few pictures you may find interestin', and they'll get sent up as soon as we stop chattin'."

Bird received a series of photos from a fifty year personal collection. To his amazement there was one that actually showed the canvas roof of the crater being covered in the dust. If he could walk to where the garage and the background exactly fitted the view in the picture, he should be right by it. The major problem was the danger of falling in if he stepped in the wrong place.

Bird hopped out of the airlock accompanied by Tobin. Any walking tour outside the 2000 m perimeter was forbidden unless working as a pair, and missions outside needed approval. Bird liked to follow all the rules. Ajax had offered up his Life Scientist as the new historian's walking partner, because he was trying to give everyone a few hours of something to do that gave them a break from worrying over Lucy and NEIL.

They headed for the open-ended hangar at the northern perimeter. It dated from a period of experimentation, with panels made out of lunar regolith concrete mixed with waste water from the base. For durability it sat on a lightweight honeycomb aluminium frame, good enough in the low gravity to brace a large roof. It was an impressive size and covered an area of 30 x 32 m, with a single pillar in the centre of the high 15 m wide doorway.

Bird carried a big floodlight. He wanted to see for himself the extent of the meteor strike that had trashed BUZZ. They stood in the entrance and shone it inside. Most of the stores stashed there during the comet impact had been recovered back to Gene's, along with the damaged LXV. They looked at the small hole in the back end of the roof, plus a larger one in the rear wall. Apart from that damage the structure looked intact and sound. Bird had an eye on it as a potential museum for his work as historian. It would be a great place to store the growing heap of junk he was collecting, to sort and recycle materials, and to display what he hoped might become a real tourist attraction in years to come.

"Big old barn, this," Tobin volunteered.

"Sure is. It needs a patch and some doors, but we could fix it up easy. Do you think it would be feasible to spray the interior with PlastoWeld and pressurise it? See, I'm walking through here and thinking museum, tourist attraction, hotel, spa." Bird laughed at the way his imagination worked. "OK, so maybe not a spa then."

"In your dreams, you starry fool. Where do you get it all from?"

"Hey, dream big, Tobe. I'm here on Presidential orders and I've got serious development ideas for all this, eh. What about having tourists riding on Bouncer to get their own aerial shot of Gene's Place, for instance?"

"If it makes money, why not? Maybe you have the right dreams. Does Bird's Place need a Life Science guy by any chance?"

"Yeah, and you'd want architect fees I don't doubt. Seriously, I do think we could make a real attraction out of this. There's never a shortage of visitors at Gene's, is there, eh? When they arrive they always find there's actually not much to do."

"Maybe so. It's an idea, but we can work on that later. You should get Ace to look, he does mapping but he's got an architecture degree. Come on, let's crack on and find this hidden crater without falling in."

The pair had an off base plan, approved by Thibodeaux, which involved walking 250 m outside the perimeter on a regular marked route to the north-east of the shed. After that they would head anti-clockwise around the perimeter line, marked by the traffic cones, keeping about the same distance outside. Normally he would rely on the in-helmet screen, but Bird had a large scale print of the relevant digital from Eve rolled up and stowed under the straps on his arm. The pair carried telescopic poles for probing the surface. The plan called for a slow search, each of them taking turns to probe ahead with their pole before walking to where they knew the ground was safe.

As they reached the halfway point between cones two and three on the north-east trail, Bird unrolled the print and looked back to the shed.

"Here it is, Tobin. See the shed here in Eve's shot? From this point we can still see the back wall. Eve's picture shows it almost side on, with the entrance just about visible. We're a ways off yet, eh, so shall we walk until the damaged wall is almost out of sight and then start probing in towards it?"

"Sounds reasonable to me. Single file, five metres apart, yes?"

"Concur. I'll lead."

Bird took slow steps, keeping an eye open for clues on the ground and glancing to his left at the shed every few seconds. The view changed until he was in line with the back wall.

"Stop here. We need to pole ahead now. He worked his pole out in front of him, holding it up at about 45 degrees, before letting the end drop to the surface.

"I'm walking to it now, Tobe. OK, Join me here."

It took a while to work their way to where the picture looked like it fitted. They studied it for a few minutes until Tobin spotted a clue on the print.

"Is that a rock in the bottom corner? If so I reckon I can see it over there." He pointed to a spot about fifty metres closer to the perimeter.

"Could be, man. Want to work our way there?"

Tobin was right. As they reached the distinctive rock they found themselves looking at the shed from the right angle, with an obvious bump on the horizon exactly in line, behind the now visible open entrance. In the eerie stillness of the Moon's history he was always surprised to find them, but the area had a single set of footprints from, and back to, the perimeter. Whoever had made them had stood for a while and then milled around a bit before heading back. They had worn smaller than normal boots.

"Hello, Eve," he said quietly. "Look, Tobe, here's why I do this. These boot marks are an echo from history and they give me goose bumps. These are her prints, and I can visualise her taking this picture. This very shot." He waved it at his friend. "I'm taking some photos to send her, so don't walk all over the prints, eh?" He placed the digital next to one of the marks and weighted the corners with small rocks, before photographing it.

They held a short conference on the likely distance to go. There were no more distinctive landmarks, but the photo suggested it was only about 50 m. They decided to approach as they had arrived, poling the ground all the way.

"Aha! Looky here," said Tobin. "I can see it." Bird joined him and watched as the life scientist pointed ahead and off to the right. "It looks smoother over there. It's all kitty litter where we've been walking so far. Is that the dusted roof of the crater?"

"Reckon so, well done you," chirped the over-excited Bird. "We still need to long-pole it though."

A few minutes later the two friends were standing where the texture changed. Tobin clapped Bird on the shoulder. "Go on, will you? It's my turn but the edge has to be yours to find. Hit it with your pole."

Bird swung the pole upwards, pushed it out over the edge the smooth stuff, and they watched the end drop. It hit the surface and a layer of dust jumped up all around it. "Bingo!" he yelled.

They were able to mark the entire area of the crater and define a safety perimeter. Bird worked his way round the edge, tapping the pole to show where the canvas started. Tobin followed him, walking a few metres further away and dragging his in the dust to mark the safe zone. They would return later and place cones.

The entrance ramp faced south towards the shed inside the base, so as soon as they had defined the site they went to work scraping some of the dust from around the edges of the ramp cover. They had left the big light outside the shed, so Tobin hopped back to fetch it, forgetting the rules for once and heading straight in across the line of perimeter cones. It only took a few minutes.

The big canvas ramp cover was pinned into the surface regolith with simple tent-pegs. It also had a bar at the outer end for rolling it up. After pulling some of the pegs out on each side of the ramp it sagged a bit, so the pair had to roll it up as they went on lifting pegs. Not the easiest of tasks as it turned out, but after a bit of frustration they managed to get it done. The fine dust was a menace, falling off the sides and getting all over the ramp, but as it was a basic dirt slope it didn't matter too much.

"You go first with the light," said Tobin.

"Together," was Bird's reply. "And this is our show, not mine. Thanks for coming out, Tobe."

"Hey, it's like a vacation after the last few shifts. Come on then, let's do it."

They walked down the ramp with their smaller suit lights on, holding the spotlight between them. By unspoken agreement they kept their lights pointing downwards. Near the bottom, Bird spoke.

"Suit lights out here, and set the big one down."

"Ah, the big reveal. OK, we can do it that way."

They placed it down facing away into the pitch dark space. He felt on top for the selector, turned it left into the "AREA" position, then clicked the switch. For two whole seconds neither man spoke.

"Oh... for the Galaxy!" Bird could hardly speak for a second, and then the words flowed. "Will you take a look at all this stuff? That's Bouncer over there. This one's LXV-77, the last open sand car. That one on the far side has to be the rig that they used to dig the ramp here. And if I'm not mistaken, this one," he rested a reverent glove on it, "this one is an LRV, one of the three original Apollo Lunar Rovers from the early 1970s. I'll have to find out which. All this other stuff too; I don't even recognise most of it. It's a genuine treasure trove. I'm standing here among the star pieces for my museum."

The Life Scientist slapped him on the back. "What a prize, dude! Now that's how to spend an interesting day. You are about to become famous, Curator Mr. Downey, sir. I salute you." And he did.

The episode prompted an immediate stream of visitors along the new path surveyed at speed by Tobin. He and Bird had walked straight back to Gene's for a hand-cart and a load of cones before marking off the path and crater. Bird stood at the bottom of the entrance ramp and cracked a continuous stream of jokes about charging an entrance fee. When Thibodeaux arrived to see what all the fuss was about, he went straight to the point.

"So, you went prospecting and hit the mother lode first hammer strike. You're a clever and lucky man this week, sunshine. I guess you'll want some of the engineering team to drag that horrid looking contraption back to the garage and see if it will fly."

"Equipment doesn't degrade here, Ajax. Where's Ace? I'd bet I can fly it.

Ajax didn't doubt the sincerity behind the idea. "Bird, we have tech guys, engineers, LXV experts, system experts, and all sorts of other specialists here, you know. What we don't have is a pilot. It may have to wait until we get one. Let's see if it will run before we cross that crevasse, shall we?"

213

It was the best he would get for now, but Bird knew Ajax would let him try it out in the end. "Tell you what, I'll see if I can find a service manual for it. We can go from there. It's only small, do you think we could wheel it to the garage on a couple of the carts?"

"Definitely not until the LXV and tech teams are free from the effort to either fix BUZZ or retrieve NEIL. Bird, you're not rushing out there on this thing, and that's final."

"But the whole idea was—"

"It's a definite negative, Mister. Even more so now I've seen the damn thing. Now, do you have duties today or are we ordering Chinese food in?" There was a general laugh from the crew around.

"Yes, and I have to own up to being late back. Nic did say not to rush though. She's shaping up well."

"Come on you, get yourself back inside. Yes, she's doing great, but until we get another cook up here you're still it. I will ask the tech team to boot over and survey this Bouncer. I'll tell them not to touch anything else until they get your say-so. Is that OK with you, Chief Historian?"

Thibodeaux opened the comms office door to find Mario sitting at the desk reading. There was nothing on the big screen. As he turned to greet his visitor the base commander held a finger to his lips and wrote on the scratch pad; I am not here. Call her now. Quietly. No screen.

Mario frowned at him and shrugged, but Thibodeaux shook his head. Mario knew he and Lucy were in deep trouble. They should never have discussed switching the uplink off. Now they would both be in for another uncomfortable discussion with the boss.

The dwarf sighed as he keyed the switch. "Lucy, it's Mario. Are you awake and dressed?"

"Hey Mario. Yes, you can put the screen back on. Is he still mad at me?"

Thibodeaux reached over him to the panel and switched the screen on. "Good morning, Grappelli."

She jumped, and he saw "Oh no, not again," written all over her face. "Oh. Good morning, Commander Thibodeaux."

"My instruction was screen uplink on at all times."

It was his turn to jump as Mario banged his fist on the comms desk and whirled to face his commander. "Leave her alone! I switched it off here because people need some private rest time. I listened on the area pickup in case anything happened. Don't keep taking it out on her. Galaxy, Ajax, it's not her fault she's trapped there. Stop treating us all like kids."

The reaction from his usually genial comms operator shocked Thibodeaux. "Cool it, Mr. Silva. That's quite enough from you."

"But—"

"I issued clear instructions here yesterday. The excuse 'We switched it off the other way round' directly contravenes my orders. I walked in here and the screen was off. Do not put yourself in trouble with me, sir. I've got quite enough problems."

Mario sat down without a word, turning his back on the commander in a rare gesture of open defiance.

"Look, Mario..." Thibodeaux began, but he struggled to find the right words. It wasn't just Mario, the whole base was upset and stressed; his relationship with the entire crew was in jeopardy. He couldn't afford insubordination. His public exchange with Lucy the other evening had sparked a series of difficult and awkward discussions with several of the others, including close personal friends. Maybe he was too easy on them, like Leif had suggested last time he was at Lancaster. His authority needed to be re-established once and for all.

Instead of disciplining his comms operator, he gave the whole situation a moment of wise consideration. He sensed a window of opportunity to deal with a problem, and maybe build bridges at the same time. Maybe the tide of resentment might ebb if he made Mario see sense, while knowing that Lucy could hear his every word.

He checked she was still watching from aboard NEIL, then he reached over Mario and cut the screen feed again. He also cut the audio uplink, but left the downlink open so she would hear him and Mario. He hoped that she would believe Mario was in for a severe talking to but, in her interest to "overhear" the exchange, would fail to notice the tiny downlink light on NEIL's comms panel. Mario noticed, but was gestured to keep quiet.

Thobodeaux chose his words with great care. "Come on now, listen to me Mr. Silva. We're all under pressure. Am I wrong to be in command? No. Have I run this facility on respect and

216

friendship for so long that I've given up some of my authority? Possibly so, and that's open to discussion. The kind of soft touch management I practice here is a sort of art form, if you will. It can be effective for building a great team that works well together. But, if you lose your team's respect it can backfire with serious consequences. That may be what happened after Lucy picked a fight with me in public the other evening."

Mario turned the chair back towards him. "Commander, I don't—"

Thibodeaux held up a hand. "Give me a moment, and let me see if I can explain it better. Most of the time I consult everybody on any given situation. I suggest options and ask for input before I finally decide on a course of action. On the other hand, it's occasionally my duty as the base commander to make a snap decision. I don't do it lightly, and you have to understand that. It's right there in the job title where it says 'Command'. There may come a time when I need to make a real life-or-death call, and when that happens there won't be any opportunity to argue about it. Whether it's in conference or solo, when I make a management decision the team must acknowledge and act on it, immediately and without question. Otherwise, what do we have?"

The dwarf spread his arms and shrugged. "I do respect you, Commander, but... Oh, I don't know. Look I'm sorry."

"It's OK. I don't want any resentment and awkwardness between us. That doesn't just mean you and me and Lucy, it means all of us. When we have a real crisis we can't afford not to operate as a cohesive unit. Yes, I am the commander, but I'm also proud to consider myself part of the team. Can we please try to roll that way, at least while we sort this all out?"

"Yes, Commander Thibodeaux."

"In that case, can we can go back to being Mario and Ajax?"

"OK, yes Ajax."

Soft management. He'd dodged the term for years, while earning respect and getting things done. It was the principal reason he and the autocratic Redwood didn't get along. He switched on the links and started in as jovial a tone as he could manage. "Lecture over. I've got things to do in my office. Would you please set up the morning report in the lounge at 9:30 AM for me? We'll start again from there. Agreed?" They both nodded.

President Braithwaite had appointed Lucy Grappelli as a base commander so she was now his equal, commanding her own station. Her sudden and unexpected elevation in status did mean that in the technical sense she was no longer his problem. She would certainly remain so, at least until her rescue. She had started this mission under his jurisdiction, and he would at least see her safe return, before allowing her to leave his team, so to speak.

Doc was right, the girl did have some balls. Short of temper, yes, but she would not be a quitter for anybody. He was still peeved at her for shouting at him before the mission started, plus hanging up on him at a critical moment. At the same time he admired her guts and determination. It was a combination of everything she was that had brought her this far from the tragic accident and loss of her friend in the space of three short days.

Every team member was present for the report, more casually turned out than the previous day.

"Good morning Commander Grappelli. We're desperate to find out what you've achieved so far today. How are things there this morning?

"We are making real progress here, Commander Thibodeaux." She was aware that her every word would be analysed in years to come. "We are all improving in communication; these guys are making more sense with written messages, and I'm learning some sign and gesture responses."

"You caused a proper sensation yesterday, you know. Word on the street suggests the entire Earth media melted down under the pressure to get information. All they had to go on was the NASA press briefing after the meeting. We did have a laugh here after some keen reporter spotted Air Force One departing from Edwards and put two and several together. The guessed headline 'President Talks To Moon Men?' caused a lot of hilarity at Lancaster."

Lucy joined the laughter. She was making her morning report from outside NEIL. "They never give up, do they? So, look what I've got here."

She turned so the camera could see a huge pile of copper spheres. "Until we learn what they call themselves, I have decided to call this team the Deep Race. Their resemblance to crabs is a valid observation. They originate from an ocean under ice, on a water world they say is 'AWAY AWAY FAR FAR'. Their wreck of their ship is in the crater NEIL almost fell into. It's about a third of the way round from our position here at the northern edge.

"These objects are air tanks two metres across, and there were 23 of them at the last count. The Deep Race have been working in pairs, pushing each sphere up the shallowest part of the crater wall and rolling them round here one by one. It's a dextrous feat, even for beings with that many feet and claws available. I take this gesture as an act of friendship, but we still have a problem because it doesn't help our air situation. I have no way of attaching them to NEIL, and nothing available that could make a cross-feed valve. In fact, the tanks are solid spheres with no valve.

"The Deep Race team drew some pictures to show me how they get clamped into a pair of half-shell shapes, which are then hinged shut. A device like a small harpoon then stabs a hole in the sphere and seals it into the air system. Therefore, in spite of the massive theoretical supply available here, we are all worrying about how much oxygen we need, and the remaining supply aboard NEIL.

"I visited the site of the shipwreck. After watching me do the bounce-hop all the way there, their leader, his usual form of address is 2,2,1, insisted that I ride on his shell for the return leg. There is much higher pressure in the oceans on their world and I don't weigh more than, well, something or other he had tried to describe. He gave me a smooth ride; all those legs compensate for the rough surface with ease. He held up the two rear claws for hand-holds, insisting that I couldn't hurt or damage them. It was certainly a faster way to travel than the awkward hop-along that we've always done here. They have a lower centre of gravity and can't topple like us.

"Intentionally or not, their spacecraft was camouflaged by design. It looks like a small asteroid, actually more like several of them linked together. In fact, what's left of it is grey and knobbly, with a texture very similar to much of the lunar landscape. It's close under the edge of the crater wall, and surrounded by similar boulders it would be hard to find on a survey photograph. It was large though, maybe 300 m long.

"We drew pictures of the solar system and established that their main survey base is under the ice on the Jovian moon Europa, where conditions are similar to home. We attempted some star maps to try and establish where their home is, but I don't have charts here to show them. That can wait while we play 'Robinson Crusoe' with what we can retrieve from the wreck of the Long View Traveller. That's my closest attempt at translation for the ship's name.

"I understand that although they are a deep water race, they have evolved to live out of that medium for a time; another comparison to crabs. I'm amazed that they can operate in a vacuum. They apparently evolved to use what was originally a swim bladder and valves, to pressurise oxygen; it's like having an internal air tank. Their physiology allows them to operate under water, in an oxygen atmosphere, or, with access to an oxygen supply, in a hard vacuum.

"Their main exploration base on Europa has a staff of about four hundred, being the greater part of the mission crew. Unfortunately the Long View Traveller was the sole mission ship, i.e. there were no associated shuttles etc. When they saw how close the comet would pass to Earth, the exploration team spotted an opportunity to sneak in and start an Earth/Moon survey by hiding next to the comet nucleus. The ship was disabled in the final comet break-up; the same event that destroyed our sample probe. After an emergency orbital manoeuvre they managed to crash-land it here without loss of life.

"Their luck didn't last. It almost looks like the comet had it in for them all along, because a few hours later the Long View Traveller was destroyed in a double disaster. They suffered a direct hit from a large piece of falling debris thrown up by the cometary impact. Part of the crater wall then collapsed, burying some of the wreckage. I'm wondering if that happened at the same time as the impact and quake that buried NEIL. Whatever the sequence, they took three strikes. The whole episode is the worst example of bad luck I can imagine. Anyway, even if we can get them back to their base on Europa, I don't think they will be expecting a rescue mission from home.

"The wreckage was almost broken in half by the falling fragment. Apart from the smashed structure and heaps of metalwork everywhere, there are Deep Race bodies scattered for hundreds of metres around. The rest of the ship suffered severe collateral damage from the subsequent explosion of the drive unit in the rear section. The crater wall collapse buried the rear end. They pointed out the source of the explosion to me, the remains of which didn't look like a standard rocket assembly. There is valuable science there, but it's pretty mashed up. When it happened, the surviving crew, my new team, were on a surface mission and far enough away over the crater wall to avoid any injury. They returned to find their ship devastated and everyone else dead."

As they approached the scene, Lucy had watched as the Deep Race crew stopped and sat down, placing all four of their arms straight out and letting them lie flat on the ground with all the claws open. They had stayed completely still for half a minute. As one, they had all stood up and come to attention, making the familiar greeting salute, this

time with all their arms rather than the two with which they had saluted Lucy. Finally they spent about ten seconds beating a furious tattoo on their shells. With the lack of atmosphere Lucy couldn't hear it, but even without sound the gesture had moved her deeply. She imagined the limp-arms gesture as sorrow or despair, followed by military honours. She was left in no doubt that these people had paid tribute.

2,2,1 turned and scratched in the dust:

MANY DEAD KNOW WE
LUCY HELP WE
SHIP HELP LUCY
SHIP HELP WE

She was getting the hang of this. It wasn't necessary to use their first two numbers of their names. She didn't know whether that was a family, tribe or maybe military tag. They were inviting their new friend to help scavenge the wreck and see if she could find anything that might help keep them all alive. Again she drew the picture of NEIL upside down, this time with a second cartoon of NEIL standing the right way up alongside. 2,2,1 wrote one of the new gesture-related words they had agreed on:

YES

"We've established some common ground. They don't have ears like us, hence no spoken language. They drum out codes with their claws, on themselves or each other as required. They also use almost unlimited gestures and semaphore using four arms and eight sets of claws.

"I've put everything into context. I've lost a colleague and friend, my fixed base is a bit roughed-up but intact, and will sustain me for the meantime. I'm expecting a supply drop later today, and I feel confident that I will be rescued. On the other hand, these guys have lost everything. They are the best part of a billion kilometres from their forward base, and who knows how far from their home world?

"It is a desperately sad situation over there as you will see from my suit camera recording. They want to place their dead, together with all the associated body parts we can find, inside the front end of the ship. When I finish my report we will return there and commence that task.

"They make tribute every time they get to within 200 m, but tell me they will stop doing that once the bodies are retrieved and tidied away. There is closure of some sort involved, but I can't begin to imagine how wretched they must feel. They want to complete the scavenger hunt first, because I think when we store the dead bodies and leave the scene it will become hallowed ground. Sometimes the messages have more ambiguity than others, but I think they said that they will never go there again afterwards."

Acting NASA Director Will Redwood settled himself behind the big desk and sprayed on some cologne. After rearranging some files, he called the Lunar Research Station. He harboured an intense dislike for the sarky and monosyllabic comms operator, but it didn't single her out from most of the others. *Oh, freaking Galaxy!* She'd shaved her head to look more like that loose cannon, Grappelli. It didn't do the ugly bitch any favours.

"Everett, get Thibodeaux."

Paula looked up from the comms desk. She had taken over at 3:00 AM, and spent the last six hours working on schematics of NEIL's communication setup. She had been concentrating hard, but still wasn't any closer to working out why they had the comms link but couldn't update the navigation files or computer on the LXV. Her neck hurt with the tension and she was starting a headache. Bird was rationing coffee and she was low on caffeine.

She smiled sweetly. "Outside on survey. No calls." *Fucking head case. Who the nuke does he think he is?*

He put on his special condescending tone, the one he reserved for dealing with the real morons. "I need to speak to him right now, so make the call."

"Ain't disposed to being spoke to like that."

"Everett, I've fired you once, but Thibodeaux gave you a stay of execution and I'm stuck with you till I can get you back here. Consider whether you are disposed to keeping a job then? I need to speak to Thibodeaux right now."

"Yeah?" Paula was beginning to enjoy herself.

He knew he was getting nowhere fast, but didn't see how he could improve the situation. "I am in charge here, and I will re-word that as a direct order if that would suit your sarcastic attitude any better. Everett, stop playing the moron and put me straight through to Thibodeaux. Do it now."

He watched as the arrogant woman sat back and smiled sweetly, folding her arms. The idiot grin widened. She abandoned the trademark shorthand speech, switching to a carefully enunciated Southern drawl complete with drawn out vowels. At once she became both condescending and even more irritating.

"Oh, my! Well ah'm real sorry to disappoint you, *Deppity* Director Redwood, suh. Mah specific orders from Commander Thibodeaux were not to dee-sturb the surface crew today unless we all get a life-or-death emergency. Why don't you record a message, and I will nat'rally be more than happy to en-sure it reaches him *jus' as soon* as he becomes available. That will most likely be when he has completed all the necessary survival tasks that he and his team are working on outside at the present time."

Paula wondered if he had broken the keyboard as he smashed his fist down on it, but at least it cut the link. No matter, it got rid of the ignorant bastard so she could carry on actually working. She sighed and rotated her stiff shoulders a bit before diving back into the schematic on the other screen, smiling in satisfaction.

Redwood stormed out of the office and took on Culver's secretary, the sycophantic Penny Tipton.

"Set up a video meeting with Thibodeaux. Call that woman at Gene's; the sullen trash with the one-word answers. She is so rude I can't even work with her. She'll be in my office and fired once and for all when she gets back here. I can't afford to have difficult staff in this organisation."

Penny stifled a laugh at the irony. "Mr. Redwood, Paula might be abrupt but she would never bite first. Why don't you call her back and try being polite? You know, a simple 'please' can work small wonders on the human race."

"Polite, is it? I don't need your advice, lady. I need to speak to Thibodeaux and she won't put me through to him. That task is now delegated to you, so let me know when it's done." He stalked back into the office, kicked out the wood wedge, and tried to slam the door. Even that didn't co-operate as it had a soft-close unit. *Damn.* He sat behind the desk and watched, seething, as it swung at its own sweet pace and clicked shut.

Penny stood outside the door and took a deep breath. She marched through without knocking, stopping in front of the desk and folding her arms.

Redwood wasn't having that either. "I closed that door. Secretary or not, you do not just walk in here. The correct procedure is that you knock on the door and wait until I invite you in. Only then may you come through it. Better still, you can return to your desk immediately and call me to ask if you may enter. I've given you a choice of actions, both with simple to follow steps even you should be able to understand. Decide which you can manage, one or the other. Out." He actually pointed at the door.

She stood her ground and spoke with quiet determination. "I am not a secretary. My correct title is Assistant to The Director, and you are not he. I want to make it quite clear to you right now that I will not be spoken to like this. I am here working for you on loan, and so far I have suffered some of the worst rudeness I have ever experienced. You treat me like something you found on Kent's shoes and I will not stand for it any longer. From now on you will address me as 'Mrs. Tipton'. I may also answer to 'Penny', but that familiarity has to be earned and, make no mistake, you are not even close. Don't you ever, and I mean ever, address me as 'You' again, or so help me..."

She left that one hanging and walked out, making a point of placing the wedge back under the door to keep it open as usual.

Redwood had to walk back across the office to remove the wedge again. He pitched it out into the office, narrowly missing her desk. Culver ran the operation with kid gloves and a smile. Well, things would change now that the command had moved on. There was no way Culver was coming back; he'd see to that, especially if the medical team felt like continued employment was also to their liking. It was time for him to take control.

He set the door lock from the desk console and switched the external light to "busy". Culver encouraged the uninvited flow of staff into the office; people often wandered in and struck up a casual conversation. Well, he was no longer running a coffee shop operation here, and there would be no more unnecessary chat. There would be discipline, starting with a proper appointments system. The secretary was back in her rightful place with nothing constructive to say because she didn't knock, buzz, or call. He messaged her with concise instructions in easy to follow steps.

By mid-afternoon he was bored stiff; the phone hadn't rung once. There wasn't a single appointment in the book and he hadn't had any visitors. Redwood opened the door at precisely 4:30 PM to find the outer office empty. Every work station was powered off. That riled him even more. He called the security office.

"Redwood. What time did Tipton leave today?"

"Oh, that would have been about three, Mr. Redwood," was the cheerful reply. "Right after the meeting with Gene's."

"Get me her home number."

"I can't authorise that, sir. Mr. Culver has the codes. The Head of Security does keep home file access information but he isn't here either now. I only do building security."

"Oh, has he taken half the day off like everyone in the office up here? I don't care where he is, find him, and have him call me immediately."

"You know, Mr. Redwood, it wouldn't hurt you to say please sometimes. There was a family emergency this afternoon and he took the train to Chicago. Look, he'll be back in tomorrow around 11:00 AM and I'll have him call you. Can I ask if it's a building security issue, because I can help with that?"

"No, I've told you already. Why do I have to repeat myself with you people? I have an urgent need to talk to Culver's secretary, Penelope Tipton, and I need to do that right now. Culver left me in charge, so I am the Acting—not Deputy—Director."

"I'm sorry. I know you are, Mr. Redwood, but that hasn't been cleared down here at security. I have no way to help you, but—"

Redwood missed the pointless suggestion. He was fast losing his temper with these morons, and he was shaking with rage. This time he did break the phone.

Although Ajax had allowed him unlimited file access, Bird hadn't been able to locate anything new about Bouncer. Without a technical manual it would be a much more difficult task. As yet Ajax hadn't let him recover the rig to the base. Without the manpower to work on it, plus the problem of a pilot, Bouncer was still stored at the crater garage.

He called Eve Meredith to tell her how he and Tobin had found the garage and its amazing haul of historical artefacts. He kept the digital showing her footprints for a surprise, and waited to send it until they were chatting. She gasped as she saw the image.

"Bird Downey, I once thought you were nothin' better than a slick opportunist. I guess you will recall a certain occasion at LEO 6, on which I based that judgement. In fact I now know you're actually a young man with some real charm. Thanks for sendin' me that, it takes me back so far I almost daren't admit it. I wish I was there to take a walk across to that spot with you. I had no idea what was stored in that garage, that's an incredible find."

"It was like a dream for me too, Eve." Like most people he had a huge admiration for the pint-sized manager and veteran astronaut. "I've always been interested in the history of this place. I haven't gotten over the President giving me an official position which means my hobby becomes part of my job. Now I've made some real progress and found the rig, but I'm stumped until I can find the paperwork and a manual to go with it. Nobody has time to invest in writing a manual at the moment."

"Hey, we'll work on that. You'll see."

"Hope so. Between you and me, Ajax gave me unofficial file access at Gene's but I can't turn anything up. I guess it'll have to wait, and anyway it was only in desperation to rescue Lucy that I thought of it. It ain't fit for that job. When we do find some time to service it and get it going I'm determined to be the pilot, and that's another conversation Ajax has been side-stepping."

Eve laughed. "Do you fly at all?"

"I'm afraid not. Pelican does though. He's got a real antique propeller plane he takes out to his observatory in Australia. It's 100 km away but still on his property, and he uses a plane to get there."

"Ajax is a careful guy, Bird, and that's why he is there managin' an unruly lot like you. He can be influenced though, if you talk to him the right way. I'll bring up the subject and we'll see what happens.

"I do believe Bouncer was a piece of Houston kit, so there might be data here somewhere. Heck, I might have to go trawlin' through *paper files*. I keep tryin' to find reasons to come and help out up there at Gene's. There's been some talk of dispatchin' a support team, and I've made a firm bid. You might even have to take me flyin' on the damn thing."

"I like that idea," said Bird. "If you do get here, I'm so going to pick your brains on the subject of Gene's history. I don't have many skills, but I do have a recommended bribery method using chocolate cake."

She laughed at him. "That's the limit. In that case, sir, I'm back to my original assertion, you're nothin' but a slick opportunist. Chocolate cake? Oh my, Mr. Downey, I'll co-operate. And don't down-talk your skills neither, you're worth more'n you think."

It was a day before he received a message entitled "Bouncer Data". There a paragraph from Eve, detailing the darker recesses of Houston's archives and the spiders that inhabited them. As predicted, she sent him a series of digitals depicting historical paper files. Bouncer had schematics, specifications and even a flight manual with some pilot notes added. Things were looking up.

There was no way it would ever be able to help rescue Lucy. It seemed to have a maximum flight endurance of around fifteen minutes, lifting on six small jets of waste CO_2 sourced from the base and stored in a pressurised cylinder under the four seats. Stability came from a set of electric gyros. It was simple tech, strapped to a lightweight chassis similar to the 20th century Apollo era LRV he had also found in the garage.

Armed with the printed data in a plastic file he sought out Kyran Mukherjee in the lounge. Work on BUZZ was coming along, and the cheerful Indian was more relaxed after what had been a tough few days. He and Ellis Ransome had decided to strip the entire body shell off BUZZ and service the chassis and systems without it. With the pressure system and accommodation unit removed, the thing actually ran. It was currently set up as a two-seat open touring rig. It did involve riders suiting up, and would therefore be useless as an exploration vehicle. The present plan involved attaching the spare body shell expected from Mt. Rainier, instead of building a whole new machine from spare parts.

"Kyran, look what Eve Meredith sent me," said Bird, "A whole set of Bouncer notes and drawings. She remembered some other stuff about it too."

"Can I borrow this?" Kyran gave his typical chuckle. "An excellent proposition for a spot of light bedtime reading, I am thinking."

"Sure, Ky. Are you available any time tomorrow?"

"Most certainly I could be. Ellis and I are through with BUZZ until we get parts up here, so we have time. Can you slack off from that kitchen and we'll check over your famous rig? He may even join us if he's free. Maybe if I take in this stuff later today we could bring it in and set it up here by BUZZ. It would be most interesting to be firing it up maybe, see if anything still runs."

Bird was ecstatic. "That would be ace, Ky. I can leave Nic in charge after breakfast, around 10:00 AM. I'll get all set up so we can play till maybe 4:00 PM. Ajax has put the crater garage on-limits, so we don't need to go ask him if we can walk over there."

The following morning Bird helped Ellis and Kyran load Bouncer onto a small derrick truck and roll it back to the garage. Thibodeaux had allowed them to keep one of the garages pressurised, to make working on BUZZ easier. Until Lucy arrived back it would stay that way in case they needed it for major projects.

Neither of the LXV engineers fancied the idea of riding an open-frame float rig on compressed gas. Kyran pointed out that lunar dust was notorious for clogging up anything that disturbed it, and much of their time was spent trying to keep equipment clean. Any attempt at a test flight would need to take place out on the POD landing area.

Ellis Ransome was even more horrified at the suggestion that Bird was contemplating flying tourists anywhere near Gene's for photographs. He was a great believer in the "what if" mantra, and would predict impending disaster for even the most straightforward tasks. That, together with a basic indifference to his fellow man, placed his cheerful and willing Indian colleague firmly in the go to seat at Engineering.

Ellis was adamant. "Bird, it's a no, man. You're not licensed, you're not a pilot, and you can't fly it. No argument."

"Come on, Ellis," pleaded the cook. "I just want to prove it works. How high could it get anyway?"

"Well, looking at the specification sheets, the theory says there's a lot of gas power available here. The numbers suggest a powerful lift-off and the ability to climb almost unlimited until the gas runs out. Set up like that the mission endurance looks too short. The problem is you can't use a parachute here. Even at 1/6G you'd be stuffed if you needed to bail out. The fall is easy but there's a hard stop at the surface with no atmosphere to slow the acceleration. You'd be a fool to take the risk, and a dead fool if you got into any sort of difficulty."

Kyran chimed in. "Hey, Bird, that is the most amazing optimism coming from Ellis. We might have an even more clever alternative suggestion though. Go on and tell him, Ell, it was your idea."

Ellis grimaced, it was the closest he ever got to a smile, and his only working facial expression apart from the stock deadpan.

"Yeah, huh? Anyway, Ky and I reckon it might function better if we limited the gas power and ran it as a hovercraft with a plenum and side skirts. We'd still have to test it way out there across the surface because the dust kick-up would be a huge problem. I spend my life resuscitating good kit from dust death. The stuff sticks. A hovercraft would trade altitude for endurance and have a greater range. Also marginally less lethal; you'd only break most of your bones if you lost control, as opposed to finishing up irrevocably,100%, dead."

Bird didn't know the engineer too well, but things were looking up and it was obvious that Ellis was having one of his less pessimistic days. "So does that means you guys will get it operational, then?"

"Yeah, I guess. We engineers do have day jobs."

Kyran rolled his eyes at Bird. He usually spent much of his working day trying to jolly Ellis along, but somehow they worked as a tight team. "Ell, it is not as if we can do anything more with BUZZ till the parts POD drops here. It's weeks away yet at least till we get the body shell we are needing. We're not so busy today. What else would you like to be spending an afternoon doing? I am thinking a bit of casual tinkering with this most fascinating item might be fun, isn't it?"

"Fun? No, Ky, it's unnecessary work. I could sleep, but then I'd get out of rhythm and be up half the night again." He gave a huge sigh. "OK, yeah, whatever. Could I care less?"

Bird caught a wink from Kyran. "Ellis, that's brilliant, I appreciate it, dude." He awarded the laconic engineer with his best winning grin. "I'll go and fix up some supplies, then can I come back out and hand you the spanners and shit?"

Ellis did the all-purpose grimace again. "Must you?"

"OK, what kind of cake do you run best on?" Bird was trying his damnedest.

He sighed again. "Fuel, man. Food is just fuel."

Kyran was having none of that. "Bird, in recent years the only 'fuel' he has ever commented on was your shortbread. The millionaire kind."

After a four hour strip-down, clean, and rebuild powered by millionaire shortbread and coffee, Bouncer was finally plugged in and the gyro batteries started to charge. The three of them sat down for a few minutes on an old oil-stained sofa dragged out from the engineering office.

"I'm still thinking hovercraft," Ellis scowled, reaching for a pad on the desk. "Yeah, now, if that flats out on paper we could think about something upscaled, maybe with a tent over, yeah, a rig to carry a rescue team up the West Way. Technical, man, oh

I gotta design headache coming on. Yeah, now if I had some plastic sheeting and spare canvas..." He started to draw, and the parts litany descended into a mumble, punctuated by the odd audible "yeah."

Kyran turned to Bird. "That's it. He will be off line now until he's finished. You could call his mother anything you care to name her and he would fail to be receiving the message. Watch this." He raised his voice, "Hey, Ellis?" There was no response.

"I don't know how you work with him," said Bird.

"Oh, he's a most brilliant engineer. He designs, but mostly I am working on all the big stuff. None of it would function if Ellis hadn't waved his magical screwdriver set around at the internal complexities. I think of it like, I'm macro, he's micro, and together we operate as a team of some excellence. We actually choose to get assigned together and this is our fourth tour here at Gene's. It must be a success because we still get sent. He is quiet and I can chatter on all the day long."

Ellis got up and bustled off, muttering. Kyran laughed. "Oh, it's that serious. See, now he's gone for his slide rule. He never uses the computers. He's got this wooden rule, it's a real antique. Still off line though, till the masterpiece is drawn."

Thibodeaux surprised them by arriving in the garage. "Hi, how's it going out here? Oh, working on Bouncer, are we? I saw Ellis, but he was in a huff over something."

"Not a huff, Commander," Kyran corrected. "He's thinking. He goes to his inner space mode. It's off line external, comms unit down totally, a place where in all honesty even I cannot reach him."

"Odd guy, but effective. So, I'm on a snap dress inspection." They both stood up. "That's good, fellas. Surface suits in the garage and emergency depress headgear deployed, check." He looked over Bouncer. "Kyran, what about Bird testing this monstrosity? I've had Eve Meredith all over me from Houston nagging about letting him try it out. It would make a great publicity shot to show his sponsor. We like to keep the President happy."

236

"Bird is a great cook and we need him intact is my present thinking," said Kyran. "It might be possible though. Ellis wants to lower the power and is busy designing a hovercraft skirt. Bouncer here would make a most excellent hovercraft, with the only major difficulty being the dust problem. He says he could use that as a prototype for a larger rig for a rescue mission. That's what he's working on, you met him going to get his antique slide-rule."

Ajax was delighted. "That's great, Ky. If the concept is valid it sounds a lot less dangerous. The expression 'possible rescue mission' immediately turns a crazy leisure-time scheme into a base priority. Bird would be able to test it then, wouldn't he?"

The Indian's deep brown face broke into the huge trademark grin. "Ellis would be happier on the safety aspect, I'd be most delighted to see it happen, and honour would be satisfied in excellent style."

Ajax turned to Bird. "What about you then? Could you live with flying a few centimetres above?"

"Yes, boss, it sounds a lot more workable. Ellis kinda put me off the free-flying idea, with a lecture on irrevocable 100% death. I'd be happy to go with a hovercraft. As for a rescue, we need that girl back here. I'd fly it all the way if you need me to, eh."

Kyran gasped. "Boss, I am busy thinking on my feet here. If it works, we could maybe look at stripping the drive trains off BUZZ and using the floor panel to build a longer range machine for a rescue."

"Now you're talking," said Thibodeaux. "That might be an option. When Ellis lands back here, please ask him about it. If he agrees with you, requisition whoever you need for preliminary design work."

It took Ellis and Kyran a day to re-plumb Bouncer's gas lines and install all the required valves, then stretch a canvas skirt over a new lightweight frame. After working with his slide-rule for a couple of hours and running some bench tests, Ellis calibrated the throttle system to allow a much lower selectable setting. This gave the new hovercraft just enough gas power to lift and balance on the air cushion below. It would never be a regular use vehicle but, as a prototype for a possible BUZZ conversion, it looked like a sound prospect.

The orbiting MAGENTA finally released POD DS335. Mission Control hoped to drop it within ten kilometres of the rock fall known as Evan's Place. The two remaining communications satellites in lunar orbit, TEL 1 and TEL 3, were not equipped with cameras, so no landing zone could be identified prior to its arrival. That necessitated a 24 hour delay while the orbiting MAGENTA mapped the area and Houston analysed the surface detail.

After her sleep period, Lucy and the Deep Race team returned to the Long View Traveller to continue their scavenging and retrieval effort. She travelled atop 2,2,1, enjoying the ride and looking forward to completing the task. They had already sorted through masses of debris, but today's scheduled task included retrieving body parts and carcases. That depressed her.

After offering their usual tribute, one of the four aliens disappeared towards the wreck, while 2,2,1 scratched letters and drawings in the dust for Lucy. The drawing showed a Deep Race body shell with its legs and claws separated. He drew two of his team carrying a clawless carcass, with Lucy holding what looked like a bucket containing a leg and a claw.

LUCY HELP

His team mate arrived back from the wreck, pulling a device like a crushed shopping basket on wheels. Inside it he had placed an arm, a leg, one of the small claws and a small broken piece of body shell. During the next four hours she filled it several times, causing a repeat of the tribute ritual from whichever one of them she handed it to.

239

By the end of the day there was a sizeable pile of items at the bottom of the rough trail leading out of the crater. Lucy indicated that her air was getting low and she would need to return to NEIL. By drawing pictures of the Earth showing the moving daylight line, 2,2,1 asked if she could spare about one more hour, and she tapped her helmet twice; "Yes". At the speed they travelled, she knew they could be back in ten minutes if necessary, and there was plenty of air in the suit for contingencies. As a base commander, she was making her own safety margin decisions.

Oxygen was still a worry. She had given Life Science specialist Tobin the tank readings from NEIL and then parked the issue as something she couldn't influence. With tank 2 empty, NEIL was drawing on tank 1, with the remaining tanks having been tested to make sure they would still feed the system. The inbound POD carried no oxygen, and because it had left Earth before her accident the question hadn't arisen. It did pack standard emergency gear including three suits, with oxygen supplies totalling 24 hours, plus the ambient air aboard.

2,2,1 made several claw gestures and his team headed for the spaceship, leaving Lucy by the trail. They spread out in line abreast, and started a very fast circuit around it. Moving outwards, it turned into a spiral, widening until they had covered a circle some 200 m across, more like a 'D' shape as the site was so close to the remains of the crater wall. Twice they stopped, picking something up. Judging by their reverent attitude to the dead, she guessed it would be more body parts; the team was completing one final sweep of the site.

On completion, three of them approached the forward part of the wreck. One ran towards Lucy and stopped with rear arms raised, indicating that she should ride. This time it wasn't 2,2,1; she thought it might be 3,1,5.

She was placed behind them to witness the dedication. All the dead and the associated body parts were inside this part of the spaceship. The last few were carried in to join them. The external door was lower and wider than a human door. They had chosen this piece of wreckage because it had a door somewhere inside that would still seal. She was not allowed to enter, as it was now hallowed ground.

The ceremony was much the same as the one she had witnessed each time the Deep Race had approached the site. The only difference came at the end, when each of them nipped off a small piece of one rear small claw and placed them in a line where they had stood. Each time Lucy had witnessed it, the weight of their tribute ceremony had moved her. Now it was as if they were leaving part of themselves to watch over their dead. She felt a great sadness for their loss and wanted to make her own gesture. Out of nowhere she had an idea.

The Deep Race walked 100 m from the wreck. One of them headed off to one side, one large claw dragging a piece of metal debris through the dust to make a wide line. 2,2,1 turned to her and drew in the dust just outside the new marker; the front piece of the wreck with a circle around it, and Lucy with the four of his race shown outside the circle. The circle had a salient at one side, showing that the rear part of the ship stood outside the exclusion zone. He added one word:

THANK

The other one re-joined them, having completed the line. 2,2,1 raised his rear arms and she settled onto his shell for the ride home to NEIL. As they approached the trail up the crater wall, his three shipmates stopped at the scavenged pile and picked up an item that

241

had fired her interest; a 15 m metal beam which they had worked free from the rear part of the huge ship. They manoeuvred it onto their backs, each holding it there using a different combination of claws.

They had struggled with the beam for two hours the previous day, clearing debris and pulling panels away from the side of the wreck around it. Finally she had watched as two of them cut it free, balancing at difficult angles within the framework they had been uncovering, and using their largest rear claws to nip at it until it was severed. Apart from holding onto them to ride, it was the first time she had witnessed the biggest sets of claws in use. They were immensely powerful, slicing through the metal a few centimetres at a time. Several smaller beam sections remained at the pile for retrieval to Evan's Place.

Lucy knew exactly what was planned for those beam sections, but she wasn't letting that piece of information reach Gene's. Oh, no. The two species on the staff at Evan's Place intended to take their combined destiny back into their own hands, and claws.

Lucy asked 2,2,1 to accompany her inside NEIL. He indicated that the others would head off to fetch some more of their retrieved gear. Once through the airlock she took off her mittens and attracted his attention while she knelt down and drew a picture showing a circle with four claw pieces outside it. Then she bit the end off one of her fingernails and placed the piece on the page. 2,2,1 moved to where she knelt and leaned across to her with all four arms, the eight sets of claws held closed. In turn, the tip of each claw touched her forehead. He then wrote:

TEAM LUCY
THANK THANK THANK THANK

With great care he picked up the fingernail and entered the airlock.

"Gene's, it's Evan's."

"Go, baby."

"Hi there Paula. How are you? I'm ready to report on the scavenging day."

"Cool. POD down, 4,200 m your west-southwest. Eve's team gone for beer. Beer..." She sighed. "Lucy, girl, go fix NEIL and fetch coffee?"

"Wow-wee. Four klicks is an amazing result. When you get a chance would you make sure to tell those guys from me that they deserve their beers. My day gets better and better."

"Can do." She smiled. "So, whassup?"

"Well, we completed the body retrieval. The Deep Race have now sealed the front of the wreck and dedicated the site with a marked absolute exclusion zone of about 100 m. It doesn't seem to be all about religion or customs; they turned out to be pragmatists too. The Exclusion zone was negotiable, because they modified it to leave the engine end of the wreck outside. I guess that's because they either want more stuff out of there, or they know that our people will want to examine it.

"We've started recovering some of their pile of scavenged items back here, most of which look like complete junk to me. There are a couple of things that may come in handy. Oh yes, and one of them gave me a present. He was quite excited and said he had looked for it all day. It's a rock from their home world. They often carry one on long space trips." She held up a smooth, almost spherical, greenish pebble about 10 cm across for Paula to see. "It's a bit like onyx, and it's beautiful."

"Pretty. They know you a rock hound?"

243

"No, we haven't discussed mission specialities as yet, although I think I know theirs."

"Two probs," said Paula, "Every geo on Earth'll want rock, every scientist wanna see wreck."

Lucy laughed. Sometimes Paula was nearly as difficult to understand as her Deep Race friends. "I've taken the usual crop of pictures. I need to get cataloguing before I forget what they are all about.

"Oh, and while we were over there I did pluck up the courage to ask if we might have a small piece of Deep Race shell to analyse. I suspected they would say no, and hoped I wouldn't offend them, but I had to ask. Their reaction really surprised me. There was an immediate and deep tapping discussion and then 3,4,2 gave me a piece out of my basket. He's their science guy. We were all outside the final exclusion zone at the time. Then he and 2,2,1 had what I can only describe as an argument, facing off and waving their biggest claws at each other for a few seconds. Then they tapped shells in the longest exchange I have yet seen. Actually I think their normal speech mode is like yours; brief.

"In the end, 2,2,1 asked me for the piece back. When I handed it over he bent a claw round and actually nipped a piece off the side of his own shell for me. Never mind my alien rock, the lab boys can fight over that all they want."

40 – MUTINY
9:00 AM (LST) 3rd OCTOBER

Redwood walked out of the elevator, and the low buzz of conversation stopped dead as every face in the wide open office turned to look at him. The entire Senior Management core team was present at their workstations. He immediately felt uncomfortable, intimidated by their silence and the range of icy stares. He stood in the centre of the large space and faced them off.

"I found an empty office here yesterday afternoon. I was told you all attended a meeting without informing me, and then went home. Would somebody care to explain that, because leaving this office unmanned represents a disciplinary offence?"

One of the men stood up and faced him.

"Yes?" prompted the already infuriated Acting—not Deputy—Director.

"If Leif puts the busy light on the door, we don't knock or call him. It means do not disturb. Must've happened last, oh, around three years ago."

Redwood snapped at him. "I sent a message at 10:00 AM yesterday with concise instructions to set up a proper appointment system." He whirled on Penny. "So, did you set it up or not?"

"Yes, Deputy Director, I did. Nobody requested an *Imperial* audience."

"I've already TOLD you," he shouted. "It's ACTING Director." There was a smattering of laughter, but by the time he looked back everybody was still.

"Funny, is it?" he screeched. "Who authorised a meeting with the Moon without telling me? Huh? Which one of you is so stupid—"

"That's enough, Will." Houston liaison manager Blake Shermann stood up and interrupted him. "Leif left you in charge, but only until he gets fit. That doesn't herald an immediate regime change, and after what we've all seen so far you'll be looking for a lot of new managers if you ever get to take over."

"Yes I will. And that'll be you for a start, Shermann. I'll be looking for a new HLM. Culver may not get back, and you lot will either get used to the idea or we will be falling out. Sit down."

"It's not us," replied Penny from behind him. He turned once again, to find the woman on her feet as well. "You really don't get it, do you? We've not fallen out with you, *Deputy* Director. We just expect a little respect by whoever is in charge. You know, as if we were all grown-ups."

"That doesn't excuse the fact that you've been holding meetings behind my back."

He caught the still-standing Shermann's eye, and received an uncomfortable 1000 m stare.

"Look, Will," Shermann said, in a conciliatory tone. "You had the lights on the door. That means we don't call you. That is the correct procedure, and it's in your famous book. We all adhered to it exactly as written because we know how you love order." He shook his head. "You can't fight us on that." There was some more sniggering.

"Enough! I've already told you, oh give me strength, you all have a brain, can't any of you even see—"

"No, Vom. No we can't." There was a loud crash as a chair went over backwards and a new adversary stood up. Jancis Szymkowiak stood 1.88m tall and towered over Shermann as she moved to stand alongside the tubby ex-astronaut. Redwood started to feel even more nervous. Shermann was difficult enough, but Szymkowiak always intimidated him; it wasn't only her sheer stature,

246

but her reputation as both a brilliant propulsion specialist and a genuine space hero. Jancis exchanged glances with Shermann and he immediately deferred, rolling his eyes at Redwood before sitting down. The Acting Director thought he had read "we warned you" in his expression.

Jancis was fuming. "So far you've either strutted or raged every time you've come through here. Stop doing that because it makes you look both stupid and incompetent. Yesterday you threw things at us, and I've trained my two year old not to do that.

"The meeting you missed was the regular daily report and started at 1:00 PM. Nothing changed, so not being in the lecture theatre was nobody's fault but your own. They are making real progress up there, but apart from shaking hands with the President and smiling at the camera you've achieved, what exactly? What have you actually done for us, Will? I'll tell you what. You've contributed nothing."

He opened his mouth, but she cut him off.

"No. Oh no, Vom. *I'm* speaking now and *I'm* not finished so *you* can stand still and listen to *me* for a change. This department and office doesn't work, and *will not* work in a dictatorship. Everyone on this floor is here because The Director rates our opinions. Leif manages the business by taking the best ideas on offer and working with them. Yesterday you shot yourself in the ass and found yourself sidelined by your own specific orders. Now you are trying to blame all the people you should be apologising to. It all makes you look weak and stupid in spite of your high-and-mighty attitude. You deserve exactly what you're getting.

"Jancis, I..." He stopped as she stepped forwards, retreating until he was backed up against Penny's desk.

"Do you want to know what happened at the meeting? Do you really want to know? They loved the fact that you failed to show up because you were sulking, and everybody, *everybody* in the theatre thought it was hilarious because you did it to yourself. We laughed, Vom. You've spread your attitude across the entire business and everybody feels the same way.

"It doesn't seem to have occurred to you that nobody wanted or needed to talk to you yesterday. We run this operation with Leif as a figurehead; a friend and advisor to us all. He can get the job done with about four polite words. You? You're a piece of shit. Go flush yourself."

She sat down to a smattering of applause, leaving him fuming and lost for words. Someone, he didn't see who, threw the door wedge with some force so he had to dodge it. As he was making the decision to retreat, Blake Shermann stood up again and attempted a spot of diplomacy.

"Will, would you climb down and work with us? Try it today, because you might even like it. I'm telling you for free that you won't get any cooperation from us till you do. So look, there is a full report on yesterday's meeting in your messages, which Penny here kindly wrote up at home last night. You're the best procedures expert in the business and we need your brain power like everybody else's, but so far you have chosen to fight us. Stop acting like a complete dick and help us rescue Lucy, would you?"

He had had enough, and retreated back into the office. This time he shut the door and left the light off. Nobody called and there were no appointments in the file. After an hour he called Culver.

41 – POWER
8:40 PM (LST) 3rd OCTOBER

One more working day remained until the 354 hour lunar night set in. Before Lucy could settle down and sleep, Thibodeaux called for a discussion between Evan's, Gene's, and Houston. He studied the scene inside NEIL, where the four aliens sat along one side of the ceiling opposite to Lucy. There were bits of paper and marker pens scattered everywhere.

"Hi, Lucy. Am I interrupting a language lesson?"

"No, We're talking about anything and everything, using a combination of tap codes, gestures, and written words. It's exciting and frustrating in equal measures. Would you like a brief report?"

"Sure. You and I are meeting Lancaster and Houston soon to talk about nightfall. It's already dark here, you know."

"I hadn't given that any thought. I'm planning to do the POD run after I sleep. These guys say they don't sleep, but have a quiet rest period. As usual, 2,2,1 says he will carry me there. I understand Houston did an astounding job on the drop."

"They did. The latest data places it 4,200 m from your position, bearing 257 degrees. It's only a few metres south of the West Way so you won't even need to search. We have an extra procedure for you to work on before dark. One of Houston's systems engineers is standing by with that. So, what else have you learned about those aliens of yours today?"

"Oh, lots. 4,4,2,2,1 is their de facto Commanding Officer. He's one rank above the others, hence the 4,4 tag, but admits he's only a junior guy from the bridge crew. The others all start with 5,4, so are therefore one rank below. One is a maintenance tech, one a caterer, and the other a sociology specialist. He was the one who gave me the rock.

"I've been busy trying to nail down their origin and purpose. It appears they're contractors for a race who look like us, from much further in towards the centre of the galaxy. The two races often work together, and similar creatures are scattered everywhere in known space. This particular sect originates from down the Orion Arm, somewhere beyond Rigel from our viewpoint. Our best approximation, given the difficulty of translation, would be 3,000 light years from here.

"They say it's a pity their starship was lost, because their base team on Europa doesn't have the resources to build another. However, the Europa base does have communication with their home planet and would send a mayday call if they knew about the situation here. If they do that, help will come. The problem is that the forward base here on the Moon expected to be in operation for two years before returning to Europa, with no communication between here and there because of the possibility of detection by us. Therefore the Europa base doesn't yet know that they lost the mission ship with only four survivors.

"Here's an important exchange for you, Ajax, and I'll show you the cartoons we drew about it. I've made notes on many of them, and I've kept everything for later analysis. I asked about their name tags. You already know that the formal address for 2,2,1 is 4,4,2,2,1. He gave me a sheet showing him pictured above the others and noted as 4,4,2,2,1. The ones below him are marked 'TEAM'. The next picture is me, above three other humans and noted as 4,3,LUCY and TEAM. Note that he assigns me equal rank to his. I drew this next one, him as -,4,2,2,1 and me as -,3,LUCY. The reply was this one. Can you work it through?"

Thibodeaux looked at the four small drawings for a few seconds. "Human, Deep Race, human, human. I get the notation on the first two, a human, 4,3,LUCY, and Deep Race member

4,4,AWAY FAR. They come from a long way away. The first number, is that a species identifier, or a location? Oh, in that case these two other humans are, wait a sec, 1,-,-,-, AWAY AWAY FAR FAR and 2,-,-,-, AWAY AWAY AWAY FAR FAR FAR.

"Is he telling us we are his closest neighbours, but that two other human races are further out there? Are they the same humans but different locations, or different kinds of human races altogether? Good grief."

"That's how I see it, and as questions go it's the biggie; one to set this human race thinking."

Thibodeaux didn't know whether to be more amazed at the sheer amount of new information, or the content itself. "Lucy, I'm blown away by all this. I wish I could get a grip on it all. Earth life changes from this moment. Everything you give us is going down to Lancaster for analysis."

"I know, and I'm working hard to make every exchange with them as clear as I can."

"One other thing before I hand you over; oxygen supply. Life Science has been monitoring your reported readings. Your Deep Race team each use a little under half what you do, so the consumption number uses a baseline of three humans. Tobin says that NEIL's main supply will last until sometime on the 12th. You have three external suits in the POD, giving you 24 hours extra personal supply."

"OK, that's ten days supply, and I can park that because I can't influence it in any way."

"Anton Levine is standing by. He'll list your options and the plans they have worked up for resupply. I'll put you through now. Go ahead, Ton."

Anton appeared on Lucy's screen, looking relaxed and confident. "Hey there, Lucy. On behalf of the Mission Control teams I want to report some options we have for you; both those already available, and some we are still working on."

"Sounds good, Ton. So what have you got?"

"OK. Mt. Rainier will receive the latest used POD back tomorrow. Tavis says his boys can turn it in record time and stack it for a high-G launch late on the 6th. You can expect a more specific supply run four days after that, with enough oxygen to put that off our worry list. With one POD currently at your location, one to recover from LEO-NINE to Earth and two on the ground at Gene's, that's the next available. Tavis wants to know if he needs to manifest anything else specific.

"The suggestion of having you lift in the POD for a return to Earth is officially on hold, because we don't have enough data on your Deep Race. As yet we're not allowed to risk bringing them to Earth. In fact the Reunited Nations is still close to meltdown on that subject.

"That's political of course, but operationally it's still available. Whether the RN likes it or not, here at Houston we are working on the procedure. It would mean lifting off in your POD with, or possibly even without, your aliens, followed by a rendezvous with the MAGENTA for transfer to one of the LEO stations. We are still unsure of the orbital debris risk following the comet impact. That's a high priority, and Exploration is working up a mission to remove tracked pieces from orbit, one way or another. That's as it stands for now."

His tone boosted her. "Thanks a lot. Having you work up a plan for every eventuality is reassuring. I've got plenty to occupy my head here."

"You're welcome. That's everything from me, but I want to connect you to one of my systems specialists to discuss another upcoming problem."

"OK, Ton, thanks for all that. Speak to you later." The screen switched. "Hello, go ahead, systems."

"Hi, Commander Grappelli, we haven't met before. I'm Stacey Merman, an Electronics Engineer in the systems office at Houston. Good to meet you."

"Stacey, pleased to meet you too. Please call me Lucy, I'm not comfortable with being a commander just yet."

"Thanks, Lucy. Can I say hello to those Deep Race guys?"

"Sure, they do watch when we're having a meeting here. Have you seen the salute?"

Stacey grinned at her. "Seen it? Everybody is doing it. You've been on every single screen in the world the last couple of days." She held out her arms and made the four-claw salute. The Deep Race immediately stood to attention and saluted her back, then sat back down and continued their observation.

"I feel honoured," she said, "You're so lucky to have been the one to discover them. It's going to change your career some. Do you have any idea of the sheer scale of the media frenzy down here?"

"I've tried not to worry about that yet. I'm kind of living from day to day at the moment."

Stacey laughed easily, making Lucy relax a little. "Glad you mentioned day to day living. That's what we need to help you with. How is NEIL's power supply holding up?"

"So far, so good. I've not used anything much apart from air and comms. It draws a lot less with the drive wheels pointing into space. Power is showing 22% right now."

"That's not too bad for a 1,400 km drive and a five day camping stop. Commander Thibodeaux told me not to serve it with sugar. It's sunset tomorrow. You will need the heater and a lot more lights."

Lucy liked the girl's businesslike approach. "I was planning to move down to the POD if the power goes out here. I've not had time to walk there yet. There is power available in the DS335 POD, am I right?"

"Yes there is, but limited air. There isn't enough battery power to see you through fifteen days of darkness. It's not designed as an emergency shelter. You would have to walk across and charge up suits with oxygen from NEIL.

We have a plan to source some power, charge NEIL, and see you through the lunar night. NEIL has a standard power line and connector. You're sitting right on the West Way; well at least you were until you got rolled. What else runs along there?"

Lucy shook her head, "Dunno."

"The power supply cable from the West and Central Array Solar Stations."

"Oh, wow, of course it does. We planned to recharge at the Central Array. We've done it before on the longer survey trips. Does that mean I can plug NEIL into the line here somehow?"

"Yes. Well, on several counts, no as it stands. At least one of those two facilities must have taken some damage and/or dust contamination because power generation is down. The feed to Gene's is still showing 72% nominal. Also, the power line is buried somewhere under the rock fall between you and the trail.

"Here's a short history refresher. Ever since the Apollo 13 crew discovered that the CO_2 filter in one end of their spacecraft didn't fit in the air scrubber unit at the other end, way back in 1970, everything on spacecraft is standardised. That's why those DS PODs can rendezvous with any lift system; MAGENTA, TUG, or Corona.

"The ten-kilometre cables that make up the solar feed connect using the same plug set as NEIL. You can disconnect the

254

feed to Gene's while you charge NEIL up. That brings us to the second problem; how to find a cable connector which, by definition, will be not more than five kilometres away from your position. In any case, you should be able to find a connector after a walk of ten kilometres or less. In theory you can unplug it and drag it to NEIL.

"It's already night at the East Array and at Gene's. They need the power that's running past you from the Central and West Arrays. They can sit tight on batteries while you charge NEIL, as long as you connect the cable up again when you're done. I need to state the obvious here, but the cable connectors are universal and NEIL would plug into either part. It's important to plug your feed line into the end of the cable that runs from the Arrays, that's the piece stretching west from your position, or you will be draining the battery set over at Gene's.

"The bottom line is, if you can find the power connector nearest to you, Gene's will have to wait for hot coffee until you plug them back in. When you call in and tell them you need it, they will go to minimum consumption until NEIL is charged. They already have a low-use regime in force."

Lucy was impressed, both with Stacey Merman's plan and the confidence she had projected delivering it. "That's brilliant, Stacey. I am sure the Deep Race guys will help me find it and get it this far. I've never seen this cable. Is it buried, and is it heavy?"

"It was buried 10 cm below the surface. It's grey, but if I'd been designing it I would have had it done in orange to make it easier for you to find the damn thing, and left a traffic cone by each of the line plugs."

Lucy had a revelation. "Stacey, there are cone markers on the trail at exact 100 m intervals. Evan and I have left thousands of them on our trailblazing trips, and it's slow work. I'd be willing to bet the last of my toilet paper supply that every hundredth one stands above a connector. It's obvious; stop, connect a new cable, drop a cone."

"Oh, yeah. There's no record of that here, but it's good logic. I can't wait to hear what you find."

Lucy already had schemes whirling round in her head. She laughed. "Simple stuff, then. I predict a busy day around here tomorrow. Check this list with me:

"Before sundown I need to head west and find the POD, dig up anything up to ten kilometres of cable, locate the connector, drag the Galaxy only knows how much of it back over here, and charge NEIL. Then I have to get it connected again so they can make fresh coffee over at Gene's.

"I just thought of another point. To give me enough slack to drag the cable, it really has to be the connector east of here towards Gene's. Heck, I'll never finish this knitting." They both laughed.

"Do you know what, Stacey? With the team I have here, I bet we can do it all. These Deep Race guys are resourceful and fast, so it should be easy enough. I really appreciate all that. Thanks a lot."

42 – FOUND
1:00 AM (LST) 4th OCTOBER

Lucy and the Deep Race team worked up a plan for the final hours of daylight. 2,2,1 was keen to build a lever to try and right NEIL. In the end Lucy made an executive decision, pointing out that they needed power more than everything else. If they started with the cable, then righted NEIL and charged up, everything else would fall into place. They had to locate the POD anyway, and that was best accomplished before sunset.

Completing everything on the list was optimistic, but planning it out was good for her morale. One of the problems in communicating with the Deep race was her constant feeling of it being two dimensional. The occasional claw gesture helped, but with no facial expressions to learn it was hard to gauge if they had any feelings.

Lucy knew she could put in a thirty hour work period if necessary; she could pay it back with a long break after dark. She snatched three hours of sleep before kicking off the big day of challenges.

The Deep Race had a supply of the algae they used for food from the wreck. It looked like dried spinach. They each moved over a large piece and sat down on it, presumably eating it through a mouth located underneath. On the points of their shells each side of their arms they had small eyes, making eight in all and therefore giving them 360 degree vision. They were also able to work the airlock controls, so they didn't need Lucy to allow them in and out. Before she lay down they took themselves outside, telling her they needed to move more rocks in preparation for the righting attempt.

* * *

257

Lucy's morning dawned bright and clear. *Yeah, right, who am I kidding?* The sun had been up for two weeks. In less than 36 hours Evan's Place would be plunged into darkness for the next two.

She lay on the mattress for a few minutes, wondering if she could have made it through the night alone. After the scares following the crash, she knew it would be terrifying here in the dark solo. The shadows were already very long, and she shuffled to the side until she could see Earth. That always made her heart leap. "To visit Earth," she had said, and later 2,2,1 had echoed the sentiment.

The Reunited Nations was going to have to make the decision to accept them, because whatever else happened she was taking them all to visit Earth. Why not? If they all got through this, Lucy and the Deep Race team would have saved each other's lives. She felt bonded to them.

The expedition started off with Lucy picking her way west through the rock fall. The Deep Race had gone ahead to the edge of the fall a bit earlier, telling her they would move some rocks out that way. It was her first chance to survey the landslide. This far from the collapsed crater ridge, the rocks were more scattered about than heaped up. They had been unlucky to get caught in it, as the fall was only about 200 m across.

On the other hand, she decided that NEIL must have rolled more than once, looking at the distance from the trail to the final stop. It was no wonder she had been so knocked about when she came to. If NEIL had travelled another 100 m the Deep Race would have found her dead inside the wreck, across the crater from their Long View Traveller.

2,2,1 was with the others at the edge of the fall, and they waited while she had a good look around. Then he pointed a claw and moved north along the edge until he was near the West Way.

She followed him to where he had drawn a picture in the dust. Her heart fell as she realised what was coming.

The now familiar cartoon figures were in a straight line, pointing towards a specific point in the edge of the fall. The team now stood in line along the same heading, indicating the way. At the end of the drawn line he had drawn a human stick figure, lying down with three rocks on top of him.

Tears fell, but she waited long enough to write, acknowledging all four of them with a Deep Race expression using their own vocabulary:

LUCY TEAM
THANK THANK THANK THANK

She walked slowly to the edge of the rocks. Like where she had exited the fall further down, there was a lot of debris lying outside the main body of the fall. She worked her way round several large boulders, looked back to check on the four creatures still standing in line, and adjusted a little to the right.

Evan lay on his back in a small space between the rocks. His chest and one leg were crushed. The suit had lost pressure, but his helmet and faceplate were intact. The rocks pinning him had been moved and the space cleared for her to find him uncovered. She knelt and placed a gloved hand on the broken chest.

The words came unbidden. "Oh, Evan, if only you could've been here to enjoy the fun. I'm so sorry you had to wait this long for me, buddy. Look, I still have some survival stuff to do, but I'm coming back for you before it gets dark. You wait here and rest easy for now, eh? Oh, you made me smile one last time."

She didn't know whether she was laughing at herself for making the age-old Canadian joke at him one last time, or crying at the loss of a true friend. Here lay a guy with a genuine sense of fun, and an open and cheerful personality. That old song lyric came back to her again, "Laughing and crying, you know it's the same release." The deep ache of loss and sadness pulled at her insides. Maybe she would kneel here for a while beside her best friend, and remember him a little longer. *A few minutes? An hour? Maybe forever.*

She knew he wouldn't have allowed it. "Get cracking, Lucy-Lu. Work to do, y'know, eh. One rock at a time." She heard the words, no, felt them. Well, it was his catch phrase and there was no doubt that's what he would have said. Before leaving him she willed herself to look in through the visor. He could have been taking a nap; the famous McEwan forty winks. He didn't look hurt or distressed. Somehow that made her feel better, but the deep ache would remain. She spoke his mantra out loud:

"Get cracking, Lucy-Lu. Work to do y'know, eh. One rock at a time."

Eventually she stood up and returned to the team. They were waiting for her in their grief stance, arms hanging limply on the gravel. She knelt too, leaning forwards and letting her arms hang to the dust. As she joined them in the pose, they rose and delivered their full honour ritual, facing where he lay. She knelt with them in the grey dust trying to sing "Oh Canada", but she couldn't contain her emotions enough. When their ritual was over, the Deep Race surrounded her kneeling form and tapped softly on her back and shoulders in a rhythm she hadn't heard before. Finally she stood up and held each of the four proffered small claws for a few seconds. Evan had received full honours. She felt a growing fondness for them. *No, that's not it; not enough. I've only known these guys a few days, but I love them.*

2,2,1 started writing in the dust again:

260

EVAN SAFE SOON
II-II-I EVAN NEIL II-II-I LUCY POD
III-I-IIIII LUCY NEIL III-I-IIIII POD
II-IIIII-I / III-IIII-II CABLE

She thought about it. The first comment was cryptic; one of those lost in translation. She decided to seek advice.

"Gene's, Lucy." Her voice cracked.

"Hey Lucy, it's Mario. Are you OK? What's up?"

"Mario, we are outside the main rock fall. The Deep Race brought me to Evan. They did say they knew where he was."

"Oh... You OK?"

"Yes. I wasn't a minute ago, but I have to be now, so I am. Stand by." She took a few deep breaths and he waited.

"Mario, I need some advice here. Please can you ask the commander what he would like me to do next. I am going to mark the place and return to either retrieve or bury Evan later today as directed. For now, we need to get on and complete the survival tasks before nightfall."

Now Mario sounded distressed. "I will call you back soon. I am so sorry; Evan was a cool guy and he always made me laugh. I don't have too many... friends..." She could hear the distress.

"That's what I told him, Mario. I knelt by him and found myself laughing at the things he said. The Deep Race found and uncovered him, but left him for me to see exactly where he was. He didn't look hurt, which is good. Then they paid him their ritual tribute. I was so touched..." That was it. She couldn't go on, but clicked the microphone twice.

Mario understood. He clicked twice back.

Sitting in the dust, Lucy willed herself to stay strong and focus for a little while longer. "Get cracking, Lucy-Lu." It echoed in her head, but in his voice. He felt close, as if he was still there right beside her. She shook her head. With a weary sigh, she drew the little monogram of the five of them, and wrote:

POD
CABLE
EVAN

They tapped in the affirmative and went to work.

At least one of the tasks would be simple. It was a flat area and the POD came into view after a few minutes ride on 2,2,1. When they reached it, Lucy unhitched and pulled down the access ramp, transited the airlock and checked inside. Everything was in good shape, stores stacked high and tight.

The Deep Race walked around the edges studying its structure. Like all the other modular spacecraft pieces, it was a half-cylinder. The Resupply POD system was six metres in diameter. It was under half the standard unit length at nine metres, so a pair would fit inside the rocket payload shell. It sat on top of its lunar landing platform, a lightweight open scaffolding structure under a metre high and containing a dozen small rocket exhausts surrounding the fuel tanks and control box.

The team surprised her again by asking what the POD weighed. The answer from Houston was seventeen tonnes on Earth. The launch system weighed four tonnes, the POD itself another eight, including five tonnes of supplies. What did Lucy weigh? 0.11

tonnes in the suit. With the difference between ten digits (decimal) and eight claw (octal) based counting systems, they had settled on binary for precise calculations. Lucy did the conversion on her head-up screen. 2,2,1 confirmed that one POD would weigh the same as 154 of Lucy:

LUCY = I
POD = 10011010

The four of them walked round it again, checking the edges with their claws. There was a brief tapping conference and then two of them lifted a corner with their big claws. They made it look easy. A third slipped underneath, sat down and allowed them to settle it on his shell. He reached up and took hold of the scaffolding frame with several claws. After another brief tapping discussion they repeated the process at the second corner, experimenting with having just one of them doing the lift. Moving round, the other pair lifted the two remaining corners together and levered themselves underneath. Next, they rose to their feet as one, tapping messages to each other on the frame and presumably feeling the vibrations. Lucy stood and watched in sheer disbelief as they moved the whole thing about 10 m, before each setting down their own corner again, levering it with their big claws as they stepped out from underneath in pairs.

2,2,1 wrote:

LUCY POD
POD NEIL

Ten minutes later she reported in.

"Gene's, Lucy." There was a pause.

"Lucy, it's Ajax. I was waiting here till you were ready to talk. Are you OK?"

"Thanks Ajax. Yes, I'm good for now. I had a moment before, but I expected it. The Deep Race ceremony nearly finished me off. I don't want to discuss it at the moment because I've parked the whole episode for now. I'll deal with it later. The busy day will help me. I need your advice."

"I am glad you asked. Lucy, I am so sorry it's all on you there. I couldn't have asked for anyone tougher."

"I wish I felt tough."

"It sounds like you're holding up better than we are, even if we all knew it was coming. Now, as to that piece of advice; I have spoken to Sara McEwan since your call. She would like Evan buried right there at the Evan John McEwan Station."

"Agreed. That's a fitting thing to do. It will have to be later when all the survival stuff is in the can. Did you tell her that the Deep Race located, uncovered, and then honoured him as one of their own?"

"I did, and she wants you to tell them how much that means to her, if you can get the message across. I agree on the timescale. Your survival and that of your team must come first. If you need to work right up to sunset any burial will have to wait. Shall we park that for now and discuss it later?"

"Yes please. It's not easy talking to you about it and I have so much to do in the next few hours."

"That's fine, Lucy. While we are on, I have some more general news for you. Wait until you hear what else Sara had to say. She's still shouting about how you 'asked' the President if you could name the site after Evan. It's already going down as the biggest ever 'tell' in known history. They still haven't stopped laughing about the look on his face at Lancaster. You nailed him to the wall there, with

264

no choice but to agree. That clip was seen by an estimated 95% of Earth's population and you are now a certified superstar. When you get back he wants to see you at The White House immediately.

"Not only that, but Sara wants to you Knighted, or whatever it is they do in Canada. You and Evan will receive The Solar Star at NASA. Shit. I shouldn't have said that bit, but I couldn't stop myself, and you haven't heard it. OK?"

"OK, I can sit on all that." She felt uncomfortable now, and needed to get off the subject. She almost wished they were still talking about how to deal with Evan's body. She switched to her most cheerful tone. "Hey, do you want a progress report from today?"

"Uh oh, it's that tone of voice. I'm getting to know the signs."

"I guess so. We found the POD and I don't even need to empty it."

"How so? Do I detect a Grappelli punch line?"

"Yep, I am aboard the POD right now, and the Deep Race team are, and I do mean literally, carrying it and me back to Evan's. Those guys amaze me."

Thibodeaux was laughing. "No, seriously? Every time I talk to you they have done something even more implausible."

With the POD set down by the edge of the rock fall, the Deep Race team wanted to start moving debris out of the way to make a proper path to carry it the last 100 m back to NEIL. So far the whole operation had taken under three hours. Lucy drew another picture indicating that it might be safer and more efficient to move NEIL outside the rock fall. 2,2,1 set all his arms and claws out at different angles and the others waved all theirs. He turned a complete circle while holding the pose, and joined in waving with the others. She had witnessed the equivalent of a head slap and the associated laughter. 2,2,1 had said "D'oh."

Two of them left again, heading east through the fall towards Gene's, after demonstrating their big rear claws dragging a 15 cm trench at almost their full running speed of around 10 km/h. They ran in single file, each pulling a big claw in the dust and turning it out like a farm harrow, first left, then right. It left an efficient scar. They were confident about finding the cable connector.

Lucy and the other two returned to retrieve Evan's body. 2,2,1 carried him, supported across his shell by several sets of claws. Lucy rode alongside on 3,1,5. She hoped there would be time for a ceremony later, but there was serious work to do before the Sun went down. They placed him in the lengthening shadow behind the POD.

The space in front of NEIL was all but clear, so 2,2,1 and 3,1,5 moved the last few remaining rocks out of the way. They had found a pivot to rest the girder on; a large rock with a sort of cleft shape in it stood ready. They rolled it to the top of the rock pile on the upside of the fall above NEIL, and wedged it into place. 2,2,1 went to work on it, shaping the indentation into a better slot for his girder to rest in it.

They placed one of the smaller girders along NEIL's roof line at ground level, moving a lot more of the loose debris around the LXV to make room. This would spread the lifting load of the big lever on NEIL's body shell. Lucy's efforts were useless in all this, as she couldn't move rocks of any real size. She tried to help moving the smaller stuff but it soon became obvious that she was getting in the way. She hadn't discussed the plan to right NEIL with the folks at Gene's. She couldn't wait to see their faces. Lifting the POD? They hadn't seen anything yet.

Lucy wasn't an engineer, but like most NASA crew she could fix most common bits of machinery. She didn't want to ask Gene's for any advice about the broken wheel in case it aroused suspicion. She sat inside NEIL reading through the manuals. There was no way to fix the suspension without spare parts, so she decided to remove the whole damaged wheel assembly in case it hindered the righting attempt.

Armed with the tool kit, she clambered up the pile of rocks on the upward side of the fall and hopped across to NEIL's upturned base. She had to climb over the various dusty drive trains and steering machinery to reach the damage, spotting the dented and torn oxygen tanks. There was a rock stuck between the base plate and the broken struts, allowing the wheel to sag overboard.

She levered the rock out using the wheel brace, and the assembly sagged even further. Leaning out over the edge, she tried to undo the six big nuts holding the wheel on its hub. She didn't want to drop the whole set of bars and struts overboard in case anything punctured NEIL. After a lot of contortion, which was uncomfortable on the still-tender ribs, the wheel fell, bouncing away from NEIL as it flew across the rock fall towards the crater.

It wasn't too difficult to detach the rest of the loose suspension assembly and the external drive shaft, leaving NEIL as the first ever seven-wheeler on the Moon. She tossed all the pieces across the cleared space to land near the Deep Race junk pile. Each wheel had independent drives, so there should be no problem using the three remaining motors.

The next real excitement came when the two linemen arrived back. A quick dust drawing for Lucy indicated that they had located the cable connector they needed to retrieve 8.3 km towards Gene's, and as predicted it was right below a marker cone.

2,2,1 had an idea. He drew his team pulling NEIL, with Lucy inside. The drawing had a comedic Wild West look about it and Lucy enjoyed a laugh, waving her arms about to indicate mirth. They joined in, but she knew they couldn't appreciate the joke. For the first time in their association she could upstage them. She drew a picture of NEIL with all five of them inside, driving to the cable. The Deep Race team members all did the arms akimbo and rotated in their head-slap gesture, then everybody waved arms or claws in a laugh.

Lucy moved her storage box step to the front of the cabin. Standing on it, she reached up into the space behind the drive console and pulled the circuit breaker marked NEIL SYS TELE. It would spoil the surprise if the intermittent telemetry at Gene's showed that she was using the drive system. Then she fired up the three remaining electric motors and pushed the drive and steering bar forwards. Outside, the three remaining drive wheels rotated.

Before they could do anything else there was more serious rock-rolling to do, because half of the fall was still blocking their exit eastbound. 2,2,1 went back to work organising his lever, while the other three started lifting and hurling rocks to the south, away from the direction of the trail. Once again, some of them sailed right out into the crater.

It took two hours to clear a track wide enough for NEIL to negotiate, if indeed they could get the wheels back on the ground. If

NEIL took any more damage in the process, she might still have to lift to orbit in the POD. Lucy presumed they were 100% confident that they would get NEIL rolling.

3,4,2 found and retrieved the wheel that had bounced away when Lucy disconnected it. She saw him rolling it back along the new path and laying it down next to the heap of miscellaneous bits and pieces brought from the wreck. She did wonder if they had firm plans for any of that stuff, had a sentimental attachment to it, or were just opportunist recyclers always willing to re-use material if they could find a way.

By the time 2,2,1 had his pivot ready, and the through road was clear, there were twenty hours of light remaining. The shadows behind everything were lengthening and Lucy was dog-tired. After a scant three hours of sleep, she had put in a twelve hour shift without a break.

She indicated that she needed some rest, and offered a suggestion:

SAME AIR
SAME FOOD
LUCY FOOD NEIL
TEAM FOOD NEIL

2,2,1 replied:

II-II-I / III-IIII-II / III-I-IIIII FOOD WE
II-IIIII-I LUCY FOOD THANK

The Deep Race team had scavenged enough from the wreck to last another three weeks. The POD held months of supplies for Lucy. With oxygen shipping in, she was much more optimistic. The Deep

269

Race ate a variety of fish and plant life from the oceans of their world. They definitely ate green food because she had seen some of it. Now their catering assistant would try Earth food for the first time. It worried her, but sooner or later they would have to try it. She knew that getting the juniors to take the plunge first made sense from the officer's point of view.

Lucy had the usual vacpac cold ready meal. So far she had found one-pot dishes, casscroles or pasta, almost edible cold, but if they got power later today she was heating up a steak.

The three Deep Race people having their normal fare got on with opening theirs. They kept their stock outside and ate the contents frozen. She guessed they weren't interested in food apart from as fuel, but then again their packaged stuff probably tasted as uninteresting as hers. She had been far too busy and tired to miss anything much, but she longed for one of Bird's amazing meals, maybe a spicy curry. That guy was a genius. While musing over food, she realised that right then she'd trade half her remaining oxygen supply for a cold beer.

She offered a choice of mixed raw vegetable packets to 2,5,1. He had seen how she opened them and slit one full of celery and lettuce with a claw. He tipped it out and walked over it to sit down and ingest. A minute later he repeated the process with a packet of cauliflower and broccoli pieces.

He wrote on the ever-present pad:

LUCY FOOD II-IIIII-I THANK
II-IIIII-I DIE
II-II-I / III-IIII-II / III-I-IIIII LUCY FOOD NO

Then he did the laugh movement, waving all his arms and claws about. 2,5,1 was joshing her.

She was exhausted, and sat on her mattress with her back against the wall. Her head started to nod. Ten minutes, that was all. She could afford ten minutes...

* * *

"Lucy? Lucy, baby? LUCY! It's Paula."

She jerked awake. "Uh? Paula, ah, yeah?"

"Lucy, you been sleepin', baby. Doc said give you three. Wake-up call."

"You what? Shit, no." The Deep Race had left. One of them must have put the blanket over her because it was folded under the table when she sat down. "How long was I out, how long till sundown?"

"Three plus thirty, uh, and fourteen plus seven. Saw you eat. No report, then sleep. They left."

"I need to find them. Screen off for five please, while I do some getting ready stuff. You know."

"Sure. How goes outside?"

She paused for a second. *Don't give it away yet, Lucy. Think before opening mouth.* "Yeah, it's OK. We surveyed the POD supplies and moved a lot of rocks to make access easier. The guys have been trying to make something to help drag power cables. They have wheels and stuff out there. Guess they are off on a new plan with their trash heap. They do keep busy." There, truth enough and no lies told.

"Good goin' baby."

Lucy put the plastic container back in the closet and zipped up her suit. It was time to put her delicate cover plan into action. Feeling sneaky, she moved to the open fuse access panel under the console. "Screen is up Paula." She was holding a pulled circuit breaker. She pulled another one out, and another.

"Negative. No screen. Lucy? Lucy, you there? "

271

After a pause, she switched to the suit radio. "Paula, something popped at the front. I'm on suit comms, EXT SUIT 2."

"Scared me. What went?"

"I don't know. I'm not that tech. Could be a row of circuit breakers by the sound of it. I definitely heard a pop, then a few more all at once." *Don't let on I've been reading the manuals.* "We have so much to do outside before dark, but I can report in fine on the suit link. After dark we can run checklists and I'll get into the manual. I wish we'd brought Kyran."

"OK, Ajax gonna dump."

Lucy worked hard to sound aggrieved at that comment. "Do you know what, Paula? He can. I've got more important stuff to do than get an earful of him today. Can you hold him off till after dark?"

"For you, baby. Go, work. I'm here two more. After is Mario. Ajax ain't crossin' that guy's line again anytime soon."

"Sounds like another story I need to hear later. Thanks Paula."

Exiting NEIL as fast as she could, Lucy found the scene outside set for the righting attempt. 3,4,2 waved to her and went to tell the others she was awake. They gathered round, and for a change it was 3,1,5 who started writing in the dust:

REST GOOD LUCY
NEIL WORK SOON

Language lessons had been almost constant at any time there was no other task under way. It was the first time she had been addressed by the team's Engineer. He was distinguishable by having a lighter dapple across the top of his grey shell. 2,2,1 was a uniform charcoal colour, the Scientist, 3,1,5 had a dark steely grey shell that paled at the top, and Catering Assistant 2,5,1 was an overall mid-slate shade.

Lucy wrote:

GOOD REST THANK
LUCY HELP WORK

All four of them shared a brief waving laugh at her embarrassment. 2,2,1 moved towards her and wrote:

NEIL READY

She tapped the affirmative, both sets of fingers to the sides of helmet. Everything inside NEIL was as ready as it could be. She might have put the storage box step in the bathroom, and the mattress back in her tiny bunk space but neither would do any harm. Everything else was secure.

He escorted her to the other side of NEIL to look over the equipment. The big triangular section metal girder tilted down from its cleft rock pivot at about 25 degrees, passing through a cleared space between the rocks below. At the surface it met another piece cut from the same stock, running along the middle third of the LXV at the roofline. The lever's lower end was cut in a neat 'V' shape to fit against it, and the pieces lashed together with something that looked like shiny plastic, to form a T-bar. The bar was cradled against NEIL with four shaped and padded metal attachments tied to it, curving around where the roof met the side to stop any slippage. Lucy had given up Evan's mattress to supply the padding.

She followed 2,2,1 up the rock-pile. Up-fall from the pivot rock was a gigantic boulder, It was half as big as NEIL, with a series of slots drilled into it. 2,2,1 demonstrated that two of his team would position themselves between the boulder and the lever, stretching out their biggest claws and grasping both. They would pull down on the lever in an attempt to roll Neil onto its side. After that they would reposition the rocks and the pivot for the second phase of the operation, tilting the LXV upright onto the remaining wheels.

Returning to the cleared space where NEIL would hopefully finish up, 3,1,5 showed her a set of dust-drawings depicting the recovery sequence in cartoons. She tried another of their semaphore signals, both arms out to the sides with all her fingers spread: "Impressed."

3,1,5 wrote:

LUCY SAFE WAIT

She followed him to the junk heap and he motioned her to stay put. Again she tapped her agreement. She could only think that this was a pivotal moment in her strange odyssey. The weak pun made her think of Evan, who would have roared laughing and cracked another one straight back at her.

We'll lay you to rest here soon buddy. I need to make sure we will survive first. She was in no doubt that he would approve.

She could almost sense him, as if he was sitting alongside her on the junk grinning over the whole affair. She'd never felt like that about anyone. Even when her Grandma died, she was immediately gone from everything, somehow beyond feelings. Here, in the deep silence of the Moon it was as if Evan was creating echoes somehow. Maybe the constant noise on Earth changed things, so you couldn't hear the ghosts. *Ghosts now, Lucy. Pull yourself together.*

The absurdity of the scene struck her. She felt like a spectator at some fantastic cosmic game show, but detached from the reality of the situation. This was their show; she hadn't contributed much to the practical effort.

Without any ceremony the game was on. 3,1,5 positioned himself where the others could see him. 2,2,1 and 2,5,1 reached up from the rocks beyond the pivot and caught hold of the girder. Finally, 3,4,2 joined them as they inched along underneath it right to the end, claws stretching wider until they could fit them into the drilled slots in the big boulder at the very end. The crab-like bodies looked surreal suspended there. 3,1,5 waved up to them, giving a go signal. They were strong, but it worried her to think they might cause themselves real harm at such a stretch. Lifting the Pod was one thing, but this looked difficult and dangerous.

For a few seconds nothing happened. Then NEIL's corner lifted off the ground. Almost too slowly to see, the gap widened to ten centimetres, then twenty, thirty. The roll-rate increased; she presumed that the angle was easier for the pullers. Suddenly NEIL rolled over to settle on its side, balanced between the roof line and the wheels. Lucy exhaled, dizzy from holding her breath.

They gathered to congratulate each other on phase 1. There was a general up-and-down arm and claw gesture. This she joined in with, tagging the new wave as "Way to go." 2,2,1 had one rear arm tucked away. She was right; it had been a big ask.

After a short break, they rearranged the kit. The plan called for moving the pivot rock forwards by a few metres and wedging it back in. The problem was that the pivot would no longer reach the big boulder with the slots. 3,4,2 drew a new picture to show Lucy that all four of them would have to grip the girder and pull it down. Lucy added her stick figure sitting above them on the end of the girder. Her offer was accepted.

She asked 2,2,1 about his rear arm. He wrote:

USE ARM II IIII
HURT ARM II
USE ARM I III
ARM II SOON FIX

He would use a different combination. Tough guy.

3,4,2 chocked the big wheels on the LXV, half-burying rocks against them. With NEIL needing to rotate more than ninety degrees this time, there was a risk of sideways slippage. It was also more critical because, if they failed, abort to orbit via the POD was the only option. The airlock was now underneath.

When they were ready to go Lucy clambered up to sit astride the girder, then shuffled backwards to the top end. The four Deep Race team members all performed the stretching manoeuvre, clawing their way along and taking their places as close together as they could below her.

The rocks below were not as big as the one with the slots, but looked a lot rougher. They would be able to get a grip. As she looked down, they started to pull. 2,5,1 was the one closest to NEIL. The rocks below him on each side of the slot where the lever angled down were a bit higher than the others nearby, so he was gripping two of them with his biggest claws, the two rear arm sets. The creature was stretched three ways.

She didn't feel the pulling start, but noted that 2,2,1's strained arm hung out unused. She worried that they would overdo it and sustain some real damage. There was a sudden jolt as one of them lost grip, then a bit of a scuffle below. She was closer to the rocks by maybe half a metre. Then it was all over and she saw a settling cloud of dust with NEIL at the centre, standing the right way up for the first time in a week. The girder pivoted sharply up as the Deep Race all let go, coming to an abrupt halt. Lucy nearly went orbital.

Laughing her head off at the thought, she clambered down. The scuffle below had occurred as 2,5,1 lost his three-way grip and slithered down between the rocks tight on each side of the lever. He was wedged almost upside-down at the bottom of the slot between of a pair of them. On the way down, he had dislodged a sizeable rock, and he was trapped underneath it.

2,2,1 had a quick look down to check the damage and then turned and gestured frantically at the other two. It was an awkward spot to reach. They both gripped the lever again and pulled it down so 2,2,1 could snag it. They lowered him into the slot, and he caught the rock trapping 2,5,1. They pulled him and the rock free, after which he let go again, diving straight back down to help his colleague clamber out. There was a short tapping session, after which the two others motioned Lucy down to the space where NEIL now stood.

2,2,1 drew on a lot of recent vocabulary and wrote:

II-IIIII-I EYE III NOT SEE
II-IIIII-I REST ROCK SOON FIX
II-II-I ARM SOON FIX

Lucy wrote back:

II-IIIII-I IN NEIL LUCY
WATER HELP EYE

2,2,1 immediately guided 2,5,1 to the now upright airlock door. By the time they arrived Lucy had the pop-out ramp deployed and was waiting inside. 2,2,1 came in first, followed by 2,5,1 who clambered halfway over his officer to make room for Lucy to shut the door. She could see his chipped and scuffed shell rim, and black fluid dripped from the eye on one protruding corner.

As soon as they were inside, Lucy grabbed a bottle and filled it from one of the big storage containers. She passed the bottle to 2,2,1, who signed his thanks with a rear arm as he set to work washing grit and dust away from the damaged eye. At least it wouldn't get infected; the Moon had no microbes. She sat in a proper seat for the first time in over a week. Opening a drawer, she retrieved the pad and pens and wrote:

II-IIIII-I NEED HELP

2,2,1 did something she hadn't seen before, and reached out rearwards with a small claw to take the paper while still dripping

278

water over 2,5,1's eye in front of him. It was the first time she'd seen the 360 vision in action, and multi-tasking with the small claws too. They were as adaptable as they were strong and resourceful. He wrote:

II-IIIII-I EYE NOT DIE OK SOON
II-II-I ARM NOT DIE OK SOON
GOOD SHELL WE

Lucy walked down to the POD to report in. It was far enough away from NEIL to avoid slipping up on her plans. Before she left they exchanged messages again, Lucy writing:

LUCY POD REPORT GENES
LUCY NEIL CABLE

The reply surprised her once again:

LUCY NEIL II-II-I / II-IIIII-I CABLE
III-IIIII-II / III-I-IIIII EVAN WORK
NEW LEVER

Their engineer had another scheme going already. They kept astounding her, well why not again? She decided she wouldn't even ask. She signalled "yes" and "impressed", then headed out.

"Gene's, it's Lucy outside the POD." She had not gone to the east side. Until they came back to deal with it later she had to pretend that Evan's broken body was not there.

"Hey, Lucy, good to see you.

"Hey to you, Pelican. I've got a quick progress report, as we're still busy. The Deep Race are dealing with the cable. I'm at the POD retrieving a few supplies." Now she was starting to tell lies.

Pelican was a chatty as ever. "That's all good stuff Lucy. Hey, you'll love this item I heard from Ajax. That ace-looking dude Sarkasian at Rainier refuses to believe they lifted the POD. He says that if you aren't actually hallucinating again then you have to be the first non-orbital Lunar POD traveller in history. He's a certified nut-job you know, and I need to meet him."

Lucy had to agree. "Tavis isn't quite as sparkly starshine mad as Kent Warwick though. He's all hard science with a wicked grin. Kent thinks original and sees stuff that isn't even there yet. He's a connector, linking ideas to sci-fi solutions."

"Oh, yeah, that reminds me. Tavis also wanted us 'to make damn sure Lucy offloads a yellow box outta my POD'. His words. Paula left the manifest with a note on it here somewhere, stand by... There you go, the ref number was DS335/BKOC/TS. He said you need to do that ASAP and transfer it aboard NEIL. It says on this manifest that it was one of the last things that he loaded and is 'a non-standard item'. Your guess is as good as mine."

"It's good to talk to you, Pelican. One thing I'm missing is the general chat. I can't wait to catch up on everything I missed, and laugh at everybody. So, would you guys make sure Tavis gets to see this camera shot for me? Here is the POD, and I'm walking round to the side now. Over there is the western edge of the rock fall. If I walk across here, you can see the entrance to the path we are clearing between here and NEIL, 100 m away."

She almost long-panned the shot to where NEIL would be visible, but caught herself in time. "Tell him thanks, I did see that yellow container and I'll carry it back right now. I'll make a full report half an hour before sundown. It will be a long one as we've had a busy day. Could you ask Paula to set it up in the lounge, so I can see everybody? After chatting with you, I'm missing them all. Even the guys I don't like."

Pelican laughed with her. "That's a great idea, Lucy. Your lounge lectures are the highlight of the day when you have time to do one. I'll find Paula and ask her to organise it. Here, I'm not so technical, but there's a screen clock running large scale here and it says you are minus 6:42 till sundown. Do you think you'll have power by then? Ajax said that when you do separate the cable we're going to have a minimum use exercise for emergency training."

"It's our intention to charged up by then. I'll call in if anything changes. Thanks, Pelican. Lucy out."

She went inside the POD, collected the yellow container and headed straight back to NEIL. When she arrived, 3,4,2 and 3,1,5 moved across from the pile to confirm the new plan:

III-IIII-II / III-I-IIIII WORK
NEW LEVER
NEIL CABLE

She tapped affirmative. Inside, both casualties waved a small claw from the rear corner of the cabin. She showed them:

NEIL CABLE

2,2,1 tapped affirmative. The driving seat was harder without the cover, sacrificed as a puke-rag over a week ago, but at least it was a proper seat. As she worked through her modified drive checklist, she worried about missing something. Several items were No-Go, including NEIL-TELE, NEIL-DRIVE, and NEIL-POSN. She had made sure the circuit breakers supported her supposed electrical failure, disabling all telemetry associated with movement. Apart from a red light against the missing drive wheel, the systems themselves all looked good. Power was down to 11%. She pushed the drive bar.

* * *

3,4,2 and 3,1,5 stopped work on their new machine for a moment, and watched as the big LXV eased forwards to negotiate the

282

roadway they had created. It headed eastbound out of the rock-fall to the cable junction. They stood together and tapped on each other's shells. 3,4,2 swore.

mating in it daylight # # well it flying fish shit i me never believed it wheelship would move # # maybe you i all we not some sunk in it bottom slime as far as it eyes after whatever is # # think you i we can we get all it these shells in it net before it creature brings they fish head seaweed back #

only if you i we eight-claw work-swim forwards-backwards as fast as it they small fish of it dark season #

it you can # # i me tired it food is running out # # it seaweed says more in it wreck # # if it fish head finds across the death line it seaweed cross a notch for it seaweed shell it egg or not it egg # # here it you think it fish head will die it arm #

it the nearly revered second senior navigation officer the heavy salutable current runner swimming star 54221/4-858635647-488221146 to it you name # # If it ever vibes it you tapping for it fish head snip it off it you mating claw # # it arm lose not lose it but a hero thing diving no-water vacuum it rocks between pulling it seaweed out # # it 3 arm a stretched claw already and a more worse to it in the hero-pull it did # # it seaweed may die the 6 eye think I me #

trying too hard and for the show off # it fish shit what it gliffer it #
smash on the beach stones with that # here it creature looks like it dead rrthyllett lying on it beach with it cover peeled off # # i

283

me glad it wears one cover over it wurt most of it time # # they
horrid legs and ugh it disgusting # #

it LUCY shares air # # it LUCY shares food # # it LUCY tries
to help and understand all we even if not strong in the pull and with
few it they claws # # i think it LUCY cute in skin like it anssentihf
from new egg if smooth and no it scale # #

stuck on it most deserted alien it moon ever found in it desert
so dried out it no moisture at all in it arse end of it spiral arm in it
galaxy nobody wants # # i me get what for company # # it 342 like
a pyllntt # # by it they drying seas of i my egg scales i me sick of
this # # use it they dead claws and help i me here # # they juniors
same all it they beach slime # #

it you they cloaca drips 44315/2-887642371-657463741
floating sea wave the indisputable night of starshine # # it 315
smells like it rotting fish that shit # #

yeah and it you it scum sucking shit worm ## crack it your
shell # #

Their three-second exchange over, the close friends tapped
a final salute, waved their claws in a laugh, and bent to the new
engineering task with a will.

* * *

Lucy was so excited at the discovery that NEIL actually worked she
found herself singing. *Damn good job the Deep Race don't have ears.* She
hadn't sung once in all the long hours that had passed since she
woozed into a vague, nauseated consciousness trapped upside-down
in this very seat.

284

Leaving the new lane through the rocks, she turned to meet the West Way, rolling at a steady walking pace for a while in case of control difficulties.

NEIL rode well with one drive wheel missing. She detected the slightest hint of a list, but the inclinometers were on the same circuit as telemetry. She guessed it was less than two degrees, well within the safety margins. The connector wasn't far, and she covered the distance in fifteen minutes.

The linemen had left a row of rocks placed across the trail. She could see the dug up cable box, and swung NEIL around off the trail to face back west. The cable feed cover was located forward of the airlock, so she stopped where it would be just a couple of metres away from the connector. At last, a job she could do without help from the two battered guys resting on the floor. She showed 2,2,1 a message before entering the airlock. It felt odd that it was now accessible at floor level:

LUCY CABLE
II-II-I / II-IIIII-I REST

He tapped in the affirmative.

A brief report to Gene's and she would attempt to connect. She faced away from the LXV where the lunar surface looked like that by the POD.

"Gene's, Lucy."

"Hey Lucy, it's Mario."

"Hey, Mario. Is the station on batteries?"

"Standing by for that on your mark. Do you have a time for disconnect?"

"We are all ready now?"

"OK, stand by." He checked with Ajax on the internal comm, then the taped emergency loss of power announcement started on the P.A. "We are on internal, Lucy. You are Go for disconnect."

The connector was in a snap-tight box, running back into the ground a couple of metres away in both directions. Lucy knelt by the box and pulled the clips open. She often charged outside equipment in the garages at Gene's, so the cable connector was familiar. She released the safety catches and unscrewed the connector ring. Her suit beeped to indicate a call. She selected radio, but not camera.

"Lucy, Ajax. Line in is down; power is yours. Please call us when you are done. Do you have a time frame?"

"Stand by."

She struggled with the dented hatch covering NEIL's charging cable. In fact the entire body shell was looking the worse for wear. LXV manager Ellis Ransome was going to kill her. She connected NEIL, and a green light glowed. *Yes!*

Back inside she checked the circuits and panels. NEIL was drawing power with a projected completion time set at minus 5:54.

Don't let on that we are by the cable. "Ajax, Lucy. We've done some cable-dragging calculations, plus charging time. It's not far, and we need it for about two plus forty."

"That's interesting, and sounds fast to me. That means the power drain Houston mentioned to you must be between Evan's and here, rather than west of you or at the arrays. After that you have less than three hours before sundown."

"Right now I'm on other tasks. I'll call you back when I have some time."

"Roger."

She moved her mattress back into the bunk space. Setting her watch for two hours and thirty minutes she exchanged a wave with 2,2,1 and lay down. If she shut her eyes and relaxed for a few minutes; the alarm was there for a backup in case...

* * *

Lucy jerked awake. "Oh, what?" The alarm was buzzing. She sat up and looked across at 2,2,1 and 2,5,1. No movement. She stepped into the bathroom to enjoy the luxury of a right way up toilet.

Power was 58%, way more than enough for what she needed. It was time to disconnect and get set up for her big reveal back at Evan's Place.

"Gene's, Lucy."

"Paula."

"Hey, Paula, ready for power-up?"

"Done chargin'? Numbers don't figure. Cable drag time'n all."

Damn, Paula's "Less talk, more think" approach was great for problem solving, but too much for any kind of real conspiracy.

"Looks good here. I haven't fixed the breaker panel yet; maybe it's something there. We have a couple more tasks and then I can look."

"You cookin' somethin' there? Yeah, baby, you dodgin' about now. How long it take you to drag that cable? Ain't stupid y'know."

"OK, Paula, OK. I had some inspired help from the Deep Race. Are you solo there?"

"Yeah, an' I'm back to bein' dumb."

"Thanks. Look, you got me. I am indeed cooking something and I could use some help. Are you showingmy report in the lounge? Can we start thirty minutes before sundown here?"

"Counter here says you got two hours plus forty-four."

287

"Will you make a couple of calls to Earth for me?"

"I'm itchin' here now. You gon' hit us again! For you, anythin'. What you need, girl?"

They discussed Lucy's new plan as she plugged the line back together. Having Paula on-side meant she could cover something much more important. Lucy agreed when Paula pointed out that it should be a NASA-wide announcement.

"Thanks, Paula. Cable is in now."

"Power is up. Ajax said to tell ya I can get coffee. And I'll have 'em all ready for ya."

Lucy laughed. "And you say I'm mischief, yeah? I know you're lying to me now. That coffee is all here in my POD."

Paula said something worthy of Redwood on a bad day.

She opened up a bit on the way back and cruised for a couple of minutes at 20 km/h. NEIL rolled as if riding on seven wheels was design optimum. She was soon back on the new path through the fall and passing the junk pile, heading for the POD out on the other side. The next hour was going to bring both fun and high emotion.

She pulled up by the POD and stared in sheer disbelief. Once again, they had out-smarted her. While she and the two injured team members had been off site, pieces of the cut-down lever had been inserted through the open scaffolding underneath. Threaded onto a new cross-bar and almost hidden underneath the scaffolding frame at the front end of the POD was the big wheel she had cut away from NEIL. At the rear end a bar had been added, braced and shackled underneath the bottom of the frame. Two more wheels stuck out at the sides, looking like smaller versions of NEIL's own wheels. She didn't recognise these, so they had to be from the Long View Traveller. Best of all, sticking out in front and attached to the cross-bar holding the big wheel was another piece of girder with a hook at the front. NEIL could tow the POD.

Lucy and her passengers joined the two outside, and she signed for "Impressed", "laugh", "D'oh!" and

"Impressed" again, in quick succession. They laughed at her, two of them waving a few less claws than normal. In the dust she wrote in very large letters:

III-IIII-II LUCY THANK
III-IIIII-I LUCY THANK
II-II-I LUCY THANK
II-IIIII-I LUCY THANK

2,2,1 had something to add to that:

THANK LUCY
I I I I I = NEW TEAM

She held out her hands and they all touched claws with her. Then she went inside and backed NEIL up so they could attach the POD to the rear suspension. The rear camera was shot, so 3,5,1 stayed in view at the front as banksman, guiding her back until 3,4,2 could drop the hook into place.

Lucy started the report using her suit radio with the camera off. Paula was working the controls at Gene's, and connected her to the lounge camera so she could watch the proceedings there.

"Good Evening, Gene's. This is the Evan John McEwan Lunar Research Station with the Lunar sunset report. Thanks for assembling early, because we have a lot to get through."

"Good evening, McEwan. The Eugene Francis Kranz Lunar Research Station is receiving your call. Lucy, this is Ajax. Do you still have technical problems? We can't see you."

"Apologies, Ajax, we've had various transient electrical glitches here today. I am pleased to say we are ready to go to camera. Stand by."

She had positioned one of the spare suits on a rock to use as a remote camera.

"The Team and I brought several projects to a successful conclusion today. I don't think I'd be exaggerating if I told you that we've made real progress. The systems glitches are under control."

She switched the suit camera on, followed by the remote she had set up to start NEIL's systems. Her view of the lunar plain appeared on the screen, filters dimming the low Sun on the close horizon.

"Can you see this? Good.

"OK, I am standing just outside the western edge of the rock fall, and I have something new to show you." As she turned to put the sun behind her she added, "Of course, I might have been filtering the news and data feed over the last couple of days, but I thought the results might cheer you all up a bit."

On the big screen in the lounge at Gene's, a new scene came into view. There, shining in the last few minutes of sunlight stood NEIL, battered and dented, but clear of the rock fall and standing the right way up. One forward drive wheel was missing. Not only that, but the LXV was somehow hooked up to the POD, which was, what? On wheels?

Lucy's speakers cut out as a massive whoop filled the lounge at Gene's and the entire audience jumped, some nearly to the ceiling. There was a standing ovation, with a lot of group hugging and not a few tears. The tiny screen inside her helmet didn't do it justice.

After a few seconds, Lucy switched to the second suit camera to show a longer shot of the same scene. As she did so, she turned back to face the limp suit lying on its rock. In the lounge at Gene's, she appeared in front of the rig, surrounded by her four friends. The McEwan Station staff all waved to the camera, Deep Race style.

She had managed yet another first. It had never happened before, but for once Andrew Jackson Thibodeaux was lost for words. He stood among his people and could offer nothing to vocalise his emotions. He could only shake his head in sheer disbelief, and accept handshakes and hugs as his triumphant team surrounded him. He had wondered what was going on when Lucy passed the message via Paula that she would like the team to be in official dress for this. On that score, he was still mystified. Could she have yet another one waiting up her sleeve after that revelation?

Lucy was waiting, and gestured for quiet.

"Guys, thanks. I, in fact we," she gestured to her sides, "can think of nothing better to say to you right now than a sincere and heartfelt thank you. It's only with the support and dedication of everyone there, both at Gene's and on Earth, that we have made any of this possible. I don't have enough time left to do a full report on

291

how we did it, but I promise that I will walk you all through the detail tomorrow.

"There is a reason for such haste this evening, which is why Paula arranged for all the NASA Earth stations to join us. We have one more duty to perform before the sun sets, and earlier today I pledged to complete it before that deadline. Would you please all sit down for a moment, and wait as I walk across here?

Paula switched SUIT 2 EXT CAM OFF as Lucy made her way to the second suit and moved it to a different rock, showing another prepared scene. Paula coached Lucy on their private channel "Left, down a little. Left again... uh-huh. There! Ready, Lucy? Vision in 5... 4... 3... 2... 1..."

The lounge screen at Gene's switched to show two pictures. Lucy's suit camera was pointing back towards NEIL and the attached POD to form one; in the foreground was a prepared grave surrounded by selected matching pieces of rock taken from the fall. The Deep Race stood behind it. The figures of Evan's wife and their son Andrew, named after his godfather Andrew Thibodeaux, appeared on the other screen. They were sitting in a gazebo with Evan's mother Hilary, overlooking the lake at the bottom of her garden in Ontario.

Oh, for strength. This was going to be so hard, but she would get through it. Lucy silently begged her emotions not to fail her, and started her prepared speech.

"Hilary, Sara, Andrew, Ladies and Gentlemen of the Eugene Francis Kranz Lunar Research Station, Lancaster, Rainier and Houston.

"Yesterday I pledged to hold a ceremony here by lunar sunset. My team members of the Deep Race were able to locate Evan and take me to him about thirty hours ago. We have managed, with help from you all, to complete the planned tasks we set out to

292

achieve during that time period. These have finally ensured our survival through the oncoming lunar night. We have now returned here to dedicate this spot and lay Evan to rest." She had to stop for a few seconds. In her speakers, there was silence.

"My friends, I would not presume to hold a religious service here. I don't have that kind of faith and I will not be hypocritical. I am presiding over the simple and ancient ritual of human burial this Lunar evening, as requested by Sara McEwan. I am laying him to rest here, at the place which now carries his name. I hope that some of you will one day be able to visit Evan's Place and say your own words. Evan was my best friend..."

Will yourself, Lucy. You can't wipe your eyes in this helmet. She cut the feed and sniffed hard.

"I'm sorry, uh, Evan was indeed my best friend. We worked as a great team and I will never meet a funnier, kinder, or more honest man. I know many of you across NASA also felt a real attachment to him."

A feeling of calm eased the emotion.

"The simple fact is that he died here because he stopped trying to outrun the rock fall, and turned around to offer me survival advice. If he hadn't warned me to strap in I am certain that I would have been severely injured or maybe even killed in the fall.

"Not only that, but by saving me, he also made it possible to save the four people standing here, who turned out to be in a much worse predicament.

"Andrew, your Daddy died a hero, saving the lives of others. You should be so proud of him."

She caught sight of Sara and Andrew clinging to Hilary, who sat holding them both in quiet dignity.

"Now I know Evan had a flag at Gene's, but I have looked everywhere inside NEIL and I don't believe he brought it on this

293

trip. Until such time as I am able return here with it, this is the best I can do."

She showed them a Canadian flag drawn in red marker on one of the sheets from her large notebook, and then motioned to the Deep Race. The four of them each took hold of a plastic floor panel borrowed from NEIL, upon which rested Evan's body, still in the surface suit and wrapped in a sheet. With a motion not possible in humans, they cantilevered it down flat into the grave, carefully drawing the panel back out. Lucy moved forward and threw in a little dust. Each of the others did the same, observing her custom as she had with theirs. She placed the flag alongside.

"The Deep Race gave me a rock from their home world. I explained that Evan was a geologist like me, and they went back to the wreck to retrieve another one to put in his suit pocket and bury with him as a talisman. They tell me that it assures him of a place in the Grand History Saga of their culture as one of the Connected. If I understand correctly, he will receive his Name later, as will I, when our story is added to The Known.

"In a few seconds, the Deep Race will dedicate this site according to their custom, filling the grave for me and then drawing a circle which none of them will ever enter, although we humans may. Thus they have offered to honour Evan in their own way, and their ritual will complete our ceremony."

She turned to face the sun, which had been falling behind the horizon until only a sliver still showed. Paula switched to the other camera, showing the longer view. Lucy and the members of the Deep Race stood around the grave, with NEIL and the POD to the left. On the right, the Sun dipped further behind the crags on the horizon.

"My last duty here is to dedicate this site as the Evan John McEwan Lunar Research Station, yet another ceremony for which I

294

do not presume to hold the proper authority. I have chosen this spot to bury Evan in the hope it will henceforth form the focal point of the station. All I have left to say now is Evan, welcome home. May you rest in peace, eh buddy?"

Her timing was spot on. The last single ray of sunshine slipped away and darkness fell. She shut her brimming eyes. Through the tiny speakers she could hear muted applause.

* * *

When it was all over and she was sitting inside NEIL, Paula put Sara McEwan through. That was another difficult moment for the two friends. Lucy stumbled, trying to apologise to Sara for not taking care of him. Sara brushed it away with a new confidence Lucy had never seen before. She thanked Lucy for doing so many things that were right, if not by the book. She also commented on how deeply the cross-cultural nature of the ceremony had touched her. She told her friend how impressed Andrew had been, and how he wanted to meet and thank the Deep Race for retrieving his Dad and helping to bury him. Lucy promised to visit as soon as she returned to Earth.

Andrew also came on the screen. He asked his Mom if it was a good time to tell Lucy the news, receiving a hug and her agreement that it was, so go ahead and tell her.

"Lucy, thank you for looking after Dad after he died. I'm coming up there when I am old enough, but

Mom won't because she doesn't even like flying. I've decided I'm going to be an Astronaut. Mom is having a new baby. The Doctor said it's a girl and I had an idea she and Gramma like. We are going to call my baby sister Lucy and we want you to be her godmother."

It was too much. Under the pressure of one emotion too many, Lucy finally broke down.

Ajax followed, but even he was too choked to say much. He said she'd upstaged her already famous performance with the President, and that Leif would speak to her very soon.

Lucy studied the scene in the comms office at Gene's. Paula, Mario, Doc, Bird, Ajax, even the astronomy guys Wilco, Ed, and Pelican were all crammed in waiting to talk to her. She decided that she had done enough for one day.

"Folks, I'm not up to any more questions. My emotions are burned out and I'm falling down tired. I will report on NEIL and all the systems tomorrow. All I'm saying for now is this: I pulled some circuit breakers yesterday so we could get all that stuff done and surprise you. They are all back in. Power is only in the fifties because we needed to stop charging and finish the other tasks, and yes, Paula, you spotted the dodge. You were always too clever for me.

"We'll start back to Gene's tomorrow and charge up again en-route. The missing wheel is not causing NEIL any problems, and the Deep Race built the POD chassis with parts scavenged off their ship.

"In a minute, with your permission Ajax, I'm going to shut off the screens and take a real break. I will be off while I sleep for at least twelve, or possibly even eighteen hours. The Deep Race guys will rest in the POD. They say it's too warm for them to be comfortable in here. Before that I am planning to eat some cooked food and have a shower; a real shower, in hot water. I will leave COMMS IN live so you can call if necessary, but don't, OK?

"There is one last thing I need doing tonight. Would you delegate someone at Mt. Rainier to find Sarkasian and hug him like he's never been hugged before. Ten minutes ago I found time to open his special delivery and it had this inside." She held up an open can of Budweiser's special edition, "King of Comets" beer.

"The label on his manifest never gave it away, even after you read it to me, Pelican. It was BKOC/TS. Now it's cheers, and good night." She cut the camera link. Ajax didn't object.

Lucy woke and enjoyed a good stretch. Getting undressed and sleeping in a proper bunk with her sleeping bag sure beat lying in her suit on the mattress, floor or ceiling. She avoided looking at the time until she was good and ready, but slipped into the bathroom for another shower. It was a misuse of the recommended water ration, but the system recycled it and water wasn't an issue.

Before lying down to sleep she had enjoyed the long-promised steak dinner, making herself take time and savour every mouthful. Once again she awarded bonus points to Bird for outstanding services to catering. She followed that with a second tin of the wonderful beer.

She took some selfies with the tin to send to Budweiser. She might accept advertising offers when she got home, but they were getting these for free. When she eventually reached Earth she would fly to Mt. Rainier, find Tavis, and give him that hug.

She was paying for it all this morning, feeling a bit bloated and overfed. She skipped breakfast, settling for orange juice and a single cup of coffee. Checking the time, she was hardly surprised to find that sixteen hours had elapsed since she informed the folks at Gene's she was taking the day off.

"Gene's, it's good morning from Evan's Place."

"Hey, Lucy. Are you dressed? Can we go to screen?"

"Sure Mario, as long as I don't pull a disciplinary for being shorts-and-T equipped."

The dwarf appeared on her big screen, wearing the biggest grin she had yet seen across his face.

"It's so good to see you. I've been listening here for the last five hours. I knew when you were awake, but I wanted you to take your time. Last time I said you looked good, you disagreed with me. Lucy, today you look great and that statement is not open to discussion."

"That was thoughtful Mario, thanks. I slept fourteen, and I'm feeling sparkly shiny, well, maybe I ate a bit too much before turning in, and I had a second beer too but hey!"

"Pig." His expression turned to feigned horror. "The guys in the lounge held a mock auction for that tin of beer. So, are you planning to start hauling it back here today? Ace has a sweepstake on your ETA. There's a lot of cash in the pot, I can tell you."

She laughed, realising that she was at ease talking to him and feeling relaxed for the first time after so many days of stress.

"The Deep Race said they needed a 48 hour break, and then they want to go and visit the Long View Traveller one last time. I suppose they might want more bits and pieces from the site. The Galaxy knows they've recycled some extraordinary stuff from that wreck. I also believe they need to say some proper goodbyes, like I did here last night."

"That's cool. I feel sorry for them. Are you going?"

"I'm not sure. It's tricky because they might feel obliged to ask me. I don't know what to think. Other than that, we'll need to finish charging NEIL up in a day or two, but now we know power is available we can do that anywhere; here, or on down the trail. How many charge stops we need depends on the rolling consumption towing the POD."

Mario took that up. "Your return trip came up at the staff meeting here last night. There was a major difference of opinion about whether you should stock up NEIL from the POD, leave what you can't carry right there, and head back here. The POD and the stores can wait for recovery later. You need to know that was Ajax' big idea."

Lucy had considered the option. "I'm not so sure. If we got half-way and NEIL broke down, we'd be in trouble again. I reckon if we take it nice and slow we should be able to get there in a week with it. Anyway we can't travel at any speed in the dark. It's not that I want to head in as a hero with the POD and its contents, but apart from providing me with emergency backup it would be much more useful to the operation than leaving it all here."

"Hey, don't get me wrong, Lucy. I think you should tow it back, and I said so. After all, the Deep Race guys took all that time and effort to hook it up, didn't they? They are all certified heroes on Earth too, you know."

"I wonder what Ajax would say if I left them here with the POD for a day or two and headed out with NEIL to check on the impact site. After all—"

He cut her off. "No. I don't care what Ajax says, don't take any more risks." He was holding both of his tiny arms out to the camera. Come on, Lucy."

"Look, it's not a firm plan, OK? But it's a unique situation and it is my job after all."

"Please don't do it. I want you back here."

Lucy considered that one. "Do you know, I haven't actually heard anything about the crater yet. I have no idea what's there anyway. It feels like unfinished business because Evan and I started out to do it before, well, before. You know. Can you understand that?"

"Yes, of course I can. I just don't agree with it is all, and it's too important for me to keep my mouth shut. You've already run rings around everybody here, you know, but it won't wash with me. Ajax says he can't hate you for loving your spirit, and that's pretty lyrical for him. I know you'll do whatever you think is right, but personally I don't think you should go."

Lucy was touched by the depth of the sentiment. "You have no idea what a rare gift real honesty is. Thank you for giving me yours."

He half turned in the chair, putting a finger to his lips. "Hi Ajax, Paula. The pair pulled up chairs and joined him at the desk. "I was just telling Lucy about the debate on her roll home."

"Thanks, Mario," said Thibodeaux. "Good morning, Commander, hope you enjoyed your rest."

"Good Morning Ajax. What's with all this 'Commander' stuff, eh? Yes I did thanks. I slept fourteen and had a shower before and another one after. Right now, the last week seems like a series of surreal dreams. I must have hit my head a lot harder than I thought. How many rules in total do you reckon I broke?"

He laughed out loud. "I closed the book on that after filling two whole pages. Tell you what, though. I defy you to find one broken rule that didn't improve your situation or enhance your chances of survival. I never thought you would manage to trump your performance with the President, but more than half the planet's population watched the funeral you held for Evan.

"Sara McEwan is telling the world that you brought her a level of closure she never expected from such a distance. My godson Andrew has already received some offers backing a guaranteed scholarship at the University of his choice, in whatever field he cares to name, when the time comes.

"On a commercial note, Lancaster is trying to work out how to deal with the interview requests. We have offers pouring in from all over the world. There hasn't been a press sensation like it in recorded history and if you choose to run with it all your feet won't touch the ground for years. The bookies are taking bets on you running for President in three years' time. You can do anything you want from here on in."

301

"Ajax, what would you say if I unhooked NEIL and went off to complete the original task? That's what I want to do. After all it's still my job. I was saying to Mario, it's unfinished business for Evan, too."

His reply completely mystified her.

"Oddly, I've been debating that as a possible development with the people at Lancaster. I'm sorry to have to inform you how that discussion turned out. In fact it resulted in the following statement, and I quote: 'Commander Lucy Grappelli, you are jointly instructed by Director Leif Culver and Acting Director Willard Redwood to return to the Eugene Francis Kranz Lunar Research Station and report in person to Commander Thibodeaux for debriefing.' Of course, between you and me they made a serious mistake, but in the long run I suspect it's me that's going to regret it."

Lucy realised that she had missed something here. "And?"

"You didn't register the actual wording. No specified timescale. Since then it might have dawned on them of course, but we wouldn't know. Somewhere between here and Earth we've suffered a total comms failure. I mean to say, this is you we're discussing here, and I already know you'll do exactly as you please. So does Mario, seems he's got a soft spot for you."

"Ajax, man. Enough already." The dwarf landed a sharp punch on his commander's arm. Paula added one on the other side, and Ajax yelped. The three of them collapsed laughing.

"OK whatever, guys," laughed Lucy. "Has the base suffered a nitrous oxide escape or something? Are you for real, or what?"

Ajax looked back at her and calmed down a bit. "No, those orders were real, and I have delivered them to you as worded. You are to report to me in person for debriefing. That is, er, when you have completed your necessary tasks. I can't order you any more, remember you hold equal rank now. Having said all that, following recent events I have no choice but to trust your judgement. To be honest with you there isn't anyone here who wouldn't trust you with their life. You must do what you think is right."

"So the management slipped up, and you're covering for me. I appreciate that. What's up with this comms breakdown? Is that meteor damage or what?"

Paula grinned at her like Tavis Sarkasian, and offcred up a passable Vampire laugh "AAAH hahahahahaha! WAAAH hahahahahaha! She was holding up a piece of thick green cable with a connector at one end. She pulled up the other end to show it was severely mangled. "Break somewhere. Gotta fix. Could be meteor. Two days to write procedure. At least. Usin' your rule book, baby."

Mario looked hard at her. Thibodeaux told her they would check back in four hours, and they left her to think it over.

In the end she decided that on balance the dwarf was right. In favour of going she had help, masses of supplies and was already well over halfway to Crater Pelican. Oxygen was inbound, so she wasn't too worried about that either. On the other hand, there was still no backup available from Gene's, NEIL had sustained damage, but seemed to be in working order. Anyway, she had her new reputation to uphold as NASA Commander Lucy Grappelli, who would usually turn expectation around. Sitting with her second cup of coffee and pondering all the variables, another idea came to her. Had those three been goofing around while using a bit of reverse psychology to try and trick her into coming straight back? If so, she couldn't win.

She still had thirty hours before the Deep Race rest period ended. Until then, for the first time since the crash, she had nothing to do. It was night outside and she'd never been keen on the lunar surface in the dark.

If it wasn't for the fact that the Deep Race wanted to visit the wreck she would have started back towards Gene's, following the cone markers along the West Way using NEIL's big headlights. Now there was one system she hadn't checked. The four headlights were at the top and bottom front corners of the LXV. She pushed the switch and only the top right side light shone. There were no spares. Spacing them out was a design feature that avoided all the lights being damaged at once. Still, one was better than nothing if you had to drive at night. Earthlight helped, because it showed the lunar surface enough to make shadows.

She couldn't achieve much, but Lucy had energy to spare after the long rest. She decided to spring-clean NEIL inside, take an inventory, and see what she could ditch. NEIL had selected supplies on board for a month of solo travel. The only thing she could still add was water. There was plenty in the POD, stored in pressurised canisters for easy hose transfer into the big tank. She unloaded all the used water and the toilet into empties to reduce the weight as much as possible, and stacked them outside for collection later.

She washed all her clothes and left them out to dry all over the cabin. After a tidy, she realised that she had been putting off the last difficult job, bagging up what remained of Evan's personal gear to place in a locker. Most of his clothes were in the trash anyway, sacrificed to emergency housekeeping during the chaotic days after the crash. She re-packed a lot of the trail supplies into his bunk-space. After a meal, and feeling tired out again, she lay down in her own bunk for a nap.

Lucy came to with a start and realised that she had woken herself snoring. She'd been out cold for six hours. It was 8:00 PM, so she gave up and called Gene's to say she was OK, but going back to bed. She slept again, only to dream about Evan.

He sat in the boulder field near the overturned NEIL, surrounded by big rocks. He was talking to them. "You've all got names, it wasn't your fault." Then he was lying down between the rocks where she'd found him. She looked into the visor and saw a contented grin as he looked up past her at the Earth hanging above. "Ah now, that's a great view. To visit Earth, but I'm not goin' again, eh? You all go then, and take your Names with you." It faded into the most relaxed and recuperative sleep since the crash.

She woke at 5:00 AM feeling calm and rested. There was no point calling Genes for a couple of hours, so she suited up and stepped outside for a walk round the site. Her suit lights spotted a message right opposite the ramp:

TEAM SHIP
TEAM POD
LUCY NEIL TEAM POD GENES

////

TEAM SHIP
TEAM POD
LUCY NEIL COMET
LUCY NEIL EVAN
LUCY NEIL TEAM POD GENES

It was a choice. Either they all travelled straight to base, or she could go to the crater and they would wait in the POD. They had considered the options, and left her to make a decision. She crossed out the top message and went inside the POD to grab some water canisters. The Deep Race were not there; they must have already started on their plan and gone to the ship. She selected extra stores to fill up the space she had made aboard NEIL.

It took three hours to replenish NEIL's water, finally depositing several large canisters outside by the message. She also left an open canister of vegetable packets outside the POD where they would find it. There was no reason to linger, she had no idea how long they would be away at the wreck. Walking back to NEIL after unhooking the tow bar, she had another idea. The suits had good lights. Retrieving two of them and tying them onto NEIL's open framework suspension between the front steering wheels wasn't difficult, and they had lines that fitted the external supply plugs. NEIL had headlights.

She swung the LXV round and drove to the charge point. That would involve a report in.

"Gene's, Lucy."

"Good morning to you, Lucy."

"And to you, Pelican. I'm back at the charge point, requesting permission to steal your juice for three hours."

"I'll call Ajax. He said you would. He also said he wouldn't stop you and had a bit of a fight with that dwarf. Mario yelled at him. That guy's tougher than he makes out."

"Sticking up for me with Ajax like he does is amazingly brave."

"Ajax will be here in two minutes, he says."

"Lucy, Ajax."

"Go ahead, Commander."

"OK, it was me last night and now it's you. What's with this 'Commander' business?" He was smiling and shaking his head at the same time.

"Keeps us on our toes. Look, I'm going to run NEIL for twenty kilometres, and see how everything looks. From that distance I could walk back with air and carry a spare suit if there's a problem. That way, I still retain the option of an escape route to Earth using the POD.

"If NEIL is running well after that I will call again and try to reach agreement on whether I should proceed to the impact site. The Deep Race independently offered me the choice of going, in which case they will stay here in the POD and wait for me to return.

"I've said I won't stop you doing that. I stand by that, but I think you should take longer and tow the POD. I don't want you separated from your escape contingency, or from the Deep Race.

"They are more important to Earth than any comet survey, whether you like it or not. So far we've been at pains here to protect you from the furore that's still raging over them, but you need to know the score. Half the planet wants to make friends with your team, the other half is frightened to death. The Reunited Nations has paralysed itself in debate and can't decide what to do. I'm hoping that Leif will be back at the helm by the time somebody comes to a decision."

"I guessed some of that, but there's no point in me taking any notice."

"That's the correct answer. So, you have supplies to spare and power access available. Can I make a recommendation that will make all your usual bristles spike up?"

"I guess you will."

"Lucy, this is a personal message, me to you. Please come back here first. Let's plan a whole new mission for when the sun is up. You can take your pick of the crew, or requisition anybody you want from Earth. The crater is important, yes, but it's already too late to see molten lava there. All the space-based instrumentation shows the temperature almost back to ambient, so the show is over. It will not change in any way in a few weeks or months. This needs planning, and I give you my word that it will be you that gets to go."

"Ajax, that's a negative, OK? I won't fight you, but no. NEIL needs weeks of work at best, if it's not scrapped. I understand that BUZZ is also a goner so I'd be stuck there with no transport. I won't risk having that happen."

"It's not OK, but I had to ask. I know you well enough to predict the answer, but hey!"

"So, that discussion is now parked for the duration. You told me to do what I need to and this is it. I will weigh up taking the POD with me and call you back after I've given NEIL a run."

"Fair enough. Not my ideal scenario, but fair enough."

She charged NEIL and called in to announce that she was heading west for a road test. There was a straight stretch about ten kilometres ahead and she maxed the drive motors on wheels five and six, leaving wheel 4 disconnected and running in 2-wheel drive. The LXV was soon rolling at a steady 30 km/h. She revelled in the movement, no, the sheer ability to travel, and kept it up for thirty kilometres. NEIL ran well, with nothing to indicate the missing wheel.

A shadow appeared in the trail, and Lucy pulled back on the control bar. NEIL braked hard on the two connected drive wheels as she steered to one side, mowing down a marker cone and narrowly avoiding a small new crater right on the trail, before coming to an untidy halt off to one side. With better lights, she might have had more room to manoeuvre. Danger still hid on the surface.

After a short break while she stopped shaking, Lucy turned round. In spite of there being no holes in the road she had just travelled, she drove NEIL back to Evan's Place at a far more sensible pace. Arriving back, she still hadn't made a firm decision about a Go/No Go.

"Gene's, it's Lucy, I'm back at Evan's."

"Hi Lucy, Ajax again. Telemetry says you ran NEIL fast for a while. We've been receiving much more consistent data with you wheels-down. The aerials must be at least partially intact."

"Yes, it went well. I used two-wheel drive and went over thirty kilometres before I had to avoid a small impact crater in the road. That spooked me into turning back. There was a huge temptation to keep going, but I worked some things through. It was the first couple of hours since the crash that I found time to think. I got rational, Ajax."

Thibodeaux was sitting with crossed arms. "Gracious, Grappelli. So?"

"The problems are oxygen, and the Deep Race. I can't leave a supply for the team here and then get the POD dropped near me to top up NEIL. They would die. Ajax, you were right before. They are the most important thing that has ever happened, to me or anybody else. My mission imperative must be bringing them to you, so they can go to Earth. The Reunited Nations can debate the issue with itself all it wants, but it was something that Houston Tech Stacey said to me the other night that made me realise. Everybody on Earth is doing the Deep Race salute. Whatever the RN thinks, the people have accepted them. They have to visit Earth."

309

"That makes a lot of sense. To satisfy my worry nodule, please confirm that you are packing up what you need and heading straight back towards Gene's Place."

"Affirmative. I wish I had better lights because I need to travel with care in case of further road damage down-trail."

"As a base commander, that's a sound decision, Lucy. We need to do some things in order, i.e. Paula 'fixes' the comms cabling and we check with Lancaster to find out whether Redwood actually died from apoplexy. If he didn't, I expect to hear that he's fired us all. I will get Tech to think about your lights."

"Ah, thanks, Ajax. I haven't said it yet, but I do appreciate you putting your neck on the line for me over this."

"I haven't put anything on the line. Paula broke her kit."

"Uh-huh."

The Deep Race didn't appear back from the Long View Traveller until after her next sleep period. There was a new, much smaller junk pile by the POD. They were waiting near it as she walked across to see them. As usual there was a message:

SHIP NO MORE WE

They had done what they needed at the ship, and she was glad they didn't ask her to join them. It would have been eerie in the dark, and she shuddered at the thought of ghosts with claws. She indicated the new pile of stuff. 2,2,1 seemed ready for that:

TO VISIT EARTH

Inside NEIL, 3,4,2 handed her something metallic and heavy, like a small harpoon in a pipe. At the same time he picked up the pad and marker pen:

310

SHIP AIR NEIL AIR

She was holding the missing link; a device for plunging into their huge recovered air tanks. If the workshop at Gene's could attach it to a pump they could access that supply. She signed 'Thank you', and put it in the locker with Evan's gear. 3,4,2 added:

TEAM SHIP LEVERS EARTH

The pile was components for study. It would all fit in the Pod with them. She wondered if they were offering up some science to trade for help in getting back to their base on Europa, or if their race was in the habit of bringing new technology to backward planets. Even after all the obvious progress and empathy, firm communication was still basic; conceptual rather than precise.

She drew the familiar picture of NEIL and the POD, this time arriving next to another POD, alongside which she wrote AIR. A second drawing showed NEIL and the POD outside a building with GENE written on it. All four of her Team signed "Impressed" and "Yes."

Ellis Ransome stood on the landing field, five kilometres north east of the base perimeter. It was a flat lava plain with less dust than a lot of the surrounding moonscape. He was still worried about the trial, but most of his fears for Bird's safety were lessened by the decision to convert Bouncer into a hovercraft and keep the whole exercise at ground level. Design and parts scavenging lists for the larger rig based on the stripped-down floor pan from BUZZ were coming along.

Kyran Mukherjee was looking forward to the prospect of watching the rejuvenated historic rig running. He was on a private channel giving Bird a few last minute instructions. Over half the base staff were out at the field, apprehension and excitement balanced evenly. Someone had recycled several of the big name-plates from the photography session on the morning of the comet impact. These were held aloft at intervals, spelling out the legend "GO BIRD!"

Kyran was aboard one of the base's electric golf carts with Doc Fisher, who was waiting to drive him while he talked to Bird. "Are you ready, Bird?" he asked. "Check gas pressure gauge live and set to standby. Remember, gentle inputs are the most important thing, isn't it? You are Go."

Bird started his commentary. Kyran monitored, standing by to coach if required. "Gas pressure set. I'm lifting at static thrust now." Alongside, Ellis and Levon DuPage steadied Bouncer as a cloud of dust blew out under the skirt. The rig lifted to rest on the cushion of carbon dioxide trapped underneath. The two men watched as Bird held the wheel.

"Steady," said Ellis. "You OK, Levon?"

"Good here."

Ellis had set up several small valves around the sides of the structure for directional control. "Bird, would you make a slow turn to port and we'll see how it swings?"

"Roger," replied Bird. Ellis and Levon felt a gentle pull as Bouncer tried to turn.

"That checks, and starboard," called Ellis. "Good, directional control established. Try forward motion, but as slow as you can manage." The twin rear valves vented, and they both felt the vehicle tug. "OK, cut the drive and set back down."

Bouncer settled to the surface and Bird was the first to speak. "Thanks, fellas. So, what do you reckon? Can I give it a proper go, eh?"

Thibodeaux was on hand to wave him off. He called round, checking that everyone was happy to continue before having the final say.

"All right Mr. Downey, it's over to you. Keep it to running pace so Doc and Ky can keep up in the cart. And remember what we agreed at the planning meeting; you can run as far as the field markers and back. Then we'll stop and analyse the data. I guess all that remains to do is wave you off. Go Bird, and go Bouncer."

"Thanks, boss." Bouncer lifted off again. Ellis had set up the valves so that it took a lot of wheel travel to achieve small reactions; he didn't want Bird over-correcting. He and Levon finally let go and moved back out of the way as Bouncer started a slow rearward drift. Bird carefully moved the wheel forwards and felt the rig start to move.

It took a bit of practice to keep going in a straight line; the directional jets were still sensitive. Floating above the surface and without any atmospheric drag, the whole thing was frictionless and willing to move. Doc had trouble keeping up on the outbound leg. Two kilometres downrange, and approaching the end of the landing

313

field, Bird had to cut the power and wait for Bouncer to scrape to a halt on the canvas skirt. He lifted again and managed a reasonable static turn to face back the way he had come.

At the other end of the field the watchers stood, amazed at how fast Bird and his ride receded as they shot away, pursued by the golf buggy. Doc Fisher was driving well offset to one side to avoid the cloud of dust. Bouncer kicked up a lot of the stuff and by the time it had settled Bird had touched down at the other end of the field.

"Great run, Bird," called Thibodeaux. "Kyran, how's he doing?"

"Good, Ajax. It is much more slippery than we expected. Airless and frictionless is making for seriously rapid transit. I once went to that place with the salt flats near Salt Lake City to see a land speed record attempt, and it was a lot like watching that from my seat here in the cart."

Ellis had something to add. "Kyran, Ajax, do you want him to open it up a bit for the cameras on the way back? I set a throttle limiter on the drive valves but there is an override available. Doesn't look too dangerous, now he's had a crack."

Kyran was amazed. "Ajax, that is the first time he has ever suggested that something wasn't actually as dangerous as he predicted. And I mean ever. Let's be going at it for a lunar speed record right here."

Thibodeuax caught the excitement. "OK guys, as long as you're having fun, let's do it. But be careful."

"Sure Ajax," came the exhilarated voice. "It's amazing to travel in silence out here with no air rush. It was unbelievable. I think we've hit on a great new idea. What's more, I can still sell this to the tourists. One more run and then I'm up for passengers."

Ellis called again. "Kyran, can you turn the rear valve limiters down from point four to point three for me? Or come and fetch me so I can do it?"

"No, I've got it," said Kyran. Two minutes."

Right from the outset, the second run was more spectacular than the first. Bird was now running back down the field towards the watchers. Bouncer had stopped beyond the graded and swept surface, so as Bird announced he was lifting a cloud of dust appeared at the far end of the field. Kyran whooped and started to laugh. Bird managed a cowboy yell, before Bouncer shot past the waiting crowd at a ridiculous velocity. It continued straight over the end of the field into the ungraded area beyond.

"Shit." Bird yelled as he cut the power. Bouncer settled to the surface, exactly as before but travelling far too fast. As soon as the rig made contact with the dust, the lower front edge of the frame hit a half-buried rock. There was a collective gasp, followed by a varied and colourful set of expletives as the audience watched it pitch forwards in a violent tumble that kicked it fifteen metres above the surface. A soundless nose-first crash followed, before the whole performance came to a close with a series of untidy rolls, fame parts and rocks bouncing away with every impact. A huge dust cloud settled across the wreck.

The golf cart rolled past them at top speed as everybody started to make their way towards the wreck, led by the sobbing Ellis.

Kyran could be heard from the speeding cart, calling, "Bird? Bird? Oh, Bird, man, are you there?"

Ajax went cold and icy calm. He would panic later and yell at everybody concerned, including himself, but he was decisive in emergency, and therefore at his most effective. He switched to the comms room channel at the base. "Ajax, emergency."

"Go." Paula on the case; no panic expected.

"Paula, Bird crashed and it looks bad. Doc is on scene and I want transport out here immediately. Throw in an emergency pressure tent and get back to me with timings. Leave the line open. Go, girl!"

"Gotcha!"

The base fire alarm had started in the background three seconds into his transmission. Smart move, she had bought twenty seconds extra while he was still issuing instructions. Everybody left inside would already be donning surface suits and getting ready to act as required. He stayed on and heard her hit the base speaker system.

"Attention! Attention! Crash out on the field. One down, status unknown. Orders from Thibodeaux. Eagle to the east garage to drive a cart plus pop tent to the field, stat, acknowledge immediately via the comms office. Fire alarm cancelled but everybody else suit up and stand by. All medic trained staff inside to clean up and muster for an emergency admission. That is all."

In a real crisis nobody was better. By the time she had finished Thibodeaux had arrived at the scene of the crash. There were bits of the hovercraft everywhere and a knot of people gathered around the largest part of the mangled rig. They were working together, slowly turning it the right way up as Doc and two others supported Bird, still strapped in the seat. Doc's buddy line was plugged into the cook's suit.

"Thibodeaux," he announced. "Everybody, quiet please. Doc, report."

"He'll live. By a miracle the suit is still intact but he's out cold. His legs are trapped under the console and that's an immediate worry. I need something I can use as a wrecking bar as soon as possible to get him free."

"Good job, Doc. Eagle will be here soon with a pop tent. Look around you, people. Check the debris and think wrecking bar. What else can we do?"

"Thanks Ajax. I want him out of the wreck. We can hold his head still until I get a neck brace, can you check they are bringing one, plus a gurney?"

Thibodeaux passed those requests, and added one for a wrecking bar from the garage. Paula reported Eagle's ETA under five minutes. She'd thought of everything, including dumping the garage atmosphere immediately all personnel were safe, so the doors could be opened as soon as possible. Recovering and storing the air took time and they could afford the loss.

He checked the time. Less than three minutes since the crash. He went to his general broadcast channel, overriding everything to speak to his crew both inside and outside the base. "Outstanding effort, team. Bird's still out cold, but his suit's intact though. Doc says he's knocked about but he'll live."

By the time Eagle arrived, Bird was conscious. He was in severe pain from his knees and had face-planted the Moon so hard he'd broken his nose on the visor. There was a lot of blood inside the helmet. As he came to, he looked up at Doc Fisher and said, "Broke my nose, Doc. My pretty nose. Ajax gonna to kill me, and when he's finished I'll have to pick up all this mess."

Ajax smiled. "Bird, I'm here, man. It was my fault if anybody's for being less than my usual cautious self. You were well ahead on the first attempt. Doc says you'll live and transport is on the way to take you to the Medical Room. We need to get your legs free, they are still trapped under the console."

"I know," was the peeved reply. "My knees are ringing. Can your knees even ring, eh? And I broke my pretty nose. But didn't Bouncer fly?"

317

"If you mean along the field, yes. If you are talking about the big cartwheel finale, then yes too, even more so." Thibodeaux almost laughed at his old friend. "Man, that's going to be a great movie to show Lucy when she gets back here."

He spotted Ellis hopping about and picking up pieces of debris. Thibodeaux knew the engineer would be distraught in his odd, expressionless way. "Ellis, that you?"

"Commander. I'm so sorry." He was still crying. "I never thought. I'm obsessive about safety, that's why I'm so terrified of accidents. I'm scared, and I hate waste, and I hate damage, and I hate pain, and I hate death. Bird might have gotten killed." He was almost chanting as he sobbed over each phrase.

"Accident. That's the word right there, fella," said Thibodeaux. He caught hold of the engineer's arm in a firm grip, pulling the younger man round so he could look through the suit visor. "Ellis, it's OK son, it was an accident and nobody got killed. I need you to go back to the base with Kyran and get a cup of coffee. Leave all this stuff here and do that for me, will you? Come on, Ellis, Bird will be fine. It's OK, really it is."

"Yeah, it's OK. He's OK. He'll be OK, I'm OK." Thibodeaux gave him a quick buddy-hug and slapped him round the back.

How do you help a guy with no real friends in a trauma situation? Thibodeaux had psychological first responders available, although he hadn't needed them over the comet strike or the NEIL crisis. A team tends to look after itself well in circumstances like that. Now he needed help because Ellis was having a personal stress meltdown for sure.

He selected another one-to-one channel and looked round for his deputy. "Levon, Ajax. I need your stress defuser training over here. The medics can cope with Bird, so find Kyran and get over here please. I need you two to take charge of Ellis for me. Get him inside and see if you can calm him down. He's broken up."

"Sure. I'm on it." Levon appeared from the crowd.

Thibodeaux looked around. He addressed the chatting crowd on the open channel. "Ajax, quiet please. Everybody apart from you two with Doc, get yourselves back inside. Bird is conscious and he'll be OK. His greatest problem will be adjusting to the status of rodeo clown hero. We'll get him inside and I'll hold an update meeting later in the lounge. It was a close one, but he's going to be fine. Go on people, this show's definitely over."

His suit chimed: RANS. "Ellis, hey, Are you with Levon?"

"Yes, sir. Thank you for, for grabbing hold of me there. Helped, I'll be OK in a bit. Ajax, I'm so sorry, man. But it don't work. No control. Lucy ain't getting rescued by no hover rig."

51 – LIGHTS
12:20 PM (LST) 8ᵗʰ OCTOBER

Lucy watched 3,4,2 and 2,2,1 working together on a message. Sitting on the floor inside NEIL, the pair were engaged in a lot of shell tapping. Sometimes they added a word or two to the pad, which they kept out of sight under the table. After nearly an hour, 3,4,2 handed it up. She was astounded to see a whole page of words:

TEAM SHIP FIND MORE DEAD WE
LINE CROSS PLACE DEAD IN SHIP WE
NO LINE IN SHIP LOOK WE
NEW LINE NO VISIT SHIP WE
DEAD SHIP NEVER VISIT WE
LUCY FOOD GOOD II-IIIII-I NOT DIE
TEAM FOOD SHIP MORE MORE IN POD WE
WORD LIST IN SHIP LEARN WE
TEAM WORD TEAM NOT WE
WORD GOOD NOW WE
IIIII-IIIIII-II / IIII-I-III WORD TEAM DIE
LEARN FROM IIIII-IIIIII-II WORD LEVER WE
WORD LEVER DIE WE
IIIII-IIIIII-II WORD EARTH PICTURE SEE
IIII-I-III WORD EARTH PICTURE SEE
TEAM EARTH
EARTH LEARN NEW LEVER HELP WE
EARTH TEAM WATER MOON HELP
HELP HOME WATER MOON
FAR FAR AWAY AWAY COME
TEAM WATER MOON HOME COME WE

Just for the fact that she had received such a long message, she signed "thanks" and "awesome."

Translating it for a report to Gene's took over an hour of careful concentration, but after several attempts she was able to produce what she thought was a reasonable stab at it:

"We went to the ship. Because we were able to locate more bodies (body parts?) there was a valid excuse to cross the line into the dead zone, place them with the others and search the ship again before finally closing it. We will never cross the line again. 2,5,1 didn't die after eating Earth food, but we have added to our own supply stored in the POD. We are getting better at language. We are not linguists but we are trying. Our language scientists 5,6,2 and 4,1,3 are dead, but we were able to access (the machine?) and learn some of their work. (The machine?) no longer works, we think we broke it. 5,6,2 and 4,1,3 learned Earth language by (watching pictures?) We would like to visit Earth and will share our technical knowledge with you. If Earth helps us reach Europa, we can get picked up there and travel home."

By their own admission, they were not specialists in alien language. Regardless of that, here were some individuals trying their hardest. All they had done was, well, what exactly? Read the scientist's notes? Looked at a computer? The only thing she could do was pass the message on, original and translation, and let the brains look into it.

They Deep Race already had the ability to get complex concepts across in a few scant words. Years of working with Paula helped with that particular approach. Now they were able to give a sentence better meaning, and offer to make deals. Sure, she could understand the gross concepts in their strange messages, but if she could get them some expert tuition there was no doubt that they could hold a real conversation. Now that would be fun.

321

She wrote them a message back:

LUCY THANK
GENES WORD TEAM HELP
EARTH HELP LUCY
TEAM WATER MOON

She couldn't promise them a visit to Earth, but she suspected they would be welcomed. She pictured a scene at the New White House in Boston, with her introducing them to President Braithwaite in The Oval Office. It gave her reason to smile. Judging by some of the comments from Gene's and beyond, she suspected that he was apprehensive of another meeting with her in case she twisted him round her finger again. She chuckled at that thought and 3,4,2 wrote her a message:

LUCY HAPPY

She waved her arms around and laughed. Yes, 2,2,1. Lucy was happy. She wrote:

LUCY HAPPY
NEIL LUCY TEAM POD AIR
NEIL LUCY TEAM GENE

She held up the sheet, and all four Team members tapped, "Yes."
"Gene's, it's Lucy."
"Paula, baby."
"Hey, Paula, always good to talk to you. I've been translating a long message from the Deep Race."
"Systems request. Paged Mario. New procedure."

"You know, Paula, working with you all this time has helped me to decipher what those messages from the Deep Race actually mean. They talk in staccato, just like you do!"

Paula treated Lucy to one of her rare and infectious laughs. "Uh-huh. Maybe I'll ask 'em stuff when they here."

Mario turned up and spread a sheet on the desk.

"Hey Lucy. We tried to download data to NAV, plus a lot of low level orbital high res digitals of the trails taken before sundown. It won't load, although the system here says it's gone. We need to check the no.3 receiver up top. We can't load the data on the other links, and we don't know why. It's likely we would only need a piece of stiff wire screwing in using the original screw ring if it's there. Think you can do that under Earth light?"

"Sure, if it means getting better trail data, heck, I'd stick my finger in it."

Mario and Paula both laughed. Paula added, "Shouldn' be tellin' you this. Ajax done had a major row with Vom. Asshole ate his rule book an' got the clause shits." The unfortunately chosen insult had them all giggling.

"So I can get moving then?" Lucy asked when they settled a bit. "I have one top corner light working and two spare suits tied on as low lights. They're pretty good. There are no spare lights or bulbs, so is there anything here I can cannibalise?"

"Hey, this is Lucy Grappelli. One light, two suits. I say it's a Go," said Paula. "Anythin' Ajax don't hear'n all..."

Lucy laughed again. "Does he ever listen back to the tapes there, Paula?"

"They glitch out bad, man. Me, you, Mario, Pelican here, ain't nothin' ever recorded."

"You're as bad as Lucy," said Mario who, in spite of his series of run-ins with Thibodeaux, usually did follow all the rules.

323

"Compliments now? Ain't you sassy."

Lucy cut in. "OK, knock it off, you two rebels. This renegade is off up the outside ladder with a wire coat hanger, except that I don't have a coat hanger. What have we got that I can break for that?"

Mario was ready for that. "The best thing would be the plug line from a suit. You could maybe... So stand by." He started typing. "Give me a minute here, I need to check physical stores. I'll call you back."

"Ain't goin' nowhere, as Paula says," quipped Lucy, "so I'll make a pot of nice fresh coffee."

"That's it." Paula growled. "No help for you. Beer, and now coffee. Argh!"

They all laughed again as Paula cut the connection. Mario called back in fifteen minutes, waving a sheet sent over from the technical office.

"OK, Lucy, tech has a solution for headlights, that is, if yours are just broken bulbs. The POD has area landing lights and, although the actual bulbs are different, the spec sheet lists the same fittings as NEIL. They should plug into NEIL's headlight sockets. If you fix the aerial I'll check some system maps and download a procedure for scavenging them off the POD."

"Sure. Let me clarify that. I need to fix the no.3 aerial for now, and stand by for a procedure on stripping lights off the POD. Then I can fix up the lights on NEIL, and I'm good to roll."

"Yup," said Paula. "Half hour, max."

Lucy shook her head at the pair, grinning at her from Gene's. "Oh, you two kill me."

She wasn't familiar with the POD, and couldn't remember seeing any lights on it. Then again, they were landing lights, and she had never seen a POD moving. That wasn't strictly true either; she had never seen one flying. Seeing one being carried along, and then turned into a camping trailer didn't count.

Outside, she took a quick look round and spotted the light clusters at each corner. They were small external units bolted to the scaffolding frame, tight up under the edges of the POD. Their cables plugged into the same sort of exterior sockets that she had used for the suits tied onto NEIL. It was another example of the "one size fits all" thinking.

Of course it wasn't as simple as it looked. In the end she had to ask the team to help. Although the lights were by the edges of the base, the attachments were far enough underneath the POD that they defied her reach. Even with the makeshift axles and wheels, ground clearance below the frame was too low for her to worm underneath, and anyway that was something even she wasn't about to try. There were too many ways to damage the suit.

As usual 3,4,2 saw a solution, and they went off to roll rocks. They'd spent about 30% of their entire association with her engaged in various versions of that task. Whatever they felt, she hadn't heard a single complaint. She unhitched the towing hook.

Two roundish boulders about 1.5 m high were rolled across from the edge of the fall to rest in small prepared hollows. Everything inside the POD was already secure, so three of the team lifted the front end and eased it onto the rocks, while 2,5,1 stood by to chock the rear wheels and stop it rolling back.

Once everything was in place, Lucy crawled underneath one front corner. There was plenty of room for her to kneel with her head and shoulders up inside the framework. She unplugged the electric feed cable from its socket, before starting on the nuts and bolts behind the light unit. She had to concentrate to avoid dropping nuts, bolts and washers, as they would be hard to find in the dust using the suit lights in the dark.

She made her way out carrying the light cluster, with all the small parts in a pocket. The two rear light clusters were already standing there, complete with the bolt sets loosely re-threaded. She had planned to ask the Deep Race to turn the POD around and jack up the rear end so she could work on those, but as usual the team had out-guessed her, using their dextrous, long-reaching claws. As was becoming the case, she signalled "awesome" and received a "no problem" in return.

3,4,2 was missing, retrieving something from the original junk pile. By the time Lucy had the last light cluster detached, he was back with a lot of wire. They had anticipated the possible need to tie the units onto NEIL, but it was also suitable for aerial repairs. She motioned him to snip off a metre and, after a careful safety inspection, climbed the squashed looking rear ladder to NEIL's roof.

The four aerials were all damaged. Three of them were intact, but flattened. The no.3 aerial screw-in locator was still in place, but the wire was missing. It didn't take long to undo the ring and install a piece of 3,4,2's wire stock.

She was playing a new game, and there was no way she was calling Gene's back until NEIL had headlights. Looking around, there wasn't anything near the front that to attach the lights to.

Back on the ground, she settled for clamping them to the 75 cm high grip bars in front of the forward steering wheels to serve as main low headlights. The wires reached the external sockets, so power wasn't a problem. She stowed the other two units in an outside locker.

The Deep Race planned to travel either in the POD or on NEIL's roof. Up top, there were plenty of things for them to hang on to, and they could swing up the ladder claw by claw. They could even communicate by tapping on the roof, receiving replies tapped on the inside wall. Lucy learned a simple code used for that kind of purpose.

She set the POD climate to freezing, about as warm as they liked. To reduce tow bar stress she had squeezed everything she could inside NEIL, leaving just enough room for one human either in the driving seat, at the table, or in the one available bunk, plus the Deep Race team on the floor when necessary.

Lucy switched the one working headlight on, plus the external sockets powering the scavenged Pod lights. Her suit camera showed her view outside bathed in light.

"Gene's, Lucy, that's the no.3 aerial done."

"Hi baby," said Paula. "That's good. Procedure for..." She saw the lights. "Well, you done it again."

"As usual it wasn't all down to me. I've taken some film of my team lifting the front end of the Pod onto two boulders so I could get underneath. NEIL has twin-bulb Pod light clusters attached to the front bars, plus one working headlight on the top corner. In fact NEIL's never been so lit-up. The other two clusters from the Pod are in an outside locker, and the remaining suits have working lights. As far as I am concerned I am good to go."

"Standby, NAV is updatin'. Check download."

"Excellent. NAV is loading data. Ajax around? I wanted a word before I get this show on the road."

"Garage, Busy workin' BUZZ. Major effort."

"I know how hard everyone has worked. I'm coming back to thank a lot of folks and then I'll host the party to end them all at my place in Lancaster."

"Sounds good, baby. Patch you through?"

"Would you, please?"

The sooner she got rolling, the less concerned she would be. She wanted to get to Gene's, hand over her aliens and get back out to start studying the comet impact. Or did she? Did her life turn on the chance meeting with them? *Everyone keeps saying they're my destiny. Rocks or the Deep Race?*

She felt like her future was forfeit somehow. Convinced that Evan had died trying to save her life, she still needed to justify his death. By standing at Crater Pelican she could say, "Here it is, Evan. We came here to do this thing, and I have accomplished it because you gave me the chance. Now you can rest in peace." It had all been so emotional, but after the funeral she had hoped it would recede. *Here I am crying again.*

She had a flash of... of what? It felt like certain knowledge. It dawned on her as if he'd said it himself. "It's only more rocks. Standing there at that crater'd be for you, for your own closure, Lucy-Lu. I don't need it now, eh?"

Suddenly she knew. *I no longer need to do it. I need to get back to Gene's, complete my reports, and then I can take these guys to visit Earth. That's my new mission.*

Paula noticed, and made adjustments. "Come on, Lucy baby. Ajax on COM 3. Voice only, OK?"

"Thanks." She switched circuits. "Ajax?"

"Paula says NEIL has better than standard equipment lights, plus the NAV link."

"Both correct, Commander."

"Leaving there this evening?"

"No, it'll be in the morning now. I'll make a departure call then. I've broken more rules on abandoning trash and junk off base, but as the commander here at Evan's I'll give myself a kicking and tidy it all up next time I'm here. I did remember to mark the canisters "used/water, and "used/toilet.""

"Get some rest. Then come home, Lucy."

Kyran and Ellis uploaded a new data sheet giving weights that the chassis and systems could cope with on seven wheels. They looked good. She spent a restless couple of hours lying in the bunk running through checklists and worry items before finally dozing off, only to dream about the landslide.

She sat in the driving seat watching the boulders roll by, but this time NEIL was upright and secure. Evan was outside in the boulder field, cheerfully dodging the rocks, which flowed the wrong way. He waved up to her and started to measure some of them as they slowed down to allow him time, before speeding up again and rolling away up the slope. He called out the numbers, which she typed into the computer.

After a while he stopped calling, and she looked up again. The boulders were all gone and he was riding off aboard 2,2,1 towards the Long View Traveller, holding the Deep Race planet stone they had buried with him. They disappeared from view. Then the giant spacecraft, intact, lifted from the crater beyond. It receded at an incredible speed, but before it vanished from the Universe she heard a deep, resonant voice like a bell say, "He will be Named."

She woke with gentle tears, and the feeling that she might have been saying her goodbyes. She was wedged against the side of the small space. Her head ached, and she was lying on her left arm, which was full of pins and needles. That sensation may have triggered the episode.

329

She had a drink and some painkillers. It was only four hours since she lay down. She decided to try one more time, and fell into a deep and refreshing sleep. Another five hours passed before she woke, rested and ready to go. The anxiety about Evan had evaporated. Her headache had gone, and with it a strange sense of foreboding about the trail and the journey home.

53 – FIGHT
8:00 AM (LST) 9ᵗʰ OCTOBER

"Gene's, Lucy."

Thibodeaux was sitting at the console. "Good morning, Lucy. Are you rested?"

"Yes, sir. I'm good to go."

"That's great. So, do you want a laugh? I've had Redwood on again from Lancaster, bitching about you wasting more time, about equipment loss and damage, oh, and twenty other things. I wish we hadn't plugged the, er, sorry, repaired the comms line yesterday, because I finally allowed myself to get a bit antsy with the bastard. I heard myself telling him to get out from behind Leif's desk, jump off Leif's Floor Fifty balcony, and impale his ass on a cactus. That man offends me in ways that nobody else can, not even you on a bad day."

She almost couldn't reply for laughing. "Ajax, I called in to make it right with you, to apologise for my attitude, I mean from back in the lounge that day and every day since. And now this? I'm confused. Delighted, but confused."

He smiled at her. "Will Redwood and I go way back, oh, thirty-some years. He started before me, but NASA U stepped him down to my intake course because he failed something or other further up the training schedule. He never lets me forget that I am still out here on ops and he's the hotshot manager. The fact is that he's only Leif's deputy because Eb Stanford retired on health grounds. He also thinks he's on a natural step straight to Leif's job, but Sunny Culver told me yesterday that our boss will be back on Floor Fifty by next week, and is not happy with the way things have gone.

She felt her shoulders relax. "That's the best news yet."

331

He held up a warning finger. "You don't know that, of course. Until then you and I can hold out, and aside from getting his prickly ass up here what's he going to do? Stop paying us? Heck, you're the most famous face on Planet Earth and for the last ten days I've been your news mouthpiece. The press already dislikes him almost as much as I do, and most reporters won't even interview or quote him.

"Between you and me, the word is that he had a stand-up row with the management team and Jancis told him to flush himself down the nearest toilet. I mean, even you wouldn't pick a fight with Jancis Szymkowiak and expect to win it."

"I don't know what to say to you, Ajax. I'd sure like to buy you a beer. Say, I've got some here." She laughed. "I only had those two tins, you know. The rest is for you to gift out."

"OK, so we know where we stand. I'm happy to tell you that every single person on the base attended a meeting this morning. We've checked every possible eventuality we could think of, and agreed that you are ready to roll. In fact, as our junior NASA member and the only one that doesn't give a shit about getting fired, Pelican Percival was the one who shouted up for a vote on 'Is Redwood a Dickhead?' I can confirm that the result of that was also unanimous. We're running out of cups to throw, as well as coffee."

Lucy felt the amusement in his tone. Pelican was turning out to be as "team" as the permanent staff.

"He's an ace. It's all good here, thanks. I have most of the stuff redistributed. The team will ride on the roof; they say there are plenty of claw-holds."

"They are tough little fellas for sure, and I can't wait to meet them. That's me, plus everybody on the Earth and Moon of course."

"They also assure me that they haven't damaged anything underneath the POD with their rolling rig. The only items missing on the POD checklist are the external lights. I even checked the launch system and everything is green. All we need to do is take off the wheels and we can still lift to rendezvous with the MAGENTA if necessary. We'd have to empty the POD and leave a supply dump inside NEIL."

He leaned back a little. "I'm gaining confidence in you all the time, Commander Grappelli.

"Thanks, boss. The next task on my checklist is to top up NEIL. Can I steal your power for the next three hours?"

"Of course. Give me a few minutes and I'll call you back with a go on that."

* * *

While NEIL charged up, she took another call. Bird looked like he'd lost several fights. His nose was splinted and he sported a spectacular pair of black eyes, plus a badly swollen lip.

"Hi Luthy, it'th Bird," he lisped, slowly.

"Jeez, I'm glad you told me. Ajax said you'd wrecked out. What's the other fella look like?"

"Oh, I was the winner. I flew Bouncer as a hovercraft redesigned by Ellith and Ky. Second run I failed on the stop and had a wreck. Doc says I walked away dead lucky, but from where I can't sit down it feels more dead than lucky. Gonna take a while to lose the bruises, eh?"

She didn't usually think of him as Canadian, but even lisping like that he sounded like Evan, and a shadow of sadness settled across her like a veil. It was going to take more than a while to heal that, too.

"Bird, you look beat. Should you even be up? Can't someone else cook?"

"I need to move about and I needed a break from research. I'm not allowed in the galley in case I get injured as I'm pretty clumsy right now, so I thought I'd give you a call. What's new?"

"Well, we've been on language lessons for the last couple of hours, chatting about philosophy and racial differences. It's pictures and a few words, with their written vocabulary and language coming along in leaps and bounds, unlike you on that jump rig," she laughed. "Oh, I'm sorry."

"OK, OK, no need." He smiled too. "I've been taking a lot of stick over this."

"I'm not surprised you're sucking some up. My problem is I can't seem to absorb this tapping code the Deep Race uses. Even when they slow it right down I can't keep up. They know hundreds of printed words now, and can hold a written conversation, and all I have absorbed is a couple of dozen basic gestures and tapped commands. The human race isn't good at alien language."

"Can I hear them tapping?" asked Bird.

"I will ask," said Lucy. "Why?"

"Because I might have had an idea," replied the new base historian.

Lucy turned to the team and held her index fingers to her temples in the "tapping code" request gesture. They complied by moving a little closer to each other for a conversation. Their small claws flexed in tiny and rapid movements, almost too fast to see. A faint buzz filled the space inside NEIL.

Bird looked on for the five seconds or so it took for them to finish and settle back to sit in their previous positions. He made some notes and asked Lucy if he could keep the tape for use later.

"That's amazing. I suspect that was a long chat. Lucy, Have you ever heard of Morse code?"

"Can't say I have. What is it?"

"It was the original radio code back when the term was 'wireless'. It was used for 150 years until they retired it around the turn of the 21st Century. Amateurs kept on using it for a while even after that. The operator had an "on/off" switch which connected a circuit and sent a sound, or beep. Each letter had an identifying series of dots and dashes, or short and long beeps. Any word or number was possible. I think we might be able to teach it to these guys and get a proper interface."

"Sounds good," said Lucy, as usual impressed by another guy who thought out of the box.

Bird stopped talking and looked at the desk. "That's a call from Lancaster. Do I answer?"

"You'd better. Where is Paula?"

"Gone for a meal."

"You're fine unless it's Vom."

"Gene's here. Er, good morning Mr. Redwood."

Oh shit.

"Downey? What are you doing?" Where are the comms people? Do we have a complete sag-off list running there as well?"

"No sir, I'm on light duties until my knees and wrists improve. I'm not allowed to go in the kitchen for safety reasons. I'm filling in while the comms crew help out on other projects."

"From what I hear you should be reporting to this office for discipline. You will be when you get back, that's for certain. What possessed you to be flying anything in the first place? You're just a cook."

Bird bristled. If he was a real bird all his feathers would have stood out. "I will have you know I'm no longer 'just a cook,' I am the base historian of the Eugene Francis Kranz Lunar Research Station, and I am busy on projects at the personal request of your

President. I also happen to be talking to my friend Lucy while Paula Everett takes a well earned break. Mario Silva is outside helping the engineers in the garage. Everybody around here is doubling up on shifts and specialities, and we're all working damn hard. That is, if it's OK with you, Deputy Director."

Lucy couldn't see Redwood, but she knew the "I might puke" expression he so loved to assume when losing an argument. Sadly, she could still hear him.

"That's quite enough of your drivel. Nobody's ratifying the joke job title. I'll deal with you when you get back here. I'll speak to Grappelli. Now."

Unlike the comms operators, who had all protected her, Bird was so surprised that he threw the link and put Redwood's face on her screen.

"Grappelli. Are you inbound to Gene's yet?"

"Good morning to you too. I am very well, Deputy Director, thank you for asking."

"I said are you inbound to Gene's yet?

"Negative."

"Then start moving immediately, and report your ETA there to this office as soon as you calculate it."

"The Deep Race Team and I are currently considering our options, while stabilising the rolling gear on the POD for long distance travel. There are still several outstanding tasks to accomplish on our working checklist here before we can make that decision."

His voice started to rise, and he put on the sour face. "No, Grappelli. No. As Acting Director of NASA I'm informing you that the decision is made. Stop pissing around out there playing games. Ditch the POD, drive eastbound immediately and report to me from the office at Gene's. What is your ETA?"

He looked like he could actually smell vomit, and she burst out laughing at the thought of him finding Kent's shoes in the desk drawer. The outbreak of mirth didn't go down too well.

"What do you find so funny?"

She calmed down, and tried to echo his officious tone exactly. "No, Vom, no. As base commander of the Evan John McEwan Lunar Research Station I make my own scheduling decisions. In fact, unlike you, Commander Thibodeaux has been offering me his help, support and guidance. We have a plan, actually an overlapping series of plans, to recover all the equipment and stores, while ensuring the ongoing and continued safety of the mission and all those involved."

He dropped the haughty air and turned nasty. "Grappelli, you quit the smart-mouth double talk and listen to me. Your plan isn't worth shit. You're as finished as Thibodeaux and I'm hauling you both back here, along with the entire comms team, the insubordinate cook and that fucking tourist. Your orders just changed. Empty the POD, get the aliens to take the stupid wheels off and lift to orbit on the next available window. I'll get that calculated and give you a firm Go time in an hour."

"No." She favoured him with her sweetest smile.

"What are you talking about, no? What in the Galaxy is wrong with you?"

"Do stop screeching, Vom. They'll hear you out in the office and make fun of you again. The POD is no longer an option. We dropped it; well at least the Deep Race did, after we jacked it up on some rocks. Two of the exhaust vents are twisted and it won't fly."

"So I can add wilful property destruction to your rap sheet. It's stacking up. You already have to account for one killed, one LXV damaged beyond repair, plus two MAGENTA DS POD missions diverted. Now I'm adding one POD also damaged beyond repair."

One killed. Above everything else she was not going to stand for that.

"You listen to me, Redwood," she relished saving his surname until she could use it as a weapon. "I still have diminishing oxygen supplies and intermittent electrical problems to contend with. If you're in luck I will actually die out here, because if I ever get back to Earth and find myself face to face with you I'm going to hit you so hard they'll find your dead ass in another time zone.

"How dare you casually mention 'one killed' to me, as if losing Evan was my fault. That man died a hero trying to save my life. I am planning to add, 'so I could punch Vom Redwood's lights out,' to that memorial. You are a heartless, savage, incompetent bastard and I will personally see to it that you get fired for that one comment. Now get off my link and don't ever call McEwan Station again. I'm finished with you."

She watched his mouth working and willed herself to smile as she waited out the several seconds until he finally started to speak. The instant he did, she cut the link and sat taking deep breaths. After about an hour she switched back on and called Gene's.

"Gene's, Lucy."

Ajax and Mario sat each side of Bird. Ajax was grinning.

"Do you know what?" he started. "Between us, we might finish him off yet. I've just had another call from him and he's actually crying. He's shedding genuine tears of frustration because he can't control us. Paula captured the exchange between him, you, and Bird, and played it in the lounge. And I'll tell you something else, too. Somehow, that piece was also leaked to the press from an unidentified Lancaster source and the phone system at Lancaster has collapsed."

"Sorry Ajax," said Lucy. "My fault, but I will not have him speak to me like that. Every day since I met them, the members of my Deep Race team have demonstrated more humanity than he has. You could try asking the Reunited Nations who they'd rather have on Earth."

"Don't you start apologising. Leif called me from home to ask what we want him to do. Then Doc Tunstall called to say that Leif was after taking back control, but he won't allow the Director in for a few days yet. This time, we've poked the ant hill all right. The word got round up here and there's a pile of resignations on my desk citing, and I quote: 'No longer prepared to work for that shit Redwood', in the comments box."

"Add me," she said. "I quit too, unless he's fired."

"That makes it unanimous; every single person at Gene's has resigned. It looks like you just kicked off the revolution."

A few minutes later Eve Meredith called from Houston. Lucy didn't know the veteran astronaut well; in fact they had met just once or twice.

"Oh babe, you've started if off now. If you only knew how much Vom hates you. He's ordered me to organise an immediate evac. He wants a list of the great and good at Gene's, includin' you, en-route to Earth within 24. Word on the street is he's buildin' a mediaeval gallows and plannin' a public hangin'. He's goin' round like an Old West sheriff pointin' a gun, with his foul mouth writing checks his ass can't cash. If it wasn't so tragic, it'd be hilarious.

"I want you to know that my shift has added their resignations to Ajax' list, plus there's one growin' by the minute at Lancaster. Oh, and I did tell him there's a Corona launch window the day after tomorrow from Edwards, but only if he's available. He said he thought we were still a week off launchin', and asked why I couldn't still do it if he was busy. 'That's because the only way it lifts off will be with you impaled on the lightnin' spike ass first, and if that possibility turns out we'll set to and build that freakin' stack in the next 24.' My exact words. And hey, he fired me. I told him he couldn't do that and waved my already signed resignation at him, along with the whole pile. But he just became irrelevant. He won't be around more'n a day or two nohow."

Paula put through yet another call, this time from Mt. Rainier. The zombie vision of Sarkasian appeared on the big screen.

"Hey, Tavis! I wish you knew how much I love you, man. I only had two beers because I figure the rest should be for the crew at Gene's. Your manifest number made me laugh so hard when I got the joke."

"Oh yeah, the beer," Tavis reflected in the smooth bass drawl. "That was why he fired me."

"Shit, no! I'm so sorry."

"Hey, don't sweat it, Grappelli. My resignation is on the pile, he just don't know yet. Anyhow, before that he made demands.

Actual fact he was yelling so loud they heard him down in Puget Sound. Guy is unhinged I reckon.

"Word is I'm getting your damaged POD fixed up to fly and pulling you out of there on a twelve deadline. The guy's lost all sense of reality. How am I supposed to do that from here? Anyhow, what've you done to my POD? I like that one and I want it back."

She couldn't help but laugh. "Did I say I'd done anything to it? Oh, yeah I did. No Tavis, see I lied to Redwood, it's not even got a scratch. We've been so careful with it. As far as I can tell there's no damage. I checked yesterday and all systems showed green. I did steal the lights though, so I could drive NEIL through the lunar night, but they just unplugged."

She got his brightest deranged murderer grin. "Well hey, that's cool then. Those POD lights far outshine the LXV ones. Want me to see if we can't get the new vehicle fitted with some?"

"Sure, why not. Any other bright ideas?"

"No. Your puns kill me." The last was delivered deadpan. "I called Ajax to say we'd all quit too and he put me through. Good to talk to you, we'll see you back at Gene's real soon."

"You too, Tavis. Say man, I so owe you a beer. I want to send Budweiser some pics of me holding that first can, but maybe you and I should offer up some staged shots by this POD when I get back."

"Yeah, cool plan. Maybe they'll send us some."

"Sure, OK, see you, dude."

Paula came on immediately afterwards. All her callers were laughing today. "Oh baby! You done started a shit kickin' scene down Lancaster way."

"I told Redwood to get off my case and offered him a nose job is what."

"Yeah, Lancaster seen the tape, all over TV now. I'm hearin' he screamed the big office down. They all took one look an' went for a beer. Word is Bar 36 is jumpin' an' he don't know who to cry to."

Lucy laughed with her. "We could do with a party when I get back, but he ordered me to dump the beer and hit orbit in the POD for recovery. He implied Evan dying was my fault. That's when I lost it. I really will smack him if I ever lay eyes on him again."

"I'll hold your glass, baby."

Finally she took a call from Mario.

"Lucy, I resigned, actually we all did. Redwood was so rude to you."

"It's OK. I'll make sure he'll never do it again."

"I'd go to Lancaster and clean his clock for you but I can't reach."

She grinned and shook her head at him. "Mario, stature isn't about height. The presence can be greater than the man, you know. Never mind Redwood, I'm first in line to wipe the smug off his face. I've never seen anything like that evening you stood up to Ajax on my behalf; you're a good 1.80 m to me."

"I'm, er, why thanks, tall girl."

"Now, I have a problem here. When I get there we'll need this beer for a party. There were two packs of twelve and I drank two of them, so we'll have 22. What are we going to do about that?"

55 – CONTROL
7:59 AM (LST) 10ᵗʰ OCTOBER

There was a full staff meeting in the outer office as the elevator doors slid open; every head of department desk was occupied. Redwood ignored them, but managed to say "Good Morning, Penny," as he passed her desk.

"There's a visitor in the office for you, Mr. Redwood." She looked back to her screen in a gesture of dismissal. It galled her to even speak to him, but she refused point blank to use his title. His use of her first name deeply offended her. She knew it was deliberate, but she also knew it wouldn't happen again. As he stalked past, she got up to follow him through the door, closing it behind her.

Redwood found a relaxed looking Leif Culver behind the desk. Doc Tunstall was sitting in the lounge area.

"Chief, great to see you, Has Doc—"

"Yes he has. Sit." Culver indicated the chair opposite his desk.

"Ah, Penny," he added. "Would you stay?"

"Of course, thank you Leif." She sat down at the in-office work station and turned the screen on. Culver then did the same as Penny, bending to his console and typing.

"Leif—"

"I said sit, I did not say talk." Culver didn't even look up. It was 7:59 AM and it looked like he had been there for hours, maybe even all night.

The Director finished with the file he was updating and the screen retracted into the desk. After the longest minute in Redwood's life, he looked up, rested his elbows and linked his fingers together.

"Doctor Tunstall has cleared me for light duties a week or so earlier than he would like, but under the circumstances we have deemed it necessary. After discussing options I have taken control of the situation on the Moon, and liaison between there and Houston. I'm delegating all other management tasks.

"I've sent a file to your office, detailing the changes. When we finish here you can familiarise yourself. That is correct procedure, falling well within your ability to comprehend without question."

Redwood started to speak, but Penny cut him off. "No, Mr. Redwood. The Director hasn't finished. Sit still and pay attention." Her oh-so-innocent smile received the blackest of looks.

"Thank you, Penny." Culver turned back to face Redwood. "Last night I spoke to Commander Thibodeaux. What I learned prompted my early return to this seat. After this meeting I am going home for the rest of the day under doctor's orders."

He paused to test his authority, but Redwood had got the message and sat stony-faced. In truth, Culver felt a little cruel, but he was about to lance a boil that he should have treated months ago; he had a clear conscience. "That's good, Will. Your continued silence indicates that you've learned something already. Last night, Ajax read me a list of names. Effective from midnight every single member of the Base Team at Gene's refused to work under you any longer. Each one has tendered their resignation. There are similar requests from across the business. Oh, and the Guest Astronomer at Gene's too."

Redwood lost his cool and started shouting. "Fucking ignorant tourist! He's behind all this—"

Doc Tunstall appeared between him and the desk, shouting Redwood down. "You will be Silent! The Director hasn't finished. I

344

will not have him stressed and he did not give you permission to speak. Are we clear?" Redwood nodded.

Tunstall turned to Culver. "I'm sorry, Leif, he will hear you out now."

"Thank you, Eric," said the Director quietly. "Now listen and make certain you understand this. When I am finished you will acknowledge before these witnesses that you will comply with my instructions. Oh, yes, and there is an 'or else' too. Pay attention, or by the Stars I will fire you on the spot. Am I also making myself crystal clear?"

"Yes, Director." Redwood swallowed and turned pink.

"When the resignation news got out, as it always does, several department heads here on Floor Fifty also tendered their paperwork to the pile."

"And me," added Penny. "I won't work for you either, Mr. Redwood."

"What happened here, Will?" asked Culver.

"They are beyond any kind of discipline, and they're being rude and insubordinate. It's like a pirate operation. They've even got alcohol. I've lost count of the broken and abused rules, the equipment damage, and the supply wastage. As for Grappelli, she was promoted to a nothing job six ranks out of her league and is strutting about with her aliens as if she owns the fucking Moon."

Culver leaned back in his chair and watched Redwood clench and unclench his fists. The man was barely in control of himself, which was why Penny and Doc were there. If he flipped, or if Culver himself felt stressed or looked ill, there were plenty of people standing by in the outer office, waiting for a single touch on her keyboard.

Culver sighed, "Will, they are dealing with an unprecedented situation up there, and they are doing some great work. The

President told them to use whatever they needed and the improvisation has been amazing. This is no longer part of our commercial survey operation and is a government backed effort. Equipment loss is a minor problem."

"Improvisation? Oh, for pity's sake! They are ignoring basic rules. Half of them aren't even wearing regulation safety gear but they seem to be inventing a new kind of theme park. Grappelli is out racing around in LXVs and customised PODs as if she's in some fantastic destruction derby, and that stupid cook is out flying ancient jump-rigs and getting himself half-killed in the process. I haven't approved any of that, I can tell you. I can't even get through to people with instructions because that dwarf and the monosyllabic woman with the smartass mouth won't put me through to departments. Resignation my ass. Half of them are coming back here to find new employment before I'm finished."

Culver stopped him with a raised hand. "Enough. This pains me, Will, but the deal just changed, right there. In fact you said it yourself. I came here today with every intention of finding a way for you to save face, that's how I operate. Sadly there's no way back. It's you that's finished, I'm afraid. I can't have you failing this organisation by making half its members resign. I can't have a man anywhere near the centre who the press won't even interview. Above all I can't have anyone belittling the efforts and abilities of an extraordinary team of people who have pulled together to work through several of the most dangerous situations ever faced by any astronauts. You are so far out of your depth here that it's taken the entire management team in the office outside to keep the organisation from looking like a circus."

"Finished? What exactly do you mean by that?"

Culver sighed deeply. "I mean exactly this, Will: I've heard quite enough this morning to know I'm making a sound

346

management decision. You should have kept quiet and apologised for being naive enough to lose control and spend the last few weeks pandering to your own ego. Instead you opened your mouth and laid the blame everywhere else.

"I've been trying to find another way we could use your skills, but through being downright nasty you blew that idea clean out of the water. On a personal level I'm sorry because this is going to be hard on you. As of this moment, I am relieving you of that and all other duties. Until we convene a board meeting you are suspended."

"You fucking wouldn't. There's a procedure—"

"Yes, Will," Culver replied with real menace. "I would, and in fact I just did. The correct procedure is that I suspend you before suitable witnesses and talk to the board." He looked left and right, acknowledging nods from Penny and Tunstall. "You may appeal of course, but unless the board decides otherwise, as far as I am concerned you're fired. It's all in your famous rule book, so don't accuse me of not following it to the letter." He turned to Penny. "Did I miss anything?"

"No, Director, I don't believe you did."

"Thanks." He pressed a button. "Blake, I need you to step in here and escort Mr. Redwood off the premises, without passing through the lobby. He can leave from the garage without talking to the press. Security will require his ID card. Thank you."

Looking back at Redwood he sighed again. "Blake Shermann will take you downstairs and drive you home. Somebody will drop your own car later. Now get out of my office, Will. Until the board makes a decision you are still under contract to us. If I see or hear one word, and I do mean one single word, crying foul, or defaming any person in this organisation, I will stop paying you immediately and we will sue for damages under the terms of that

347

contract. Actually, I've changed my mind on that one. Why don't you call a press conference and tell them what happened? We already know what they think of you, don't we? A NASA Deputy Director the press won't interview. Says a lot, doesn't it?"

"I suggest you go and find the cactus I believe Ajax recommended. You could sit on it for a while and try to work out what makes you such a mean man. We will get back to you when we are ready, and not before."

He nodded to Shermann, who had entered the office to stand behind Redwood. The ex-Deputy left without another word.

"That was well handled, Leif," said Penny. "I'm glad you fired him. He's beyond redemption."

"Don't apologise. Thanks for your support, both of you. Before you ask, I'm calm and cool, and Eric here knows or he'd have me out on a stretcher. I hated doing it, and in all these years I've never fired an employee before. In a way I'm sorry that the board will ratify my decision when this is all over. Still, we can't afford to have that sort of nastiness here. On reflection, he's been my greatest mistake, and my biggest career disappointment. I'll wait until security calls me to say he's gone, and then I'll go home. Sunny is waiting in the coffee shop to drive me."

Once again, Lucy drove through the cleared path through the rock fall. Even though the plan had changed, she was content. The camper and trailer, as the people at Gene's seemed to be calling the new rig, turned east towards Gene's. Driving in the dark wasn't so bad with the twin-bulb POD lights, and when they next stopped she was going to find a way to hook up the other two pairs of lights at the top of the LXV and give herself the maximum possible forward vision.

As they reached 15 km/h she felt a distinct snaking movement as the POD swung left and then right, pulling NEIL off the driving line. Slowing to 12 km/h helped a little. She decided to check for a sweet spot at a higher speed, where the rig might be more stable. At 25 km/h there was a huge thump and a lot of claws started hammering on the roof. She stopped and waited while 2,5,1, who was riding inside, wrote:

POD NO
III-IIII-II FIX

There was a pause for a minute or two while they hooked the cobbled-together trailer back on. She tried again but with the same result. This time she went outside to join them for a look at the problem.

3,4,2 and 2,5,1 were already drawing a much more secure-looking hook attached to the bars on NEIL. They also indicated that wanted to retrieve some more spare parts from the junk pile. Feeling defeated, she turned and drove the whole rig back to where they had started.

Another delay followed while the Deep Race re-built the attachment. Lucy found herself frustrated and miserable. She could have walked further than she'd driven. For the first time she considered dumping NEIL and lifting to orbit in the POD.

Back at Gene's, Mario was monitoring comms and Paula was watching the telemetry from NEIL for any signs of progress. GPS was telling the story.

"Hey Lucy, it's Mario. You OK?"

"Hi Mario, We're outside working on the tow bar. We had a major problem with the rig snaking at any speed, and then it disconnected. They're building a Mk.II version right now in an effort to keep the POD attached, but we can't see an easy way to damp out the motion. It's a long drive home, and I'm pissed."

Mario rolled his eyes at Paula. "Oh, I'm sorry to hear that. Still, even if you plan to drive slower you may still be home before dawn." He was already trying to think of ways to keep her spirits up.

For once Paula decided not to be flippant. "Frustratin'. Film the bar and I'll ask Ellis."

"OK, stand by." Paula watched as the suit camera showed the Deep Race working on a tow bar with a much longer hook at the end, curved right back on itself to stop the disconnection problem.

The engineers and LXV experts spent all afternoon on the stability problem. They came back to Lucy to ask her to re-distribute the load in the POD so that the front wheel carried more weight. She was disappointed, but to be fair they didn't have many options. She gave in and started her sleep period earlier than usual, hoping to depart the next day.

The Deep Race had been working on the same problem. Their solution was a lot more radical. They started some axle modifications on the disconnected POD, ready for when Lucy woke up.

Once she approved of the plan, they produced a set of ramps fabricated from their stores. Guided by one of them as a flagman, Lucy drove NEIL far enough up to get the odd wheel on axle 2 off the ground. This was then removed, and added to the new axle they had fashioned for the POD, giving it four wheels in all. They put the large wheels at the back, and the smaller ones at the front. They also attached a set of double towing hooks to damp out the motion, plus some flanges to fit on the POD's front axle and keep the hooks roughly in place on the framework. It took all morning.

The best speed NEIL could manage while towing was still only 18 km/h before the rig became unstable, but the motion was nowhere near as severe. Lucy was once again disappointed. She had to be content with the prospect that progress would be slow, but safe. Apart from the so-called 'POD mods', the LXV engineers, especially the ever-cautious Ellis, were happier to see NEIL running level on three axles than offset in any way.

Lucy and the aliens all retrieved something different from the pile to carry as spares. The POD ended up carrying another girder long enough to make a pair of replacement axles, together with several long pipes and various other pieces of metalwork. These were threaded through the open frame base and lashed on with aerial wire. There were also two more of the smaller rear axle wheels and loops of extra wire in various gauges.

Mario took the evening report, accompanied by Bird. Doc Fisher had discovered a chipped shin to add to his woes. He would be out of action for several days yet, but kept busy collating a lot of the base history. Pelican had suggested they keep him on the comms crew so he could spell the others.

351

Mario was speaking. "Lucy, we're all trying to support your thinking as much as we can. I've got a suggestion, but I bet you've considered it already. Don't go any further from the parts supply shop until you are as sure as you can be that what you have actually works. Remember, you're at the last service station for 1,400 km."

"I hadn't thought of it in those terms, but I've been working on that principle. We've selected what we can carry in the way of spares. They hauled an amazing amount of parts up from that old ship, you know. I'm desperate for action now, in the sense of actually going somewhere. I'm stir-crazy."

Bird nodded at her. "There's a lot of 'I don't know how she's done it, I would have taken the POD and gone home' talk around here. We all know you're full of schemes to avoid that."

"I didn't think in those exact terms either. You two cheer me up. Look, I need to go and see how the work is coming along. Can we talk later?"

"Sure, as long as Ajax doesn't find more excuses to keep me out of here," Mario complained. "I keep getting assigned to the garage and this is my office after all." She could see that he was smiling.

"Tell him from me that if I don't get to talk to you both every shift, I'll dump the beer."

A bit of conspiracy was good for the soul. "That I will do. See you later then."

"Good evening, Paula."

She looked up at the screen and actually squeaked. "Leif! Oh, man, how are ya?"

"I'm doing well, thank you. Rumour tells me you'd had the Lucy hair-do, or lack of. Suits you. Listen, can you do something for me and arrange a staff meeting in the lounge as soon as possible, but without letting on why? I'd like to sneak up on them."

"You bet! Dark, ain't nobody out. In twenty OK?"

"Thanks for that. 7:00 PM will be excellent."

Paula organised yet another short notice full staff meeting with the Lancaster Team. As usual she manned the comms console at the back of the lounge and watched until the Director was ready, then dimmed the lights and brought him up on the big screen. There was a pause of about a second before the entire team got to its feet and applauded their boss. He smiled and waved the ovation away, motioning them all back into their seats.

"Oh, get out of here with all that, folks. Sit down and relax, will you? All right, here's all the news. I'm feeling well but still fatigued. I have no pulse as the robot heart pumps using a propeller. After detailed negotiations with Doc Tunstall he's allowed me to manage the rescue operation between a few hours a week here at the Tower and some time at home. Everything else I have to delegate.

"I've assigned control and management of all other duties to the relevant section heads. From now on, you have my full attention and any help or advice I can offer. Ajax, please carry on running your excellent and innovative operation as you see fit.

"From what I've seen, there has been some amazing cross-department support there and you've made more progress than I could have hoped for."

Ajax stood up. "Thanks, Leif. From every one of us, welcome back. There was a sigh of relief here that stretched the recirc system to its limit. I need to know what role your Deputy has assumed?" There was a murmur of approval.

"Yes, you are all entitled to a full explanation on that score, and please accept my profound apologies. Redwood is suspended, until such time as the board convenes to decide if he has a future with this organisation. I'd like to give a nod here to Mario and Paula, who I understand have had a hard time with him, while protecting the rest of you from some of the worst of his nastiness.

"Any questions? No? Great, so I have a few pieces of news to tell you. The people in Seattle have enough spare parts to build a whole new LXV. I have already ordered one as you know, and somehow Kent Warwick managed to outfox everybody and order another while he was requisitioning a new TUG. That means we already have two brand-new examples to come, plus one cooked up from the spares source, making three in all.

"Sarkasian will send it up in the next few weeks. They are doing as much pre-assembly as possible. Kyran and Ellis, you two will be on LXV construction duties for the foreseeable future. NEIL will go to Bird for his museum upon arrival. You two can give yourselves a break before you have to start work on the new machine. As soon as it's up and running, the two new ones should arrive as they are already in emergency production. The national wallet rarely opens, but the President gave us carte blanche to get equipped and we are making the most of it.

"I do need to say a few words about the rules, people. One of the things that bugged Redwood the most was his assertion that there has been a lot of deliberate rule-breaking." He was trying not to smile.

"I can't imagine that any of you would taunt him." Thibodeaux growled and the giggling stopped. "Thank you, Ajax. Now I haven't been studying the screen as I don't seem to have the right glasses on, but next time we speak I expect to see correct dress on the base. There are still some rocks flying around up there, and it would be a shame to lose anybody else at this stage. Penny will have restored order in the office and found my glasses by the time I come back to you at 2:00 PM tomorrow.

"Alcohol. It's reasonable to assume everybody in shock has had need of medication during the last few weeks. There's been a number of comments about drinking. I know about Tavis's supply of beer for the base, and we can't drag that all the way back here, can we? You lot had better dispose of it, I don't know, I guess you will have to think of a way to recycle it into the water loop.

"Ajax, you are quoted as saying you had lost count of the rules and regs Lucy has broken, but that every broken rule had either improved her situation, or increased the odds on her chances of survival. As you start back to work after this, would it be fair of me to ask you all to hold that thought? The operation must be safe and efficient, and the book ensures those ends. Enough said, I think.

"I'm through for this evening, because I can see Doctor Tunstall hovering outside. It's my second visit to the Tower today and he's looking tetchy now. I thought I'd get away with it, but I swear that man has spies everywhere." He looked around, provoking a general chuckle.

"There are two more quick points I need to cover before cocoa on my veranda at Mojave. We need to start rotating staff back here, and the Houston roster office is nipping at my heels about it. I wouldn't dare order anybody home until after Lucy gets back.

355

After that you will be over-staffed and there will have to be some movement. The immediate question is whether anyone wants to come home sooner?" There was a general shaking of heads. "OK, then. If anyone decides they do, please see Ajax.

"My last item is this pile of resignations. You all cited the same problem, and I have dealt with that as demanded, er, suggested by you all. Does anybody want me to ratify their resignation before I go home?"

There was a huge jeer and an outbreak of mirth in the lounge. One or two people threw styro cups.

"That's the spirit, and case closed I think; these can go in the shredding. What about you, Pelican? You've seen the show and played your part. Do you want to come home yet?"

"Not a chance, Leif," shouted the Australian, to a warm round of applause, "I'd like to stay here for the full six months if we can spare the air. I've never had so much fun. When I get back I'm coming to talk to you about a proper job."

"That's not a problem, and you've earned the right. Folks, thanks for turning up on short notice. One last question and I'll let you all go. It's a pity you clowns already threw your cups. I want to know who it was that called Redwood a dickhead?" That finished it on a high. He gave them a wave and cut the connection.

Ajax called during the evening to tell Lucy the news that Leif was back in charge, and send the taped meeting for her to enjoy. She settled down in good spirits, but wondering if she would ever actually get away from the place. She hated the prospect of sitting out the long night waiting for the dawn.

She slept well, waking to the feeling that at long last all the bases were covered. After breakfast she called in to announce her departure. There was a surprise waiting. Everybody was scattered around the lounge area, out of uniform and with many loud shirts on view. Paula had set up the kit so that when Lucy called in they could see her on the big screen.

"Good morning, Gene's. Oh, hi there everybody. Am I missing something?"

Pelican appeared to be in charge, wearing a ridiculous wide-brimmed hat with things dangling around the brim. Ajax was sitting in the audience for a change.

"G'day Lucy!" yelled the jovial Aussie, in a much stronger accent than usual. "Now these fellas have all cancelled their resignations, but they've had to take a day off until the blasted paperwork catches up and they get reinstated. The whole station is in limbo. I've staged a bloody revolution, deposed Ajax, and taken control of the base so I can host a waving-off party. Actually it's a bit of a tradition in me family to have a huge barbi in honour of any new journey. It's not even for you. We're celebrating the fact that *the beer* is on its way at last. We're toasting with bloody *soft* drinks. The kitchen served up hot dogs with some special sauce Bird made and we're keeping a jar of that for you. From all of us here, good luck driving. Cheers!"

There was a great "Cheers," and a lot of other noise. As usual, the cups were flying.

He went on, "We invited Vom to join us, but he's gone an' got himself fired, the arsehole!" They were helpless with laughter by this time. He managed one more line. "Come on, Lucy. You've got the bloody beer. For gawd's sake stir yerself will yer?"

She pulled herself together. "Thanks, Pelican, you're a one-off. I'll get your beer there in one piece. OK, the Deep Race are already outside on the roof and I'm up for two four-hour sessions today, travelling at around 15 km/h, for a total of 120 km. You betting, Ace? I'll be busy but I'll leave the cameras on and chat. NEIL is rolling now."

There was an almighty cheer at Gene's.

Travelling down slope and on the flat, NEIL's realistic stability limit was 15 km/h, but on a smooth upslope 18 km/h was possible. Towing the POD and running on six wheels, the LXV showed less of the usual tendency to hop in the air. The increased weight on board was a possible factor, with supplies from the POD stuffed in the cabin and bunks. Lucy felt that NEIL ran better on six wheels, and made a note to take it up with Kyran and Ellis, maybe for some trials later.

She made slow progress, and by her scheduled stop she was behind the plan with only 45 km covered. She met the team outside and they checked the towing and running gear. 3,4,2 stayed on the roof, working on a device to hang the spare lights on. They were so good at planning ahead, and a bit more high-level light would aid the longer view of the trail.

By the end of a long eight-hour stretch she was 92 km closer to Gene's. Slow progress, and her head and eyes ached. Once again the Deep Race retired to the POD, and she settled down for a night's sleep. The next day she would drive without her lookouts, as they were due for their own rest period and would stay in the POD for the next 36 hours.

* * *

"No, no, no, oh shit."

Team Leader Anton Levine looked across the Houston control room. "That sounded final."

The TEL Operator looked up at him from the shop floor. "Sorry Ton, telemetry glitched on the rocket. It's resetting itself now."

Another tense voice joined in. "Trajectory is off by three, no, four degrees. Whoa, that's a tumble maneuver. Stabilisation shut down too. Stand by... Anton, it won't make orbit."

Anton felt the snake of fear slither across his shoulders. "TEL?"

"Back on-line. Oh, no way, man! The fuel level is dropping and we're end over. Loss of control and major damage. That's a mission abort."

Anton stood up and raised his voice to order mode. "DELIVERY, separate the POD immediately if you can. Everything is secondary to saving it. NAV, let the rocket go, work with the POD and give me a landing zone and ETA close to Lucy in the next thirty seconds. TEL, data on where the rocket will come down, that's your bag. SAFETY, if TEL says less than 200 km from Gene's, call me back. When the Pod is loose, press the destruct button on the rocket if necessary. If not, track it to impact. Use all the down-and-up fuel in the POD if you need to, it doesn't need to get back to orbit. As close to Lucy as possible, team. If we lose this one she will die."

By the time he had finished they were all heads-down.

"Lucy, Ajax."

She knew by his tone. "What happened?"

359

"Well, I've got good news and bad news. The DS338 POD is on the surface, that's definitely good news. They lost the MAGENTA as it hit orbit, probably comet debris. It's a good thing they delayed Eve's mission to bring new staff up. Anton's team did some rapid thinking and jettisoned the POD at the first sign of trouble. By a supreme effort and some great luck, they dropped it in some flattish country north-west of Crater Agrippa. It came down a lot harder than normal after they ran out of puff using every gramme of the down-and-up fuel to get it as close to you as possible."

Lucy swallowed. "And...?"

"And it could have been a lot worse. The MAGENTA crashed over 500 km west of your position, hard enough to make its own crater. But for Houston's lightning reactions the POD would be there too. We are working on a new route for you right now. Ace and Pelican are looking at hundreds of digitals taken before sundown by the MAGENTA that dropped your trailer. Keep on heading east and we will find you a route to the POD. They are certain it will be intact and your supplies should be OK.

She realised how fatiguing the stress really was, and sighed. "Did you just say Agrippa? Crater Agrippa? Ajax, that's way off to the south and there's not much oxygen left here."

"Tobin says you have a little more than he calculated. He was being conservative on the numbers, and you haven't been exerting yourselves like you were a few days ago. He says NEIL has over two days supply for you all yet."

She shut her eyes for a moment. "If only we'd been able to access their big air spheres, or they were small enough to bring some along. The Deep Race are on a 36 hour break in the POD. They say they use a lot less air that way, so with luck we'll stretch the supply here. I'm dead tired and I'm quitting for now, but I'll suit up to preserve on-board supplies while I'm awake, and go as fast as I can tomorrow in the hope you can locate a route."

"Hang in there, Lucy. At the moment that's the best I can offer you."

After sleeping for six hours and finding herself wide awake, she had a quiet chat with Paula before driving again. She punished herself, driving for a total of fourteen hours and putting another 160 km of tracks behind them. There was no news from the Deep Race, and no update on a route to the DS338 POD. She still had some 300 km left to drive, even if Ace and Pelican could find and upload a route.

She stopped for the night and reported in, then sat and reflected on the situation. Back to worrying about diminishing oxygen. *Here I am, stuck in a tin can with no way to reach safety in time unless I can find a damaged POD in the dark, off trail, down south in the canyons west of Hyginus. Why does it have to be Hyginus? I even hate driving the marked trail on the other side in the light. Great.*

After a four hour nap out of a suit, she donned the second charged example to conserve the on-board air supply. Determined to drive as long as it held out, she ignored all the O2 LOW warnings on the head-up. When the red alarm went off, indicating that it could no longer keep her from hypoxia, she waited another fifteen minutes before discarding it. In nine gruelling hours she had covered a disappointing 85 km.

Trapped, Lucy trapped, trapped in the LXV, no, under a rock. She was in Evan's suit, stuck out on the regolith with an air leak she couldn't reach. The O2 CRITICAL sign flashed red in the head-up and she gasped as she looked at the Earth above. Choking... Trapped... Gasping...

"NO!" She sat straight up, hitting her head on the top of the tiny bunk space. Dream, Lucy-Lu, it was a dream. Deep breath. Her panting slowed.

"Gene's, Lucy."

"Mornin' girl."

"Hi Paula, I don't even know what day it is."

"Monday, baby, 13th. Early, 4:15 AM. You OK?"

"I don't know. I had a nightmare about oxygen. Time has either rushed like crazy or stood still since the crash. I feel like I'm both approaching and receding from something important, or there's something I'm missing. Some piece of a puzzle, maybe. Am I making any sense here?"

"Gotta say no." Paula smiled at her and in a rare moment ditched the cut and freeze-dried persona, switching to the South Carolina drawl. "Lucy, you done things even you would have never imagined yuh could. Had a massive shock and lost a close friend, and then we couldn't be there to he'p yuh. We all wanna put arms around and say things will be OK. Soon, girl. Hang on in there a few more days, but someone always here. Always."

"Thanks, Paula. I need that hug and I'm coming back for it. It's the first time I've had a bad dream. I've had some dreams about Evan and they make me feel so odd. I tend to wake up crying happy tears because the Deep Race will Name him in their Great Saga, whatever that is supposed to mean. Somehow it seems like they are taking care of his memory for me, and that feels right. So much has happened since the crash, but it seems like less than an hour ago, I get flashbacks and they scare me. I'm afraid I'll making a wrong decision and kill us all."

"I paged Ajax, his orders soon as you up."

"Not at this time of the morning!"

Thibodeaux arrived in the comms office still rubbing his eyes. "Hey, Lucy. You OK? Early call."

"I'm sorry Ajax, I had a nightmare and called in for a hug. I didn't ask Paula to wake you."

"No, that's cool. I'm going to give you a piece of good news and then ask you to rest a while longer. Then I'm getting on with stuff here. I've not been sleeping much anyway."

Paula butted in. "He done made Pelican deppity boss. Levon dee-lighted!"

"That's sound thinking, Ajax," Lucy told him. "We all knew Levon didn't relish that role."

"Yeah, he's too busy in the garage with Ellis and Ky to do much. I'm trying to spread the load. Pelican is a certified manager and runs a major organisation. I asked for a show of hands at the meeting and got a unanimous vote in favour. Leif said he'd take a whole day off and rest because Pelican would employ common sense. He powers people up somehow. Maybe he's far enough outside the operation he can see things we can't. Pelican is also the reason you are alive, because he thought out of the box and asked if the POD you are towing could drop at Evan's Place. He's good for morale too, like staging your waving-off party."

"That is good news. Strange how we use his first name, Leif, but always referred to his ex-deputy as Redwood, or Vom. Says it all, I guess."

"That wasn't even the good news. The POD's beacon is on. We didn't tell you it was off after the hard landing, but Houston have been trying everything they could to initiate it. TEL 1 picked it up last night. That gives us a more accurate location. Actually their original position, based on the pre-landing data, was less than ten kilometres out. What's more, Ace and Pelican have a route staked out and are plotting it for upload to NAV."

Lucy shivered. "I think what gives me the chills over this is the fear of trailblazing in the dark and falling into a crevasse, I don't even like driving the marked trail east of Hyginus, even though the canyon is kilometres away. I always arrange, uh, arranged, for Evan to drive that section. It's not heights exactly, but I hated doing survival training in the Grand Canyon. It's an odd fear, in fact of all the dramas I've faced, the thought of going over the side of that crater in the rock fall was what scared me most."

Thibodeaux shook his head at her. "My, my, Commander, do you have an identifiable weakness?" He managed to keep a straight face.

"Guess so, who knew?" she retorted with a wry laugh.

"So, based on their route being a Go, it's a good thing you didn't make better time so far. The turn-off point from the West Way is five kilometres behind your present position. Why don't you and I both get some beauty sleep and then we'll upload the route in the morning?"

* * *

NEIL left the West Way at 7:00 AM, heading south east between the two great canyons Triesnecker and Hyginus. There was plenty of wiggle room each side, but Lucy drove with more care than she ever had. In places she slowed to below walking pace as the dangerous shadows fooled her in the headlights. 3,4,2 had joined her in NEIL, riding in the passenger seat. The others stayed in the POD on standby, using as little of the precious oxygen as possible.

After an hour, 3,4,2 passed another message across:

TEAM IN NEIL SOON
POD AIR NO

She brought NEIL to a stop, so she could write back using the muli-choice format.

TEAM AIR FULL 12 / TEAM AIR FULL 24

3,4,2 was certain:

TEAM AIR 4
POD AIR NO

Lucy asked a question she had worried about ever since their first meeting. How close had they been to running out of air?

LUCY TEAM MEET
TEAM IN NEIL
TEAM AIR 12 / TEAM AIR 24

This time he reply made her gasp:

TEAM LUCY MEET
TEAM IN NEIL
TEAM AIR NO 2

Lucy wrote:

TEAM IN NEIL NOW.

According to NAV, she had 137 km to travel. The final oxygen tank was dropping towards the red zone, but there were no alarms ringing. She plugged an unused suit into the system and drained it into the main tanks. The gauge showed twelve hours. She had stretched nine hours from an eight hour suit, so when NEIL's supply fell to the red line again it should indicate at least three hours left. It put a new perspective on her fighting with Thibodeaux about the LXV mission safety margins. *Ironic that this time I'm up against that red line for real.*

She drained the last spare suit back into the system, and the computer showed 21 hours. There was about six hours left in the suit she was using. As the Deep Race came in through the airlock in pairs, she realised that they were short of air too. That 21 hour calculation equalled about twelve hours for the four of them, but a lot longer if they stayed inactive. She would have to use suit air. She needed to ask them to oxygenate, then go back to the POD and keep as still as possible. She wrote:

> LUCY AIR 24
> TEAM FULL AIR 4 / TEAM FULL AIR 8
> TEAM IN POD REST
> USE LESS AIR

3,4,2 replied:

> 3,4,2 AIR FULL
> TEAM FULL AIR 1
> TEAM IN POD REST

This one would be difficult. She thought carefully:

TEAM NO AIR FULL
TEAM AIR FULL LUCY DIE
TEAM AIR REST 18
LUCY FIND POD
AIR IN POD

Once the others were inside they carried on, 3,4,2 and 2,5,1 taking turns to observe from the driving seat. 2,5,1 attracted her attention:

MORE LIGHT DRIVE FAST

Lucy signalled in the affirmative. He climbed down and had a sharp tapping conference with the others, before handing up a message:

NEIL STOP
TEAM AIR REST 20
2,5,1 / 3,1,5 REST POD
2,2,1 / 3,4,2 REST TOP NEIL LIGHT
LUCY DRIVE FAST

They unpacked the spare POD lights from the outside locker and plugged them into the remaining external sockets. Lucy heard them climb up to the roof to find claw holds. Suddenly, the way ahead was floodlit. Somebody tapped "GO" on the roof, and she pushed the bar forwards.

Dips, craters, stones to avoid. Without a marked trail the concentration made her head and shoulders stiff. There was no chance of a sleep break and she was tiring by the hour. Round, over, avoid, 10 km/h maximum, often less, still more than twelve hours to go. She had changed suits, leaving one left for when she arrived at the POD. After the other three had charged their air bladders, NEIL showed five single-person hours, plus the spare suit. The team would be OK if they kept still, but Lucy wondered if the margin was too fine.

She stopped and tapped on the side wall. There was scurrying above, and 2,2,1 appeared, hanging outside the front windows to see her message:

LUCY REST 2

He waved and the lights went off.

"Gene's, Lucy."

"It's Ajax, go." He was sitting with Paula, Mario, and Tobin.

"Data says 44 km to run. I can't drive any more without a break; my head is killing me and I can't see straight. I'll take something for it and then shut my eyes for two hours. Will you call me then?"

Tobin replied. "Talk oxygen first, Lucy."

"OK, Tobe. I'm in the last suit and it still has about three hours left. I did have an idea though. I drained the other spare into NEIL to see if I could work out a safety margin below the red line. I'd stopped using the others before they red-lined, so I had NEIL scavenge those, too. NEIL indicates what I now believe is sixteen single person hours on tanks.

He was busy at a console. "I concur on your numbers. If you have three hours in that suit, don't use it until you get to the POD. Depending on the residual supply, top it up before you go out.

"Thanks, Tobin, that's a working plan then. I'm too exhausted for new ideas. Ajax, I wish I hadn't fought you on safety

368

margins, that all seems like a lifetime ago. I guess this is the payback. I feel like I did when I saw the Deep Race creeping on the rocks; the horrors of foreboding. I'm not frightened of dying, but I can't bear the thought of the failure." She felt a tear run down her cheek. "It's not that far to the red line. I so need a hug."

Mario stood up and held his arms out. "Hugs are here, Lucy. We're all waiting for real ones."

She swallowed hard. "Thanks, Mario. Ajax, I'm signing off for now, but would you leave Mario there to watch me sleep? Do not let me have more than two hours; we cannot afford it this time."

After a quick bathroom visit, two painkillers, a half-litre of water and an energy bar she lay in her bunk with the shutters open. *There is no way I'm going to sleep.*

* * *

She propped herself up on one elbow to look across at Evan in the driving seat. He turned round and grinned at her for having forty winks, like he was so famous for.

> "Then roll we did,
> My Lucy-Lu,
> I'm rollin' up there,
> Just like you,
>
> One rock at a time,
> It busted my ass,
> I'll be waiting for ya,
> Above the pass,
>
> Rest easy now,
> And I'll watch you sleep,
> Then I'll roll to the top,

369

Breathe shallow, breathe deep."

* * *

"Lucy!"

"EVAN! Uh? Oh, hey, Mario. Evan was here, right there in the seat. It's like he's closer when I'm too tired to lift my head. Do you know what? It happens when the Deep Race are all close by and resting. I wonder if it's something to do with them. I need to think about it when I get the time."

"Dreaming again, Lucy. You made me jump. Your two hours are up. You OK?"

She sniffled a bit and pulled herself together. "I'm fragile when I wake up after dreaming about him. Don't you worry about me; let's go find this POD."

He brightened. "Thanks for asking Ajax to leave me to watch you. I need to remind you of the need to make good time on this final stretch."

She yawned and rubbed her eyes. "Do you know what? I don't believe it's a dream any more. Evan is following us, I know it now. He's watching over me, or something. I don't believe in ghosts." *Or do I?* She tapped on the side of the cabin and the big lights were switched back on above.

The trail climbed higher, winding between lines of craters and over rolling hills. Several times she had to turn back and find a better route. The frustration grew as time stretched forwards. With luck she was drawing ever closer to the POD, without, ever closer to the red line that would mark the end of her own trail. The theory said twelve hours of air inside, as indicated by NEIL, but there wasn't much left in the suit for when they found the crash site. It took another eleven interminable hours to reach the point at which Ajax called a halt.

370

"Lucy, Ajax. Stop there. The computer can't separate the relative positions of NEIL and the POD."

Paula chimed in. "See it? You there, baby."

"No. Stand by Paula. Quiet now, and let me think here." *Damn, terse with one of my best friends. Deal with that later. One hour of air left inside, and I closed the suit visor over an hour ago. Two hours in the suit... maybe. No real margin left.*

She drew a quick picture and then banged on the wall. 2,2,1 appeared, dangling by the front window and hanging by some rear claws. She held up a drawing of him atop NEIL holding the POD light, an arrowed circle indicating it swinging around. Underneath she had written "POD". He disappeared and the twin cones of brightness started a careful sweep. After a few minutes he tapped a single code on the roof, "No."

3,4,2 was waving frantically from the dust ahead. She looked at the large letters he was drawing in front of NEIL.

SUIT NO AIR LOCKER
SUIT LIGHTS

Of course they did. The POD lights needed the power supply from NEIL but the suits were independent. The suits shut down when not in use, but even after scavenging the last few breaths of air out of them they would still have power available. She signed 'Yes', and he ran to one side. After about thirty seconds, he reappeared with a used suit. A few seconds later 2,2,1 carried out another other one as high as his large rear claws would stretch. Lucy was drawing a suit arm as large as she could, showing the power test on/off and light switches on the external panel. She pressed it against the window and they switched the suit lights on, before scuttling off in different directions looking for higher ground.

371

Ten minutes later 3,4,2 was back in the headlight beams, pointing off to Lucy's left with both right side arms. He needn't have taken the effort to write the single word.

POD

2,2,1 also arrived back and wrote alongside.

LUCY WAIT
NEIL GO UP
TOW BAR NO

They tapped each other, then both went out of sight. She heard them unhitch the bar, and the sound of claws going up the rear ladder. Somebody tapped 'Go' on the roof and she swung round to her left. The brighter POD lights were already pointing at a steep slope maybe 500 m away. She steered left and right, looking for a better way up, but saw an unbroken ridge line. She had to trust her team; this was the final chance. What is on the other side of that?

There was still that horror of ridges, canyons, and shadows. She took her hands off and let NEIL drift to a halt. Many claws rapped on the roof, stopped, and then repeated the signal: "Go, go."

The O2 LOW alarm flashed on Lucy's tiny head-up screen. She'd disabled the sound alarm in the hope Tobin wouldn't catch it at Gene's, and cancelled the warning. 55 minutes left, plus the twenty margin she had managed to drag out of the other suits.

No choices left. One deep breath and she turned around to buy back the 200 m she'd wasted prevaricating. Silence from above, she guessed they knew what she was doing. Back alongside the POD trailer she turned again and rapped on the wall. "Go."

372

Both sets of claws above concurred. Here goes, Lucy. Face your fear. She jammed the drive bar forwards and resolved to keep it there as she aimed NEIL at the spot shown in the beams.

It was further than she had judged, and by the time NEIL reached the base of the slope, she estimated it was over 100 m high, but less steep than she had thought. They were doing over 30 km/h and it took forever to reach the crest. Then there was nothing in the view except stars. Galaxy, she might hit orbit. There was a sickening lurch as NEIL launched off the ridge crest in a slow motion arc to the impact, partway down a much steeper slope on the other side. After a lurch and some more scrabbling up top, the claw-held lights pinned themselves to a site over two kilometres away, where she spotted the POD lying on its side.

It was a mess. The POD had hit the shoulder of a low bluff about 300 m away, bounced, and then rolled to a halt down the slope. There were pieces of the sub-frame and engine assemblies for hundreds of metres around. Lucy knew Anton's team had run out of fuel before it landed, but in spite of the obvious damage it looked like they had pulled off a miracle by getting it to her with the shell intact. In spite of all that, the reality of the situation left her shaken. This was how close she had come to...

Her suit alarm sounded again. *So soon?* This time it wouldn't cancel. She instinctively checked the display in the tiny screen, although she knew the message already: O2 CRITICAL. It was flashing red over the oxygen indicator; nothing left. She reckoned on twenty minutes more. She switched both the suit data feed and radio links off. *No time for discussion and, if I run out, I don't want to hear the fuss.*

As she hopped across the last twenty metres, 2,2,1 was writing in the dust as usual.

> POD DIE
> AIR IN POD OK
> POD AIR IN NEIL
> LUCY NOT DIE
> TEAM NOT DIE

Shit. The POD's airlock door was jammed; in fact the entire frame was bent and twisted, although by some miracle it still looked like it might be airtight.

She hadn't damaged the POD they had towed all this way, but Sarkasian was going to lose this one. The guy seemed to have a genuine fondness for the equipment he was responsible for and she actually laughed as she imagined herself apologising to him. The oddest things made her smile. She yawned, tired to the bone. *When did I last get a decent rest?*

She pushed and pulled at the door but it was stuck fast, so she started to look around for something to use as a wrecking bar. She had planned to let the team inside and suggest they use up the ambient air while she hauled the supersize wheeled oxygen tanks across to replenish NEIL. Now that would to go to waste as she broke in. She turned to find the two Deep Race guys already measuring up the POD with their claws, and drew a quick diagram to show where to cut through the skin.

After a "wait" gesture and a furious tapping exchange, 3,4,2 raced to NEIL and went in through the air lock. 2,2,1 was writing again.

IN POD SOON
AIR IN POD
LUCY AIR 2 / LUCY AIR 1

No. Not even that. She knelt to scratch a reply, addressing him by name, which she had never done before. She hoped it would focus his attention:

2   2,1
LUCY
    AIR
        NO
NEIL   AIR NO 1

AIR
    A i r _____

She stopped for a second and shook her head. *No, not yet. I'm just tired; there must be some air left/ Write, Lucy...*

AiR   N   P OD
L u ~ NO

     -_____ _ _____
NO

She looked at the message she had tried to write, but couldn't seem to concentrate. *Ah, well. I don't care. Doesn't matter now. So tired.*

The lights on Neil were dimming; she couldn't see as well. She couldn't focus on the message. *The words. I need to lie down. Letters, remember the letters. There's the Earth. Lying on my back.*

Deep below the fatigue she realised that the struggle was over. *Earth is so pretty.*

Talk to me Evan, I came here to see you one last time... Earth... Blue... Green... Sea of Cortez... So close... Home... Fading... Tired...

Sleep...

Home...

Talk to me...

Where are you?

Evan?

My friend...

Dizzy...

Failed...

Visit...

Earth...

After one more deep sigh, Lucy's eyes closed.

2,2,1 had got the message and was already moving. They had discussed air consumption weeks ago, and he already knew that the ability of his species to operate for a time without a direct air supply didn't apply to humans. As Lucy lay down on her back and closed her eyes, he immediately raced to NEIL and left a series of small dents as he banged a furious message to 3,4,2.

EMERGENCY OFFICER ORDERS # # it LUCY no air need in it NEIL airlock # # it you outside two fllzzs or I will it your eyes eat it you putrid waste of water ## it LUCY die I we you us all die # # EMERGENCY OFFICER ORDERS #

Four long seconds after leaving her side, 2,2,1 was back. With lightning speed he rolled her body towards and then up over himself, steadying the suit with several sets of claws so she balanced sideways, face-down across his shell. Dragging her boots behind, he moved as fast as possible to where 3,4,2 was coming out of the airlock holding the air tank harpoon. 3,4,2 was lucky. He was already on his way out, and could never have made it in two fllzzs. 2,2,1 banged instructions on the other's shell as the pair of them tried to wedge Lucy inside. Even using all their claws they had trouble making her limbs stay put.

it you avoided it eyes eaten quick work # # it LUCY in airlock it you outside cut it POD bring it air tank # # it you stand in all legs it eyes look no it help it i may still eat it you # # help it I me get it LUCY in here # # remember it LUCY airlock emergency drill it you get away all it claws from it door go go go faster faster faster it you putrid stinking beach turd #

Lucy had instructed them on emergency airlock usage, so the millisecond 3,4,2 was clear of the doorway he smacked the red EMER CYCLE button. The door slammed, but nothing else happened. No LOCK or CYCLE light. Through his feet he felt 3,4,2 hammering through the frame.

it LUCY it claw trapped in it door # # i me it LUCY legs hold inside # # it you it LUCY claws hold # # it you not so clever now it you vomiting scumbag # # save it kill it as easy # # it you kill LUCY 221 it i eat it you mating claw # # it you open door it who slow now it you decaying pus carcass #

2,2,1 pressed CANCEL CYCLE and the door swung open again. Too slow! He clambered over Lucy and made sure the squashed glove was fully inside, then held her legs and arms away from the aperture. It didn't leave many claws spare, but he managed to stretch far enough to reach the EMER CYCLE button again. Some kind of moisture sprayed from the glove as carbon dioxide leaked out of the now punctured suit.

* * *

Paula and Tobin had been watching the scene through Lucy's suit cam but the radio and data feed had cut out off after the oxygen alarm sounded.

"Why she do this? Ajax gonna shit. As usual."

Tobin laughed at her. "I suspect a data malfunction, might even have been at this end and not the suit itself. Anyway, Paula, that girl is tough. Do you believe she cares what Ajax thinks?"

"Nope." She sighed, and shook her head. "Yo, what now, Tobe? She stargazin'?"

The suit camera showed a view of the sky. Suddenly the scene tumbled and all they could see was dust.

"Call her again, she might still receive."

"Lucy, it's Paula. Gene's calling NEIL.

There was no reply, but the view tumbled around once again to reveal a corner of the air lock floor and a bit of a Deep Race shell. There was blood dripping down the wall. Another, more strident, alarm sounded. They both looked at the console, then at each other. Lucy's life signs implant, which was independent and didn't run through the suit, had ceased to function.

"Oh no, oh shit." She looked over her shoulder to the open door. She knew the commander was in his office one door along. "Boss. Hey, Ajax. Need you here. NOW!"

She managed to page Doc Fisher before completely losing control. Thibodeaux arrived a moment later to find his tough comms specialist on her feet and sobbing. "She's out of, oh, air. Oh, Ajax, her implant sh-shut down. I can't..."

He shuddered. "Oh, Paula." He put an arm round her as Doc ran in. "We lost life signs, implant's gone." Doc stopped, shook his head and sat down hard.

Tobin looked up from the console. "Ajax, the implant didn't even red line, the actual signal cut off here with no warning. The suit alarm was going off about twenty minutes ago, but on previous experience she's been getting about 75 minutes of air after that. Then it and the radio both tripped off. I can't see this suit would be different from all the others." Another alarm sounded. "What the . . ? Shit, that's NEIL O2 CRITICAL."

"Roger." Ajax let go of Paula and she turned to watch the screen again.

"Look," shouted Doc, pointing to the view from NEIL's internal camera. "One of them is dragging her out of the airlock. What in space happened there? Galaxy, she's covered in blood."

They watched as the Deep Race creature pulled Lucy to the middle of the floor and then started cutting the surface suit away around her shoulders with his small claws. He worked almost too fast for them to see, slicing through lines and systems until he could seize the helmet and pull it off her head.

"He didn't know how to undo the lid," observed Tobin. Guys, it's less than a minute since we saw the camera point at the sky and she's already inside. I didn't even know they could move that fast."

2,2,1 cut around the right wrist of the suit and pulled off the glove. He held up her hand for them to see, half rolling her body as he pulled at her arm; the top joint of her right index finger was missing and he had the damaged digit caught in a claw to stop the blood flow. Doc produced a tissue and stood by the camera, wrapping it around his own finger. 2,2,1's claws moved almost too fast for them to follow, putting the damaged hand down and tearing out the inside lining of the discarded suit arm. He bound a clipped-off piece around Lucy's smashed finger with it. She moved and tried to sit up.

Tobin moved behind Paula and held her shoulders. "Paula, she's OK. It's only a finger. Of course, it's the one with the implant. This all makes sense. Galaxy, Ajax, you couldn't make it up."

Paula put her arms round a surprised Tobin. She was sobbing again, this time with sheer relief.

"Lucy, it's Doc. Are you with us?"

"Yeah. I'm groggy, Doc, oh, I need to lie down again. There's an alarm. Hey, I'm inside. Man! What in damnation happened to this suit?"

"You're safe inside," Ajax told her. "We think you ran out of air, but your clever friends got you through the airlock. You've lost a bit of a finger and the life science implant with it. We had a shock moment here when it shut down."

She looked at the hand. "Shit, shit, shit, that hurts. I'll need to get off my back and dress it when I stop spinning. So how did that happen?"

"We thought you might be able to tell us. Get it bandaged first and then we'll run back over the last few minutes if you feel OK." He turned to Tobin. "Talk oxygen."

"NEIL is right on empty, Ajax. The manual doesn't have an expected margin figure for that, so I can only offer a guess. I'd guess thirty minutes, and I'm hoping that's pessimistic. They need to get the tanks across and pump the system up as soon as." He turned back to the screen. "Lucy, we were watching the suit camera and it looked like you passed out, but your comms tripped off before that."

Thibodeaux scowled. " Did you—"

"Huh? Off?" she interrupted. "It must have failed, but I hadn't noticed." She realised she was feeling better already and knew she would get away with it. There were shredded pieces of suit all over the floor. "OK, I don't have a suit until I replenish one of the empties, and they are all outside on headlight duty. Anyway I can't do it until we get oxygen aboard, so I need to supervise that from here, and soon. That's the O2 CRITICAL alarm; we're empty."

She got up and sat in a seat. "Oh, now that's outstanding. I'm looking outside at the POD and 3,4,2 has already clawed through the skin and opened the damaged door from inside. I need to get him to wheel one of the tanks across to NEIL and connect the external line."

Tobin spoke up. "Ajax, her suit's O2 LOW alarm didn't sound here. We did get one, but it was twenty minutes before she flaked. That must have been the O2 CRITICAL datum. The only way I can account for that would be if the suit suffered a system event. That would account for the comms being off too. I'd need to check diagrams."

"Forget it. To be honest I'd rather not know. She's OK and that's what matters. That suit isn't coming in for repair. Thanks, Tobin."

"Lucy," said Doc. "You need to get that started and then attend to your finger. It's still bleeding."

"I know, it's hurting like nothing I've ever felt. Thinking about it makes me feel queasy again. It's not bleeding much so let's ignore it for a few while I organise the team and then you can talk me through that.

She wrote a message for 2,2,1:

SUIT NO AIR
NEIL NO AIR
TEAM BRING AIR

She drew one of the wheeled air tanks, NEIL, showing the O2 IN cover, then the two connected. It was a simple pop-fit with a release handle that opened the flow. 2,2,1 signalled in the affirmative. With no way left for Lucy to get across the few metres separating NEIL from the POD, she was losing count of the times she owed them her life.

There was one more problem which needed work. She had imagined a triumphant arrival at Gene's, towing the DS335 POD into the big garage. Now it was stuck on the other side of a long escarpment, and judging by the slope she had come down there was no way NEIL could climb back over from this side of it. Not unless there was an easier way back somewhere nearby. Redwood had accused her of running a lunar destruction derby and, to be fair, the evidence was stacking up.

She began to worry about 2,5,1 and 3,1,5, left behind on minimum oxygen drain in the POD. She couldn't remember when they needed supply. Would they be able to get here?

Outside there was a tapping sound. "Go." She grinned as she thought of how frightened she had been when she had first heard tapping, lying on the ceiling at the crash scene, and how much worse it had been when she spotted the first Deep Race creature crawling towards her across the rocks. I must remember to ask which one of them that was.

The console chimed, and showed "O2 PUMP TANK 4 STBY." Lucy switched it on and watched for the gauge to start moving.

"OK, people, O2 transfer is live. Doc, would you talk me through what I need to do to this finger?"

61 – SUNRISE
9:00 AM (LST) 16ᵗʰ OCTOBER

Cartographer Ace Horowitz sat at the comms console and spread his hands. "We didn't anticipate you ending up on that side of the escarpment. We did see it there, but we honestly thought the crashed POD was on the side where, well, where your trailer POD is now. Unfortunately, we can't find a break in the ridge anywhere that would allow you to cross back over it and retrace your tracks to the Seas Road. It looks like you drove down the only non-fractured part of the whole plain."

Lucy shrugged. "Ace, it can't be your fault. I think I'm jinxed. Every time we achieve something there's another hurdle to jump. I guess seeing you and Pelican there this morning means you have a plan."

He grinned. "Sure do. Fancy visiting Agrippa?"

She caught their excitement. "Agrippa? And what is making you two so cheerful about that? It's high and rocky country all the way from here round that crater. Nobody's been there yet."

"No," said Ace, rubbing his hands, "but you're so going to love this. Pelican has been stereo-mapping every moment he's awake. I dread to think how many digitals he's flashed on the screen to compare before-and-after views. We have programs for that, but he insists he sees better than they can. We've spent the last two days getting a complete new route planned out to get you back onto the West Way. We've put archive shots against post-impact versions, checking for new obstacles. You can get back to the road east of Agrippa, just to the northwest of where the West Way passes between the craters de Morgan and Cayley."

"Ace, you're hired. If I can go that way it'll take hours off the drive home."

"Yes, it's less than one third of the distance from where you are now to that point. It looks like a good trail route too, passing over some of the bluffs close to the south curtain wall of Agrippa and then down into some flatter country. We're completing an accurate NAV data upload for you today. Even better than that, he's also spotted the one thing that'll set off your buzzer. Go ahead, Pelican, it's your surprise."

Pelican was so excited he could hardly get the words out. "Lucy, remember all that indecision you had about visiting 'my' crater? Incidentally you called it right in the end, of course. Well, I've found you a big, fat comet fragment crater sitting right by the new trail, southeast of Agrippa."

Lucy was standing up by this time. "Oh, wow-wee! When do I get started?"

Thibodeaux had let the guys have their moment. "Not yet, Lucy. There is no way you are crossing those hills in the dark. Like it or not, you're going to have to travel in the light, and that's still four days off. I want you to stay put until the sun comes up. How's it going with the supplies?"

"Good, thanks, Ajax. The team lugged all sorts of gear across the ridge from the POD, carrying a suit with them for local lighting. The problem here is how to pack it all in here and leave room for us travellers."

"You don't have to bring everything that was in the POD, you know, The beer and coffee would do."

"I know that, but these guys are waste-nothing recyclers and opportunist scavengers second to none. They simply refuse to leave anything behind if we can squeeze it in. 3,4,2 even designed some roof storage using some of his wire stock."

After the meeting, she explained to the team that they would rest here and go onwards after sunrise in four days. They immediately had a long tapping conference. For a change it was 3,1,5 who started drawing.

* * *

"Good morning, Paula. I never apologised for cutting you down when we reached the POD. I was so uptight that day. Say, what day is it anyway?"

"You worryin'? No dramas, forget it. Tense was all. Sunday baby, October 19th. Also sun-up day. You OK?"

"Yes I am. So, I'm counting my blessings this morning. I'm rested after a five day enforced stopover. My finger is much less painful and I've got the glove with the missing piece in vac-store for later. I'll live without it, but Doc says he can do miracles. I've spring-cleaned and tidied NEIL. The equipment and supply inventory is complete, including new suits out of the crashed POD. It's a good job they weren't stripped out to load extra weight. As with the dump at Evan's Place all the used and damaged stuff is now stored for collection later, in this instance inside the remains of that POD."

"Couple o' days, party here then."

"I can't wait for that. So, I get to watch the sun come up and then I'll be out of here in a few hours, back on the trail surrounded by boxes and aliens."

"Yeah, Where they at?"

Why did Paula always get one step ahead? "Outside somewhere, resting in a shadow, it's too warm in here for them most of the time." In fact they were over the ridge doing a final bit of equipment retrieval.

Because of the ridge separating NEIL from the DS335 POD, the two trails didn't yet meet. Lucy wanted to come back and connect the two in future, making the shortcut and saving her travel time on surveys out west. Or did she? Was her future here, doing her work among the rocks and keeping an ear open for Evan at night? She wasn't sure. Much as she had come to love and respect them, she was still debating whether her route lay on the same trail as the Deep Race.

The team arrived back so they could all gather outside and watch the sun come up. It never changed the sky like in Earth's beautiful atmosphere. Even during the day all the stars shone steadily in the black sky as seen by eyes shaded from the sun. But today something was different. For a few fleeting seconds immediately before sun-up, Lucy glimpsed a gentle coruscation above the horizon. Was it a ring, the merest hint of a shimmer, or maybe a distant sparkle? She mentioned it to Mario, and a few minutes later she received an excited call back from Wilco.

"Lucy, I was outside Gene's at sunrise on Friday to try and see what you reported, but as far as I could tell there wasn't a hint of it here. It's atmosphere. I'm writing this up as 'Grappelli's Shimmer'. Score yourself another point, because you're the first human ever to see ice crystals refracting sunlight in the Lunar atmosphere, and I'm insanely jealous. In the planetary sense there is so little it's almost undetectable, but Comet Percival dumped so much ice that it's boiling off the surface. I suspect there is a lot more moisture closer to the impacts than over here by the base, and you seeing it there when I couldn't backs up that theory."

"It should have been you that saw it," she said, "and I want you to call it 'Wilco's Shimmer'. I thought it was a migraine coming on, or I was going as starshine mad as Kent. It was just like that, a faint sparkle like a ring that lasted for maybe a second or two, and then it was gone."

* * *

"Oh, no, not again. You're supposed to be ready to drive, not outside in a suit. What's the problem now?"

"Come on, Ajax, it wouldn't be us if we didn't have a performance ready now, would it?"

Pelican was hosting a repeat of his waving-off party in the lounge, but the commander had leaped out of a chair at the sight of his geologist, suited up and standing on the surface next to NEIL.

"This time it's nothing to do with me, I'm only bringing you the news." She was grinning. "You see, the Deep Race didn't fancy the idea of overheating inside NEIL for the next few days. They liked their old accommodation better, so they came up with an alternative plan." The camera view changed to show the DS335 POD rolling towards NEIL across the plain below the ridge. In front were four small shapes trotting along holding lines in their rear claws, pulling it by the chassis.

After the applause died down, Lucy filmed their arrival and 3,4,2 attaching the tow hook once again, before switching back to the view of herself. "Commander Thibodeaux, Deputy Commander Percival. Ladies and Gentlemen. We will finally be departing for Gene's in ten minutes. Any questions?"

The first thirty kilometres on the new trail went by in two hours. It was easy country, with gentle rises and minimal debris scattered around. Driving in the sunlight was so much easier than the dark. Her fear of canyons had evaporated like Wilco's Shimmer, and, although the shadows were still total, the POD lights burned into the closest ones a little. In several places she saw obvious new impact sites, but there was no time to stop. So many things would have been different if she hadn't agreed to stop and let Evan collect one more rock. He would still be alive, but the Deep Race team would be dead. She had spent days going over that issue, but there was no going back. Those rocks had rolled to a stop.

Even though they didn't like to spend much time in the sunlight, three of the Deep Race had insisted on keeping a lookout in turns from NEIL's roof. Each hour she stopped to allow a quick change-over, the one going off duty retreating to the POD to cool down. As usual, if she heard five sharp bangs on the cabin roof, she was to stop immediately and wait for a lookout report.

There was a constant exchange of tapping between them and 3,4,2 who, after saying he didn't mind the warm cabin so much, rode with Lucy. In deference to his physiology she had put on extra layers and turned the climate down until she was only just comfortable.

The land angled upwards, and NEIL crossed one set of low hills after another. There were more craters around. The trail and all the associated headings were loaded, so all she needed to do was follow the screen.

Stopping for a meal break, she explained to 3,4,2 that she was getting cold. He reached for the pad to write back:

TEAM POD COOL
LUCY NEIL WARM
IIIII TAP ROOF STOP

He left her to go and settle down in the POD, saying that apart from rotating to lookout duty they would continue with their rest time and go quiet until she needed them.

They rolled on through the day, climbing across a moonscape of ochres and lighter greys featuring every kind of surface in a strange jumble of textures. There was one deviation from the planned route, taking them ten kilometres north towards the high wall of Crater Agrippa to avoid a narrow but deep cut scar that hadn't shown up well on the maps.

By the time she stopped to sleep she was eighty kilometres further along. She slept well and woke feeling like she could drive

389

forever. The previous day had been so much easier than the endless night driving. There was no sign of the Deep Race, so after checking outside and a quick look in the POD to make sure they were there she set off.

The drive became more difficult. NAV showed the route climbing north east to within five kilometres of the curtain wall, before turning and crossing the uplands to descend back to lower country towards the new crater. The computer was close, but there were occasions where she had to turn back and run along the sides of deep rilles facing away from the wall. It all added time but, with the oxygen tanks replenished, the time pressure was off.

Towards mid-afternoon, disaster struck suddenly near the top of a large bluff. Lucy started to feel a tilt as one wheel sank into soft dust. Several alarms went off at once. Almost immediately NEIL stopped dead and there was an almighty bang from the POD behind. NEIL sat, listing to the left and nose down, with the screen showing DISCON DRIVE WHEEL 5 / ZERO ROTATION STEER WHEEL 1.

NEIL was stuck fast. She reset the system and tried reversing, but after two attempts the computer refused to allow the LXV to move and the wheel 5 drive unit overheated, shutting itself down on an automatic cooling timer.

There was nothing for it, she would have to get the shovel. As she opened the airlock, the Deep Race were waiting, with a large scale drawing already prepared in the dust. A set of wheels, drawn with the left front wheel half in the ground and the third axle left wheel about 25% under. An inspection confirmed the news. The tow bar looked fine, but the end bars under both the POD and NEIL were bent at the attachments.

With the POD disconnected and rolled out of the way it took Lucy with the shovel, plus the Deep Race using pieces of scrap metal and claws, all afternoon and most of the evening to free NEIL. It seemed that as fast as they dug, either more of the surrounding dry dust settled in the hole or the wheels sank even deeper. After two hours, the Deep Race called a halt and 2,5,1 went to the POD for parts supplies. The others started surveying the local area for large boulders, retrieving a local one, plus one from well over a kilometre away.

As usual, 3,4,2 had an idea. They rolled the two rocks into indentations made for them away from each side of the LXV. Next, they tied three of the strongest wires around the boulder on the left side. After checking with Lucy that there wasn't anything underneath the front that might get damaged, 2,2,1 and 2,5,1 selected a piece of pipe from the scrap collection tied underneath the POD. They pushed and twisted it under NEIL's base plate from the other direction until it poked through into the trench.

Once again Lucy was surplus to requirements. She asked if unloading all the stores and equipment aboard might help. After a brief discussion they told her to go ahead. In the end, she made twelve return trips through the airlock before their new idea was ready to try. She dragged as much of the heavier supplies outside as she could manage. These included all the water canisters, the oxygen tanks, the beer and most of the packed stores she had already moved across from the POD. Even in the low gravity she could feel her muscles getting stiff.

They worked the pipe forwards, with Lucy able to help by digging in front of it to loosen the dust. After another hour they had moved it far enough so it ran underneath behind the two steering wheels at the front, poking up at a shallow angle on the right side and downwards into the ditch on the left. They then dug away from NEIL on the left side and pulled the pipe far enough through so that about two metres was visible on both sides. They fed four of the wires through the pipe and tied them over the huge rocks displaced twenty metres out to the sides.

3,4,2 explained that they would suspend NEIL's front end in a cradle to allow the original lifting lever to pass under the wheels as a ramp. Lucy would watch from the driving seat, ready to back NEIL up out of the ditch at his command. The Deep Race would push rocks underneath the sets of wires, increasing the tension and lifting NEIL the required half-metre. 2,2,1 and 2,5,1 had scoured the local surface and built up a suitable collection of rocks for the purpose.

After a progress report to Gene's, she watched the activity around NEIL. Out to the right, a large rock was already trapped under the wires and leaning against the anchor boulder. She couldn't see who was pushing it, but the rock was rolled under the wire towards NEIL and secured to stop it moving back. There was a slight lurch, and NEIL definitely lifted another few centimetres. That was the first rock on the other side coming into play.

It was a slow process. Once there were three of the rocks stretching the wires each side, 2,5,1 fed a second pipe underneath NEIL, ready stuffed with suitable wires. They secured it a metre behind the first. It was then tied to another pair of large boulders out to the sides. As soon as the new pipe could hold NEIL, the rocks under the first set of wires were moved away until they could be re-tied at the same length as the new set.

NEIL's front end now rested on eight of the cables, with the two pipes holding the front end almost clear. The wheel on axle 3 was now out of the dust, and the front left steering wheel nearly so. 2,2,1 and 2,5,1 made their way into the ditch and moved as much of the dust as possible from the front wheel. There was another short pause as the four of them took stock and agreed on how to work the triangular cross-section lever underneath. It would rest on good ground behind and outboard of the rearmost left steering wheel, angling down underneath and below the now airborne drive wheel. The front steering wheel only had to stay out of the dirt.

Lucy hated to think of them going underneath, but for once the operation went without a hitch. They pushed a lot of smaller rocks into the ditch and forced them underneath the lever, to afford enough grip for the drive wheel to pull NEIL out. They backfilled the ditch with gravel to stabilise everything.

Lucy recorded the entire operation on film, using her own suit camera and setting up a second suit to cover a long angle. There was a constant back-and-forth between her and Gene's, where the entire crew were watching from the lounge. It was after 10:00 PM by the time they were ready to try and extract NEIL but, as usual Houston and Lancaster were on line, so she had a large audience.

Finally 3,4,2 scratched the message she had waited for:

NEIL READY
LUCY DRIVE
3,4,2 SEE

They had been learning to write numbers, and said they liked the new way to write their names.

It seemed to take forever to cycle the airlock and reach the driving seat. 3,4,2 was standing in position ready to direct. She reset the drive computer and switched the two remaining useable motors to standby, ready to power wheels 5 and 6. Once they slackened the front set of wires, they wanted her to move half a metre backwards if she could. 2,2,1 and 2,5,1 were going to walk alongside, pulling the forward pipe back by tugging on the wires so that it would still be available in place if there were any problems. When it touched the second pipe, 3,4,2 would signal her to stop and they would consider removing all the wires and pipes in the hope she could back straight out. Tough as they were, she wasn't keen on the idea of having them anywhere near, and especially under, NEIL when the wheels were turning, but that was the plan.

She watched to the side as they rolled away the rocks keeping the front wires taut. Nothing felt different, and she didn't detect any movement beneath. A brief tapping conference followed at the front where she could see them all, as all they made the final adjustments to the plan. Three disappeared, leaving 3,4,2 with one big rear claw raised. Stop.

He held his front arms out to the sides with the claws held horizontally. These would signal the wire-draggers. She needed to concentrate only on the vertical claw, which started a slow circle. "Go."

Lucy pulled the control bar slightly back. There was a gentle bump underneath and NEIL started to move. Immediately, 3,4,2 held the claw up again. Stop. The side claws worked in rapid semaphore, directing his team. Underneath, Lucy heard a couple of scrapes as they adjusted the pipes. Glancing off to the right she saw movement, and realised that the second set of wires were slackening. That took longer than the first set, and she realised that NEIL must have pulled the pipe back, stretching those wires even tighter. There were a few more scrapes against the bottom and then silence.

Once again, 3,4,2 stood in the ready position. As the upheld claw rotated, Lucy fed in the power. NEIL lurched a bit as the steering wheel bumped over a rock, and then the drive wheel caught.

She drove NEIL backwards up out of the ditch with the front steering wheel bumping over the collected hardware. Lucy let out a whoop of delight and exchanged excited waves with first 3,4,2, and then all four of them. She could hear the roar of approval from Gene's and the Earth.

Clearing up outside could wait, she was exhausted. She went outside to thank her team, exchanging "awesome, work done, way to go" signals. They must have been mind-readers because almost immediately 2,2,1 wrote:

LUCY NEIL REST 12
TEAM POD REST 18

She would indeed rest, but then she would clear up all their gear and have it by the POD ready to stow when they got up. Again, it would be late afternoon by the time they made any progress. She looked around the place; it was right at the top, flattest part of that big bluff. "Rocks Pass", she was going to call it. She would ask the team if they would help her roll the rocks into a line by the trail, the biggest ones sitting in the ditch, with a place sign scratched on the largest one. They could add their names and the date next to it.

She was too tired to do anything else other than eat and sleep. It only seemed to happen when she was exhausted, because once again she had a variation of the Evan dream.

This time, he was pushing the four biggest anchor boulders away from outside and whooping with delight as they rolled off down the gentle slope. She noticed he had his big Canadian flag attached to the one-piece, but he wasn't wearing a helmet or a surface suit.

"Work to do, kid! One rock at a time, always one rock at a time, eh? It's all part of life, y'know. The pressure drops and you fall asleep, but it doesn't hurt, eh. I fell asleep watching Earth. Lucy, Lucy, Lucy-Lu, you get to visit Earth. I have to go, they need me, but I'll see ya, you'll see. One more rock. One more pass. One more time..."

He waved the flag up to where she was sitting in the driving seat, then curled up and rolled himself off down the slope after his rocks, disappearing below the horizon. As before, the Long View Traveller was there, receding out of sight into the black sky.

When she woke up there were no tears. Coming to terms was an odd process, and hadn't he said she would see him again one more time?

Before going outside she drove NEIL for a few hundred metres and checked out the steering and systems. Everything stayed in the green, with no warnings or snags showing up. It was a lucky escape. Without the foresight of her team, and their attachment to the collection of spare parts, well, it didn't bear thinking about.

She parked by the POD. After going out she inspected everything underneath, but apart from the bent strut where the tow bar attached there didn't appear to be any signs of visible damage.

For a change it could be her turn to get things done while the Deep Race team rested. So far she had usually appeared after a sleep break to find all the work completed, so she made the most of the opportunity. By the time they did open the POD door she had packed all the removed stores back inside NEIL. Most of the lifting equipment from the previous day was stacked near the POD airlock ready for stowing.

She had then set out on a personal mission to roll some of the rocks that she wanted to place in a line alongside the new trail. Although they only weighed 1/6 of what they would on Earth, so did she. It took a lot of effort to overcome the inertia, and she was sweating by the time she had accomplished what she could of that without help. She was planning to ask the team to help with the biggest ones that she thought could sit in the ditch.

It was 2,5,1's turn to write messages. He was the one she had interacted with least.

TEAM REST GOOD
TEAM THANK LUCY WORK

In return she signed "work done, no problem."

Communication was a two way street and she was beginning to know a lot more of their simpler signs. These strange mixtures of signing and written words had a basic workability, but it would be much better if they could all achieve real understanding. She was aware that they still knew very little about each other, and hoped the experts would make rapid progress once she reached base. She was still amazed that they could achieve so much using what communication they had.

While they stowed the long lever and pipes underneath the POD, she put all the coiled wires inside. After that, they helped her to roll the four largest boulders into the ditch, adjusting the placement of the others to complete the long line marking the place. After a discussion about a sign, 2,5,1 rushed off the way they had come, to recover what he described as:

GOOD NEW ROCK

It turned out to be one half of a boulder, 1.2m across and broken in two. On the flat surface 3,4,2 inscribed the agreed message:

ROCKS PASS
HERE HUMAN LUCY GRAPPELLI
AND DEEP RACE MEMBERS
34221 / 44342 / 44315 / 44251
DUG OUT LXV 252 NEIL
WE WORKED TOGETHER
ONE ROCK AT A TIME

She wanted to know whether the Deep Race had artwork, or even understood what she was doing. She thought for a while and wrote:

MOON ROCKS MESSAGE PLACE
NO WHY
TEAM PLANET MESSAGE
NO WHY

3,4,2 got it straight away:

398

TEAM ROCKS NO WHY SEE
ROCKS GOOD SEE
MESSAGE FOR LUCY FOR EARTH
TEAM PLANET ROCKS NO MESSAGE
ROCKS GOOD SEE

The last two lines jumped out at her; art, it had to be. They understood the concept of art. It taught her something; a snippet of information about them that helped explain the small polished rocks she and Evan had been gifted. She wrote:

LUCY TEAM ROCK GOOD SEE
EVAN TEAM ROCK GOOD SEE
 EARTH GOOD SEE

The reply astounded her:

TEAM PLANET PLACE FOR ROCKS SEE
TEAM PLANET TEAM VISIT PLACE
GOOD SEE ROCKS
LUCY TEAM ROCK GOOD ROCK
EVAN TEAM ROCK GOOD ROCK
EARTH TEAM GOOD ROCKS SEE
TEAM SHIP TEAM PLANET ROCKS
EARTH PLACE GOOD TEAM ROCKS SEE

She made the 'wait' sign and studied the message in disbelief. If she caught the meaning, their planet featured a museum or gallery for looking at the best rocks. The one she had received as a gift was high quality, and they were once again offering to find more, this time to display on Earth.

The finished milestone was finally placed facing the trail, leaning between the two huge boulders at the middle of the row. She took some film and several digitals. She hadn't called in since 7:00 AM and it was already after 3:00 PM, so she made it time for a report.

"Gene's, Lucy."

"Hi Lucy, how's your day?"

"Hi Pelican, good to speak to you. I've road tested and checked NEIL and everything is good. I've also helped the team tidy up yesterday's technical gear and re-pack stores. We're getting ready to roll again. They rested till 11:30 AM, so I'm going to try and drive until midnight and see how close we can get to that crater. I guess you'll want to see what else we have been doing?"

"Lucy, we always want to see what else you've been doing. The entire world is hanging on it every day."

She turned to show the line of twelve boulders, arranged in height from the smaller ones each side to the huge pair in the centre. Then she walked closer until the camera saw the engraving.

"Oh, that's excellent," said Pelican. "Your odyssey is starting to leave legacy artwork now. That'll be there forever; maybe it could be a tourist attraction in years to come. This is going to be a huge hit in the news feeds."

"Thanks," replied Lucy. "I looked at all those rocks and saw them set up in a line. I wasn't considering the implications. Well, we are ready to leave now, so I'll sign off and crack on. One rock at a time, eh?" She tried to make it sound like Evan.

"Yes, of course. I didn't catch the significance of the reference. Bird told me that was his catch phrase. Wait till he and Sara McEwan see this."

"He was there in my dreams again last night and he said it to me. I think the dreams are getting easier to handle and I'm starting to hope he'll be there whenever I sleep. It's odd because it only seems to happen when I'm sheer exhausted.

Last night he said that he had fallen asleep watching the Earth. Dying was a natural thing to do, part of life and there was no pain. I don't understand it, but think what I'm hearing from him is for real. I don't want to know why I believe it's so, but every time I wake up from one I kind of know what he has told me is exactly how it happened. I don't cry as much now and I can talk about it to you without so much pain. I think the dreams are a way of him saying goodbye, gradually somehow, as if he is still here and helping me to deal with it."

By the time she signed off, 3,4,2 was waiting to point out a new message:

LUCY DRIVE 12

She rubbed out the 12 and replaced it with 8. He signed "OK", and went to join the others in the POD.

In the end she drove for ten hours, with one short break. After coming down off the Rocks Pass bluff, the route followed an obvious set of passes running between various crater walls. She steered a little off the computer route to stay at least 500 m from the rims wherever possible. There was never a straight line for long, and she made slow progress.

After a quick report to Mario she ate and settled down to rest, pleased with the day's work. She was hoping Evan would be waiting, but she slept for five dreamless hours.

401

A quick check outside indicated no movement from the POD, so she reported to Paula before setting off to find the end of the trail. She didn't want to give it too much thought, but she was beginning to get excited about the amazing performance that NEIL had put in. After everything they had been through, the machine had looked after her so well, operating far beyond any possible design parameters.

It took four hard hours to cover the next twenty kilometres. At one point she came to an impassable rock field and had to turn round and cast about for a better route. That involved unhitching the POD and asking the team to help her clear a space to push it into before backing NEIL up to where she could make a turn, then reversing back to re-attach the POD. She spoke to Pelican, who directed her back round the other side of a small crater. He checked on satellites and received a position from TEL 1. He stayed on to advise as required, blowing up and zooming digitals as she progressed.

There were a few tense moments as she threaded a path round several blind bends, through a very narrow pass some 600 m long between two low crater walls. Once she realised how tight it was, NEIL and the POD were already committed. There would be no turning around, and she hoped Thibodeaux wouldn't enter the comms room. She finally found herself at the exit from the pass, looking south down a long slope beyond the ever-present high wall of Agrippa on her left. At the bottom of the slope, five kilometres away and reaching all the way to the horizon, stood a wide plain.

And there it was. Lying beyond the slope she spotted it; a spectacular and obviously brand-new crater. Tiny by the standards of the massive lunar features around, it looked like a perfect circle, she estimated 100 m in diameter, with a low wall of rubble thrown up to surround it. Stretching away in almost every direction was a gigantic splash shape; an area of darker colouration where the sun hadn't yet baked and bleached the dust and surface rock into the almost uniform light grey. The huge force of the impact had peppered Agrippa's mighty crater wall with debris, spawning a vast landslide off the steep slope. This stretched almost all the way to the new crater, obscuring most of the splash on that side. It was many orders of magnitude larger than the landslide NEIL had suffered, and the sheer size of it made her gasp out loud.

Her eye caught a movement. She brought NEIL to a standstill for a better look.

Beyond the partially collapsed crater wall, a monumental landslide was rolling off the slope. She was glad to have stayed away from the wall, because even watching from a safe distance made her shiver. If the landslide that killed Evan had been anything like that it would have filled the Long View Traveller crater to the rim. Neither they, NEIL, or the ship would ever have been found. It took several minutes for the debris to settle. She managed to capture some film through the window. It would make a great piece of study material, and she didn't doubt that it would be on the Earth news media later in the day.

As she started NEIL rolling again, out of nowhere sudden gooseflesh dragged across her back, from the lower right side of her ribs, up and across her left shoulder. She stopped again, instinctively turning her head up and left to the top ridge of the curtain wall. *What am I looking for, Evan? Why just there?* She could feel his presence. In an instant, she was as frightened as when she had realised he was dead. The answer wasn't spoken, but she knew. The whole ridge was unstable and she was in real danger.

403

The verse from one of the dreams chimed in her head:

"One rock at a time,
It busted my ass,
I'll be waiting for you,
Above the pass."

Just a dream? No. But how could it? Her concentration snapped back into place and in a blind panic she drove NEIL down the long slope as fast as she could manage. The POD swung and shimmied behind as NEIL rolled away from the danger. Without giving it a conscious thought she spoke out loud, as if Evan was still sitting across from her.

"Dangerous place, you say? Well, we're past it now, dude. One rock at a time, eh, buddy?" She realised that she was talking to the air, or? Suddenly he was there, right there beside her for half a second, close enough to touch. She caught herself turning to the other seat, but... A pair of tears rolled down her cheeks as she spoke out loud.

"You're fast, buddy, but I nearly caught sight of you there, Evan."

Realising that there was more of the wall to come down, she also decided to circle around to the right, away from the crater and try to approach it from the other side as far away from any possible collapse as she could. Picking her way round took more time, but after the scare she calmed down, and allowed good sense to outweigh any more irrational haste. It was bound to happen sooner or later, and after about three more hours she ran out of room. About a kilometre from the Southern wall of the new comet crater, the debris was too packed and jumbled to drive NEIL any further.

She reported in to say she would take a sleep break before spending a single day taking samples and studying the area. A proper survey was impossible without a full team consisting of specialists from several disciplines. This would have been the case at the original destination too of course, as the comet was never expected to collide with the Moon in the first place.

She was already making notes on who to bring back. Nobody would argue with her about it. In spite of the hundreds of requests they had received from around the world for the geologist to conduct various diverse tasks, her mission needed to end soon.

Thibodeaux asked her for a favour. "I consulted Pelican, as he has a vested interest here. He's already hopping with delight because the comet impact became Crater Pelican; that was from an original idea by Leif. I have a much more personal request for you regarding this one if you have no better plans. It should be Pelican's to name, but he has ceded you the prerogative. If you don't have a better idea, would you consider doing me the personal honour of naming it 'Crater Andrew David McEwan', after my Godson?"

She didn't reply for a minute, and he knew why. He waited.

"That's a wonderful idea, Ajax."

"So, any surprises for us tomorrow?" he asked. "After your previous grandstand events, half the planet will be watching your report from the crater. No pressure on you of course."

"No, this one will be a simple dedication. I don't care who watches, as long as Andrew is one of them.

He nodded his approval. "I have to say Sara's still worried about her pregnancy, otherwise we would have invited them to Lancaster. Young Drew McQ doesn't know about this yet, but I hear his Uncle Leif and Eve Meredith will be dropping by his house after school. Only you and I, and those two know about the name.

Could you possibly time your piece for 5:00 PM in Toronto, that's 4:00 PM your time?"

"With pleasure, Ajax. I'll be keeping it low key tomorrow. I think I will name it 'Drew McEwan.' Sara will have to cope with his shortened name, but it's something we are doing for him in his father's name and I know for sure that's how Evan would want it."

She joined the team outside and told them she would need to rest for eight hours before starting work. They said that they were content to stay out of the sunlight and rest in the shadows. 3,1,5 asked if she wanted to get NEIL close to the crater, but she didn't see the point of clearing that many rocks. She could walk that far.

There was another surprise. 3,1,5 had a personal message for her. He drew a rough map of all the trails driven so far and marked some known places, annotating:

EVAN PLACE
ROCKS PASS 221 315 342 251 PLACE
GENE PLACE

At their present location he added:

LUCY PLACE

The suggestion touched her, but she tried to explain the plan. She drew a pair of the stick figure humans, with their hands touching. Below she added a small figure. She wrote:

EVAN – SARA
      I
DREW

Then she rubbed out her name on 3,1,5's map and wrote:

DREW PLACE

2,2,1 drew two Deep Race figures with claws touching. Below was a cracked egg, with a tiny Deep Race figure next to it. He astounded Lucy by writing:

EVAN EARTH
SARA EARTH
DREW EARTH
DREW PLACE GOOD

2,2,1 – 4,3.6
    I
    2,5,1

221 LUCY TEAM
251 LUCY TEAM
436 DIE IN SHIP
NAME WITH EVAN

He moved across and laid his largest rear claw on 2,5,1's shell. No wonder he had dived straight between those rocks after 2,5,1 the day they righted NEIL. They had all lost friends and colleagues in the Long View Traveller, but she'd never imagined that they travelled as family units. Every time they had a discussion she got closer to them. She knelt and laid her arms on the ground in the grief gesture, offering it for their loss. All four of the Deep Race immediately assumed the same position and held it for the required thirty seconds.

When they finished paying their ritual tribute and stood up, Lucy knelt by the map and added to it. Now the legend at their position said:

4,3,6 PLACE / DREW PLACE

2,2,1 looked for a whole second, then tapped on 2,5,1's shell. They both came close to Lucy and held all four arms out towards her, claws closed. They touched her forehead with each of the claws in turn, the same gesture 2,2,1 had made before, when she offered him a piece of her own fingernail to honour their dead. Then he wrote:

2,5,1 / 2,2,1 LUCY THANK THANK

Lucy woke feeling refreshed, and lay still for a few extra minutes. For the first time in weeks she felt a great sense of achievement. Evan hadn't visited her dreams, but she guessed she hadn't been as dog-tired. She got up, took a shower, and put on a brand new suit retrieved from the crashed POD.

As she depolarised the windows from dark to clear, she saw a new trail stretching away through the debris field, wide enough for her to drive NEIL to the edge of the crater. All the time she was sleeping they must have been working their claws off. When she exited the airlock, she discovered that the POD was unhitched and there was a message waiting:

> NEW TRAIL FOR LUCY
> THANK
> LUCY NEIL
> DREW PLACE 4,3,6 PLACE

When NEIL arrived at the end of the trail the four of them were waiting to greet her. There was even a back-up space so she could turn the LXV, but the trail ended below the low crater wall. As usual there was an explanation:

> NEIL HERE
> ROCKS FALL NEIL FALL

Quite. They had cleared a path for her, so she walked with them up the slope, climbing ten metres to a prepared clearing at the very edge of the new crater.

* * *

"Good afternoon from the comet impact crater near Agrippa, 600 km to the west of Gene's. Looking at the full Moon from Earth, that would be a point slightly to the right of centre. I'm here with the the Deep Race to provide you with a few statistics."

The crater is an almost perfect circle 110 m across and fifteen deep. A fragment from the Comet Percival break-up made it. A field estimate suggests that about 60,000 tonnes of material was blasted out of this hole and spread across the surrounding landscape, some of it heated up enough by the force of the impact to have fallen back to the surface as molten lava. Under the circumstances it's incredible that we can to get so close, but during the long lunar night everything cooled and solidified enough to allow our approach.

"The comet was almost all ice, and as I watched the Sun rise over the mountains a few days ago, I was able to see some of the vast amount of cometary ice crystals evaporating off the lunar surface at the series of impact sites to form the first ever lunar atmosphere witnessed by mankind. It's too thin and tenuous to capture on film, but I caught the merest suggestion of an ice-ring around the rising Sun.

"Once we knew Comet Percival was on a collision course with the Moon it became apparent that we weren't prepared for a full survey of the impacts. I will be coming back here to do the hard science as soon as we have the right equipment in place. My role here today was to do some basic measurement, record a lot of film and photographs and make a few notes.

"It is my pleasure to perform one more duty this evening." At Gene's, Paula switched to the usual suit camera, placed to show a longer view of Lucy and the Deep Race team with the crater providing a backdrop behind them.

410

"During this expedition I lost my close friend Evan McEwan. I learned last night that two of my Deep Race team also lost a family member with their ship. Now I don't yet know if they are male or female, or even if there is a distinction, but the two standing this side of me, 2,2,1 and 2,5,1, are a parent and child who lost a partner and a parent respectively. For those reasons, I am dedicating this crater not only to one, but two special individuals.

"At this point I would like to take a minute to speak to Evan's son Andrew. Hey there, Drew McQ, I know you and your Mom and Gramma are watching from home. We have already named a place for your Dad, but your Uncle Ajax came up with the idea that it would be fitting to name somewhere for you also. I happen to think it would be nice to share naming it with the Deep Race team. In a way it will connect you to them, and I hope that will be all right with you."

She turned and stood for a moment, looking across the crater. This time there was none of the previous emotion. She was calm and fulfilled, satisfied that the task which she had taken so long to achieve was about to be completed. Across the Earth and Moon, she once again exercised the deep power to make many millions of people wait patiently for a few seconds.

Finally she spoke. "In a gesture of friendship and bonding between Mankind and the Deep Race, I hereby name this crater '4,3,6, – Drew McEwan'. She could hear applause at Gene's, and hoped she had scored a hit in Toronto.

Paula switched to a third camera, running in another suit near the edge of the clearing. On the face of a split rock, standing like the one at Rocks Pass, was an inscription:

CRATER 4,3,6
DREW MCEWAN

411

She finally stopped answering questions after an hour, then backed NEIL into the turning space. The POD was over a kilometre away, back where the trail had originally finished, but something made her hook up and drive it to the edge of the splash zone, ten kilometres further into the plain, before calling it a day.

Lucy lightened the windows. She gasped, and then swore repeatedly and with real feeling at the changed scene outside, northwards across the crater. She did it for several minutes. Eventually she called Gene's.

"Hey, Lucy."

"Paula, remember when I told you I had the horrors at the top of that slope, close under Agrippa's curtain wall after filming the big slide? I was convinced Evan was there telling me it wasn't safe. Well, while I was sleeping last night, the crater wall collapsed almost completely. It's gone as far as the horizon in both directions. The place I crossed that narrow pass and drove down to the flats is covered in debris that has to be 200 m deep. Crater 4,3,6 DREW was half filled with rocks, and some even spilled over this side. If I'd stayed parked there last night I might have been gone."

Within a few minutes the comms room was stuffed with experts. Thibodeaux expressed their collective horror at the thought that NEIL could so easily have been there when it happened, especially if the event that Lucy had witnessed the day before had triggered the final collapse. Ace had a second route programmed, it would add seventy kilometres to the southeast, but the compensation was a simple drive from there to the original junction. With luck she would be back at Gene's in just four days.

She went outside to see if the team were about, but there was no sign. She hoped they weren't attempting to move that lot and actually laughed out loud at the thought. They came outside to look at the collapsed crater rim. 2,5,1 wrote for a change, expressing the understatement of the year:

MANY ROCKS
NO MOVE WE

She did the laugh movement and they all joined her. She sketched the map again and indicated the new trail back to the West Way, showing where it took them to the junction and adding:

GENES
DRIVE 4 DAYS

3,4,2 had a better idea:

3,4,2 DRIVE / LUCY DRIVE
GENES
DRIVE 2 DAYS

Why not? She immediately signed for "yes, awesome." 3,4,2 had a rapid discussion with the others and followed her inside to see if he could do it. The control system was designed to be as easy as possible. The handle was pushed backwards or forwards for drive speed and direction, and to the sides for steering.

He had watched her drive for many days, and she wondered how long he'd been itching to say, "Go on, let's have a go then."

Lucy switched on the electric motors and 3,4,2 pulled himself up onto the seat. She sat opposite and let him get on with it. NEIL rolled slowly forwards and gathered speed until they reached 10 km/h. The guy had obviously studied her carefully, because he slowed a little and turned in a wide half-circle to take them back to the start point where the rest of his team were watching. Thirty minutes later NEIL left Crater 436 - Drew McEwan and headed southeast.

3,4,2 drove first, and by the time Lucy had watched him for nearly six straight hours they were already halfway back to the Seas Road. The sun was higher and the shadows less of a problem. Lucy drove the second stretch, finally hitting the West Way shortly after midnight.

Once again they changed over, and she sat with 3,4,2 as he started along the known trail. He reached out a claw and made the sign for paper and pen. He was still driving at 12 km/h, but held the drawing pad in two claws and wrote:

LUCY SLEEP
3,4,2 DRIVE 12

He was following the cones now and she didn't doubt his ability, so she signed her thanks and retreated into the bunk. She wondered if she might worry and have trouble sleeping, but these guys had saved her life more times than she cared to think about. She would trust them with it any day. She would rest for maybe four hours...

* * *

From far away up the trail she spotted Evan sitting right at the top of the mighty landslide at Agrippa, exulting in the devastation and making rhymes.

"One rock kicked,
One landslide licked,
They shoulda KICKed that comet, eh?
It's all over for me now anyway."

He rolled about like the rocks he was kicking down the big slope, laughing as he went.

"One life, eh, it's all you get,
You haven't wasted yours just yet,
Work to do kid, you stay strong,
You made me proud to sing my song."

She was in the driving seat, and he was throwing styro cups at her, still making rhymes.

"Look after Drew McQ,
And watch the baby too,
You'll be coming home real soon,
From that big ol' dusty moon."

She turned to see his sharp grey eyes looking right at her, into her, *through* her. He'd given Drew those beautiful eyes. He sat very still, and the next rhyme was delivered in a more serious tone.

"Those rocks vibrated at the top,
You felt them shiver by the drop,
I told 'em no, and did my dance,
To give my Lucy one more chance."

Gone. This time he was gone. This time she knew for certain that he had left her and that it would be forever. She looked outside, desperately searching; outside NEIL, outside herself, *outside her soul*, but finally she realised it was all over. There was no spaceship.

"Goodbye to you my friend,
My lovely Lucy-Lu,
Go on living for me now,
I so loved you, I so loved you..."

416

His final line hung in the silence, gently fading away as she eased into wakefulness. She experienced a brief flash; that rare moment of certain knowledge that exists, trapped in the tiny instant between the sleeping and waking worlds. In that hazy place it all made some kind of sense. *Certain knowledge? Yes.*

She had felt his presence as she panicked at the threat of the fall. For an instant he had been next to her at the top of the pass, before rolling off up the crater rim to steady the teetering rocks until she was in the clear. She knew now, as clearly as she would ever know anything, that last night's vast landslide had almost happened at the same time as the fall she had witnessed. Now she felt safe at last, and he was finally gone. And yes, she had never admitted it to herself before, but she had always loved him too. Lying there in the bunk she realised for the first time why she had never married.

Calmed and content, she slipped easily back into a deep, therapeutic sleep.

* * *

Lucy woke after resting for the entire twelve hours. The constant feeling that had worried at her; that she was leaving Evan behind, or that he was close, was completely gone. *It seemed so real, but he can't have been there. Dreams and daydreams, Lucy-Lu, stress and fatigue, that's all it was, eh?*

She climbed out of the bunk to find 3,4,2 still driving NEIL like a little hero. To her astonishment they were 162 km closer to home. In four hours there would be a coffee and beer delivery at Gene's.

Then Lucy and her Deep Race team were going to visit Earth.

Wilco was beyond excitement. "Ringtone, we're looking at some data here that shows a massive electromagnetic spike from the direction of Jupiter. It wasn't exactly on the planet or its moons, but somewhere close by there."

Following Redwood's departure, Director pro tem Ringtone Buchanan was in the Floor Fifty office with his deputy, Blake Shermann. The door was open. He immediately reverted to running the show as close to Culver's model as possible, and was proving a popular choice. Culver was on extended leave, recuperating at Eve Meredith's house in Maui.

Ringtone caught the implication straight away. He studied Wilco, sitting in the office at Gene's. He knew his countryman well enough to realise he never panicked, but for once he sounded close to it.

"You clearly think it's important, Wilco. Can we check elsewhere to verify it, or could it have been an anomaly caused by the comet? We've seen various odd things showing up from that period. Do any other stations have data that we can cross check?"

"Yes, I'm getting to that," Wilco snapped, irritated. The normally ultra-polite astronomer gestured for quiet. "We've started asking around. It'll take a few hours to get a cross check, but we should know by early afternoon. We just wanted to make you aware."

Ringtone thought for a second or two. "I've never seen you this excited; you're practically hopping. What's your gut feeling?"

"I wish it sounded less odd, but I'm certain it's the Deep Race. I think their rescue ship arrived at Europa and we picked up their exit from hyperspace. Good Galaxy, I sound like a sci-fi geek, how awful."

Ringtone wasn't convinced. "But I thought they didn't have the means to communicate with Europa after they lost the ship. The base wasn't expecting them back for a couple of years, so they won't yet consider them overdue or in trouble."

"I know all that, but I can't think of a better explanation. Ed showed me the readouts and whatever it was it looked pretty strange, like nothing we've ever seen. All sorts of odd lines peaked on the background monitors for about 30 seconds, fading out in small waves until they were back to normal." He turned round. "Oh good grief, what now?"

Ed Seals and Pelican arrived on-screen.

"Hi Ringtone," said Seals. "This gets stranger. You all know me; I can't sleep if I'm busy on a project, so I wandered back into the astro office at 4:00 AM. There was this big EMP spike on the overnight readouts. That's what Wilco's so excited about. I thought it was corrupted data from Comet Percival, but I was mistaken. I did get Pelican up early to help us—"

Pelican interrupted him. "Bloody Astro Prof, he's just like the rest of 'em! 'Hey matey, it's 5:00 AM. Roll out of bed and check data for a laugh.' D'you know what you can do with yer lousy Tech grade 2 job?"

There was a general lessening of tension.

Seals countered, "Junior Lab Techs, you're all the same, can't get a decent one. OK, Ringtone, we crunched a few numbers and rapid-scanned a lot of the overlooked archive from the last month that we haven't had time to go through yet."

He turned to Wilco. "Want another shock? In the last ten minutes, we identified the exact same thing happening on October 15th, and in the same area too. On that occasion all the lines on the chart went the other way. I've never seen spikes like it and I've studied so many Pulsars and Quasars I can't even begin to tell you.

"Twice now, something has ripped space apart over there in a way I don't understand. In two dimensions it would look like a tiny, planet-heavy ball bearing dropping into a thin rubber membrane with a sheen of water on it. The event caused a miniscule hole which then healed over almost immediately, but not before pulling some of the water through to follow it and evaporate. Both times it happened immediately beyond Jupiter's outer moons. It got lost in all the data and printouts during the comet situation. All I can come up with is the unlikely theory that something disturbed the fabric."

"OK," Ringtone allowed. "The hairs on my neck are standing up now. Where are you heading?"

"It was Wilco who said hyperspace ship, science fiction, and losing his marbles all in the same breath when the event happened this morning. But get this, if the Deep Race are studying Earth from Europa, as they indicated, surely they would have seen their surviving crew on TV a couple of weeks before the event Pelican and I just found. I would surmise that they immediately pressed the 'help' button to home.

"I have a strong hunch their rescue ship didn't arrive there this morning. Having seen the data from October 15th, I think it crash-stopped in-system then. Extrapolating that theory, this morning's spike had to be the same ship departing again. Now, they might have been going home, but my intuition says not. Can you imagine them leaving their four remaining crew members stranded here and going home? I can't. I think we're expecting visitors."

THE END

420

Thank you...

Thank you for reading "To Visit Earth". If you enjoyed this story, please consider taking a moment to leave a review on Amazon, Goodreads, or anywhere else books are bought and/or reviewed. Authors love feedback and this is one way to provide it, as well as let others know that you enjoyed the book. Also, please tell a friend about the book.

You can find more information and follow Ian through his Facebook page:
https://www.facebook.com/SciFiMac/

He also loves email and can be reached via
scifimac@gmail.com

37843571R00253

Printed in Great Britain
by Amazon